Trying
not to
Love you

Trying not to Love you

BY

AMABILE GIUSTI

TRANSLATED BY HILLARY LOCKE

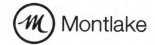 Montlake

Previously published as Tentare di Non Amarti by Amazon Crossing in Italy in 2015. Translated from Italian by Hillary Locke. First published in English by Montlake in collaboration with Amazon Crossing in 2020.

Published by Montlake, in collaboration with Amazon Crossing, Seattle

www.apub.com

Amazon, the Amazon logo, Montlake and Amazon Crossing are trademarks of Amazon.com, Inc., or its affiliates.

ISBN-13: 9781542018944
ISBN-10: 1542018943

Cover design by Plum5 Limited

Printed in the United States of America

Unto a broken heart,
No other one may go
Without the high prerogative
Itself hath suffered too.

—Emily Dickinson

1

There was no way to avoid the puddles, so she waded bravely through – and as if that weren't bad enough, the water sprayed up into her eyes every time a car went past. Beneath her pink wool beanie with its little pompom on top, her poor hair hung limp as a jellyfish.

What a night! It was only two short blocks from the bar to her apartment but each trip felt like crossing a minefield, and the rain that particular evening was a cruel bonus, adding insult to injury.

She paused at a distance from her building, praying he wouldn't be there. His presence was insistent but erratic: one day yes, another day no, and then there he'd be again. It was a dangerous little game they were playing. He knew just how to make it impossible for her to report him and, in any case, a woman has few legal grounds on which to call the police over a psycho ex unless he actually kills her, even though she's not exactly in a position to speak out if she's dead. Either way, she's screwed.

Penelope – Penny to her friends – stopped just out of reach of the glare of a streetlamp; the light buzzed on and off, then came a sizzle, and finally darkness. At least he wasn't waiting at the entrance. Now it was just a matter of figuring out whether he was inside.

Penny sighed into the rain, bit her lip and told herself she couldn't stay out there much longer. *If he doesn't stab me first, I'm gonna die of pneumonia.*

Shrugging her shoulders, she quickened her pace as she sploshed her way to the door, though not exactly quite so carefree as Debbie Reynolds in *Singin' in the Rain*.

The building was truly hideous – one of those sad, crumbling apartment complexes, a chipped canvas for mediocre graffiti artists, with a sparse lobby further enlivened by drab, peeling wallpaper. The ideal place, in fact, for a sick psycho to take revenge on a girl who'd dared to stop dating him.

Penny crossed the threshold, her heart in her throat.

It was totally dark inside. The light switch was still faulty, the single bulb on its bare wire failing to relieve the gloom. Just as it always did, the concentrated darkness took her breath away.

Penny had a serious problem with the dark. She would lose all sense of reality, grow paralysed and then panic until she eventually managed to force herself to breathe and think and count to ten. Then she would finally come to, the blood rushing back to her arms and legs, and she could move again, though it was always a momentary truce, only long enough to fool the brain until it was light again. Those times when she couldn't find the light right away were when she'd start screaming.

On this particular evening, she took her cell phone from her bag and turned on the flashlight, illuminating a grey and desolate space. Mildly heartened, she set off up the stairs.

She lived on the second-to-last floor, and hoped Grant hadn't bothered to climb that many steps to lurk in wait for her, crouched in some miserable corner.

One month earlier, Penny had dated Grant for seven stupid days. They'd met at the bar where Penny worked. He'd walked in, gorgeous as the sun, elegantly unkempt and with the most charming smile. He'd exchanged a few words with her while she was mixing his mojito, and then ended up waiting outside for her, all done with a studied delicacy, clearly with the hots for her but making no assumptions. They had fallen into an easy conversation outside the entrance to Well Purple. Nothing on that starry night, not the faintest hint of anything wrong, had led her to suspect that so much beauty and elegance could hide something far more sinister, but Penny had been forced to snap out of her fantasy by only their third date. That boy with his perfect looks – every mother's dream for her daughter – was no more than a spoiled and violent little bully who took pleasure in humiliating women, so Penny had dumped him without much thought and he had not forgiven her. Since then he had begun to follow her everywhere. For the time being he was still limiting himself to inspiring fear in her, observing her from afar with his feral smile and mocking her threateningly, though never in the presence of a witness. In public he acted like a true gentleman, straight out of *Downton Abbey*, but once he was sure no one could hear him, he'd let his mask drop and harass her, making clear his intentions and promising acts of unspeakable violence against her.

Penny had made no mention of it to her grandma as she didn't want to scare her. She'd researched it online and discovered that without physical acts of aggression, visible bruises, a visit to ER or reliable witnesses, no one would really believe her. Grant was the son of a lawyer – he had himself just graduated from law school – plus he was rich, dressed like an Abercrombie model and even had the looks of one. Who would ever imagine he could be a danger?

Penny continued up the stairs. Suddenly her phone signalled it was about to run out of battery.

'Not now, not now, not now!' she pleaded, but the old contraption didn't give a damn about her fears and chose to die right then and there.

She was plunged into the darkest of darks, halfway up a flight of stairs.

There was nothing for it but to continue to climb, hoping her feet wouldn't find the edge of some broken step and that her panic wouldn't come rushing back. Above all, she hoped not to encounter Grant emerging from the darkness.

She held her breath and climbed the stairs as fast as she could.

Three more floors, three more floors. Hold on. You can do it. The darkness is only dark; it's not a wall, it's not a well, it's not the centre of the earth.

Suddenly she heard fast, heavy footsteps coming up the stairs behind her. There was no way it was one of the elderly residents of the building. Penny was the only young tenant in the midst of an army of retirees, all over sixty, and none of them could move in such an agile way. Her heart was on the verge of bursting, and there was no way she could stop it. A herd of horses galloped in her chest. For a moment she felt faint and stopped to lean against the wall, but then she mustered up all her courage.

Like hell am I gonna let you win, you fucking creep!

She picked up her pace again as a milky glow pooled on a flight of stairs below her. The asshole had a flashlight. Penny started to run with the chaotic fervour of a wounded deer, until finally she reached her floor. Panting, she dug in her bag for her keys, but they were nowhere to be found, as if even they were in league with Grant. She continued to rummage, feeling her way through a tide of junk – her wallet, scattered M&Ms, tissues, a bottle of nail polish, cocoa butter lip balm – the whole artistic jumble that filled her Mary Poppins-style bag. Everything was there except for the one thing she needed, and then finally she felt them, cold and hostile against her palm. Victorious, she pulled them out and groped for the keyhole with her fingertips.

Grant was very close by now, the light from his flashlight about to reach her, and then Penny's keys fell to the ground, ringing out like scattered coins on a sidewalk.

You idiot! she thought to herself. *You're like the girl in some cheesy horror movie – the one who runs from the monster straight into the nearest parking garage, deserted road or forest. You deserve every-thing coming to you!*

She knelt on the floor, her eyes flooding with tears, unable to stem the flow of her fear. The keys appeared just before the beam of light blinded her.

Penny remained on the ground, her back against the wall, one hand in front of her face. The light was pointing straight at her now, like the laser eye of some evil cyclops. Behind it she could make out the silhouette of a man. Grant – it was Grant for sure.

An arm stretched in her direction, reaching out to overpower her.

'Touch me and I'll kick you!' Penny exclaimed. It wasn't easy to hide her panic under layers of fake bravery. She hadn't eaten all evening but a little food came up anyway, as if all the meals from the last ten years were climbing up her throat.

While she fumbled in indecision – *What do I do? Do I try to hit him? Should I run? Should I shout? Should I pray?* – a hand grabbed her and pulled her up, though more gently than she'd expected.

Penny was dumbstruck for a moment, and then the man moved his flashlight away from her eyes, and in the dim light she realised it wasn't Grant. This new sight, however, made her feel like she was going straight out of the frying pan and into the fire.

What she saw was a kind of giant – a man of about twenty-five, tall and sturdy as a redwood. Well, her imagination was prob-ably getting carried away looking for comparisons, but she had no doubt he was over six foot four, and he couldn't have weighed any less than two hundred and fifty pounds, not because he was fat but because his muscles were enormous, bulging even through his clothes. He could have snapped her in half with a single forearm, the same one helping her get back to her feet, and on which she noticed a dense weave of tribal tattoos in shades of grey and black. His wrist was as solid as a trunk of petrified wood and streaked with raised veins, visible even in the semi-darkness.

Having previously imagined it was the beautiful, cruel and crazy Grant on her tail, it almost seemed to her as if this man, dressed all in black, with his appearance of a heavyweight champion and his military-style crewcut and ice-cold eyes – blue, or maybe grey? – might be some kind of heavenly spirit sent down to rescue her.

'You scared me,' Penny whispered, still wondering if she was right to feel relieved or if this was some new threat that would be harder to fight off than Grant himself. How could she even begin to keep this one at bay?

The man froze and glared at her, his eyes like shards of glass. His glacial stare was unnerving, but Penny continued to look at him bravely, and for a handful of strange moments they remained like this in the shadows, gazing at each other. Silence surrounded them, broken only by Penny's anxiously rapid breathing.

'What are you doing here?' she asked finally. It was undoubtedly a stupid question to ask of this Herculean stranger, who perhaps harboured a similar intention to hurt her as Grant did, but she couldn't think of anything better to say.

The man pointed upwards as if to indicate the heavens.

'Are you an angel?' she continued, knowing it sounded a little ridiculous.

An angel? Looking like that? He looks more like a demon guarding the gates of hell.

'I live upstairs,' the man replied. He had a powerful voice to complete the package. A hoarse, deep voice that was as imposing as his body.

Penny squinted, incredulous. She knew no one lived up there. It was a sort of dilapidated attic, more like a pigeonhole than an apartment, inhabited by mice and old moth-eaten furniture.

The man, correctly interpreting her obvious astonishment, added in a monotone: 'I'm the new tenant.'

'Tenant' was not a word that much suited him. A 'tenant' sounded like someone who moved in with rubber plants and striped silk sofas, painted the walls a creamy yellow and bought sets of pots to steam their vegetables in. This guy, on the other hand, made her think of old cellars where people drank and fought, of wrestling rings spattered with blood, spit and sweat, and damp sheets after wild sex.

Flushed to her ears, Penny didn't think there was any need to remain in the company of someone who was either a new tenant or a dangerous lunatic.

Then she asked him with a little bitterness, 'If you live upstairs, why don't you go, then? Why are you still here?'

'I'm waiting to see you safely inside,' he replied.

'Why?' she asked with suspicion.

'Because of the look on your face.'

'What look?'

He was silent for a moment, and then felt around in his pockets as if looking for something. Penny wondered if he was going to pull out a knife and slit her throat right there, but instead he took out a pack of Chesterfields and a lighter. He brought a cigarette to his lips and lit it. His face was illuminated with a reddish glow that momentarily revealed large eyes, a straight nose and full lips, his mouth slightly furrowed on one side from a small scar. He drew on the cigarette and said, 'Whenever I see a woman with that face on her, I usually stop to make sure she's not in danger, even if I don't know her.'

'*You're* much more likely to be the danger here!'

He raised an eyebrow, and his sarcastic laugh was accompanied by a slight hint of annoyance in his generally impassive demeanour.

'I'm no danger to women – not in the sense you mean, anyway – and even if I were the type, you wouldn't be my first choice.'

7

Penny gritted her teeth, feeling a sudden intense hatred towards this man. She was well aware she wasn't enormously attractive – she'd fought to maintain a simple, even anonymous look for over twenty years now, but had shed many a secret tear over it as a teenager. Her lack of self-esteem was the reason she'd thrown herself into the arms of someone like Grant in the first place. Why should someone as intriguing as this stranger even bother to give her a second glance, she asked herself, though she nonetheless found it intolerable that he'd had the nerve to insult her quite so openly.

'You can take yourself upstairs by the balls with my blessing,' she told him.

She didn't have to say it twice. The stranger directed his flashlight towards the stairwell and walked off without a word. Penny couldn't help but follow him with her gaze until he had melted away into the darkness, then she quickly put her key in the lock and went inside. She pulled the door shut carefully behind her, secured the chain her grandma had left off so she could get in, and only then was she able to start breathing normally.

The apartment where Penny lived with her grandmother, Barbara – known to her friends as Barbie – was a cramped and simple place with few windows. Two bedrooms, a bathroom and a living room with an open kitchen, all crammed into one little area. Penny's grandmother would always say, 'Hi, I'm Barbie, and this is Barbie's house – that's why it's so small!'

Even Penny's dreams were as miniature as dolls. She had hoped to go to college but had failed to get a scholarship. But it was better this way – otherwise she would have been forced to choose her own destiny, and she knew what she would have chosen: to stay with her grandma.

With no options, there was no room for conflicts of interest. Penny knew that, had college been an actual possibility, Barbie would have insisted she move on to campus and look for a job so she could keep up her studies. But she also knew that her sweet grandma, who always seemed young despite her seventy years, would have suffered immeasurably without her, and so she had stayed and had not regretted it for a moment. She loved her grandma more than anything in the world.

Penny flicked on the kitchen light. She undressed in that room, letting her drenched work uniform fall to the floor: her grey coat that pooled around her calves, her skintight T-shirt, her pleated miniskirt that screamed slutty Sailor Moon from her favourite manga series, and her nude tights with a red garter on the left thigh, having kicked off the rubber boots she'd slipped on before she left the bar, where she was forced to wear four-inch skyscraper heels. What was under her clothes was the body of a twenty-two-year-old who was skinny and pale – neither beautiful nor ugly, but somewhere in between. Brown eyes, a nose equal to a thousand other noses, and decent lips – the only part of herself she didn't detest. Smooth, dark copper hair, cut into a short bob by a neighbour who had once been a hairdresser. The result was a shaggy, asymmetrical pageboy style with one longer, pale pink section that hung over her face. She took off her single earring: a long silver cross dangling from her left ear, and placed it on the table.

After this, Penny went to the bathroom and climbed straight into the shower to wash off the smell of the bar – the greasy food and the smoke and all the sugary cocktails she'd mixed.

Only then, refreshed and unadorned except for her pastel lock of hair, did Penny look towards the door of the room where Barbie was sleeping and tiptoed in. Her grandma hadn't heard a thing – not even what had happened out on the landing. She was enjoying the blissful sleep of a child with their favourite teddy, cosy under the covers.

Barbie was small and slim like Penny – an older and softer version of her, dreamier and more eccentric, with fantastically long hair, once blonde, now silvery. When she was young, they'd called her 'Pocket Barbie' because she was so slight and beautiful with her spectacular hair. Penny kissed Barbie on the forehead, careful not to wake her, then went through to her own room.

'Room' was a generous term for what was really nothing grander than a hole in the wall. Penny had given her grandma the larger room and taken this one, barely larger than a box. The bed could scarcely fit in and there was no place for a wardrobe; Penny had had to settle for a rack on which she hung her few things. She did at least have a window overlooking the fire escape and on to a side street – no epic panorama, but nonetheless a place where sunlight filtered through in the morning and crisp air in the evening, along with the occasional yowls of mating cats, which didn't disturb her and actually helped her nod off. After the meaningless chatter and quarrelsome drunks of the bar, the straightforward calls of the animals outside seemed purifying, almost a kind of lullaby.

Penny put on her pyjamas and flopped into bed. In the silence, just before falling asleep, she couldn't help but think back to the tattooed guy on the landing. Did he really live in the attic? Did his head actually clear the ceiling up there, or did he have to stoop the whole time?

She imagined this giant crawling on all fours to avoid hitting his forehead on the rafters and laughed to herself. Where had he come from, and why was he here? He was definitely out of place, more glaringly than a rock band at a classical music concert. He was mysterious, and as beautiful as a tiger or a fire-breathing dragon, or a lethal abyss in a breathtaking panorama.

Penny fell asleep thinking of the man's ice-cold eyes; she had the feeling he'd be able to kill someone without blinking.

2

MARCUS

Francisca gets out of prison in exactly two months, and as soon as she's free we're getting out of this shithole. We haven't seen each other in four years, what with me locked up in one place and her in another. God, I've missed her so fucking much.

Meantime, I've found myself a job and a place to live that's more of a dump than a home, nearly worse than prison, but who cares because it's not gonna be for long. In two months we'll take our things and move on.

I've had other women since I got out – I don't make a habit of saying no – but fucking is just fucking, and Francisca is a whole other thing. She has something the others don't. She has those merciless eyes, those naughty ways – she's basically me with a pussy.

We didn't kill the guy on purpose. It happened during a fist fight. When the other guy hits as hard as you do, you're not gonna hold back, and if an asshole is about to slash your woman, how do you stop yourself from snapping his neck?

We killed him, sure, but in a brawl. They provoked us – that bastard and his buddy, who only ended up in hospital because I didn't get to finish him off too. That's why we didn't get a life sentence. Francisca got four years and I got six, but I got out early on account of my exemplary conduct.

I know. Me? Exemplary conduct? I've never been exemplary at anything, though in prison I tried to behave myself. I respected the rules and avoided conflict. After all, it's pretty easy to be left alone if you're six-four and have the face of a killer.

Not that I actually am a strangler, but I'm not gonna just sit there and take it either. If someone comes up to my woman when she's leaving the bathroom and puts their hands all over her and then sticks a knife in her face and tries to make her fuck him or die, I'm sorry but that person does not deserve to live.

Francisca had already started to beat the sack of shit before I got there. That asshole had no clue who he was messing with. His nose had already been smashed to a pulp when I joined in and started pounding him into the ground.

Right now I work as a bouncer in a nightclub. They hired me in spite of my past – I did warn them, but apparently having a former convict as a security guard is cool. It's a place where spoiled brats like to go, the kind who need to be set straight when they overdo it. These rich kids drink one beer too many, lose their tiny minds, and then become total assholes around women. I know I'm not one to judge – I've done all kinds of shit, but I've never messed with a woman like that, not ever, and I can't stand the kids who won't take their hands off a woman even after she says no. They can't all defend themselves like Francisca, so I come to their defence, and usually all it takes is one look at me to make a kid shit bricks in his designer jeans.

Sure, work sucks. I don't get to go home before four in the morning and I don't even have the cash to buy a car yet. If I had one, I wouldn't be able to drive it anyway because they also took my licence. So I walk, whatever the weather. I like walking. After four years of small spaces it's refreshing to move. I breathe all the air I want, and even if the neighbourhood is a sewer and a bore, it smells like roses and the beach compared to where I've just come from.

◆　◆　◆

I've moved into my new home, if you can even call it that. It's just a shack on the top floor of a shitty building, but if I fix it up a little it'll be decent enough. I'm good with tools; I can fix things. Meanwhile, it has a skylight, and while I fall asleep I can look up at the stars. It's not about being romantic – even that word makes me sick – it's about a simple physical need. After four years of staring at a concrete roof where nothing ever changed besides the damp spots and the spiders, I need to look at as many things as possible. I admit I chose this place for the skylight.

It has all I need: a bed, a bathroom, a kitchen. The ceilings are low, and in one place I have to stoop so I don't damage myself or the ceiling. I'll put a punch bag in the corner. I like kicking and punching – I do it until I can feel my muscles melt like hot liquorice. In the meantime, I've been doing push-ups: one hundred, three hundred, five hundred. Then I go out and run miles under the open sky, and then finally I get ready. I have a shower and put on the black shirt, pants and leather jacket the club gave me – and I go to work.

It's packed every night, but on weekends it's impossible. Sometimes I have to throw people out. Sometimes a girl will hit on me, but at work I can't reciprocate, so then I'll try to get away and we'll do it in her beautiful car. Sometimes I don't even know what they look like. In the darkness they all look cool, and then later, after hours of smoking and sweating, they turn out to be just average, but for a quickie they're fine. If they're drunk, on the other hand, then I let them go, even if they're gorgeous. Zombies are not my thing.

Francisca would understand – she never cared when I fucked other women. She'd just say, 'Don't worry, baby, it's just your cock that's having fun, not you.'

13

And then, around dawn, I go home.

Fortunately, the uniform the club gave me also includes a flashlight, otherwise I'd never be able to find my way back up the stairs to my apartment.

This particular night, I climb a few flights and hear a gasp and a moan.

I run faster and find myself in front of a girl. Never seen her before. She's scared. She has the face of a woman getting strangled, but there's no one around – she's all alone, her keys are on the floor, she can't see a thing and if she's not crying yet, she's just about to. She's small and very thin, with short hair. She's panting. I wait for her to go inside but she's afraid of me. I can't blame her, I'm a scary kinda guy, and even scarier if you know me – but I'm not mean to women, I repeat. If I'm not sure they really want me, I don't touch women and I keep my zipper closed. But this one? I wouldn't touch her if she knelt down and begged me. I have my standards. If it weren't for her tolerable legs that I'd advise her not to shove under men's noses if she wants to make it home at this hour, I'd think she was a man. Her hair is wet and messy, a little brown and a little pink. She looks like a fawn with no tits, but her legs don't lie. I've seen thighs, and these are a woman's thighs.

I leave her at her front door and go upstairs. If you say you don't need me, little girl, I'm outta here.

The apartment is a total mess. I'll get myself organised tomorrow. I'm not gonna be here for long, but I need to look settled for my parole officer. I need to play the part of someone who wants to be good and work and calm down, and not someone who can't wait to leave. I take off my clothes, toss them on the tattered couch and don't bother to put anything else on. I take a cold shower because there's no hot water, then I lie down, still wet. Then I fall asleep and I don't dream about a fucking thing.

3

In the morning, Penny woke up early after a deep sleep. She wasn't due at work until after lunch, but sleeping late was not a luxury she could afford. A scene of devastation would greet her most mornings, as if a tornado had upended everything in the apartment. The disorder wasn't because they'd been burgled or a hurricane had swept through – it was all caused by her grandma. The sweet and dreamy Barbie suffered from an inadequate supply of blood to the brain, and as a result had been struck by early onset dementia. Her current fixation was the kitchen: she was reliving the period when she had been a primary school teacher and had combined her twin passions – for children and the sweeter things in life – by preparing all manner of delicacies for her little ones. She had guided them along the journey of knowledge with no reproaches or beatings, encouraging them instead with exquisite heart-shaped chocolates and meringues packaged like sweets. Unfortunately, only her passion had survived from that time, and not her precision in following recipes. If she decided to bake cookies and couldn't find flour, there was a risk she'd use talcum powder or even laundry detergent. She created mess in every corner, and Penny would get up early every morning to tidy it up, pretending first to taste her grandma's delicacies and share some with the neighbours, and then cooking something that was actually edible before helping her grandma to wash and dress. After that, they would both play pretend, like kids who were best friends. So there was no time to sleep, though she'd only gone to bed that morning at five.

In the afternoon, Penny's second commitment awaited her: she worked at the library. The neighbourhood was known for its violence, and yet the library was always packed. Maybe it was the chance to spend time in a heated building, or the quiet and friendly atmosphere, or the pure and simple pleasure of reading a good book in peace, but the fact was that it was always full of people. The library was small but elegant, clean and uncluttered in style, with wooden floors and books with multicoloured spines, and Penny felt like Alice in Wonderland whenever she was there. It wouldn't have surprised her one bit to see a white rabbit with a pocket watch slipping between the shelves. After the squalor of her night-time work, mixing drinks for drunk bikers or girls stoned to the dark roots of their dyed hair, all in a similar state of undress that revealed everything there was to reveal, the placid world of the library made her feel reborn.

'Shall we head outside for a while?' Penny asked her grandma, after brushing her hair for a long while and dusting it with the rose-scented powder that Barbie loved. 'I still have a couple of hours – shall we go for a walk?'

Her grandmother nodded happily. She loved to go out, but couldn't do it alone. She had a limp and very quickly got tired, and there was always the risk that she'd grow confused and not know how to get home.

Along with her grey coat, Penny pulled on her pink beanie, which had dried out over the few short hours she'd been home, and then took her grandma by the hand. It was no longer raining, but the air was still cool. They set off down the stairs, Barbie looking like a little girl with her mother.

An obstacle presented itself on their way down, however – not in some metaphorical sense, but in the shape of a bag used for training, the kind favoured by boxers and kickboxers. Behind the bulky object, Penny had no difficulty in recognising the stranger she'd met the night before.

Punch bag and man filled the entire tiny landing, making it impossible for Penny and her grandmother to pass without being flattened between the wall and the powerful mass of that body. He was way bigger than the bag, his head almost grazing the ceiling.

'So how are we supposed to get past?' asked Penny, annoyed.

The guy placed the punch bag on the ground and pushed it as far as possible against the wall. She could see him better in the cold light of day. His broad shoulders were like those of a Greek statue, and his tattooed forearms popped out of a black sweater with the sleeves rolled up. He wore dark jeans and low Chelsea boots. Around his throat was a leather cord, the ends secured via a ring in the shape of some sort of creature, possibly a snake.

Penny felt her cheeks flush and, in the pit of her stomach, the remote flutter of butterflies. The stranger looked at her, and Penny looked away. His eyes were extraordinary: a rare blend of grey and sea-green.

Barbie whispered loudly in Penny's ear, 'What a handsome man!' Her voice could easily have reached up to the top floor of the building.

Penny's grandmother never tried to hide it if she met a man she found attractive. She was outspoken and direct – at times as embarrassing as those people who blurt out absolutely every single thought in their head. Her husband had been a teacher too – a skinny guy with round glasses and the light build of a featherweight, so it would have made more sense if a man in the mould of an immortal Greek warrior weren't exactly her type. In actual fact, however, Barbie's ideal man was completely different to her husband in every way. Long before he ever came along, she had experienced a love she could never forget. He'd been a rude and rebellious boy – the sort to get his hands dirty, with calluses on his palms and muscles bulging from physical labour – and Barbie had been madly in love with him. It had ended badly, mostly because her parents, with their old-fashioned rules about class, had refused to let her see him – but Barbie, who now often forgot what she'd been doing the day before, still remembered that forbidden passion from her youth. His name had been John, like John Wayne, and according to her stories he'd even looked a little like him. Maybe that's why, every time she came across a man who looked like a soldier, a cowboy or a boxer, she would smile at him and suddenly be sixteen years old all over again.

Penny's grandmother took the man's hand and was able to slip comfortably through the small gap on the landing, but when it came to her own turn, Penny stopped, muttering under her breath.

'You're such a kind man!' Barbie exclaimed. 'What's your name?'

The guy smiled, and Penny thought it looked artificial and insincere. Smiles like that were always prone to hiding secrets.

'Marcus,' he replied, and then, turning to Penny, said more firmly, 'If you'd like to pass by, we can all get on with our day.'

'I'll go when I feel like it. I'm not squeezing through just because you're in a hurry!' she shot back crossly. But her irritation, although authentic, could not completely quell the fluttering of those terrible butterflies in her belly.

Damn hormones! You can study and read and think and be as civilised as you like, and then you're suddenly no better than some monkey. Are we no better than the animals? Do our instincts really have to insist on responding to the biceps of some random caveman?

Penny bit her tongue, unable to switch off her brain. She hated that she'd already imagined herself wrapped in those arms, which looked capable of inflicting pain more than caresses.

With her grandma waiting for her at the bottom of the stairs, happy as a pig in clover, Penny finally stepped forwards to pass him. Marcus moved back as far as he could to give her room, but nonetheless, Penny's breast brushed against him. Once more, it seemed, he was right in front of her – practically on top of her, in fact. Those damn butterflies flew up to her throat. Was he wearing cologne? Maybe not – he just smelled clean, with the tiniest hint of sweat. His huge shadow seemed to shroud her completely, like an oak tree blocking out the sunlight. She barely reached up to his breastbone.

'Don't worry, I'm not gonna touch you,' he whispered, with a cold smile.

Penny slipped away, still blushing. She wanted to slap herself. Not because of that one fleeting moment of contact, but because, secretly, her sick brain kept asking: *Do you like him then?*

Not in a million years – a passing fantasy, that's all it is! she answered in return. She hated novels with women who instantly lost the plot, like fate had pressed a button, all because some cool guy had happened to glance at them.

A passing fantasy. That was true – in rational terms, at least. She had never once lost her head over some guy; in fact, she was still a virgin – by choice, and not for lack of prospects. All those drunk guys at work came on strong every night of the week, but Penny wanted something else: love with a capital L, like in the books. She fancied herself as Jane Eyre; not via some grumpy guy with a crazy wife in the attic, but by casting herself as the heroine of a great love story, strange and unforgettable, the kind that would knock her off her feet and, even if it ended badly, leave her changed forever. She had hoped that Grant might be that special person, but Grant was as crooked as a barrel of snakes, and violent with it.

Since then, she had promised herself she would be more careful not to be trapped by lies and promises and other such demons. Demons like Grant, who would trick you with their elegant ways, but also demons like Marcus, who seemed designed to summon up the most primal part of yourself, the buried and secret part you didn't even know you had.

She raced to catch up with her grandma, and yet she couldn't help but watch him climb the stairs, carrying the punch bag as if it were light and stuffed with flower petals, and once again her brain filled with daring questions that she had to tune out and refuse to answer.

◆　◆　◆

The peaceful atmosphere in the library always helped Penny feel clean and new, whatever was happening in the outside world. Her job was to put the books back in their places, right the furniture and help readers with any requests that involved going up the ladder, as Miss Milligan, the chief librarian, was old and unsteady, and even ascending one step would give her a severe case of vertigo.

Penny was looking for a book on one of the top shelves right this minute, in fact. She was on her own, up her beautiful ladder on wheels, sliding between the aisles as if on a skateboard. It was fun going up and down like this, and she was contentedly humming a song from Disney's *Beauty and the Beast* under her breath. She came across the volume she was after and headed back to floor level, pleased to have tracked it down for Mr Aubrey, who was longing to read this rare memoir.

And right there in the library, all her simple pleasure suddenly vanished in a puff of regret at the sight of Grant leaning against the bookshelves, arms folded across his chest, with his honey-coloured hair, turquoise eyes and that mockery of a seductive smile, which tricked anyone stupid enough to overlook the wicked sneer when his mask slipped. Stupid people like Penny, in short.

'Hi,' he said. 'Long time no see.'

Penny knew all too well that a madman must be indulged and not provoked, but something about Grant made her want to fight back. Maybe he'd lose it in public, in front of witnesses who could give her some credibility with the police.

'I see you almost every day, Grant,' she replied. 'Wherever I go, there you are.'

'Because I'm in love with you, baby,' he said, those damn perfect teeth still bared in a grin.

'You sure have a funny way of showing it.'

'It's the best kind of love there is, baby,' he whispered, coming closer. 'I can't live without you.'

'So this kind of love includes trying to rape me, right?'

'Come on, you know you loved it, Penny,' he whispered near her ear, and Penny's guts tightened like a boa constrictor around a lizard in its death throes. 'You are one angelic bitch, honey.'

'Maybe, but you still disgust me,' she said bravely.

Come on, you asshole. Hit me, do something so I can go to the police right now. Let's finish with these exhausting, ridiculous ambushes.

Grant snarled at her. 'Our time will come, baby. Meanwhile, I'll let you savour the wait. You'll always have me breathing down your neck.'

'But why? Why can't you just leave me alone?' she asked, even though she knew perfectly well why that was. He didn't behave like this with girls of his own social standing. With them, he played the good boy, the young lawyer – his mother's official companion to charity soirées. On those he considered socially inferior, however, he felt free to unleash the worst excesses of his behaviour. He chose his targets with care, deluding them with a couple of dates where he'd be graceful and gentlemanly, but then he'd show his true self:

21

violent and dirty sex; sex without consent; threats, insults, verbal humiliation. Even his kisses were promises of abuse to come.

'Because a nobody like you can't afford to tell me no.'

At that moment, Miss Milligan appeared from the central hallway.

'Everything OK, Penny?' she asked. 'Mr Aubrey is waiting for his book.'

Grant unleashed one of his most devastating smiles. 'Of course. I'm not gonna waste any more of your time, ma'am.' Then he turned to Penny. 'Until next time we meet, my love.'

He walked away like a perfect gentleman, unburdened by guilt. Penny handed the book over to the librarian, and realised suddenly that she'd been holding her breath the whole time. She let out a long and agonised sigh, and, looking down, saw that her hands were shaking. If Grant wanted to bring her down psychologically before he got to her physically, he was sure succeeding.

Those damned two blocks till she got home. It was such a short distance from the Well Purple to Penny's apartment, but anything could happen in that stretch. It took a year off her life every single night. After Grant's warning that afternoon, she was taut and tense as a strung bow. It wasn't raining this evening, at least, but the gleam of the streetlights barely made it down to road level. She pulled her coat down over her legs as far as she could, certain the problem would drive her mad if it didn't get sorted soon.

Suddenly she heard footsteps nearby, as if someone were lurking in the alley to her right. There was no time even to wonder *Who, what, how?* before something touched her arm, and she screamed at the top of her voice.

But once again, it wasn't Grant, but that guy – the new neighbour. The one who sent Penny's hormones into a tailspin.

'Hey, listen – cool it, OK?' he said, annoyingly calm and reassuring. 'I'm not gonna hurt you.'

Penny froze, her face white as a sheet, her hands on her chest trying to stop her heart from exploding. While she caught her breath, Marcus lit a cigarette. He took a deep drag, exhaled and then looked at her.

'What do you want?' she asked furiously.

'Nothing. I saw you coming and waited for you.'

'Why?'

'Because you always look like a rabbit caught in the headlights.'

Penny swallowed and glanced over her shoulder, as if a whole pack of wolves were following her, then she looked back at him, and the shuddering panic she had felt up to then for quite different reasons became a stark quiver of physical awareness, such as you might feel in the company of some wild animal. Marcus was dressed all in black, like the night before.

She stood still for a moment as he walked ahead, then after a few yards he turned and threw her a puzzled look.

'If you wanna go on alone, go for it, OK? I'm tired and in a hurry, and I don't make a habit of escorting people home, just so you know. It's a coincidence that yesterday and today I came back so early. I'm usually way later.'

'Who cares what time—'

'So I can go now?'

'Go ahead!'

He grimaced and shook his head. 'Hurry up, I'm tired,' he said, waiting for her.

She sighed with secret relief. It made no sense to feel safe next to a man with tattooed arms and a murderous-looking face, but that was exactly how she felt.

'So where do you work?' she asked, to make conversation. It turned out to be a nightclub just a few blocks away. She'd even been there once with Grant, back when she still thought he was a nice boy. 'Strange, I never saw you there . . .' she murmured.

'Because you'd have noticed, you mean?' he asked, holding the smoke in his lungs for a few seconds.

'Well, actually . . .'

'I just started,' Marcus explained, breathing out. 'I'm a bouncer.'

He didn't ask, but Penny told him anyway. 'I work at Well Purple – the bar at the end of the block.'

'That explains your outfit,' Marcus commented, pointing to her skirt, barely concealed by her coat. 'Do you also provide other services?'

She scowled at him, and said loftily, 'Just because one is a bartender in a place of dubious taste and is forced to dress like a manga nymphet does not mean one is a slut.'

'Never dreamed of such a thing. I was simply trying to understand why someone with the face of a sixteen-year-old fresh out of bible study goes around half-dressed at night, but that's your business obviously.'

'Obviously.'

'Just don't get raped on my watch, OK, or I'd feel like I had to intervene – and I'd like to avoid any unnecessary trouble.'

'If that happens, I hereby authorise you not to intervene on my account.'

'I have many faults, but I'm not a coward.'

Unable to restrain herself, she asked him in a rush, 'So what *are* your faults, then?'

Marcus let out a hoarse laugh. 'I always have this effect on girls, I don't know why – don't feel you have to hold back, huh?'

'What are you talking about?'

'OK, so we start with the usual questions, right? Like, who are you, what do you do, what's your story, maybe my love can save you – but you ought to know that I don't sleep with little girls.'

Penny's eyes widened and she stared at him in bewilderment. 'What? You're out of your tiny mind!'

'I am? It's written all over your face and I know how to read. Go take a cold shower. If you're under eighteen I won't even touch you with my fingernail. I really don't need any more problems right now.'

'But I'm twenty-two!' Penny replied, irked, then realising immediately it wasn't the right thing to say.

'Are you serious? I'd never know. I'm still not gonna touch you.'

'You're disgusting! How did we even end up talking about this?'

'I was trying to be clear here. I don't want problems. I'm only here for two months, and I'm not intending to make friends or enemies, so don't even try.'

'Who's trying? Has anyone ever told you you're a bit of a bully?'

'Oh, they have, and they usually do it before they beg me to fuck them senseless.'

'OK, stop it. We're almost home, so you can leave now, and try not to speak to me if you see me again.'

'I'll have no problem pretending that you don't exist. I don't even know your name, and I don't care to know.'

'Well, I have no intention of telling you!'

'Great. If you're normally heading home round about this time, I'll try to avoid it.'

'Great. Sounds perfect to me.'

He brought two fingers to his forehead in a sort of military salute, and stopped to light another cigarette. Penny walked ahead of him, annoyed, wounded, tired, and eager to have no more to do with this man – even by accident – for the rest of her life.

Whenever Penny felt anxious, she had two tricks to get the smile back on her face: the first was to breathe in the aroma of books, and the second was to get herself a wacky manicure. That afternoon, thanks to a persistent bad mood, she found herself with ten Tiffany-green nails with panda decals. To complete the ensemble she bought bright purple mascara, which gave her a vaguely alien appearance, but not even that managed to shift her mood. She was anxious because of Marcus, and also because she couldn't stand feeling anxious because of Marcus. How dare that boorish and arrogant newbie to the building think he was God's gift to womankind? He had flat out assumed she wanted to sleep with him!

Not that she hadn't thought about it, to be honest; she would have been a hypocrite to deny that. Of course she had – she thought about it every time she saw him, and even when she didn't but was hoping to see him again. She made out like she was this great ice queen, but one peek at him and she lost her mind, and she hated it. She couldn't stand having nearly got to the grand old age of twenty-three without any temptation, only to suddenly find herself gripped by this indecent obsession. Every single square millimetre of Marcus seemed fashioned specifically with the intention of making her want him. He looked like someone straight off the front cover of *Men's Health*, as if the most attractive version of those guys in the glossy magazines had crossed who knew what gap in the space-time continuum and ended up right there in her building. The only thing he did lack was their smile; unlike your average model, Marcus always looked super pissed off, his ice-cold eyes devoid of light or warmth. He looked like someone who'd seen and done things that had stolen away his very soul. But she wanted him. OK, fine, she could admit that to herself now – she wanted him. The red light in Penny's imagination was forever on, and her senses were on constant alert. When she saw him, she felt a fiery torment deep within.

But she couldn't bear that he took it for granted that she would want him, and compared her to all those oversexed women who slept with him! And, above all, that he had humiliated her by rejecting her and treating her like some little schoolgirl.

With a knot of anger tightening inside of her, despite the cheerful nails and purple lashes, she was just heading back into the building when she almost bumped into a stranger at the entrance – a tall guy in a tatty suit and tie, with the air of an underpaid government employee.

'Do you know Marcus Drake?' he said. 'He just moved into this building.'

Penny nodded and pointed upstairs.

'How is his behaviour?' the stranger asked.

'Sorry, in what sense?'

'Does he behave well? Does he bother anyone?'

He bugs the hell out of me. He's a jerk who doesn't acknowledge anyone under five-eight.

Even if she didn't have the faintest idea who this guy in the suit was, she could have told him about the vibrating noise that sometimes came from the attic, probably while Marcus was kicking the hell out of his punch bag, and how annoying it was that he chainsmoked in a building full of old people with asthma. But she didn't.

'He's no bother to anyone,' she replied with a shrug. 'He's a very quiet tenant actually.'

She wasn't clear why she was siding with Marcus, whatever side that was, but it seemed to come naturally to her to want to protect him.

The man nodded and smiled with a strange paternal satisfaction as he wrote something in a notebook that he'd pulled from his pocket. Right at that moment, Marcus came in through the front door. He was about to light a cigarette but stopped in his tracks. His face fell visibly when he saw the man and he dropped his glacial facade for a moment. Then he looked at Penny and frowned, realising she'd been talking to the guy. Penny was sure of one thing: Marcus was wondering, with a hint of alarm, exactly what she might have said about him.

'Oh, so you're here,' the man said to Marcus. 'Where can we go to talk?'

'I didn't think you'd be here so early,' Marcus muttered in a low voice.

All three of them started up the stairs, Penny trailing behind them, listening in as the man in the suit asked Marcus questions about his work, which Marcus answered in dry monosyllables.

At the door to their apartment, Barbie appeared with a tray of cookies, the same ones she'd been busy baking before Penny went out. As soon as she spotted Marcus she lit up, her manner suddenly flirtatious, as she always was when she saw him. Penny had tried her hardest to dissuade her from being so friendly with Marcus, but her grandma felt eternally young and was still inclined to appreciate the statuesque good looks of certain young men. When she'd been in a particularly sentimental and romantic mood, she had even advised Penny to ask him out.

'You can't deny he's a handsome boy, my dear. If I were your age, I'd ask him to the movies or to a nice restaurant with candles on the table.'

'Er, yes . . . maybe . . . I'll think about it.' Penny had decided to let her grandmother live with that hope, though no way would she be asking him unless she were forced. And Barbie, living in her own sweet la-la land, had convinced herself that her niece was having an affair with that hunky young man from the top floor.

'Oh, Marcus!' Penny's grandma exclaimed. 'I made cookies. Would you like some?'

'You two know each other?' asked the stranger.

And then Barbie said something that made Penny wish the earth would go ahead and swallow her up. 'My Penny and this young man have a little thing going on. It's real love at first sight! Isn't that romantic?'

Marcus looked as though he'd been kicked in the gut. He reeled backwards, shooting a hostile look at Penny.

'Are you a relative of Marcus?' Barbie went on. 'My Penny's a good girl. She's twenty-two, works in the library and has a good head on her shoulders.'

'Great!' the man declared, giving Marcus a smile of explicit approval. 'So I trust she knows everything then.'

This time it was Penny who was reeling. *What is it I'm supposed to know?* But Marcus unexpectedly beat her to a response. 'Of course she knows everything,' he confirmed earnestly, and put an arm around her shoulders, squeezing her hard as if to say, *Don't say a word or I'll crush you.*

Penny nearly collapsed in shock.

'Come upstairs with us,' the man said.

So, without knowing what on earth was going on, Penelope found herself climbing the stairs behind Marcus and his mysterious visitor, urged on by her grandma, who was bubbling over with joy.

Marcus turned for an instant and threw her a look, with an unspoken command not to mess this up for him.

They entered his apartment, and Penny forced her face to stay neutral. Should she pretend she'd already been here? She made out that she wasn't surprised at the transformation of what she remembered as having been a dump into a decent apartment – very masculine and lacking in frills, but clean. There was a blue throw on the couch, to cover up the holes. The punch bag Marcus had carried in a few days earlier towered in a corner. The worn wooden floor had recently been swept, and, right under the skylight, a bed had been pushed up against the wall, covered with a light-green duvet. The whole place still reeked of the white emulsion used to freshen up the walls.

The stranger looked at everything carefully, nodding repeatedly and loosening the knot of his tie a little. Finally he sat on the couch and turned to Penny. 'So, is he behaving himself?' he asked again. 'With you, I mean. To gauge Marcus's progress, I need to take a few things into consideration: not only whether he's employed and sober, but also how he behaves with the people around him, such as his neighbours and his girlfriend.'

Penny swallowed hard, more embarrassed than she'd ever been in her whole life. Marcus stared at her, his polished-steel eyes boring into her, filled with emotions she couldn't even begin to guess at. Suspicion? Fear? Anger? The man in the suit was also staring at her, with a pinch of apprehension and the air of a parish priest awaiting the confession of his most rebellious believer, whom he nonetheless loved and wanted to save from the fires of eternal damnation. Everyone was waiting for her to speak.

'Well, as I already told you,' she said finally, feigning a quiet sincerity, 'his behaviour is exactly as it should be. He smiles at everyone and he's an absolute angel with me.'

Penny was suddenly afraid of having exaggerated. To imagine Marcus smiling at the elderly inhabitants of the building – the same Marcus who went around with a constant sneer on his lips – seemed too absurd to believe. And to imagine him being polite to Penny, when he probably gave her less consideration than he would a microbe, was even more far-fetched; but the man, who was either stupid or a little too innocent, seemed to fall for it anyway.

'Great,' he said for the umpteenth time, with another satisfied smile. 'And you, son, I beg you, keep surrounding yourself with decent people. Above all, forget that other girl. She brings out the worst in you and just causes trouble. She's not right for you. I don't like knowing that you requested to visit her in prison. Penny, on the other hand, seems like exactly the right kind of person. If I can be sure you're doing well, you'll see less of me, but if they tell me you went to see Miss Lopez or I find out you've made another bad move, I'll have to report it to the director. You're on parole. If you mess this up, they'll make you serve another two years. That's not a threat, son, it's the law; I only hope you pay attention and act in your own best interests.'

Marcus nodded, but Penny sensed a pent-up anger in him. He was saying yes, but he wanted to break something. Penny saw him clench a fist so hard that his knuckles grew waxy and the veins on his wrist burned bright blue. If Penny, who barely knew Marcus, had noticed, how come this other man – who must be his parole officer – had not? He certainly knew Marcus better than Penny did, yet he didn't seem to have any idea. He scribbled another note in his little book, shook hands with both of them and finally left, after loosening his tie again with a tired gesture and wearily stretching his neck.

Penny started to follow the parole officer out, but Marcus held her by the arm. 'Could you just wait until he's gone? I'm sure he'll stop and ask your grandmother something else on the way down. If you follow him right away, he'll catch on – unless you regret this whole little charade and want him to.'

She didn't quite understand why she was helping him like this, but Penny shook her head. 'So you were in prison?' she asked immediately, without a hint of accusation or even excessive curiosity. She didn't want to know why or for how long. She was sure he had killed someone, and preferred not to know the details.

'Yes, and you don't seem too surprised.'

'It's more that I don't really care.'

'So why did you lie to him then?'

'Because it's fun to play pretend sometimes. Don't worry, I didn't put that idea of you and me being together in my grandma's head. She doesn't get things right and she lives in a world of her own. I wouldn't want to be with you even if you were the last man on the planet. And, hey, I'm not even going to beg you to fuck me silly.'

Marcus suddenly smiled, and for the first time Penny glimpsed a spark of genuine amusement beyond his usual mask of aggression. She watched the play of his lips, enchanted like a little girl watching a rainbow. With that smile tugging at his mouth, at least three days of beard, and the monumental body that towered over her in the small room, it was an all-too-pleasant sight. Penny shook herself and bit her tongue, pressing a nail into the palm of her hand, doing her best to appear detached, as if the sudden sensations – hot, humid and fluttering – halfway between her stomach and her knees were nothing out of the ordinary.

'I'm sure he'll run a background check on you two, in case the innocent-looking kid and the sweet old lady turn out to be the top dealers in the neighbourhood,' Marcus said wryly. He went in search of the cigarette he'd been lighting earlier on his way into the building. He found it in a pocket of his jacket and put it to his lips.

'My grandma only deals in cookies, and often she puts salt in them instead of sugar. I don't deal anything, and neither of us has been to prison,' Penny said with a shrug. 'Once, my grandma stole a pair of tights in a store, but she didn't do it on purpose. She doesn't always realise what she's doing and thought she'd paid for them. That's the only crime she's ever committed and no one even noticed.'

'And what about you?' asked Marcus, lighting his cigarette, and from behind the sudden cloud of smoke he stared at her so attentively that Penny felt her internal organs scramble like ingredients in a cocktail shaker.

'I'm an epic bore. Your probation officer will be very satisfied with what he finds out about me.'

'I'm sure he'll be back.'

'In that case, I'll tell my grandma to bake more cookies.'

'Why are you doing this for me?'

'I'm not doing it for you, I'm doing it for me. It's fun, that's all.'

'And what do you want in return?'

Penny smiled, tipping her head to one side. 'You're not used to people doing something for nothing, are you? It must be hard living in a world where you're only worth what you give. Don't worry, we can keep on ignoring each other. I won't ask you any funny questions, and you don't need to pretend to be in love with me just to please my grandma, or even sacrifice yourself by giving your body to me.'

Marcus let out a puff of smoke with a sarcastic look on his face. 'It might not be that much of a sacrifice after all.'

It felt like there was a tuning fork twanging away between her ribs, but Penny replied bitterly, as though she'd never thought of it herself: 'Well, let's hope we never find out. I'm leaving now. I think the guy must be gone.'

With that, she waved airily and headed back downstairs. Only then did she realise she was trembling with nerves. She'd managed to quell the urge to ask who this Miss Lopez was that the probation officer had mentioned. Somehow she had the strongest feeling that, in comparison with herself and her own humdrum life, Miss Lopez was anything but dead boring.

4

Marcus

Living in a building full of old people simply has to be the worst possible way to fly under the radar. I hadn't considered this particular complication. Every time I see someone on the stairs, they ask me who I am, what I do, what I'm aiming for in life, if I'm married, if I have pets . . . It's such a drag having to stop and be nice to everyone all the time.

I'm just carrying my new punch bag up the stairs when I meet the girl from last night. She still has that ridiculous pink hat on with the pink bit of hair sticking out. She looks at me with her wide eyes, and I can read her like a book. The usual story. Another bitch with a college-girl face who's gonna give me nothing but trouble. I have no problem with women who know what they want – we meet, we fuck, we say goodbye – but these girls straight out of bible school are the worst: they rip off your pants and then want you to marry them. I've always stayed away from that kind and I don't plan on changing any time soon.

I need to start avoiding her. If I give her an inch she'll take a mile. She's a loser who still lives with her elderly grandmother . . . I can already imagine the consequences of a throwaway fuck in that direction. They'd probably send round the parish priest to exorcise me.

◆ ◆ ◆

I see Malkovich and straight away a machine-gun fire of obscenities rattles through my mind. I thought he'd at least give me a minute to catch my breath before tracking me down for the usual inter-rogation. He always hated Francisca. He blames what happened on her, and does it with that faux-paternal air that pisses me off even more. I'd break his neck if I could, but I can't. I don't want to go back to prison, but anyone who says Francisca would have stopped me from killing that guy if she really loved me doesn't know the first thing about the two of us. Francisca and I are the same, cut from the same cloth. We totally get each other, we think the same, we have the same needs. I'd have killed that guy no matter what.

Not only does it bother me that Malkovich is here early, but also that he's talking to that idiot girl who lives below me. What the hell is she telling him? It's clearly nothing that serious though. I can tell by the way Malkovich is looking at me: kinda satisfied, without that horrible eyebrow he raises during his usual sermons full of *my boy*, *my son*, and *don't ruin your life now*.

The old woman could have kept her mouth shut. Does she really think I'd date her granddaughter? How on earth did she come up with that? It's too much of a can of worms to even go there. Malkovich is happy, whatever – and I can't tell him the truth if I don't want to risk going back inside for another two years.

I have to admit that, once he's gone, the girl surprises me. I'd imagined her as the typical chick who plays hard to get and then puts her hand down my pants, but there's more to her than I thought. She's a bitch all right, to hear her talk – the kind who'd give me a serious kick in the balls if I got too close – but now she has me paying her more attention than I'd expected. OK, she's pretty weird, with her pandas, that pink hair and the purple eye-lashes to boot, but she has beautiful chocolate-coloured eyes, a sensual mouth and gorgeous legs. Her skirt today isn't as short as the one she had on the other night, but it's enough for any man with a discerning eye to notice that her thighs are worth a second look. I'm guessing she also has a nice ass. If I weren't in the mess I was in, I'd do her for sure. If she's this feisty in bed, we'd probably have a great time.

There's just one thing that's bothering me: I can't see Francisca. She'll be out before long though, and it's best not to piss off Malkovich. If we want to be left in peace, we need to start acting less with our guts and more with our heads.

5

The bar was crowded and noisy. The waitresses usually served food and drink at the tables, but on nights like this the thirsty patrons resembled a horde of zombies around a carcass, so Penny with her singular flair for mixing cocktails was stationed alongside Carlos, the regular bartender.

Five minutes earlier, Grant had come up to the bar and mockingly ordered something from Penny. At the sight of him, she had frozen for a moment, the shaker in her hands and a snake of icy sweat running down her spine. Then she had whispered something into Carlos's ear and dashed to take refuge in the small staff area where they stored their shoes and coats.

Penny's colleague Debbie came in just at that moment to look for aspirin in her bag, to swallow dry in the hopes that her damn headache would go away, and found Penny there, holed up like a cat in a box.

'What are you doing in here?' she asked. 'It's madness out there – now is no time to take a break.'

'I'm coming,' Penny muttered, thinking back to the sinister way Grant had looked at her a few moments earlier.

'Did something happen?'

'No, everything's fine.'

'Then hurry up, yeah? The place is heaving.'

Penny nodded, getting to her feet. In any case, it was useless to try to escape. Prey always flees; but Penny did not intend on being Grant's prey, nor did she plan on showing her fear, though in actual fact she could feel the fear flowing right through her, warm and salty, a fear that made her legs leaden and her arms go limp.

She left the staff area and went back to the bar. Grant was still there; he hadn't budged an inch, even though he was besieged on all sides by a crowd. His Bloody Mary was still untouched. Penny watched in horror as he licked his yellow straw in the most vilely suggestive manner before running his tongue over his lips. She looked away, sickened.

For a couple of hours she tried to ignore his presence. Grant moved away from the bar, but he remained in the room, sitting at a table ordering things that she was sure he wouldn't eat, simply to justify his presence. He was alone but people noticed him because he was handsome, well dressed, and unlike the other guys he didn't look rotten as a wormy apple. He chatted up a few of the girls, but Penny knew he was there for her. He stayed until last call, and the place began to empty out. Suddenly the crowd melted away and Debbie, who was in charge of the floor because she was sleeping with the owner, ordered Penny to bring the cheques to her various customers.

'Could you go instead, please?' Penny ventured to ask.

'Listen, missy, I've been working the floor for six hours with a killer headache while you've been standing behind that bar. Now move your ass and take those people their cheque.'

'That one man has been bothering me . . .'

'Bullshit. I can tell a troublemaker when I see one. No one bothered you. You're just being paranoid.'

And how was Penny supposed to respond? That a beautiful guy had stared at her all night with a smile on his face? What crime had he committed? She knew – she knew that his smile was equivalent to a sick promise, a silent way of telling her, *As soon as you leave here, I'm going to hurt you as much as I can get away with*. But that was hard for Penny to explain to anyone else.

So, in spite of herself, she took the check over to the bastard. Grant continued to smile at her with his barefaced-lying sweetness.

'Here you are at last, babe,' he said. 'I spent a fortune just to be near you, did you notice?'

'Just pay and leave, please,' Penny replied coldly.

'I'll pay, I'll leave, but I'm waiting for you outside. It's late, it's going to rain and I have the car. I'll take you home, so you'll be perfectly safe. And since I love you, I'll leave you a nice tip too, see?' He pulled a fifty-dollar bill from his wallet and left it on top of what he owed. Then, dropping his voice so that only she could hear him, he whispered, 'It's an advance. If you turn out to be worth more, I'll pay up later.'

Penny took the money but left the fifty dollars. She walked away feeling soiled, as though someone had poured a stinking, sticky liquid all over her. She was definitely in trouble.

She had no friends, there was no one she could call for a ride, and she couldn't exactly call a cab just to go two blocks down the street. She had to find a solution, some way to avoid being alone and at the mercy of Grant's not-so-mysterious intentions.

In the staff area, Penny changed her shoes and put on her coat, then she asked Carlos a question and he replied, 'Aren't you tired yet?'

And that's how she found her way to the rear exit. It was a blind alley, a dead end, and a high wall separated it from the next street over.

She needed all her strength to get out of there, climbing on to a garbage can and then scrambling over the barbed wire that ran along the top of the wall. She wasn't exactly what you would call agile, but fear and need triggered a sudden burst of athleticism in her. Just as she was climbing over the barbed wire, she tore her pantyhose. *Crap*, she thought. She'd have to buy a new pair. *Just focus on getting home safely – your pantyhose is no big deal.*

She made it over the wall, tearing the other leg of her tights on the way, then pulled her coat more tightly around her, cursing Grant and his whole family.

Reaching the safety of the alleyway down the side of the building, she suddenly spotted him standing in front of the bar, waiting for her. She couldn't go out that way or he'd follow her with that outwardly angelic air of his, no one any the wiser that his real intentions were full of violence and sex.

So her only safe option was impossible after all. She quickly turned left and left again, and then began to run, wondering how far she could get before he came after her. There was no cab to jump into for those terrifying ten minutes to home, not even a stupid bus.

Sometimes she'd turn to see if he was following, but unless he was hiding, there was no sign of him.

After a while she saw the colourful sign of the Maraja nightclub ahead of her, and there was Marcus, smoking a cigarette with a girl in skintight jeans, boots with sky-high heels and a green fake-fur coat, whose laugh sounded like she'd been a nervous sheep in a previous life.

Penny ran faster, desperate to reach them. Marcus had his back to her – that damn gorgeous back that looked like it had been sculpted by Michelangelo himself. Peering around the side of Marcus, the girl caught sight of her and gave her a curious look. Only then did Penny realise the state she was in: the torn pantyhose and a gash on one knee, blood dripping all the way down to her shoes. To complete the picture, she was pouring with sweat and wheezing.

Marcus turned, and for a moment his eyes, like liquid mercury, stared at her without recognition. Finally, from behind his usual veil of smoke, he asked, 'So what do you want?'

He punctuated his question with a searing look, and Penny first raised her eyes to the heavens, as if seeking forgiveness for having abandoned her senses in choosing to turn to this caveman for help. And then she dropped them in an attempt to apologise to her nether regions, because, despite all reason and logic, they were clearly not indifferent at all to that primitive call. There was nothing she could do about it: she just found this man wildly attractive. One glimpse of him and her DNA, hormones, molecules and atoms danced the samba.

'What actually happened to you?' Marcus asked again, looking at her legs and the blood.

'Oh, nothing. I got into a fight with a dumpster. Can I tell you something? Without an audience?' Penny said, pointing to the girl in the heels and the fur, who took another drag on her cigarette, thoroughly enjoying the spectacle of this wounded bag lady. Marcus turned to the woman and, without him needing to say a word, she shrugged her shoulders and flicked her cigarette on to the ground, crushing it with the pointed toe of her boot before marching back inside.

Once they were alone on the unusually deserted sidewalk, Penny went on the attack. 'I changed my mind,' she said with a determined air.

'Are you drunk? Because I don't understand you,' Marcus objected, chucking his cigarette and kicking it down the street.

Penny thought back to Grant and his secret threats, and let out a deep sigh. 'I told you I didn't want anything in return for that favour with your parole officer.'

Marcus's lip curled in that way people's do when they find out they're right after all. 'So you've changed your mind? Well, what a surprise, though I'd rather die than go to bed with you.'

'Why do you always think I want sexual favours from you?'

'Because that's what everyone wants from me. Or maybe you want me to solve a mathematical equation for you, or paint you a portrait in the finest watercolours?'

'Of course not, but it must be sad.'

'What?'

'To think that the whole world always and exclusively revolves around your . . . er . . . thing.'

'The whole world does always and exclusively revolve around my . . . er . . . thing.'

'That's absurd. I really don't want it. I mean . . . I don't want anything like that. I just want to make a deal with you.'

Marcus lit another cigarette. That one small act – the pursed lips and squinting eyes, the flame held close to his face, his hand cupping the end to protect it from the wind – was enough to make her hormones run riot. A deep and persistent tug somewhere low down in her body – way down, below her heart and her stomach – led her to wonder if there wasn't some truth to what he said. She had a terrible suspicion that she wanted him as her mysterious lover. One look at Marcus and her whole old-fashioned romantic ideal of two lovers holding hands in the moonlight and promising eternal love completely went out the window. All she wanted was to shove her tongue down his throat, et cetera et cetera. Oh, and how she longed to do that.

But right now she was here to offer him something quite different and, despite the damn blaze of desire that had lit up in her loins over the last ten days, she needed to keep up appearances and remain inscrutable.

'I want you to be my bodyguard at night.'

'What?'

'It's only two blocks – just from the bar to my front door. I won't ask anything else of you.'

'Well, like I said, you wouldn't want me to paint you a water-colour,' he said, laughing without conviction. 'That's the second thing women usually ask of me: first it's sex, and then self-defence. You're not exactly being original here.'

'I don't want to be original,' Penny snapped. 'I want to stay alive!'

Marcus maybe recognised that her anxiety was genuine, because the smirk was instantly wiped off his face. 'Who is this person that wants you dead?'

'Just someone. I'm not going to bore you with the details.'

'And this guy actually wants to kill you?'

'Not kill me necessarily, but . . . um . . . as you might say, bother me.'

'I don't like that kind of guy, but I can't have anything to do with this. If I get my hands on him, I'll kill him, and I'm not going back to prison.'

'I knew it.'

'Knew what?'

'That you hadn't done time for killing a good person. I just knew you had to have been dealing with some piece of shit. Anyway, look, I'm not asking you to kill anyone, just . . . walk with me, OK? If you're there he won't even come close. He's a coward.'

'They always are.'

'But this guy's an above-average coward.'

'You don't want to report him?'

'He's never actually done anything to me, except the one time . . . and it wasn't serious enough to go to the police. So far it's mainly just threats, but tonight he was at the bar and I'll admit my heart skipped a beat or two. I slipped out the back exit and got all scraped up. I'm all my grandma's got – I can't go dying or get into trouble.'

'And what do I get out of it?'

'I told you, I'll keep playing the part for your parole officer.'

'I can handle my parole officer all on my own, thank you very much. I just have to avoid seeing Francisca for a couple of months, pay the rent and hold down my job.'

'Her name is Francisca?'

'Huh?'

Penny found the name strangely discomforting. Francisca Lopez. She imagined her to be tall and sexy, with dark hair, killer legs, great breasts and cruel eyes. You could tell he was just crazy about her. She wondered how it would feel to be loved by someone like Marcus.

She instantly dismissed this as total fantasy and went back to the reason she was standing there now.

'If Francisca needed help, wouldn't you be glad there was someone to help her out?'

'Francisca can take care of herself, but I know what you're saying. Well, OK then, but I want more in return.'

'I don't want to sound like a broken record but I'm not giving you my thing.'

Marcus laughed, and this time he seemed to find it truly funny. 'Look, no offence, but I hadn't even thought to ask. I was thinking of something more useful, OK?'

'Like what?'

'Like money.'

'You want me to pay you?'

'You want a bodyguard, don't you? That's a paid service.'

'It's not like I'm swimming in cash.'

'I didn't say you were. I'm pretty broke myself and an extra dollar is an extra dollar. Shall we say a hundred a week?'

'You're insane! Where do I find that kind of money? Oh yeah, I know, I could go prostitute myself with Grant, but then I wouldn't need your help anymore. How about thirty?'

'Thirty? That doesn't even buy my cigarettes. You get what you pay for.'

'And what exactly am I paying for? I'm asking you to walk beside me for two blocks, that's all!'

'It's for accessory services.'

'I told you I don't want "accessory services". Forty – take it or leave it.'

'Sixty? I'll even carry you over the puddles for sixty.'

'Fifty and that's final, and if there's a puddle, feel free to dive right in, OK?'

Marcus laughed again, shaking his head, and every cell in Penny's being started to throb in unison. They shook hands to seal the deal; his felt huge, warm and a little rough, and Penny's atoms went into secret orgasm.

'I want the first week paid up front,' he said. 'Pay me tomorrow if you don't have it tonight. Now, just wait here a moment. I'll tell them I'm leaving and we can go.'

Night was just turning to dawn and the sun was moments from breaching the horizon. Penny had stopped looking around in fear. She wasn't afraid when she was with Marcus, and she wasn't afraid of him either. Yes, he'd been in prison for killing a man, he looked terrifying, and his personal vocabulary was decidedly foul-mouthed, but Penny knew she was safe with him. He really was monstrously tall. She felt like a tiny crumb alongside him, and wondered what it would feel like to lay her head on his chest. The whole time they were walking, the particles in her body screamed like a gaggle of Beatles fans. She coughed to cover up the noise, paranoid that Marcus might somehow hear them.

'So the name of this asshole is Grant?' he asked.

'Yeah. Sounds decent enough, doesn't it?'

'So where'd you find this guy?'

'At the bar where I work.'

'And you weren't suspicious? Quite honestly, it's a shitty place. I have no idea why you're even working there.'

'It was close to home and they hired me. The Maraja, where you work, didn't want me – seems like I don't wear enough make-up.'

'Yeah, well. Basically they only want women who look like models.'

'Is your sensitivity included in the fee?'

'I didn't think it was in the job description to have to pay you compliments.'

'It wasn't, no, but you don't have to be offensive.'

'I wasn't trying to offend you. You're just short, OK? Did you think you were some kinda supermodel?'

'First, I'm not short, you're just huge. Second, you're a jerk.'

'I didn't say you were ugly. You've got your own thing going on, for someone who likes . . .'

'Likes what . . . ?'

'Women like you.'

'That's enough, thanks. Anyway, Grant looked like a normal guy at first, maybe more polite than average, even – the type who opens the door of the car for you, or pulls your chair out so you can sit down, or brings you flowers and chocolates.'

'Those types are always perverts, but you women get screwed by all this bullshit about the perfect gentleman. I'd never dream of bringing flowers, chocolates or crap like that to a girl.'

'Not even to Francisca?'

'Never!'

'You say it like someone told you to cut off your balls and pickle them.'

Marcus laughed for the umpteenth time that evening.

You don't like me, but at least I can make you happy. I'd like to make you happy in other ways too, but there's no hope of that.

'Ah well, almost!' he exclaimed, pulling his cigarettes from his jacket pocket.

'Well, to put it your way, I did get screwed. After a couple of cosy dates, he quickly showed me once and for all that he's no superhero. He completely flipped out.'

'He attacked you?'

'We were in this romantic spot, full of nice couples, up on a hill with a view of the night sky and everything else, and then out of the blue he basically ordered me to . . . um . . . to . . .'

'Give him a blowjob?'

'How did you know?'

'It's easier to ask for a blowjob than have full-on sex with a bunch of other people around.'

'Well, he didn't ask exactly, and as for you, you cut right to the chase, don't you? Always straight to the point.'

'I use the words as required. Does it bother you?'

'No . . . strangely not. Actually, I guess once you say these things out loud often enough they lose their power.'

'I'm not talking this way to upset you. It's just the only way I know.'

'There's a whole beautiful array of other words out there, should you choose to split hairs, but no matter.'

'Returning to the asshole, how did you manage to stop him?'

'I had a bobby pin in my hair that night, so I jabbed him . . . um . . . there . . . and ran away.'

'You did what?' Marcus paused with his cigarette in mid-air, staring in open admiration at her audacity.

47

'I didn't hurt him enough unfortunately, because ever since then he's been haunting me wherever I go – only verbal threats, and never when anyone else can hear.'

'That kind of guy can't get it up to save his life, trust me, but they're dangerous anyway, because they'll cut your throat in frustration when they can't get a hard-on.'

'Quit talking like that with the old people in the building, will you, or they'll all drop dead and you'll be back on the stand for manslaughter!'

'Right now, you're the only person I talk to like that – you're the only person I talk to at all, in fact.'

'Really?'

'We're here.'

Penny shook herself and saw their apartment building up ahead. His language was direct and colourful, devoid of sentimental frills, but she was concerned by the idea that Marcus didn't have anyone else to talk to besides her. Though that didn't exactly scare her, even if she was starting to feel an overwhelming interest in him that went far beyond his ability to protect her in her current situation. It wasn't just your everyday sexual attraction, which would have been entirely normal for any hot-blooded woman who didn't get to see much action. No, this feeling was plain confusing – something to do with her ribcage, the pounding of her heart and her inability to breathe whenever she was around him. This was not good, whichever way she chose to look at it. Having a crush on someone with the body and face of a Greek statue, who spread pheromones with his every stride, who loved a woman with an exotic name, and who saw Penny as the slightly less intriguing equivalent of a garden gnome, must be the first step on the path to grief and sorrow.

6

MARCUS

Francisca's gonna wonder what happened to me, and that pisses me off. Unfortunately it's the only way to distract those assholes and make them believe we're not going to see each other again. They have this stupid idea that we're dangerous together, but we're even more dangerous on our own. Our past is a whole lot more tragic and violent than your average person's. We met at sixteen, and we'd already been through so much by then. Two misfits without a future and too much of a past behind us. She got bounced from family to family, and I got taken away from my mother. I never knew my father. The first time Francisca and I laid eyes on each other, we both thought, *You are me, I am you. We'll never be alone again.* We stayed together, united in body and spirit, until that asshole tried to cut her face and we took care of him. If we hadn't had the kind of past we did, we'd probably have been allowed a plea of self-defence – we were attacked and provoked. But what happened will mark us forever.

◆ ◆ ◆

I'm having a cigarette and some woman starts chatting me up, when luckily Penny arrives out of nowhere. I don't know why I say luckily – maybe because this woman's putting me off. Maybe because I enjoy talking to Penny, even if she's not much to look at. Maybe because when you look in her eyes, you think, *She's twenty-two all right, but she definitely hasn't visited all the bases yet.* I don't know much about her but I'm rarely wrong about such things. And also, she's strong. She always looks me straight in the eye, and I can tell I make her uncomfortable sometimes, but only when her throat flushes red. I don't do it on purpose, you know – I'm just like that. I live on bread and beer and not beating about the bush.

We make a pact: I walk her home and she pays me. Not much, but cash is cash. It's relaxing being with Penny, actually. My mind stops racing when I'm around her. Usually I'm a mile a minute, running, acting, thinking, thinking, thinking about the past – digging up all the memories I've tried so hard to bury over the years. My head always feels like it's being bombarded by amphetamines, even though I never take that shit. When I'm around Penny though, I stop thinking about it all. She's like one of those cartoons for kids who are lucky enough not to have a mother who's a prostitute, like mine was. Me, I never got to watch that kind of cartoon.

In any case, I'm planning to offer her a bonus in exchange for my fee. If she trusts me, I'll give her some lessons in self-defence. She's not going to be able to count on me forever. I'll be gone in a couple of months, and that maniac could still be out there. A few strategic moves, some tips on where to hit harder . . . I never had to teach Francisca a thing; she was already wise to everything she needed to know.

The judges are idiots to think we're more dangerous together than alone. At twelve, Francisca set fire to her stepfather's house after whacking him with a baseball bat. At fifteen, I plunged a pair of scissors into the back of my mother's lover.

7

She ran into him on the way back home from the library. He was on the way out. They met at the door of the building, just as she was putting her key in the lock. The smell of his body hit her first. He was wearing old trackpants and a white shirt glued to his skin with sweat. Penny's tongue nearly hit the floor. She needed to get a grip, erase the fantasies that flooded her mind whenever she saw him, and take control of the atoms bouncing and squealing within her, stunned at so much abundance. She swallowed hard, pretending not to notice the six-pack bulging under his T-shirt, or the veins pumping along his wrists.

'Hey,' he said, and Penny composed herself, afraid he wanted to back out of their agreement or raise his fee.

'I can't give you more than fifty dollars,' she murmured, staring down at the key in her hand and her nails. 'It's a lot of money for me already, you know.'

'I'm not asking for more money. I wanna give you a gift.'

'A gift? What kind of gift?' she asked, blushing.

Marcus laughed mockingly and shook his head. 'You say I'm the one with a one-track mind, but I just know you're always thinking about it too! Well, it's not the gift you're hoping for.'

'I'm not hoping for anything.'

'Sorry, but you're not the greatest actress, little lady. You definitely want me, even if you won't admit it. You've wanted me a long time now, but it's simply not gonna happen. We. Will. Not. Fuck. Is that clear enough?'

'Maybe if you say it a little louder, they'll be able to hear you down the block. I wouldn't want them to feel excluded.'

'They wouldn't hear me even if I screamed right in their ear. The youngest person around here is seventy years old. Anyway, I thought I'd teach you some self-defence moves.'

'Me?'

'Tell me, aren't you the one getting followed around by that asshole?'

'Are you serious?'

'Yeah. Let's start right away.'

'Now?'

'It's never too late to learn how to hit someone who tried to force you to give him a blowjob.'

'Fine. Let me go tell my grandma I'm with you.'

'Just give me time to shower, OK?'

Penny nodded. She resisted the urge to beg him not to change, to remain just as he was, all sweaty and barbaric. She needed to look but not touch. Maybe if she repeated that enough times to herself she'd get it through her thick head.

Upstairs, Penny walked into the apartment, where Barbie was humming and busy making cookies.

'Why don't you go get some rest?' Penny told her, because Barbie was scattering flour all over the place, pouring it into a sieve that she'd no doubt mistaken for a small bowl.

'You know, I think I'll do just that. I cooked and baked all day for those little ones, but they were driving me crazy. I'm tired now.'

Penny felt a lump in her throat but kept on smiling. 'I'm going up to see Marcus for a few minutes,' she explained, thinking maybe

Barbie wouldn't remember him, or that she'd mistake him for one of her class who'd been giving her a hard time maybe, but her grandma surprised her.

'Oh, that handsome man of yours! He reminds me of when I was a girl. I'm glad he moved here and you two got together. So, when do you plan to get married?'

'I don't know yet. We need to get to know each other a little better first,' Penny said, walking around the kitchen and tidying up along the way.

'Take my advice: let him want you. No kisses until you have a ring.'

'I promise.'

'He seems so unhappy. Try to make him smile.'

'Does he look unhappy?'

'Oh yes, he has that look of someone who's never really been shown love. You can do that part.'

'I'll do my best.'

'I taught little ones for many years and I learned a few things in return. Some of the biggest bullies had eyes just like Marcus. I never mistreated them. I could always achieve so much more by showing them love and tenderness – and by giving them cookies, of course. All kids love cookies.'

'I'll fill him up with tenderness and sweet things then.'

'That's my girl! Now run along and take him some of the treats I baked today.'

Barbie made up a parcel of cookies and Penny was forced to leave the apartment with it to humour her. She made her grandma swear she would go to sleep, and Barbie promised, her face as innocent as a child's.

At last, Penny climbed the twisting staircase up to the attic, so narrow with its low ceiling that she wondered how Marcus even managed to get up there. She knocked, excited beyond all reason.

He opened after ten seconds, still wet but no longer sweaty. He smelled of soap, a light soap with a faint hint of mint and citrus. He was evidently in the habit of changing without towelling off, because his clean T-shirt clung to his body just like the one before had. He was wearing a different pair of sweatpants and was barefoot. This time, Penny commanded her tongue to remain in her mouth.

'These are for you from my grandma, but don't eat them. She put detergent in them, I think.'

Marcus made no comment and pointed to the single table that served for the kitchen, living room and study – the only table present in that tiny space, in fact. Marcus had moved the couch and laid out a rubber mat.

If Penny had been under any illusion that Marcus might have a secret motive in wanting to teach her self-defence, she would have been in for a harsh wake-up call. Fortunately, she hadn't remotely entertained this possibility, and she trusted him. Somehow she trusted an ex-convict she'd known for less than two weeks, who could put her out of action with a mere snap of his fingers. She'd let him turn her upside down like a doll without fearing for a moment that he might harm her.

Penny listened to him carefully. She learned some basic moves – how to wriggle to loosen his grip, to aim for the eyes, nose, crotch or ankles of a potential attacker.

During one manoeuvre, she suddenly found herself lying on the rubber mat with Marcus on top of her. There were at least three inches between them, but he was closer than ever before to her, and she realised how small and fragile she was in comparison. A delicate little leaf against the solid bulk of an ancient oak.

'In this position you have to lift your knee,' Marcus explained, touching Penny's thigh to show her the movement.

Her mind exploded at his touch, and she blushed, knowing full well that if Marcus had asked or even gestured for them to make love, she'd have no hesitation. It was as if the very existence of Marcus had awakened her from a very long sleep. It no longer seemed a step too far, like scaling the snowy heights of Mount Everest or bungee-jumping off some fearsome bridge. For a long time she had imagined sex as a special skill, a talent she didn't possess, something one was born with or not. Now it seemed natural, easy, necessary . . .

At that precise moment, the door to the apartment swung open and Mr Malkovich appeared, wearing his usual tattered suit, tie loose around his neck, glasses on the tip of his nose and a pen between his fingers. Marcus jumped like a leopard surprised by its prey. Penny lay there, half paralysed with astonishment.

'Well, that's got me reassured,' the parole officer commented effusively, without so much as a greeting. 'I'll admit that after our previous meeting, I did have the slightest suspicion it was all an act – you two being a couple, I mean – but this surprise visit has dispelled all my doubts. And I know you stopped writing to Miss Lopez – good boy. I ran a background check on you, Miss Miller, and I'm very satisfied with what I learned. You're definitely the person best suited to lead our Marcus down the right path. Right, I'll be off then and you two can get back to it.'

With that, and without giving Penny or Marcus the chance to utter a single word, he left. Marcus stood up abruptly and whacked his head on the ceiling.

'Shit!' he said, massaging his skull.

'Did he really come in here, or was I hallucinating?' asked Penny, sitting up.

'He's less stupid than I thought,' Marcus muttered to himself.

'Except that now he'll be convinced we're madly in love and having sex all the time.'

Marcus gave her a smile, and Penny felt something blossom inside her. He smiled so seldom that, when he did, Penny was quite sure the planets shifted from their orbits to contemplate the wonder of it.

'Get up.'

'Wouldn't it be better if we lie down again, just in case he comes back?'

'Didn't you lock the door when you came in?'

'I don't remember.'

'OK. First rule of self-defence: lock the fucking door of the fucking house.'

'Sorry, it slipped my mind. I had those cookies and . . .'

'Next time be more careful.'

'Will there be a next time?'

The smile wiped off his face and he frowned. 'I don't know. I don't know what that pain in the ass expects from me. I have to pretend not to want to see Francisca anymore. She's going to wonder what happened to me. I'm so pissed.'

Slowly, Penny looked down at the floor. 'I could do it,' she said.

'Do what?'

'I could tell Francisca that you haven't stopped loving her, you haven't stopped thinking about her, you're just pretending.'

Marcus stared at her as if he had X-ray vision and could see right through her. 'You'd really do that for me?'

'Yeah.'

'Why?'

'Why all the whys? Because I like you.'

'You're a strange person. I've never met anyone like you before.'

'Can I see a picture of her? I want to make sure I'll be talking to the right woman.'

He nodded and started rummaging in the pocket of a jacket hanging from the knob of the bathroom door. He pulled out his phone and handed it to her. Penny held her breath, as if it were part of a ritual in which she was miraculously allowed to participate.

The photo was a few years old. It showed a younger and skinnier Marcus with a woman for whom 'gorgeous' was an understatement. She was way more than that. She was Jessica Alba's dangerous twin. In the picture they were close, half-naked – an in-bed selfie. Neither of them was smiling. Penny wondered if they had just made love, and why they looked so serious and like they were consumed by some centuries-old fatigue. Marcus was holding one of his constant cigarettes between his fingers. Francisca was holding the phone and nuzzling into Marcus's face with a languor that seemed like her natural attitude, rather than just exhaustion following wild sex.

'She doesn't like having her picture taken,' Marcus commented. 'I don't have that many of her. She always says photos steal her soul.'

Penny nodded and muttered, 'She's very beautiful.'

'She's the most beautiful woman I know,' Marcus insisted.

'See? You're romantic in your own way.'

'I'm not romantic, it's just a fact. I mean, look at her.'

'Yes, she's beautiful.'

'Would you really do that for me?'

'Tell me when you want me to go and I'll go.'

'You're really strange, Penny.'

'I'm the strangest.'

'You're not so bad yourself, you know.'

'If you're just saying that to soften me up, you don't have to. I said I'll go, OK?'

'What does that even mean, "soften me up"? And I never say things I don't mean. With me, what you see is what you get.'

'What I see is already a lot.'

Penny got to her feet. There was a big spiky lump in her throat – seeing Marcus's mysterious and intimidating girlfriend had made her feel downright terrible. Penny didn't think she'd fallen in love with Marcus exactly, it was just her hormones talking. The same old story of all her cells and atoms in turmoil – nothing to do with the secrets of the soul. It was so easy to confuse the two. So easy to look at Marcus and think that her thumping heart was more than just lust, when it was nothing other than a twenty-two-year-old virgin's need to open herself up like a ripe pomegranate for the sexiest man she had ever seen.

At least, she hoped that was the case. Because if there was more to it than that, she was digging her own grave.

She wanted to go home. She wanted to lie down next to her grandma and hug her, hide her face in Barbie's silvery hair and cry, even though weeping was a tragic and disproportionate and totally pointless reaction to the reality of the situation.

'Next time I see you, you can tell me where to go and what to say to her.'

'OK . . . thanks,' said Marcus, and Penny got the impression that 'thanks' was a word he seldom used.

Just before she left, Penny reached up on tiptoe and lightly touched Marcus's cheek. His skin was freshly shaved, barely roughened by the shadow of dark stubble. He didn't back away, but seemed troubled by her gesture.

Penny smiled at him and said quietly, 'My grandma says that bullies need more tenderness than other kids do,' then she headed back downstairs before he could ask any questions.

◆　◆　◆

Leaning against the wall with one leg bent and a cigarette at his lips, Marcus was waiting outside for her when she left Well Purple. Her stomach did a somersault so fast that, for a moment, she thought she'd done one herself. For four long hours she had survived the fuggy atmosphere of the bar, terrified that Grant would repeat his little trick from the previous night and jumpy whenever anyone came up close. An actual somersault might have helped soothe the sudden rush of adrenaline when she finally made contact with the sweet night air and the scent of rain to come. Penny, however, feared it was Marcus's presence that was rocking her to the very core – against her will and without him knowing anything about it. How would she be feeling right now if she actually wanted to get together with him? But that was a stupid question that would never be answered.

'Well, aren't you just the punctual one?' she told him as he stubbed out his cigarette, crushing it under the heel of his massive black leather boot. They walked along the street, under a mist so fine it turned to dust before hitting the sidewalk.

'I don't like to do a half-ass job when I'm working. Were you OK in there?'

'Usual story.'

'Did that asshole show up?'

'Not tonight.'

'So what does he look like?'

'He's tall, skinny, blond. Well dressed.'

'You like that type?'

She turned, and looked at him angrily for a moment. 'I didn't think you judged women for actually being interested in a man. If I was wrong, I can take myself home.'

Marcus reached out and touched her elbow. It was very brief, but Penny had the impression that this fleeting gesture expressed something like friendship.

'I'm not judging you,' Marcus said. He took another cigarette, put it in his mouth, then patted down his body in search of a lighter.

I'll help if you want.

'You shouldn't judge a book by its cover. Otherwise I'd have to be afraid of you.'

'You should be afraid of me.'

'I was at first, but only for a moment; only because I was afraid you were Grant. I was afraid of the dark more than I was of you.'

Marcus found the lighter. The tip of his cigarette glowed orange as it touched the little flame. He took a long draw and, with the smoke still in his lungs, in icy tones he murmured, 'You should be afraid, you know. I'm not the type who would ever attack you, so you don't need to fear me like that, but just don't think this can go anywhere – don't imagine anything else between us. You pay me and I'll escort you home. You help me and I help you. It's a business agreement.'

Penny nodded as she poked around in her coat pocket. Marcus's words sounded right. They were certainly preferable to those of other men who might come into Penny's life and invent a million stories to gain her confidence, as Grant had done. She preferred Marcus's sincerity, even if it hurt her heart.

'Here,' she said finally, taking out five ten-dollar bills. 'Your first paycheque.'

Marcus shoved the bills into his pocket with no hesitation. Further demonstration of his frankness. A transaction – there was nothing else between them.

'Now, tell me what I have to do to go and see Francisca.'

Marcus was silent for a few seconds, then told her about the prison where Francisca was locked up. It was about two hundred miles away. The best day of the week for visits was Sunday: there were more people and the checks were less thorough. She'd have to be ready for a full-body search and to be questioned on why she was visiting.

'When Malkovich finds out, he may ask why you went,' Marcus said, almost to himself.

'He'll think it's a gesture of friendship. Do you think they listen in to conversations?'

'No, they don't take things that far. They're not the Taliban.'

'Well then, I'll tell Malkovich that I went to tell her it's over between you two – that you didn't have the guts to do it yourself. He'll believe that.'

'He'll believe it because that's what he would do. Because he's a mediocre government employee who's probably wanted to divorce his wife since who knows how long back, but can't work up the courage and would be happy if someone else did it for him.'

'Or else he'll believe it because he knows how much you love Francisca, and he knows that seeing her in tears would kill you.'

'Francisca would never cry over such bullshit.'

'You think the love of your life leaving you is bullshit?'

'You'd never understand.'

'What? What exactly wouldn't I understand?'

Marcus turned abruptly, once again reminding her of some pent-up wild creature. 'What it means to survive. Anyone who's cried out all their tears by the age of twelve will never shed a single tear again. She cares about me all right, but if I let her go, she'd come out of it stronger than before. I've never once seen her cry. And anyway, it's completely hypothetical, because I have every intention of dying at her side.'

Penny made no comment. She had always believed that love was about living with someone, not dying, but she said nothing. His truth was something else – for him, life was a struggle and love was a weapon. Standing together in the face of harsh adversity, and not just being together for the wonder of it. She had no idea what had happened in their pasts, what Marcus and Francisca had suffered and shared, but surely that kind of love was all they could allow themselves.

It's certainly more than I'll ever have.

'How do I get there?' Penny asked.

'How do *we* get there, you mean.'

'You're coming too?'

'I'm not letting you go alone. You never know what might happen.'

'Are you trying to supervise my mission?'

'That's one way to put it.'

Right then, the rain began to hurl itself from the sky, the heavy drops forming dense sheets of water. Marcus flicked away his cigarette and grabbed Penny by the hand, dragging her towards the door of their building. Her legs felt like clay and she was as wet as a chick in a puddle. Marcus ran a hand through his close-cropped hair, making a hail of drops fall on to the floor.

'Go and get changed,' Marcus urged her. 'If you get sick we can't go anywhere on Sunday.'

'How very selfless of you.'

'I need you and I want you to stay healthy – till this Sunday at least.'

'Then I can crawl off and die?'

'Be my guest.'

Penny muttered something under her breath and set off up the stairs. As per usual, the switch wasn't working, so Marcus took out the powerful little flashlight from his pocket and its warm beam lit up the stairwell.

But when Penny tried to open her apartment door, she realised something terrible had happened. Barbie had drawn the chain. The door opened a short way but then resisted. Unless she could magically morph into a sheet of paper, Penny would not be getting through any time soon. She stood there, paralysed in front of the crack that was taunting her. Then Marcus said from behind, 'I can break that right off for you – fittings like that are no good to anyone.'

'Can you do it quietly?'

'It's an iron bolt, not a cookie made with detergent. It will make some noise.'

'My grandma would have a heart attack this late at night – and the same thing would happen if I tried to phone her to let me in.'

'So what are you planning to do then?'

She turned and looked at him nervously – worried about what she was about to say. 'It's easy. I'll come sleep at yours.'

Marcus started in alarm, a surprising reaction for a man of his size. 'Forget it.'

'OK then, I'll stay right here, get pneumonia, and Francisca will keep thinking you're an asshole.'

'Francisca already knows I'm an asshole. Can't you ask another neighbour for their hospitality?'

'I don't know anyone well enough to ask.'

'You don't know me well enough, but you're still asking.'

Penny tilted her head to one side and stared at him provocatively. 'So what's the problem? You think I'll jump you in your sleep?'

Marcus gave a mocking laugh and brought his face close to hers. He whispered into her ear, their cheeks touching, still damp from the rain. 'Don't play with fire, monkey. You're the last girl in the world that I'd touch if I had all my wits about me, but you jump me at night and I might not be such a perfect gentleman. I'm all man and my gears are in full working order, so watch what you say.'

'I might just agree that it's better not to play with fire, so what do you know?'

'With that face there? I don't buy it. You wanna be fucked by me, no doubt about that, but you'd die of a broken heart if I treated you afterwards like I treat any woman who's not Francisca.'

Penny felt a chill, imagining the outcome: Marcus walking away after making love, without the slightest show of tenderness.

The very idea was appalling to her, even more so than the certainty that she would never in a million years end up in bed with him.

A gigantic sneeze interrupted her thoughts.

'Having said that, we've reached an impasse, as they say,' she said. 'Where will Penny sleep tonight? As we've just heard, pneumonia is closing in.'

Marcus let out a muted snort that sounded like a rumble of thunder in the silence of the stairwell. 'Well, OK then, come sleep at my place – but behave yourself.'

'You're ridiculous. You're like the living embodiment of lust, and you're telling *me* to behave myself?'

'You really don't know who you're dealing with, do you? I'm trying to protect you, but go too far and I'll show you what I mean all right.'

Penny was almost tempted to ask him to show her. But another sneeze brought her back to reality. 'Marcus, don't go fooling yourself you're God's gift to all women, OK? I just want a place to lay my head for the night. Having said that, can we move it along a little? It's going to be dawn soon and I'm really tired.'

◆ ◆ ◆

'You can sleep there,' said Marcus, pointing to the couch. 'The bed is mine. Now go to the bathroom and change, then lie down and shut up until tomorrow.'

'And what do I change into, pray pardon, good sir?'

'I'll lend you one of my shirts.'

Penny locked herself in the bathroom, peeled off her wet clothes and put on the long-sleeved T-shirt whose sleeves dangled beyond her fingertips. It was so big it fell off her shoulders. It had his smell. She sniffed it as if it were a rose in June.

I'm a pervert.

When she came out, Marcus was in wearing grey cotton pyjama pants and nothing else.

You doing this on purpose? You definitely want me to jump you.

Penny pretended to ignore him and lay down on the couch, wrapped herself in the blue blanket and closed her eyes.

Marcus carried on around her with his regular bedtime routine. She heard him peeing in the bathroom, could hear water running, then the door opening and the bed creaking under his weight.

'What if I get thirsty at night?' she asked suddenly.

'You're just gonna be thirsty,' came the abrupt response from her unfeeling host.

'And if I want a snack?'

'I'd like to avoid being vulgar, Penny, so spare me that kind of question.'

'Vulgar? In what . . . Oh right, I get it.'

'Good. So stop it, OK?'

'Is this really the first time you've hosted a woman guest over-night without . . . ?'

'First, you're not a guest, you're a blackmailer who got her way. Second, apart from Francisca, I don't host, I fuck. Third point, I'm tired and I'd like to sleep. Is it possible to turn you off somehow?'

'I'd like to avoid being vulgar, Marcus, so spare me that kind of question.'

She was sure she heard him laughing softly in the dark. His laughter was reassuring and oddly familiar. In spite of Marcus's rough ways, Penny felt in no danger whatsoever in that room, under that roof with its window to the sky. She thought of so many things, most of them highly improbable, the kind of vivid, lazy fantasies one has before drifting off to sleep. She imagined kissing him, taking his hand, touching him. She fell asleep, right there on her back.

When Penny awoke, it was daytime. Marcus was still asleep. She stood on tiptoe and gazed at him. She reached out her hand, tempted at the sight of that skin, that granite slab sheeted with painted silk, but immediately drew it back. His arms and most of his chest were covered with black-and-white Maori tattoos. Curves, coils and swirls that nestled together like birds in a flock – flames, leaves, eyes, waves on the sea, daggers and rising suns, and finally, grinning dolphins and a huge stingray on his chest. Alongside the stingray, she noticed the one exception to this glory of wild and fascinating tribal visions: a red heart that seemed to throb like the very heart of Christ in a sacred painting, pierced by a crown of thorns. Penny had no doubt that the heart symbolised his feelings for Francisca. She swallowed down her pain and annoyance and took a few steps back. It was better to leave before he woke up.

It would have been better if I hadn't come . . .

What if I'm falling in love with him? What do I do?

She shook her head, picked up her clothes, which had dried overnight, and went to change in the bathroom without bothering to close the door. Marcus moved and turned over, but continued to sleep.

Penny headed downstairs, imagining Mr Malkovich arriving at that moment. He would have no further doubt about their connection. She looked like a young lover just out of a warm bed and smelling of sex, and not like an unwelcome guest – or blackmailer – who had slept on a very uncomfortable couch.

Fortunately, Penny's grandmother was already awake and had unlocked the door. She didn't notice the time when Penny came in, but merely asked if she had taken out the garbage. Then she asked if she'd like her to make pancakes.

'Why don't I make them for you, Grandma? You watch that TV series you like so much.'

'Oh yes, you're right. Today Gonzalo's going to tell Hermosa that he loves her. I can't wait. It's so beautiful when love triumphs, don't you think?'

Penny did indeed think so, though she had the sinking feeling that the sentiments borne by Gonzalo for Hermosa, expressed in a thousand overblown romantic expressions, would be the closest her own little life would come to true love, and she would just have to settle for the sick attentions of someone like Grant instead.

8

MARCUS

Malkovich barged into the apartment right when I was teaching Penny a few self-defence moves, and my heart almost stopped. He's so fucking suspicious. I wanted to tell him to mind his own fucking business, to think about his wife's withered pussy and not to get involved in my personal life, but as long as I'm not completely free, I have to make the best of it. Penny, however, was good – she kept up the act. And she also offered to go talk to Francisca. I hope she doesn't change her mind. I want to know how Francisca is, what she's thinking, and the silence is killing me. I really don't get why Penny volunteered – if she wants a thank-you fuck from me or if she's just trying to be kind. Kindness is alien to me and I'm just not used to it. I don't even think it's real, so I think Penny definitely wants me to fuck her. I have to be careful, because a saint can be way more dangerous than a whore. And I don't want to hurt her. She's like some character out of a romance novel, with her big eyes that look straight into me, even if there's nothing to see inside and she's wasting her time, and sometimes she even looks at me as though she were convinced – and I mean really convinced – that if I cut myself I would bleed human blood. But I don't bleed like a proper person; I ooze bile instead.

Penny also asks a lot of questions. She's almost as prying as Malkovich. Sometimes I humour her with an answer, but I have to be smart. I can't tell her everything.

I do like Penny. Not to fuck, which is unusual for me. That's generally all I care about – I either like a woman sexually or I don't. In the latter case, she doesn't exist. I wouldn't sleep with Penny, and yet I see her, she exists. Sometimes talking to her gives me a kind of rush. I never know what she'll say – she's so unpredictable. She's like some weird little mystery I find dangerously intriguing.

◆ ◆ ◆

She wasn't supposed to sleep here. It's the last thing in the world I wanted, but I couldn't just leave her on the landing, and if she gets sick we'll have to skip the trip on Sunday. I'm a damn opportunist, I know.

Luckily, after a lot of yakking, she suddenly drops off. I don't dare shut an eye. I hear her breathing softly, making little sounds sometimes, like a cat softly meowing.

I get up, I'm thirsty, so I open the fridge and take out some water. I drink it straight from the bottle. Penny moves and the blue blanket slides on to the floor. She's curled up like a cat, with my shirt that's three times too big for her. A silver cross hangs from one ear, resting on her neck. She has a beautiful, full, peach-coloured mouth. I look at her and have a vision that stops me right in my tracks. Her lips on my skin. I shake myself, stretch my shoulders vigorously, tell myself I'm an idiot. I pick the blanket off the ground, cover her up and run back into bed.

Did I just run away? Yes, I did. Shit. Penny and sex need to remain two separate things. I can't think anything like that again, even just messing about.

Unfortunately, in the morning, after I worked so hard to fall asleep, I wake up and find her standing right there in front of me. Her back is turned, she's changing, and she doesn't even notice that I'm looking at her. For a brief moment her naked torso slips out of my shirt. She's curvier than she looks when she's dressed. She has a nice back, smooth and as white as cream. She's wearing pink polka-dot panties. She turns to pick up her clothes and exposes her breasts without knowing it, since I'm pretending to be asleep.

I guess I'm too healthy about certain things, because my animal instinct is instantly unleashed. It is so obvious that I have to turn over in bed. If she saw me, she'd notice a huge bump in the crotch of my pants. Of course that's normal for a man when he wakes up, but I prefer to keep these things to myself.

But there's something worse. Sure, it's normal to get turned on when I see a naked woman who's prettier than I expected. But the unthinkable part happens later, once she's gone. Because I have the tragic urge to masturbate while thinking of her. She doesn't exist for me like that. I can't – I can't handle this bullshit.

So I take a cold shower until my hard-on softens and I stop thinking about my tongue on her round, innocent nipples.

9

As soon as her grandmother found out about Penny's trip, she phoned Mr Donaldson, who lived on the ground floor and had an old car. She couldn't bear the idea of her darling little Penny on one of those filthy, draughty trains. She imagined her as a child, travelling on some school trip, with her classmates throwing paper balls and opening the windows wide. At the same time, she was equally convinced that Marcus wanted to take Penny to meet his parents before announcing their official engagement. For either or both of these purposes, the car seemed like the best idea.

Too bad that Mr Donaldson's auto was an old sky-blue Bentley, cumbersome and ridiculous, one of those cars that guzzle gas like camels drink water and doesn't go more than fifty miles an hour. As soon as Penny saw it, she thought of Marcus's reaction. He would be horrified, to say the least.

And Marcus *was* horrified.

It was Sunday morning. Mrs Leboski, who wasn't working that day, had offered to keep Barbie company. Since all retirees are a bit sleepless and bored, they were all glued to the windows to watch Penny and Marcus set off in the infamous vehicle.

Marcus looked like he wanted to kill someone. He glared at Penny as if he intended to scalp her once the onlookers had dispersed.

'How could you ever think . . . ?' he hissed through gritted teeth.

'It wasn't my idea. It was my grandma.'

'Was that outfit your grandma's idea as well?' he exclaimed, with a sideways glance.

Penny tried to shrug off her annoyance. She knew he was right about the car and her outfit. The car was a wreck and her outfit wasn't remotely suitable for a prison visit. Early that morning, however, looking long and hard in the mirror, she just hadn't been able to bring herself to put on the jeans and sweatshirt she'd put out the previous evening, so she'd decided to dress up. Not for Marcus – or not directly, at least. With a melancholy and naivety of which she had not at first been aware, she had done it more for Francisca's benefit. Penny had no desire to meet her while looking sloppy, ugly or pathetic – not Francisca, the most beautiful woman in the world, according to how Marcus saw her. So she had put on a pretty dress – the only one in her wardrobe, which otherwise consisted entirely of casual clothing. She had bought it in a second-hand store, and so often gazed at it lovingly on the hanger, waiting until the right occasion arose. It was a bottle-green velvet sheath, very short and tight, and totally out of place for the day's objective. She had paired it with high-heeled boots that made her wobble a little, and a flame-red leather jacket. She'd even put on make-up. She was going to restore hope to a thwarted love – sabotaging her own happiness in the process – and she didn't want to do it looking like some loser.

Marcus, in his regulation jeans that clung to his muscles, a blue sweater and a sports jacket, looked back and forth between the car and her dress.

'We're not going to the disco,' he muttered in disgust.

'This is my outfit and I'm sticking with it.'

'Besides, you have to drive. I can't for at least another year. If they catch me, I'm in trouble.'

'I'll take care of it – what's the problem?'

'If you sit down in that thing the skirt will come up to your navel.'

'I thought you didn't look at me in that way, and since you're used to Francisca's long, long legs, mine are hardly going to be of any interest.'

'I don't look at you like that, no, but you're about to meet a lot of prisoners who have worse taste than I do.'

'How kind you are. Anyway, who cares – let's have fun today.'

'Penny, don't piss me off any more than I already am. We were supposed to be discreet and now there's a whole building looking on from the windows. We were supposed to take the train, and now I'm sitting in some junk heap that might fall apart in two miles' time. You were supposed to get dressed so you didn't stand out from the crowd, and instead you look like some fucking weirdo.'

'Well, buckle up, sunshine. If you want to see Francisca, we're doing it my way.'

'You're more of a bitch than I realised, you know?'

'It's not my fault you underestimated me. I've always been a bitch.'

Penny hadn't driven in a long time, and to start with it was a game of sudden jolts and the engine shutting down. The radio didn't work, the heating didn't work, the rear windows didn't close properly and the engine made an angry noise.

Marcus was sitting beside her, stiff and seething. His eyes were brutal, and he stared straight ahead. He didn't say a word to Penny for many miles.

'Not that it's anything new,' she said suddenly, chasing her thoughts.

Marcus ignored her. He lit a cigarette and the smoke was sucked out of the open windows.

'Not that it's anything new!' Penny repeated, louder this time.

'What the fuck do you want?' Marcus suddenly growled.

'Like I said, it's nothing new that you won't talk to me. You've treated me like shit for three days now.'

'I haven't treated you like anything.'

'Exactly. What did I do to you? Did I contaminate your couch? Did you find any dirty plates, 'cause if you did, they weren't from me. You won't even give me self-defence lessons anymore.'

'You only pay me to be your escort at night and I don't have to talk to you. If you want to continue the self-defence lessons, you have to pay for them. Only the first one was free.'

'I don't have a penny left.'

'That's your problem.'

'No, really, what did I do? If I offended you in any way . . .'

'*You* are the dirty plate. Watch the road! Stay in the lane. Where did you learn to drive?'

'Where you learned your manners.'

'Can you be quiet for a moment? Focus on what you need to tell Francisca. It's the only thing that matters to me. The rest is bullshit.'

Penny didn't respond. She gripped the steering wheel hard and felt her heart shrink to the size of a button. It was true that Marcus hadn't spoken to her for three whole days. When he walked her home at night, he was silent, as if his tongue had been cut off, and he answered her questions with meagre monosyllables. Perhaps he was already imagining his future with Francisca, and the moment he would ride off into the sunset with the love of his life. He only escorted Penny for the money, otherwise he would have sent her straight to hell, she was sure of it. Penny's heart shrunk further, to the size of a grain of rice.

After a couple of hours consisting mostly of grumpy silence, the engine began to sputter. The tank was almost empty. They had to stop at a gas station.

'I'll go pee while you fill the tank,' Penny said to Marcus when they pulled in.

'Wait, you idiot, and I'll go with you,' he replied in a less-than-kind tone.

'No need, thanks.'

'Are you nuts? There are a bunch of men over there. You do the math.'

He wasn't wrong. A few men sipping beers at a nearby bar stared at Penny with interest – or rather, at her lower half, squeezed into her very tiny dress. Penny felt exposed and out of place, and for the first time on the trip she thought she should have worn jeans after all.

Marcus grabbed her hand roughly, yanking her off towards the bathrooms.

'Hurry up and take a piss then, will you?' he said.

'You're such a gentleman.'

'Penny, I'm not kidding here, hurry up. I need to check the car out and I only have two eyes.'

She did what she had to do. When she came out, they filled up the tank.

'I'd like a bottle of water,' Penny said. 'Is that asking too much?'

'I'll get it. You get in the car.'

Penny sat in the driver's seat and watched as Marcus went inside. There was a bit of a crowd, especially truck drivers and hangers-on.

While she was waiting, someone tapped on the window. Penny winced, noticing a man in his thirties with bleached blond hair and the look of a biker from the Seventies. She didn't even have time to understand what he wanted before she saw Marcus come up behind him. He had a bottle of water in one hand, and with the other he gripped the back of the man's neck and pulled him backwards.

'Get the fuck out of here,' he said, in a calm voice that would have made Dracula tremble. Then he let him go and the man, who had looked as though he was gearing up for a fight before he saw Marcus staring at him with eyes that looked like the very fires of hell, stammered a few words of apology and disappeared.

Marcus climbed back into the car and literally threw the bottle between the seats.

'He didn't do anything wrong,' Penny protested. 'Maybe he just wanted to know what time it was.'

'Listen, little princess,' he yelled at her in a fury, 'I wanna get to the prison, OK? We're late. From now on, no more stops, even if you have to hold it. And he didn't want to know what time it was. His pants were unzipped and he was flying free.'

Penny blushed, murmuring, 'I don't . . . I didn't . . . I didn't realise . . .'

'Look, if a woman wants to go around with her pussy in the wind, she has the right to do it without anyone touching her. This, however, only holds true in a perfect world. In this shitty world, you'll end up with your legs open against a guardrail within ten seconds. I don't care how you dress, but I'd like to avoid getting into trouble just because you want to prove you have nice thighs.'

Penny nodded, dazed. Of everything Marcus had said, the thing that struck her most was his implicit compliment about her thighs.

◆　◆　◆

She was searched, just as Marcus had said she'd be. A female guard patted her down, making her take off her jacket, which was in turn inspected. She had to leave her ID, and explain which detainee she intended to meet and the reason for the visit.

She'd imagined being led into an impersonal booth, the kind where two people communicate with each other through a glass wall using an intercom, but instead found herself in a room full of scattered tables where many other visitors were sitting. No doubt most of them were husbands, mothers, sisters – somebody's young children, even. A narrow window let in natural light. On the tables stood bottles of water and plastic cups.

She sat down to wait. She was scared. She was dying to meet Francisca and at the same time she desperately wanted to get up and leave, but she'd made a solemn promise, and though it cost her she wanted to stand by her word.

As the first inmates arrived, she saw hugs and smiles and a small crying child with his arms flung around his mother's legs. A buzz began to spread through the room, like in school during break time.

She'd expected a more hostile, gloomy atmosphere, but instead everyone was chatting to each other in a normal way. They were laughing even, or sharing tales of their kids' successes at school, or stories about a nosy neighbour, as if none of the prisoners were wearing orange jumpsuits with the words 'Property of the State of Connecticut' on them, as if they'd never committed any crime more serious than kicking a tin can down the road.

Penny looked at her watch, and then out the window, then back at her watch. Finally, she glanced up at the door and spotted her.

Francisca.

She understood at once why Marcus was so enthralled by her, by her energy. She was an immediate sensation, an instant emotion.

Somehow Francisca was hypnotising even in the way she looked at other people, the way she walked and in the resolute gesture with which she tucked a lock of hair behind her ear. She wasn't just straightforwardly beautiful, but commandingly so, wild and impetuous in her looks to anyone with eyes to see. She was a purebred horse; a fierce siren. She was Marcus in female form: tall, strong and well-muscled like he was, but also overwhelmingly feminine – a superior femme fatale. One of those rare beauties who can drive a man to kill.

Her hair was shorter than in the photo, but not by much; it fell over her shoulders in soft, shiny black waves that no prison could manage to tarnish. She was caramel-skinned with large eyes, two clear black almonds studded with gold specks in the irises. Under the sleeves of the orange uniform, Penny could well imagine tribal tattoos like the ones on Marcus.

Penny looked the woman up and down, and felt her heart slipping to the floor and drowning in a lake of tears.

Francisca looked at her and sat in the chair opposite. 'Do we know each other?' she asked, seeming uninterested and speaking with a vaguely Latina accent.

'We don't, but . . . I'm a friend of Marcus,' Penny replied. She felt as vulnerable as a bird stripped of its wings and feathers.

Francisca raised an eyebrow. 'Marcus doesn't generally have friends,' she said, now looking Penny up and down with more interest.

'Well, he does now.' At the back of the room a woman blew out a birthday candle on a cake. Someone applauded her, inviting her to open packages with big yellow bows. Someone else let out a shrill laugh. A man said something to his wife in a heartfelt tone.

Penny forced herself to put up with Francisca's fierce gaze. She explained that she lived in the same building as Marcus, that they had become friends and that she was there to deliver a message from him. She did not tell Francisca that she feared she was in love with him, that she dreamed of him every night, that when she touched him, by accident or mistake or by pretending it was by accident or mistake, she felt the fires burning strong in her chest. She didn't tell her that being there, pretending to be a go-between, was punishment for her soul.

Francisca remained silent for a few moments. She didn't smile or even seem to breathe as she looked out the window, towards the end of the sunlit courtyard.

Finally, staring back at her, she said something that Penny was definitely not expecting. 'I'm sorry for you, *chica*.'

'Pardon me?'

'I'm sorry for two reasons. If you fall in love with him and he doesn't like you back, I'm sorry because it'll be like someone breaking your legs. And if he does like you, then as soon as I get out, *I'll* break your legs.'

'He doesn't like me, you can be sure of that,' Penny murmured, and for a moment she felt a chill. Of the two alternatives, the most realistic was the first.

'Are you fucking him?' Francisca fired back at her.

'No!'

'If you're just fucking, I don't care. Have fun while I'm in here, but once I'm out you can forget it.' As she said that, she reached out in Penny's direction and squeezed her hand. Penny's fingers squirmed in the tight grip. At the same time, she noticed something on Francisca's wrist. Just below her palm was a jagged scar a few inches long. An old wound; the unmistakable trace of a cut. It was pink now, and shiny like mother-of-pearl. To be that light in colour, the scar must have been old, though Francisca couldn't be any more than twenty-five. The mere thought that a child might want to attempt suicide made Penny's blood run cold.

Francisca noticed Penny's look and pulled her hand down into her lap. That gesture, that modesty, from a tattooed convict who was clearly threatening her, evoked an unexpected feeling of tenderness in Penny.

'Marcus thinks about you all the time,' she told Francisca in all sincerity.

'And how would you know? You his confessor or something?'

'No, it's just that sometimes we talk . . .'

'Talk?'

'Yup.'

'About what?'

'I don't have a list of our exact conversation topics. I just came to let you know that he can't write to you because of his parole officer, but he can't wait for you to get out so you can go off together.'

'And he's said all this to you?'

'Why does that seem so strange?'

'He and I, we trust no one.'

'You're trusting me right now.'

'I don't even know who you are.'

Penny smiled and introduced herself in a mock-formal manner. 'Hi, my name is Penny. I'm twenty-two years old, I like reading and I'm afraid of the dark. Marcus and I met by chance. We happen to talk but we don't fuck. If you want to write, I'll can give him your letters, and I'll send you his letters from my address. Here's my address. Trust me if you want to, but I can't force you if you don't.'

'Why are you doing this?'

'You and Marcus are so alike. He also asks me why I do this or that. There is no reason. Can a person not be kind without having a secret motive?'

'No. If someone's nice they want to fuck you over.'

'Not me.'

'You're the type who could really fuck someone over.'

'How so?'

'You have the face of a fucking angel.'

'I'm no angel.'

'I bet you're even a virgin.'

'One, that's my business, and two, that wouldn't make me an angel. You want me to tell him anything?'

'Tell him that when I get out, I'll suck him off until the last drop.'

Penny blushed and shifted a little uncomfortably in her chair. Just then, a guard entered the room and informed everyone that visiting hours had ended. Francisca gave her a look that was ironic and mad at the same time.

'Don't even think about trying to take my man from me,' she told Penny just before she got up. And thus she made her exit, as beautiful and bitchy as when she came in.

◆ ◆ ◆

Marcus was waiting for Penny in the prison parking lot, leaning against the Bentley, which looked like a big blue bathtub. Fidgety as a kid, he had smoked something like a billion cigarettes, all of them dropped at his feet in a mosaic of spent butts. As soon as he saw her returning, he questioned her with his eyes, full of a piercing passion. Penny told him almost everything she and Francisca had said. She didn't include the part about the sucking off.

Soon after, they fell into a dead silence. Penny was plunged into misery, the kind that comes suddenly and grips your heart in a vice. She was jealous of Francisca. Francisca was probably also jealous of her, but not because she seriously feared she could be replaced; no sane man would ever prefer sweet little Penny, with her short hair like a doll and her stupid love stories, to a woman like this. Francisca was only annoyed because Marcus had confided in Penny about his own life, and consequently their life together – that he had allowed Penny the smallest glimpse into their world, even though it was shortly to be closed off from her forever. Like a dog marking its territory, Francisca had wanted to make Penny understand that Marcus was all hers.

And he really was. Whatever had drawn those two together in the first place remained sealed in an inextricable bond.

Penny and Marcus set off quickly, and as the afternoon advanced they found themselves driving along country roads. The leaves of the trees were the colour of blood, and Penny found herself wondering if Francisca had a tattoo the same as Marcus's, the one with a pierced heart. She was certain she did. She imagined them getting the tattoos together, like kids carving declarations of love into the bark of trees.

Suddenly, Marcus put a hand on her arm, making her jump.

'Can I ask what's wrong with you?' he asked, between two breathfuls of smoke.

'If I talk too much you tell me to shut up. If I'm quiet, you ask me why. You're never satisfied,' she replied, annoyed.

'Did Francisca upset you with a few choice comments? That would be just like her.'

'No – what makes you think that?'

'She likes bugging people,' he observed, as if proud of it.

'To tell you the truth, I was minding my own business. I'm really not thinking about you and your incredible beauty all the time.'

'Are you hungry?'

'Huh?'

'It's four o'clock. Are you hungry?' Marcus repeated.

'A little, but we're in the middle of nowhere and I'm not up for hunting.'

'Let's get a sandwich.'

'I don't want to end up at another gas station with flashers, thanks – assuming we find another one. We passed the last one a while back.'

'While you were inside I took a look in the trunk. Your grand-mother filled it with food. How long did she think we'd be gone?'

'I wouldn't trust it. Grandma is a treasure, but it's probably not edible.'

'Let's risk it. I'm hungry, and when I'm hungry, I can't think.'

Do you want to eat me?

'OK, let's see what she made.'

They stopped in an open area covered with drifting leaves. The views of the Connecticut countryside would have been wonderful for anyone willing to admire them, but Penny, who normally loved to get lost in nature and became intoxicated at the beauty of every-thing not created by humankind, found she had little interest, and couldn't even bring herself to enjoy the hillside dotted with trees leading down to the banks of a small river.

There actually was a bag full of food in the trunk of the car. The cookies smelled of soap and were immediately discarded. She was afraid to taste the mess of who-knows-what or the cake. Fortunately, the bread was bread, and the cheese didn't look like soap. The apples were undoubtedly edible too.

'Well, at least we won't die of hunger, except now I need a pee.'

'You're like a leaking faucet. You make me laugh.'

'When you get old and have prostate problems, I'll laugh at you.'

'I'm never going to get old.'

'Will you be forever young?'

'I'll die first.'

Penny bit her lip, thinking that yes, it was quite possible that neither he nor Francisca would live to see thirty.

'I'll come with you,' he said.

'What a gentleman you are, but no, I don't need protection from the raccoons. That is, I'm assuming your intentions towards me aren't sexual.'

She walked away to pee. Afterwards, as if suddenly all her senses had grown sharper, she heard the river flowing a few feet away. She scrambled down the slope and stopped a short distance from the sparkling, hypnotic water. A little further down, the river grew broader, the two banks connected by an attractive iron bridge, painted red like Marcus's tattooed heart. She sank down on a carpet of crisp leaves, thinking how much she would like to live in such a place, in the middle of nature, surrounded by animals. Waking in the morning, before the sun got going for the day. Harvesting the produce from her own vegetable garden. Keeping livestock in her own pastures. Chopping wood and watching it flame up in a stone fireplace. Hiking for hours in the open without meeting a soul. Tasting newly fallen snowflakes on her tongue. Brushing Barbie's long hair while her grandma sat stroking an orange cat on her lap. Loving someone under the warm covers, while the wind outside banged the shutters. Beautiful dreams, large and small.

'Penny!' Marcus's voice brought her back to reality. He had come down the slope and was staring at her strangely. 'What are you doing, disappearing like that?'

'I haven't disappeared, I'm right here.'

'I was worried when you didn't come back.'

'You were worried about me?'

Marcus frowned for a moment, and then said teasingly, 'Well, if something happens to you, who gets to pay me my fifty dollars every week?'

'And, above all, who will receive Francisca's letters?'

'Exactly.'

'It's nice to be important to someone. Let's go eat – come on.'

He helped her to her feet, and they climbed back up to the car where they devoured the sandwiches and fruit, washed down with fresh water from the stream. Marcus also took a pee but didn't bother going behind a tree, just turned his back on Penny and went right in front of her.

Just as the sun was about to set, they got into the car to leave, but the engine was dead. The key turned in the ignition, but no engine fired up to break the woodland peace.

Penny and Marcus gazed at each other for a long moment before the light faded and darkness swallowed everything up.

For once, he hadn't brought his flashlight with him. The road wasn't lit; the car looked like a dead dinosaur. Their phones had no signal, and even if they had, who could they call? In daytime they would have walked towards the last gas station they had seen, some ten miles away, but at night this would be dangerous, if not downright suicidal.

'So what are we going to do now?' asked Penny, in a tone that didn't quite fit with her resolve to always be brave.

Marcus's voice answered from the darkness. 'Nothing. We'll sleep here.'

'Here?'

'Well, we don't have much choice.'

'But it's cold, and who knows what kind of people hang around here!'

'Didn't you say there are only raccoons?'

'I have a problem with the dark, Marcus,' she said in a small voice, close to the edge of panic. 'Especially when it's so . . . dark.'

Unexpectedly, he took her hand. In the darkness, Penny felt the sudden, rough and enveloping heat, and her heart jumped like that of a tightrope walker.

'It's not totally dark. Look up there.'

Penny lifted her face and looked up at the sky. There was no moon, but the stars were suddenly shining like tiny, distant pricks of light, as if someone had lit a million birthday candles. She stopped being so afraid, her breathing calmed and her anxiety fell away.

'Let's get in the back,' Marcus told her. 'There's more space there.'

Now she'd dealt with her fear of the dark, another fear suddenly began to creep into Penny's thoughts. Would they end up having to sleep together on the back seat of the car? The same seat where generations of young people had made love, and probably even Mr Donaldson years before? That knowledge tugged at her guts, and the fever she'd been running for the past two weeks, ever since meeting Marcus, burned in a secret and intimate corner of her.

They moved to the back together. Fortunately, the Bentley was huge, a dance floor on wheels, so the back seat was practically the size of a bed. Until right this minute, Penny had always cursed the darkness, but now she thanked it, or he would have seen her blushing.

When Marcus took off his jacket, the rustling of the wool seemed amplified in the silence of the car.

'Put it on, because you're practically naked,' he said.

He didn't have to ask twice. Thin tights and cold leather boots certainly weren't enough to keep Penny warm. Even Marcus's jacket wasn't enough, to be honest, even if it did reach down to her knees.

'OK, let's do this,' he continued. 'I'll lie down and you lie next to me.'

'Huh?'

'You want to freeze?'

No, but I don't want to die of a broken heart either.

'Of course not.'

'Then lie down with me.'

'OK, but keep your hands to yourself.'

Please don't keep your hands to yourself!

'Don't talk nonsense,' he snapped.

Pretty quickly, they found themselves hugging each other on the back seat of the old Bentley. Marcus's legs were too long so he had to bend them, but Penny found a strangely comfortable position in a gap between his body and the back of the seat. Touching him, clinging to his chest, she felt a sort of intoxication, as if she'd drunk one of those strong cocktails she mixed up every night but never got to taste. Just like she'd imagined, his chest looked as though it was carved out of granite – solid, broad and yet so very warm.

She tried to fall asleep but it wasn't easy. In fact, it was almost impossible. How on earth could she end up in the arms of sleep when she lay huddled in Marcus's arms? How could she think of sleep when her heart beat so wildly in her ears, hysterical as a madman's cry? She feared he might hear it and make fun of her, of her excitement, of her cheeks flushed with desire. She was about to say something to him, anything to silence that rumble from her chest that seemed more deafening to her than a bass drum, when suddenly Marcus asked her, 'Just why are you so afraid of the dark?' His voice sounded close to her ear and a shiver ran down her spine, making her hair stand up on the back of her neck.

'Maybe because of the accident.'

'What accident?'

'The one my parents died in.'

'I didn't know about that . . .'

'Why would you? It was a long time ago. I was five, and we used to travel around in a caravan. One day, we got into a hit-and-run. My parents died on impact and I was buried in the wreckage for hours until they found me. I don't even remember it, but I'm still really afraid of the dark.'

'Shit.'

'Yeah.'

'Are you cold?'

'No, not now.'

I'm way too hot.

'Thanks, Marcus.'

'Thanks for what?' he snapped.

'I don't know. Everything, I think.'

'I don't know what that means. You're so weird, Penny.'

'When you leave, will you come say goodbye to me?'

'I don't think so. One day you just won't see me anymore and that'll be bye-bye.'

'And what will I do without you?'

'Find yourself a decent man, fuck him good and you'll forget about me.'

Penny thought about it for a moment. 'Well, I guess I will.'

'Good.'

'Aren't you going to sleep?'

'In the middle of the woods?'

'You afraid of an ambush by the local raccoons or something?'

'No, I'm afraid of an ambush by the local assholes. I'm sure nothing will happen, but it's better to be careful.'

'You always seem to be at war with something or someone.'

'I *am* always at war.'

'I could tell that from your tattoos. I like them a lot.'

'I know.'

'How do you know?'

'Everyone likes them. And the women give me a blowjob after they're done looking at them.'

'You do it on purpose, don't you? You want to embarrass me or punish me for something. I don't understand you.'

'It's the simple truth. I've had the best blowjobs in my life from girls who admired my tattoos right before they did it.'

'This is not one of those times, you do realise that?'

'So stop talking about my tattoos or my reflexes might kick in.'

'You're sick.'

'I'm a man with a half-naked girl on him. Your breast is pressing on my shoulder and my hand is on your ass. You don't have to be some rare breed of pussy to get me thinking naughty thoughts, OK? It happens to the body even when the head doesn't care.'

'In other words, you only think with—'

'I wouldn't say *only*. If I only thought with that we wouldn't be talking right now. You'd be lying under me, stripped naked, but instead I'm putting up with your bullshit, so I'd say I'm using my head all right.'

Penny fell silent. The discovery of not being altogether invisible to him wasn't particularly flattering. What was more upsetting to her was that Marcus's head didn't care – that his mind and body clearly travelled on two separate paths. Yes, Marcus would have sex with her, but purely on a physical basis, without his own heart being pierced. She was just like the others, that was all, and she'd have done well to realise that before getting seriously involved. Besides, she'd seen Francisca now, hadn't she? How could she ever hope to compete with her? She had to find some way out of this mess.

◆ ◆ ◆

It seemed nothing short of a miracle, but the car started with no problem at all the following morning. It was almost as if it had broken down on purpose, the old pimp. At dawn, they sprung apart and climbed stiffly out of the car, slithering down the slope to cup their hands and drink from the stream, and then they left. The air was cold, the colours still dull, but as the sun came up with its rosy light, the glistening leaves once again resembled drops of congealed blood.

Neither Penny nor Marcus spoke the whole way home, as if divided by something better left unsaid. Each kept to themselves, and when they arrived at their destination Marcus said goodbye to her on the stairs without even looking at her.

'No need to get sentimental now!' Penny shouted at his receding back. He didn't turn around, but raised an arm and gave her the finger before disappearing from view.

10

Marcus

I can't tell if Penny is naive or just stupid. As soon as I see her all dressed up like that, it makes me want to turn the air blue with my curses. I hold back because there are old people around and because I swore to myself to pay her as little notice as possible. Having discovered that my private parts would gladly bump into hers, despite what I claimed, I've barely said a word to her. The less she speaks, the less I stress. When she talks, it makes me want to look at her mouth, and from there a whole flood of obscene thoughts rushes through me. I keep repeating to myself: *I don't want to fuck Penny, I don't want to fuck Penny.* When actually I want to fuck her so much.

This is totally weird for me, because generally I don't think like this – when I like a woman, I either do it or I don't, and then bye-bye.

This time, I think about what I'd like to do to her and with her, but I don't do it. And I have no idea why not. What the hell is the matter with me? I've seen quite a few naked women, many of them way more beautiful than her, so why have I been in this constant state of excitement ever since watching her get dressed, while she was completely unaware I was spying on her?

What does it all mean? Why do my pants swell with a throbbing erection every time I remember her back and that slender spine?

If I had any time to waste, I'd go see a doctor in case I have some mysterious illness, but I'm too busy for that, so instead I'll just try to resist her.

You know, I'd really like to strangle her because of what she's wearing today. Not only because of the effect it has on me, but because of what I think it'll do to other guys. I realise that, in a sense, she's my responsibility today, and if someone steps out of line I have to intervene, but I'd like to avoid that. The little idiot doesn't realise that if you're made of meat and have two legs then you're not going to go unnoticed, especially if you put them on display in a dress that barely covers your ass. I repeat: Is she naive, stupid or just a provocative bitch?

So this guy who peeks at her through the car window with his zipper down – half high, half drunk, and who knows what else – I really wanna give him a good kicking, but I manage to hold back. I need to stay calm. I need to stay calm. I have to think of Francisca and how she'll be out soon. Like I always say, everything else is shit.

She comes out of the prison as pale as a corpse and staggers around, looking like a little girl in her mother's high heels. I have to hold back the absurd impulse to steady her.

She tells me about her meeting with Francisca in a weak and toneless voice, and then she falls silent, like all her batteries have run out. I ought to be happy, but no – I'd love to know what she's thinking, but she won't answer me. She turns her back, treats me like a stranger. OK, so I am a stranger, but I think I have a bit of a right to know if Francisca actually went for her. I need to know everything that's going on with Francisca and I have the distinct feeling that Penny's hiding something from me.

I smoke like a demon and then ask if she's hungry. We eat, we drink, we don't talk much. And then the car decides to die and everything goes to shit.

We're forced to sleep in the car. The darkness is so thick you could cut it. I can tell she's terrified, because her breathing is heavy like the first time I met her on the stairs. I don't know why I still feel responsible for her. I try to comfort her in my own way. If you look at the stars, I say, you can't be afraid.

The worst is when we lie in the back. Maybe we should have stayed in our separate seats, but it's way too cold for that. The problem is that when she's close to me, she smells so good and my body declares war on what my brain says, so to cover it up I come out with the heavy, mocking words of a complete asshole.

The truth is I'd like to comfort her in a whole other way. As soon as I get back I need to find a woman to fuck; I can't behave myself when I'm exploding like this. I'm sure if I just get this out of my system the madness will pass, but meanwhile I need to get through the night. I have to order my body not to do what it wants. I have to order my mind to stop imagining Penny, sweet and wild, utterly naked except for her high-heeled boots, those magnificent thighs spread and waiting for me, lying back on this very seat.

I can't wait for dawn so we can try to get this shit car working and get home. Then I can write to Francisca, wait for her reply, and go back to life as I know it.

I leave Penny on the stairs without even thanking her. After all, she offered to do this thing – I didn't ask. At home I take off my clothes and take a shower. Despite the cold water and my good intentions, I am desperately excited. With one arm resting on the tiled wall, I jerk off under the stream of water. It's the last time I'll ever do such a thing, the last time I'll think of that little girl in that way, imagining her under this same water, her lips parted in a low moan. Starting tomorrow – no, tonight – I'm gonna start fucking whoever I find. If this thing with Penny is the result of moderation, I prefer to go overboard. I'm sure Francisca would prefer that.

11

Ever since the day Grant showed up at the library, Penny had been wary. If she had to go put a book back on a shelf in some distant corner, she did it with her heart in her throat, for fear that her worst nightmare would suddenly come true. One afternoon, when she had just climbed to the top step of the ladder, she heard a voice calling from below and nearly fell.

She descended slowly, carrying a heavy volume and ready to hurl it in his face if necessary, but then realised it wasn't Grant, or even some other man. A girl was smiling up at her, and Penny tried hard to remember where she had seen her before. She was tall and very slim, with an edgy haircut and veneers on her teeth. They were too white and perfect to be real.

'Penny Miller, don't you remember me?' the girl asked, shaking her hand.

Penny's brain flashed through moments from her past: sweet sixteen, high school days, her fury at her grandmother for insisting on moving her to a school way out of their neighbourhood – an expensive school that had drained Barbie's savings, terrific in educational terms but full of racist assholes.

Then, 'Rebecca Day?' she exclaimed, very nearly tempted to ask her where she had left the other half of herself, since she barely weighed a hundred pounds. Penny was no giant, but her former schoolmate looked like she hadn't eaten in months. Penny's first thought was that she was sick, but that smile, those clothes that must have cost at least six times her own salary, and her air of triumph told her that Rebecca was yet another of those under-fed aspiring-model types. Penny couldn't understand what she was doing here, so far out of the way for her, given that she was from uptown.

'Yes, it really is me! We were looking for you.'

'You and who else were looking for me? And why?'

A new figure now emerged from behind a shelf. This person Penny recognised immediately. It was Igor, another classmate – her first crush. He was still very cute, with blond curls and moss-green eyes. Not that there had ever been anything between them; she had merely dreamed endlessly about him and composed gushing fantasies, mostly involving the remote possibility that they would one day get married. All this had been scribbled down in a ridicu-lous diary with a cover that was as rose-tinted as her romantic hopes. They had not got married, of course; in fact, they had barely exchanged two words with each other at school, and after they graduated they had completely lost sight of each other. So what on earth were her old classmates doing here now?

'We went to your apartment and your grandmother said you worked here,' Rebecca explained, tucking her hair behind her ear in a studied gesture. She had a perfect manicure, each nail with a different colour glitter on it. The skin on her hands was typical of someone who had never worked a day in her whole life, other than putting on costly scented creams.

For a moment, Penny felt herself sucked back in time by some cruel and unseen force. She was a little girl again – alone, humili-ated, angry like Stephen King's Carrie, but without the supernatu-ral powers she needed to fight back against a bunch of assholes.

She had defended herself in any case, but not in the way she'd have liked. Not by burning it all to the ground.

That powerful impulse didn't last long, however, and almost immediately the new Penny came back in force, the one who didn't care, the one who said what she thought and didn't let herself get steamrollered.

'Are you looking for a particular book?' she asked, looking down at them, just as they had looked at her back then and were trying to do again now. Only, they were at a disadvantage on several levels, and couldn't hurt her anymore. Igor was looked more like his high school self than Rebecca: he was tall, although Penny's concept of height had changed somewhat since meeting Marcus. She used to think six foot was very tall, but now it barely seemed to hit the mark. He was dressed in a style similar to that of his schooldays, a blend of quirky and traditional: a tweed jacket and jeans, with a slight beard and a small earring in one ear.

'We need you,' Igor said, speaking for the first time.

Penny could see they were losing patience.

'Want to tell me what this is about, or should we play a guessing game?'

Rebecca smiled again, and Penny could practically hear her cheeks squeaking like rusty knobs, forced to simulate a friendliness she didn't feel.

'We're organising a reunion,' Rebecca informed her. 'We're trying to contact everyone in our class. It'll be a whole lot of fun! We can all see how we've changed – share our successes . . .' she added, with the obvious intention of revealing all of her successes and laughing about the failures of others. 'I'm getting married!' she continued. 'My fiancé is an entrepreneur.'

She stretched out a hand in the typical gesture of a future bride showing the world a very respectable ring, hoping to arouse envy and even a few stomach cramps. Penny saw the flash of a diamond the size of a hazelnut, surrounded by a ring of smaller diamonds. It stood out grotesquely, like a cyst, on her bony ring finger.

'Congratulations,' she said indifferently.

Then she noticed that, behind Rebecca's back, Igor was winking at her and gesturing down his throat with two fingers like he wanted to vomit. Penny smiled at him instinctively, and Rebecca thought she was smiling at her.

'So, are you coming?' she asked.

'Er . . . when is this?'

'Saturday, at my boyfriend's house. He's letting us use his mansion!'

So we can all see for ourselves just how rich he is.

'Well . . . I'll need to check. I work on Saturdays.'

'Let me know – here's my number. Feel free to bring a plus one.'

'A plus one? Who do you have in mind exactly?'

Igor snorted, puffing out his cheeks. 'She wants to know if you've been hung out to dry like a stocking with a run in it, or if you have a boyfriend.'

'Oh, come on!' Rebecca replied in a shrill little voice. 'Not everyone has to go and get engaged! But then again, as far as I can remember, the boys never really liked you, Penny. You never dated anyone at school. Don't worry. If you come on your own, that's fine too.' Her casual tone seemed to express her full compassion and understanding, but she could barely disguise the triumph and gloating that loomed beneath.

'Well, I'm not on my own,' Penny said, before even thinking about the whole backstory to this lie.

'You're not? You've got a boyfriend?'

'I do, yeah.'

'Oh, right. Well then, bring him along too.'

'I told you, I don't know if I can come, because of work.'

'Of course!' Rebecca exclaimed, as if she finally understood the mystery. But Penny could read it loud and clear on her face. *She doesn't believe me and thinks I just don't want to go to the party and admit I'm all on my own, a total loser with a lousy job and one single dress that's not exactly the hottest thing on the catwalk.*

Which, unfortunately, just happened to be the truth.

And then, since she didn't want to let Rebecca win here, Penny found herself declaring, against her better judgement, 'We'll do our best to make it on the night, and then I can introduce you to my guy. He's called Marcus.'

◆ ◆ ◆

Pretending with Rebecca had been easy, but it would be way less easy to convince Marcus to help her. Returning home from the library, Penny hatched a plan.

Shutting herself away in her room, she began to rummage around in her jewellery box. This luxurious-sounding item was actually just a cardboard box decorated with pictures of puppies she'd cut out from a sheet of wrapping paper. And it was almost blasphemous to describe the contents as 'jewellery' – mainly it consisted of bracelets with plastic beads from when she was a kid, earrings that were silver-plated set with the odd chip of cubic zirconia, a Fimo ring in the shape of a birthday cake, and a belt buckle garnished with rhinestones. Among all that jumble, however, was a pendant precious enough to be kept in a tulle bag.

Penny held it up and admired it against the light. It was a heart made of white gold, set with diamonds – hers and hers alone, a gift long ago from her parents, who had otherwise left her nothing besides a fear of the dark.

She considered her plan. Did it really make sense to risk losing the one and only object that still bound her to her lost family, all to one-up Rebecca? It would be so much more sensible just to ignore her, to let Rebecca fester in her own evil cesspit of spite and maliciousness and hope never to bump into her again.

That would be more dignified, yes, but Penny's memories of high school were still far too raw, while she could barely recall her parents. In some ways she had managed to move on since graduation, growing in courage and spirit, but she could not yet put behind her the daily bullying that witch had subjected her to, creating such a powerful atmosphere of scorn and mockery around her, which no one had ever challenged by daring to get to know her. Including the very same Igor who was now laughing at Rebecca behind her back. Six years earlier, he'd hung on to Rebecca's every last word.

Rebecca and Igor's feigned indifference to Penny's announcement that she had a boyfriend was obvious. They weren't all that subtle, and if Penny didn't show them something tangible, they would continue to regard her as a loser – and that, Penny was not prepared to tolerate.

So she did what she thought was right, or at any rate necessary, and that very same day she went to the pawn shop to trade in her pendant. It was worth far less than she'd hoped – a measly two hundred and fifty dollars. Mentally begging her parents for forgiveness, she promised herself she would come back for it.

After work that night, she went to meet Marcus at the Maraja, rather than their usual spot in front of Well Purple. She paced around for a while outside the entrance, but he didn't appear. Finally, Penny plucked up her courage to talk to the other bouncer there, a guy who was fat rather than imposing. The man looked her up and down and then laughed.

'Marcus always gets the ladies. Since he's started here there's been a regular parade of pussy slamming itself under his nose.'

Penny wondered if the man was calling her a pussy, but preferred not to investigate. 'Can you tell me where he is? Did he leave yet?'

'Well, no. He's out back smoking a cigarette.'

'I want to ask him something important . . .'

'Oh, I get it – you're another one who's got it bad. Go on back then.'

Penny nodded and slipped into the narrow side alley, made even more cramped by the fire escapes climbing the walls of the neighbouring building like metal snakes. A strong smell of garbage emanated from a couple of open bins lined up against the wall. She held her breath as she went past, and rounded the corner to the back of the building.

And that's when she saw something she would really rather not have witnessed.

Marcus was leaning against the wall, his shirt raised over his abdomen and his pants pulled down to his muscular thighs. He was gripping a woman who was nearly naked by the buttocks, holding her in the air against him. They sure weren't smoking any cigarettes. They were having sex.

Neither of them noticed the spectator. They were moving in a furious rhythm, faster and faster, and Penny could hear the obscene thud every time their bodies slammed together. The girl, a blonde with long hair and a butt as tight and round as a drum, moaned without restraint. Marcus himself made no sound, other than a low growl now and then.

Penny stood frozen to the spot as they climaxed, their cries of satisfaction seeming like primal screams. Finally, Marcus slipped out of her, pulling off the slimy condom. The girl tried to tease him to extend the encounter, giggling, 'Wow, you're an animal!' but Marcus said nothing, just threw the condom to the ground.

Still unable to move a muscle, Penny was shocked but power-less to leave. There was a lump in her throat, and she could barely breathe. She wanted to turn and run, she wanted to wipe Marcus from her thoughts, she wanted to tell him exactly what she thought about him and his extraordinary love for Francisca, but all she could do was stand there, trembling and shaking, hating him to the very depths of her being, telling herself that if sex was that sordid and sweaty, there was no way she would ever let anyone do it to her.

The blonde was pulling on her panties as Marcus turned his gaze away in seeming disdain, catching sight of Penny at that pre-cise moment, so that she at least had the satisfaction of seeing him flinch as if he were ashamed. Or maybe it wasn't shame, but just the rage of an asshole who wants to be able to fuck some slut in peace without getting dirty looks from someone else.

Because she gave him a very, very dirty look indeed, before backing away and following the alley round to the front of the building.

The fat bouncer laughed when he saw her. 'Some cigarette they were smoking, huh?'

Penny ignored him and walked off down the sidewalk in the direction of her apartment. That evening she was going to head home alone – she didn't need a babysitter. She was so mad that if Grant had had the misfortune to materialise at her side right there, she would have ripped him to shreds before he could even say 'ouch'.

It wasn't clear to her quite why she was so furious and disgusted and disappointed and desperate and even a little dead inside, all at the same time. She knew all too well that Marcus did that kind of thing – and with Francisca's blessing, even – but that was simply how she felt. The image was forever seared into her brain.

After several minutes, she realised how fast she'd been walking. She was almost home, exhausted and a little nauseous and crying her eyes out. *Stupid useless tears.* She wiped them as best she could on her sleeve. *Stupid whining idiot.*

She climbed the stairs and took refuge in her apartment, where there was no trace of Marcus. *Perfect. The less I see of him the better.* She performed her usual night-time routines and went to bed.

That's when her heart leaped into her throat and she nearly died of a heart attack.

There was someone on the fire escape. An imposing silhouette blocking out the moonlight. She sat bolt upright in bed thinking it was Grant at her window. But it was Marcus.

◆ ◆ ◆

He stared at her through the glass, gesturing for her to let him in. His expression seemed to be saying, *Open up or I'll break in anyway.* She shook her head and made a gesture as if to say, *Get lost, you prick!* Then Marcus slipped two fingers along the frame, fiddled for a few moments, and raised the sash.

Penny's mouth fell open in shock.

'Hope Grant is less good at forcing the locks than I am,' he said, stepping over the windowsill and boldly entering her room.

'Get out of here! I'd rather sleep without throwing up on my pillow,' Penny said, covering herself with her sheets. As if she needed to – any right-minded nun would have coveted her sensible pyjamas.

Penny's room suddenly felt tiny in relation to Marcus's bulk.

'Say, what's wrong, little lady? You shocked at what you saw? You're really not getting much, are you?'

I've never done it in my life.

'I get plenty,' she lied, 'but not with strangers and not like that. You were nearly in the garbage!'

'When you're in the mood, it doesn't matter where you do it, especially with someone you've only just met. At least they don't expect anything – they just let themselves go.'

'So do you always do it in an alley, not like – you know – in bed?'

'In bed I run the risk that people wanna sleep over. That doesn't happen down an alley.'

'You have it all figured out, don't you?'

'Pretty much. So what were you doing back there anyway? Were you spying on me? Did you like what you saw?'

'I didn't see a thing!'

Marcus shot her a sardonic look. 'You saw it all, baby. I could tell by the way you looked at me.'

'I was paralysed with shock, more than anything else. You know how you freeze if you see something horrible?'

'You're a lying bitch, but no matter – you sure can run fast. By the time I got out front you were gone. Didn't we have a deal? Why'd you come tonight anyway? Did Grant visit you again?'

'No, I wanted . . . I wanted to ask you something – something that would have given you the chance to earn more money. But I've reconsidered and decided it doesn't matter, so you can go now.'

'Oh no, you need to tell me now. Any money involved and I become very curious indeed.'

Penny looked down at the sheets. Marcus sat on the end of the bed and started to light a cigarette.

She stopped him. 'No, not inside. Grandma doesn't like it.'

He went to the window and straddled the sill. He lit his cigarette anyway, but at least blew the smoke outside. Penny thought about whether or not to tell him about her plan, and then the memory of Rebecca made her give in. She told him everything in a whisper.

Marcus burst out laughing. 'You want me to pretend to be your boyfriend? You reckon I look like someone who's a boyfriend?'

'You look like a savage and sexy bastard, and that's good enough for me. If I can't upset them because I'm richer or more beautiful, then I'll make them burn with envy over the kind of man everyone wants to screw.' She realised she'd been a little too frank.

Marcus shot her a roguish smile. 'Should I take that as a compliment?'

'If you think it's a compliment for your dick to be bigger than your brain, then fair enough. Now go away and leave me alone.'

'So you don't want to fool your friends anymore?'

'They're not my friends, they're assholes.'

'And how much were you willing to pay me?'

'Two hundred and fifty dollars.'

'For one night?'

'Yup.'

'That'd be great. Where did you get the cash?'

'That's my business.'

'I wanna know. If it's stolen, I could end up back inside for money laundering.'

'I earned it fair and square. I provided a bonus service to some rich guy who likes honest women, and he handed me an astronomical tip.'

Marcus froze, his cigarette suspended between his lips. 'Bullshit,' he murmured.

'You can get dirty at work, but I can't?'

'Enough now.'

'Why? You make me mad or try to embarrass me every step of the way – but you can't take it when I do the same thing to you?'

'You're so bad at this game. Don't go around saying shit like that, OK? I'm nice, but you say stuff like this to another guy and he might break you in half.'

'And you wouldn't dream of it?'

'Of course I dream of it, but I can control myself. So what now?'

'What now? Nothing!'

'I was referring to those assholes.'

'Oh, them. I don't know.'

'How do we play it at this party?'

'Nothing special. You just have to pretend to worship the ground I walk on.'

Marcus blew out a cloud of smoke and shook his head. 'I couldn't fake that even if I took an acting class.'

'So could you at least pretend to be crazy about me?'

'Hmm . . . You have a plan C?'

'You're going to need to work for this money! If you don't think you can do the job, there's no deal here.'

'Let's see . . . I could pretend to find you painfully provocative. I could pretend that when I look at your mouth I want to kiss it till it bleeds, that I dream of fucking you for hours every night, and that I like everything about you, even that ridiculous hair and the way you insist on getting under my skin. Would that work?'

Penny had to swallow before she could speak. Her throat was dry, and she felt flushed and slightly dizzy, like after a long massage.

'Um, yeah. I guess that would work. I don't know if it'll be convincing enough though. I'll withhold payment until after, when we're sure it worked.'

'I reckon you can trust me that it will.'

'Either way, you have to go now.'

'Tomorrow I'll put a better lock on this window for you. The one you have is weak as anything. It's not safe. When I go out, fasten it good and tight.'

'Are you worried about me?'

'Sure! I need this job.'

'OK, that explains it.'

Marcus jumped out on to the fire escape and gave her an ironic farewell salute. Penny raised her middle finger in return, in the same way that he so often did to her. He laughed and disappeared from view.

After fastening the window against any further nocturnal intruders, Penny was alone again, taking refuge under the covers.

◆ ◆ ◆

The next day at noon, Marcus was there as promised with some tools to fix the window lock. When she opened the door, Penny thought privately that she really needed to stop right now with this business of feeling giddy every time she caught sight of him.

But Barbie was more obvious than Penny – who just feigned irritation – in letting on how overjoyed she was to see him. 'Oh, how wonderful to have this nice boy come into our home! How kind you are! Penny, you have to pay him back somehow.'

Penny instantly blushed, thinking of the scene behind the Maraja. Marcus, as if he'd read her mind, gave her a smarmy smile.

'Just fix the window and get out, will you?' she ordered him, leading him to her room.

Marcus fiddled with the frame while Penny watched from the doorway. Today he was wearing a long-sleeved T-shirt, sinfully tight, that highlighted every muscle in his shoulders and his huge, tattooed arms. Penny bit her lip and stared at the floor, hating herself for being so totally under his spell.

At one point, Marcus stopped, pulled something from his back pocket and handed it to her. 'It's a letter to Francisca. Write the address on it and send it off.'

'You mean *please*?'

'I'm already doing you a favour by fixing your window.'

'Well, you broke it! And, in any case, I pay you very well.'

'I'm paid to escort you from your place of work to this apartment, and I'll also be paid to pretend that I want no one but you, but I am not paid to be a carpenter.'

'You're vulgar and corrupt.'

'Ah yes, my two main strengths. My two fundamental values are sex and money, as you well know.'

'Plus you're sleazy. Only a total sleazeball could do what you did and then write to his girlfriend the same night.'

'That's a lot of action for one night, sure, but spare me the sermons about Francisca, OK? That's how we operate, and someone like you is just never gonna get it.'

Penny fell silent; whenever she talked to him about Francisca, Marcus dropped his normal jerkish cheerfulness and became a plain old jerk.

'Anyway,' he went on, 'if I have to pretend to be your boyfriend, I guess I need to know a few things about you, just to have some shit to say. What were you like when you were younger? Though I can probably imagine for myself . . .'

'That's not true.'

'Let me guess. You were lonely, and introverted but not timid, just disgusted by everyone around you. Even though they all thought you were stupid and submissive, you were intelligent and full of rage. You wanted to grab the jerks by the hair and stick their heads down the toilet, at the very least. And you liked some guy who never liked you back. Am I wrong?'

Penny looked at him, wide-eyed and mouth agape .

Marcus frowned and returned to his work.

She asked him, 'How . . . did you . . . know?'

Without taking his eyes off what he was doing, Marcus muttered, 'You're pretty predictable.'

Just at that moment, Barbie entered the room. 'Will you have lunch with us?' she asked Marcus chirpily.

Penny and Marcus simultaneously gave two different answers.

'No,' she said, just as he was saying, 'Sure.'

Barbie bounded back to the kitchen like a happy child.

'Just what do you think you're doing?' asked Penny furiously.

'Eating.'

'Go eat at your own house.'

'I have an empty fridge and I'm hungry. When I'm hungry I can't think, you know that. Plus, you have to pay me back for the work I'm doing. After lunch I'll fix your grandma's window too, and that shitty chain on your front door. So either you give me twenty dollars or you offer me lunch.'

'I know why you're doing this. It's so you can criticise my cooking later.'

'Your cooking?'

'Absolutely. If my grandma made lunch, there'd be sugar in our mac and cheese.'

'Well then, why don't you move your ass and get something ready?'

'Go tell your mother to move her ass,' Penny spat, before turning and stalking off to the kitchen.

Having Marcus over for lunch was weird. The whole apartment seemed smaller with this giant around whose head virtually grazed the ceiling. Penny's grandmother looked tinier than ever standing next to him.

Penny's heart, on the other hand, swelled with his every step, bite, word or silence. She was more and more afraid of him, and not for the obvious reasons – like the fact that he was arrogant, unpleasant, argumentative and barbaric in his behaviour. No, she was afraid of getting too used to his presence, of starting to depend on seeing him. Too much about him was becoming familiar to her: his smell, a combination of citrus-scented soap and tobacco; the way he arched an eyebrow or took a drag on his cigarette as it hung from his lips, the smoke filtering around her, before snatching it up again; his solid arms, and shoulders so majestic it seemed as if they could hold up the sky.

Penny had to watch herself, emotionally at the very least. She simply could not allow her heart to go lurching around like this, like a drunk slamming into every wall that presented itself.

When lunch was over, her grandma settled down on the couch to watch her favourite soap. Marcus looked across the table at Penny and said, 'Well, you're good in the kitchen, I'll admit that.'

'Thanks for the compliment, I guess.'

'No, I'm serious – you're good. Next time you make that pasta, bring me some too, yeah?'

'Anything else, sir?'

'After lunch I always have other needs, but you're not the right person for that.'

'You're so crass.'

'How old were you the first time you did it?'

Penny swayed as if someone had pushed her. 'Excuse me? What does this have to do with lunch? Mind your own business, pervert.'

'So how old were you?'

'Where on earth do you come up with these questions?'

'I'm just asking what comes to mind.'

'You can't always say everything that comes to mind, you know!'

'You're right, not everything, but come on, it's an innocent question and it's part of what a boyfriend should know. How old were you? Or maybe you've never done it and you're just posing as an experienced woman?'

'I've done it all right, but I don't want to tell you.'

Marcus started to light a cigarette, but then stopped. 'Let's go to my place so I can smoke and you can tell me your darkest secrets.'

The most sensible answer to that would have been a colossal 'no', but Penny's good judgement had flown to the four winds recently, and so, abandoning all caution in the face of blind desire, she nodded and followed him.

They quickly made their way up to his attic room, where Marcus lit up what must have been his hundredth cigarette of the day. He sat on the bed, his back against the wall. Penny kept her distance, perched on the arm of the couch and pretending not to look at him. All of a sudden she mustered up her courage and offered him another deal.

'I'll answer your stupid question if you tell me one thing about yourself.'

Marcus frowned. 'You go first.'

'If I go first, you could back out if you don't like my question.'

'So you're scared?'

'You said I'm smart, didn't you?'

'Yeah, you're that all right. So tell me all about your scandalous past. Or, if you want, we can tell everyone at the party you lost your virginity to me. I'm sure your bitchy former friends would love that little detail.'

'Only bitches, never friends, and they're so bitchy they just might ask.'

'Meanwhile, tell me how it was. I'm very curious. I can't imagine you engaged in such shallow behaviour.'

'Horrible emotionless sex with any old passing stranger is mindless and shallow, yes, but when you truly love someone, it's tender and overwhelming – it's romantic, and you should know that since you have Francisca.'

'Ha! I'm always horny. I'm never gonna be romantic in bed, and Francisca is more than fine with that. But anyway, you haven't answered my question yet.'

Penny bit her lip, staring into the corner of the room. She could invent whatever she wanted, couldn't she? The best thing about lies was that they didn't have to fall within the limits of the actual truth. So she tried to imagine her ideal situation, the one she'd really set her heart on, and pretended it had already happened.

'I was very much in love – very much. My heart exploded whenever he walked into a room. It was all very natural and beautiful. He was my ideal man. There was beautiful music in the background, and scented candles and flower petals on the bed. There are no sordid details to tell. Love made it all pure and innocent.'

For an instant Marcus looked distracted, as if he wasn't even listening, then he stared at her as if she were an alien.

'So what happened to this perfect guy?'

'He's . . . um . . . he's dead.'

'Dead?'

'Yeah, he was sick – leukaemia – but I don't want to talk about it. It still hurts too much to think about. Your turn now.'

Marcus smoked in silence for a while, staring out of his skylight. 'I'm disappointed. I was hoping for something . . . a little spicier.'

'It's your turn,' Penny repeated.

'You wanna know about my first time? Better you don't, little girl, or we'll ruin this romantic atmosphere full of princes, petals and sighs.'

'That wasn't my question.'

'What was it then?'

'Whose ring do you wear around your neck?'

Penny immediately regretted her question when she saw Marcus leap from the bed and nervously stub out his cigarette. Clearly agitated, he ran his hand down his neck to tuck the leather thong with the ring on it out of sight under his shirt, before stepping close to her – too close – and pushing her back against the wall. Penny felt the full warm weight of his muscular body leaning into her.

'Don't you ever ask me that again,' he growled, bringing his face down to her level.

They locked eyes for a moment, in silence. Marcus's irises had turned silver, and his cold expression said everything there was to say. Penny felt like she couldn't breathe – and not because she was afraid of him, but because she was quite overwhelmed at the strength of her feelings. She wanted to kiss him, wanted him to kiss her. For an instant, it seemed as if Marcus was about to answer her silent need, as if he had read the message of her thoughts, her parted lips, her ragged breath. Penny slowly licked her lips as if her tongue were seeking something more, but the moment was all too brief. After his flash of confusion, Marcus actually shook himself. Then he stepped back and looked at her with some indefinable measure of hostility or resentment, his brow creased and his breath, like hers, a little faster than normal.

'Time for you to go,' he said, before turning his back on her and shutting himself in the bathroom.

12

MARCUS

It's not hard to find women. I'm spoiled for choice. So I go out back with one and take her without so much as a kiss. It's a one-off fuck, not exactly enough to satisfy my hunger or this strange and primitive desire that's been eating me alive, but it's something.

Suddenly I hear someone coming from the alley. I turn around and swear. It's Penny. What the hell is Penny doing here?

She's just standing there, staring at me, then she runs away like I'm some demon who steals the souls of the innocent.

I calm myself down, tell my boss I'm leaving and go look for her. She must have sprinted to be so far ahead of me. My inner voice tells me, *Everything's OK, so long as she got home safe. If you don't find her dead on the sidewalk or raped in an alley, she's probably in bed right now making a list of all the reasons why you're such a fucking asshole.*

I guess I should just go home, take a shower, go to sleep and not care what Miss Penny Miller thinks of me.

So why do I climb up the fire escape?

I can't say – I don't have all the answers. I just know that I go up to the second-to-last floor and knock on the window.

And then I see her, her eyes staring through me like poisoned darts. Pervert, foul beast, lout, and who knows what else she's thinking about me. Not that I care, I'm me – I can't keep my cock out of action for too long. I'm a regular, living, breathing man after all. I'm not attracted to any particular quality she has – it's no more than some primal urge, OK? She's a woman, she's not repulsive, she has two legs, a pussy, an ass and a mouth. I love to tease her and rile her up – it gets me going. If that makes me an animal, then so be it.

◆ ◆ ◆

That night, I write to Francisca. I write and crumple up the paper and then I try again. I repeat this tired exercise half a dozen times at least before I can finally throw down a couple of acceptable thoughts. I've never been a scholar, but this time the discomfort is not from my dislike of a blank page and a pen.

I feel guilty.

Why would fucking some random slut make me feel guilty? I've always done it with no issues or regrets, so what's different this time?

Only when I finally sign the letter do I realise what the matter is. Damn it to hell.

I don't feel guilty about that girl whose name I don't even know.

I feel guilty because when Penny asked me to take her to her reunion, she offered me two hundred and fifty dollars, and when I asked her where she got the money, she led me to believe she'd provided some kind of sexual service to a man, and for a second there, I was thinking, *Tell me who he is so I can kill him.*

She was joking, but that's not the point.

The point is that until I realised she was joking I did want to kill him.

But why do I care who she blows? It's enough that she pays me, right?

It doesn't make sense, it definitely doesn't make sense, and things that make no sense make me nervous.

Kicking the bag for an hour is the only thing that makes me feel better, blow after blow after blow, and then I punch it until my arms are on fire and the attic seems like it's about to explode under the weight of my fury. In the end I'm exhausted but my head is clear and I go to sleep sweaty, and the thoughts that torment me are gone.

◆ ◆ ◆

I agree to take her to her stupid party. The money is good. I'm not thinking of anything else – I don't have to think about anything else. Anything I do for her is simply another contribution to my slush fund. I just have to make sure she stays alive until next month and then I'll get the fuck out of here.

She and her grandmother are like characters from some sappy film. How can people live like they're prisoners of a life that never changes? How does Penny not want to run and run from here? She takes care of the old woman like that old woman was her child. Penny does everything – I can tell from her hands. She has the hands of someone who has always worked and will always do so: rough, tired, chapped. So when does she get time to live a little for herself? She sleeps, eats, breathes and works. And that's her whole life?

I know I'm one to talk. As someone who spent the last four years in prison, it might seem hypocritical, but I did have a life before that. Skidding, twisted, hazy, violent, but a full life nonetheless. I've seen things, done things, changed things, broken things, killed things, but I've never stayed stuck in one place.

Seems like Penny's been in that apartment for centuries, and now she also takes care of a half-gone grandma. Doesn't she ever just want to leave it all behind?

I don't know why I ask her to come up to my place. There are so many things I don't know or understand these days. I only know that while we're talking about how to pull one over on her former classmates, I find myself wanting to learn more about her. Specifically, of course, I wanna know how she is in bed. The best way to find out is to fuck her, I guess, like that's ever gonna happen. Even though I want her bad, it's simply not going to happen, OK? So all I can do is ask her some intrusive questions. She's telling me about her first time, but I realise I can't really imagine her with this perfect man she's describing – so nauseatingly romantic; pathetic like some character killed off early in a movie. I can't imagine it simply because, while she's talking to me and I'm following the movement of her lips, I'm seeing her naked in my mind's eye all right, but I'm the one on top of her, inside her. I think it's better I don't ask Penny any more sexual questions. I'm a jerk. A real jerk. My own worst enemy.

But then she asks me about the ring I wear around my neck, and it pisses me off to no end. I always get mad when someone asks me about it. Even I have a few secrets I'd rather keep to myself, you know.

But when I hold her up against the wall, I can feel her trembling all over. I look at her, and her eyes are burning and her lips are like flowers and her chest is heaving, and . . . I don't care anymore about the cord around my neck or all the secrets. I just know I want to kiss her, lick her, touch those fresh petals with the tip of my tongue, and part them to let me enter. Damn it, I want to get inside of her in every which way.

I don't have to go along with this feeling. It's just some pointless, drunken, drugged-out, fucked-up reaction, even though I'm stone-cold sober and haven't smoked anything besides cigarettes for years and no one fucks with me ever. I can't try to kiss someone beautiful like Penny without feeling my ears hissing and the floor dropping out and my dick asking, begging, torturing me as it turns hard with a will of its own. I need to find some way out: either I leave here or I fuck her. Maybe after I fuck her and get it out of my system, I can go back to thinking of her as just some faceless and nameless pussy, huh?

13

She had no money for a new dress and nothing remotely suitable to wear. It was time to improvise. Fortunately, her grandma had plenty of vintage clothes – were they back in style? If so, Penny would be wearing an original, not some recycled imitation.

Penny and Barbie were similar in size, so when Penny tried on one of Barbie's dresses in front of the mirror, she saw how her grandma had probably looked as a young woman – slim, innocent, but feisty – though Penny's hair was shorter, and her smile didn't come as easily as her grandmother's. The dress was a sunny yellow colour, tight at the waist, with a hoop skirt like a downturned flower, and three organza petticoats that tickled her skin and made a rustling sound when lifted. That combination of softness and roughness reminded her of Marcus and the kiss-but-not-a-kiss he had given her – more of an injustice than a kiss really, punishment for her sin of curiosity. So what was the big secret regarding that ring?

She had the strong impression that he'd come to hate her, though she didn't know why. For the several nights following that afternoon and leading up to the party, Marcus had acted with apparent complete indifference to her when walking her home. For her own part, she had made no attempt to talk to him, and so they had walked together but each was locked in their own silence, two pissed-off statues with their hands in their pockets. Every time, Penny would watch him out of the corner of her eye, wondering how many more random women he might have given his body to behind the club, and precisely what he might be feeling in his heart when he was with them. And then she'd wonder exactly what he'd written in the letter to Francisca, and if, when he finally read her response, his soul would come alive again and he would at last break this hateful silence reserved only for Penny.

And as she wondered all these things, she felt sad – discarded like a stale piece of bread no one had cared enough to eat.

◆　◆　◆

Losing her nerve while she was getting ready, Penny was suddenly tempted not to go out at all. What was the point? Marcus was ignoring her and was bound to be on his worst behaviour at the party, proving that it was all just a pathetic charade, and then Penny would only become more depressed.

She studied herself carefully in the mirror. The dress adhered nicely to her figure; it was cute. She wore a rhinestone headband, also from her grandma's vintage collection, which for once held back her strands of pink hair. She looked pretty – not quite 'stratospheric pussy', as Marcus would no doubt have put it, but she was far from unattractive. Still, she felt depressed.

I had to ask for a whole night off from work for this stupid party and I'm only going to come away humiliated. Well, I'm not going. They won't even miss me.

But when she left Barbie's room, teetering on a pair of white-and-yellow-chequered heels, she saw Marcus standing there – her grandma had let him in without even warning her – and nearly fell over, like a circus performer on stilts.

'Just look how beautiful you are, my darling!' Barbie said with love and pride.

Penny replied with an equally adoring smile, certain that she could walk out in a banana costume and Barbie would still find her beautiful. Marcus, on the other hand, seemed little inclined to pay her any compliments at all. To be honest, he hardly looked at her, whereas she was studying his every detail. Her heart broke a little more every time she looked at him.

He was dressed in dark grey jeans and a cream-coloured woollen V-neck that clung to his body like a second skin. A few tattoos peeked out from his collar, just enough that he looked fierce and hot. On his feet he was wearing butch black biker boots, and to complete the ensemble, a long leather coat that had seen a lot of action, wild like his eyes. The bastard was to die for, totally irresistible. And he knew it. Her former classmates might have boyfriends with big wallets, but she knew that as soon as they saw Marcus, they'd want to rip his clothes off.

Those idiots are gonna die foaming at the mouth with lust – I just hope I don't die before they do.

She smiled at him out of habit, but he merely glanced briefly in her direction and snapped, 'OK, let's go.' Penny grabbed her favourite coat – the old pink woollen one with the buttons shaped like flowers – and followed Marcus out the door on the way to an unforgettable evening.

'Let's take a taxi,' Marcus said when they got outside.

'I don't have enough money,' Penny said, annoyed.

'Let's call it my treat.'

'And to what do I owe this generosity?'

'I hate taking buses. It's bad enough we have to go where we're going.'

'Look, I'm not forcing you, OK? If you want to back out, we can go back to being enemies, like before.'

'And deprive myself of the pleasure of being your date for these idiots? No, I really must insist,' he said.

They reached a busier street, near the Maraja. Without saying anything nice to her – or indeed anything at all – Marcus stuck close by her side, unlike all the nights he walked her home from work, when he was always a few paces ahead of her, turning back to glance at her as if she were of little more interest than the average garden snail. They finally managed to hail a taxi and gave the address to the driver, who exclaimed, 'Friends in high places, huh?' He caught sight of Marcus's stony gaze in the mirror and kept his mouth shut after that.

They were quiet throughout the ride. With his hostile expression and square jaw, Marcus looked like some tattooed assassin. It would have seemed entirely natural to wonder if he was hiding a long-barrelled .357 revolver under his coat.

Shortly before arriving, Penny felt so oppressed by the continuing silence that she held her breath for a moment, before saying quietly so the driver couldn't hear, 'Listen, I don't know what I did wrong the other night. If I offended you by asking about that ring, then I'm sorry and I won't ask again, and if you really don't want anything more to do with me, we can stop talking to each other as of tomorrow, but just for tonight, you need to do what I ask. If you want the two hundred and fifty dollars, you have to earn them, OK? You need to look like a gorgeous tough guy, but you also need to be nice to me. You have to make them jealous of me and the amazing sex we have all the time, and make them think that I have something way better than some rich boyfriend. You get me?'

In the darkness, Marcus's eyes gleamed like onyx. 'Well, I certainly have the biggest dick,' he said coldly and dispassionately, as if contemplating some objective truth.

'I know, I've seen it – remember? – but that's not the point here. The point is that you have to pretend to be stupid in love with me, or – if that's too much for you – at least pretend to be attracted to me, you know? They have to see us together and think I'm the luckiest girl alive.'

The taxi stopped; they had arrived. Around them stretched a residential neighbourhood with pristine sidewalks, colonial-style mansions and expansive lawns. A whole other planet from where Penny lived. For a moment she was afraid of making a wrong move or that such a distant world from her own could somehow contaminate her – or worse, make her go back in time to when she was an angry and miserable sixteen-year-old. So, as Marcus paid the driver and got out of the car, she remained inside, almost paralysed in her seat, in her stupid old vintage dress.

But then Marcus leaned in and whispered something in Penny's ear that gave her an unexpected burst of courage. 'Your wish is my command. Those bitches are gonna wish they could be you.'

The place was more of a palace than a house, and was already packed with people. From outside, Penny could hear music and the hum of voices. Her heart was racing as if it might burst. Marcus took her small hand in his giant paw.

'Listen, you're not sixteen anymore – fuck the lot of them,' he said angrily.

Penny nodded but wasn't convinced. Inside, she shuddered with alternating waves of fear and rage.

Rebecca opened the door, together with her much-vaunted boyfriend, and Penny felt the first pang of victory of the evening – and of her life – over her former classmate and torturer.

Not only was she an underfed fake beauty, all dyed-blonde hair and a set of equally fake coal-black eyelashes, but her man also was faux-handsome – a thirty-year-old dressed in the latest fashion, with slumped shoulders and protruding ears. All right, together they may have given off the air of wealth from their hair down to their shoes, but in reality they were grotesque and morbid figures, polished but full of a fat lot of zero.

As soon as they saw Marcus, they both recoiled as if there had been an explosion. Rebecca's eyes widened as if she'd been struck by lightning. Her boyfriend, Tucker, flinched and grew pale. Penny wondered if he had been bullied as a child. But then they immediately recovered their cool, simulated, perfect smiles, shook Penny and Marcus's hands and showed them in.

For Penny it was like being plunged straight back into her past. Everyone was there – with or without dates, but eager to share tales of their successes. There was Gaya, the smart one, who had graduated from Yale; Robert, the rebel, who had stopped rebelling and now worked in his father's business; Jessica, the slut, who had given everyone blowjobs in the bathrooms and was studying to become a lawyer; and Igor, who kept his distance but stared at Marcus with ill-concealed suspicion.

Just about everyone was staring at Marcus, in fact, with varying degrees of curiosity. He spoke little, like tough guys tend to do, but he never let go of Penny's hand, like a man staking his territory. Feeling him this close thrilled her to the core, and he played his role to the max. Al Pacino at the very height of his career could not have done better himself. Marcus didn't deviate in any way from his normal self – there was no sweetness nor smiles, nothing out of tune with his general impassive demeanour – but when Nickelback's

'Trying Not to Love You' came on the sound system, he slipped an arm around her waist and swept her away to dance with the other couples. He held her so close that his body felt like an extension of her own, and Penny learned the true meaning of the word 'torment'. Any former classmate choosing to study her closely right then would have had no doubt as to the all-consuming passion she clearly felt for her date. He made her feel small but aroused, utterly helpless but also like she could take on the whole world, scandalously eager and yet terrified in the face of all that desire.

'Don't crush me, okay?' she whispered as they danced.

Marcus bent down a little and muttered into her ear, 'If you want them to drink the Kool-Aid, you have to let me touch you – I don't write poetry when I like a woman, I just put my hands all over her.'

'That's fine, but . . .'

'I'll stop if it bothers you.'

It doesn't bother me one little bit – the problem is I like it, a lot.

'I get it, but if you keep this up, we're gonna have quadruplets in nine months' time,' she said through gritted teeth.

He chuckled a little. 'I guess I'm gonna have to give you a lesson on just how babies are made.'

'I don't need any lessons from you.'

'Well, start acting like you do, because your bitchy friend is coming over.'

At that moment, Penny heard Rebecca's voice nearby.

'My darlings!' she exclaimed, in the condescending tones of a First Lady greeting factory workers on a press tour. 'We're going to play spin the bottle. Care to join?'

They soon found themselves sitting on the floor in a circle like thirteen-year-olds, the only difference being that the bottle wasn't Coca-Cola but Möet & Chandon. Marcus stuck out among them like a redwood in a flower garden.

The rules seemed to be a little different from usual. The person chosen by the first spin of the bottle could either ask a question or pass on their turn to someone else. Penny and Marcus sat side by side and managed for a while to get away without being chosen. They witnessed a flurry of indiscreet questions, and penalties like kisses, groping breasts to feel for implants, pants dropped to show boxers or briefs, and all kinds of other nonsense. Suddenly, the champagne bottle picked Rebecca and then Marcus. The bitch was too clever to beg him to stick his tongue in her mouth in front of everyone, even though it was obvious she was dying for him to do so. Tucker wasn't playing; he had disappeared into another room, but Rebecca was still too shrewd to risk offending him. With a smile designed to look both soft and inviting, she asked Marcus, 'What exactly do you feel for Penny?'

Penny shook like the proverbial house of straw built by the three little pigs. Marcus on the other hand didn't waver for a moment. He locked eyes with Rebecca and said loud and clear for everyone to hear, 'I'm crazy about her and want to fuck her all day and all night. That what you wanted?'

Penny's cheeks grew as flushed as Rebecca's, though for different reasons. Penny was utterly stunned at this apparent revelation, while Rebecca, behind her inexhaustible smile, looked ready to blow her top in fury.

The game continued with more questions and ridiculous penalties, until this time the bottle pointed to Igor, and then Penny.

Igor, who was seated directly opposite her in the circle and hadn't stopped staring at her all evening, declared defiantly, 'I want a kiss.' He also eyed Marcus – who, sitting next to Penny with one hand on her knee, glared back at him with steel in his eyes. Everyone applauded, except for Rebecca, who seemed on the verge of a panic attack. Igor crawled on hands and knees towards Penny, across the circle of friends, who were laughing and egging him on.

'Only if you want to,' he told her when he was close enough.

Penny thought back to when she was sixteen and would have given anything for a kiss from Igor – or even the smallest sign that he had registered her very existence. Then she noticed Rebecca's look, as if the storm clouds were brewing, as if the evening wasn't going at all to plan, and suddenly a shudder of sheer joy shot through Penny's soul at the idea of causing her maximum grief. These days, Igor's lips weren't half as appealing as they had been when she was sixteen, but in any case she gave her consent.

Igor's eyes shone bright.

But both of them had overlooked one tiny detail.

As Igor leaned over and Penny offered up her innocent mouth, Marcus casually shoved his rival away with one arm, while in the same gesture pulling Penny close to kiss her.

This was no brief or superficial kiss. It was deep, so deep – an invasion of her mouth, a battle with her tongue. Penny's body felt as soft as cotton and as hot as molten lava. There was a buzz of voices from somewhere distant, but in that moment life had otherwise stopped, and she could see and hear nothing else, could not possibly want for anything more, might even have let out a small groan in front of everyone. This was no ordinary, everyday kiss. Marcus had penetrated her very being in an intense act of love.

Except that Penny knew it wasn't true love. She knew all too well that Marcus was only playing the part of a possessive boyfriend refusing to risk humiliation or defeat at the hands of another man. She knew he didn't give a damn about her, that he'd only kissed her like he'd kissed a million other women – and he would never kiss her like he must kiss Francisca, with his tongue but also his soul, but tonight she was just fine with that.

When they finally pulled apart – as unfortunately, they eventually had to – Penny realised that absolutely everyone in the room was staring at them, even Tucker, who had appeared from somewhere with a stupid little grin on his face, as if he had been drinking his head off until that moment.

And finally Rebecca, unable to bear the fact that she hadn't been the centre of attention, declared the game over.

Penny was the last to move. She was still feeling dazed after what had just happened.

Marcus pulled her to her feet. When they were standing face to face, albeit at different heights, he said scathingly, 'I'm really earning those two hundred and fifty dollars, don't you think?'

'If it's that difficult, then stop trying so hard. No one asked you for an Oscar-worthy performance.'

'As long as you're with me, you'll avoid rubbing yourself up against that guy. My woman doesn't let another man put his tongue in her mouth.'

'I'm not rubbing myself against anyone! And I'm not your woman!'

'As far as they're concerned you are. Your bitchy blonde friend thinks you are. No one touches what's mine, period, but we can drop the act right here and now if you want, so you can go fuck your friend without making me look like a jerk. He's been staring at you all night like a kid in a candy shop.'

Penny's eyes widened. 'What do you . . . ?' she sputtered. 'You're so . . .'

'Vulgar? Rude? Crude?'

'Exactly!'

'I've never been a fucking prince, little lady, and anyway, you just loved kissing this vulgar guy right here.'

'That's not true! I had to put on my best . . . acting . . .'

He drew closer, like a tiger stalking its prey. 'C'mon, Penny, you liked it all right, and it's useless to pretend otherwise, but let me tell you, you kiss back like someone who hasn't had much practice. That romantic boyfriend of yours preferred to watch TV, did he?'

Penny stared at him mutinously. She was just about to reply in defence of her imaginary lost love's sexual prowess when Rebecca re-entered the room.

'Oh my gosh, you just can't keep your hands off each other, can you!' she exclaimed in a tone of false amusement. Then, 'Your boyfriend can manage five minutes without you, can't he?' she asked Penny loudly. 'We're going to have some girl time.'

Rebecca dragged Penny upstairs to one of the many bathrooms in the house. In front of the largest jade-framed mirror Penny had ever seen, Rebecca finally dropped her mask.

'OK, Penny, who is this man? Some paid escort?'

Penny ordered her cheeks not to burn and her voice not to waver. She could not give in and confess that yes, the coolest guy in the room was not her boyfriend at all, that although he wasn't an escort in the strictest sense, he did come at a price.

'How dare you?' she replied in horror.

'Look, it's just not possible for someone like him to want someone like you! Have you seen yourself?'

'What do you mean, it's not possible? We have a special bond between us, something you and your moron of a fiancé will never grasp, because the only thing you two have in common is money.'

Rebecca let out a nasal, treacherous laugh. 'And what binds you exactly?' she asked. 'Come on, let's hear it . . .'

Penny stood up as tall as she could, summoning all her courage, then pushed Rebecca back as she made a run for the bathroom door. A moment before exiting, she declared haughtily, 'Love with a capital L. A deep kind of love – the kind you'll never experience.'

◆　◆　◆

After leaving the bathroom, Penny shut herself in one of the bedrooms. She had to wait until her breathing went back to normal.

Her face was burning, her hands were shaking and her legs had turned to water. Rebecca was mean and clever. She was sure to go and spread doubt among the other women, and then they'd all be laughing at Penny behind her back for the umpteenth time.

Penny realised she had entered a large, luxurious master bed-room, belonging perhaps to Tucker's parents. She looked at herself in the full-length oval mirror supported on a pedestal in the shape of a lion, that was possibly even cast from pure gold. There she saw a pathetic-looking girl, persecuted for years by a coven of witches with silky ponytails instead of brooms, who had insulted her because she came from humble beginnings, took the bus to school, always wore the same shoes and was not even particularly good at anything. She hadn't excelled in any particular subject, the boys didn't notice her, and above all, she hadn't suffered their harassment in silence. She'd reacted by expressing her hatred in return, staring them right in the face without dropping her gaze, and whenever possible she had practised acts of subtle revenge. Once, they had locked her in a dark closet, hoping she would beg them to let her out, but Penny hadn't screamed, begged or even cried. Instead she had waited in silence for the janitor to find her by chance and let her out, and by then it was so late that she'd missed the last bus and had to walk all the way home. Only God knew how afraid she'd been in that small dark space. She had wanted to be sick, to pass out, to crawl out of her own skin, but she had not given them the satisfaction of her tears and her despair. A few days after that, however, the cheerleaders' uniforms were stolen and later found in tatters in the schoolyard.

Revenge had always made her feel better, but not this time. No one could ever believe that Marcus was her boyfriend. It was all too clearly an act. Couples like Penny and Marcus didn't exist in the real world, where men like Marcus ended up with women like Francisca, and in the meantime fucked almost everyone else – including the Rebecca type – but certainly not someone like Penny Miller.

She sighed, falling back on the king-sized bed with its pearly-white wooden canopy and bronze-coloured silk bedspread.

At that moment she heard a knock at the door. Fearing it was the lady of the house – even though she'd have no reason to knock if it were – Penny jumped to her feet, even redder and more uncomfortable than before. She was just coming up with possible excuses when Igor walked in.

'I was looking for you,' he said with a smile. 'I saw you come up here with that bitch and then I saw her come down by herself. Everything all right?'

Penny nodded mechanically and sat back down on the bed.

'Did she make you cry? Your eyes . . .' Igor went on.

'Nobody makes me cry.'

'I know – I've always admired that about you – but you look upset.'

'When did you ever admire me?' exclaimed Penny.

'Back in school – you were tough, and even though I have no proof and can't begin to imagine how you did it, I'm sure it was you who wrecked Rebecca's brand-new phone. How did you manage to get it into the toilet in the boys' bathroom?'

Penny shook her head. 'Even if it was me, I wouldn't tell you. You were always her accomplice.'

'That's not true – I was just there. I never participated in her bullshit.'

'The fact that you define her crap as "bullshit" shows you have no idea. It's not bullshit to put peanuts in the food of someone who's allergic to peanuts and send them to the emergency room. It's not bullshit to unjustly accuse someone of having copied homework, or humiliate her in front of everyone because she has a patch on her shirt. And the fact that you didn't intervene when

131

you could makes you an accomplice. It's almost worse than if you'd participated.'

'I was only sixteen, Penny.'

'Trump was sixteen once too, but the evil was always there.'

Igor laughed. 'What, you're comparing me to Trump now? Fine, I was an asshole, but I assure you I'm not one now.'

'Well, how did that happen? Were you born again?'

'I just grew up and wrapped my head around a few things.'

'Oh yeah? And what would those things be?'

'That most of the people in there are jerks. They're high school beauty queens whose glory days are behind them, failed former quarterbacks and spoiled cokeheads. By the time Rebecca's hit thirty, she'll look like your grandmother, you'll see.'

'My grandma looks better than she does now.'

'I've always loved that you're such a fighter.'

'Thanks, Igor, but you're a liar and a jerk. Here's what I think. I think Rebecca was disappointed that I didn't show up with patches in my clothes and an ugly boyfriend, and now she's going for plan B.'

'So what's plan B?'

'How would I know? Maybe she wants to convince you to come up here pretending to be on my side, and then launch a counterattack? Maybe you're supposed to fuck me and post photos of it on Twitter.'

'You can't really believe that.'

'Of course I believe it. The apple doesn't fall far from the tree. And now I'm going to invite you to get the hell out of here. If you're recording our conversation, or Rebecca is behind that door having a laugh, you should both know that—'

'Listen to me, Penny,' Igor said firmly, interrupting her. 'I like you a lot, and I liked you back in high school too. I found you intriguing from day one, because in the midst of a whole pack of

132

fake rebels you were the only real one, and you were pretty as well. I always thought you had the sexiest lips and eyes in the world. During the game down there I wanted to kiss you so badly. Too bad Marcus is so possessive. For a moment I thought he wanted to kill me.'

'You can stop the charm offensive, OK?'

'I'm not trying to charm you and it's not bullshit. I'm just trying to explain why I never asked you out when I could before. Rebecca told me you were a lesbian.'

'Wait, what?'

'Well, you were different. You were very much your own person and you didn't date boys. Don't blame me if I believed her.'

'I don't give a crap if you believed her or not. You can both go to hell. I'm leaving now – this party is shit.'

'No doubt. But speaking of Rebecca . . . you were right about one thing. She's going to want payback for all of this.'

'I knew it. So what are you going to do now?'

'I'm not doing anything – she's the one you need to worry about.'

'I'm not afraid of that skinny beanpole. Let her do whatever she wants.'

'I . . . um . . . I'm afraid she's already doing it.'

'Doing it? Doing what?' asked Penny, looking around as if Rebecca were hiding somewhere in that big room full of moulding.

'She didn't tell me what – we're not close like we used to be – though a little while ago she told Tucker she was going down to the basement to get a couple of bottles of good wine.'

'I hope the mice eat her.'

Igor shook his head, looking at Penny, his eyes full of regret. 'She asked Marcus to go with her.'

Penny stood up quickly, her heart doing flips inside her chest. 'What did he say?' she asked, her voice broken with grief.

133

'He went.'

Igor kept talking. As she walked down the stairs like a robot, rigid and desperate, she could hear his voice behind her, but she couldn't hear him. Her pain was like a fog entering in through her ears.

Downstairs, the party went on, oblivious to her problems. They were listening to music, eating, drinking, dancing, smoking. Someone had dived into the pool with all their clothes on. Someone else was browsing through old photo albums. On the surface, it seemed like a reunion she'd seen in so many movies – nostalgic and cynical, both at the same time.

Except that, down in the basement, Rebecca and Marcus were definitely having sex. Penny had no doubt about that.

Her first reaction was to ask Igor where the damn basement was.

'I'll come too,' he replied, 'except that, if you go down there, you'll show her how she's getting to you.'

'I didn't ask for your advice, asshole,' Penny said. Passing by the buffet table, she grabbed a shot and poured it down her throat, then glared at Igor with all the hatred she could muster – which was a lot, even if it was mostly reserved for Marcus. 'So you came upstairs to distract me with all your talk, just to give that bitch more time.'

'No, I swear I didn't! Please believe me!'

'Fuck you! Just tell me where the basement is and leave me alone.'

He told her, and then Penny once again ordered him to go with such force that Igor had no choice but to walk away.

She went down the flight of stairs and located the wooden door that Igor had described to her. It was locked from the inside. There would have been no reason to shut themselves in if they weren't up to something in there.

She stopped in front of the locked door, and tears of anger, frustration and disappointment spilled out of her. She tried every way she knew to calm herself down but she just couldn't stop crying, until finally she realised that going in and making a scene would be ridiculous.

He's not your boyfriend, she told herself. *And you haven't even paid him yet.*

She shook her head in a gesture of defeat, turned away from the door and walked out of the house without so much as a backwards glance. She was stumbling in her chequered heels and had left her coat inside, but she wouldn't go back in there for all the tea in China. It was cold out and the air was damp, but Penny just wanted to get home at all costs, even if it meant freezing to death.

She asked a passer-by walking their dog to tell her the way to the nearest bus stop, which was a little further on. Meanwhile, it started to rain. A hard rain, like God was firing a load of nails into the earth.

She sat on the plastic bench in the bus shelter, but water hammered its way through the roof, drenching her face, her clothes and the shoes that had survived decades of boredom and were now destined to die in one stupid night. She didn't want to look up and so she sat hunched over like a broken doll, her tears as heavy as cream. She could no longer feel her own heart – earlier in the evening the blood had been surging through every vein in her body, but now she just felt dull and limp.

She ran a frozen hand over her cheeks and noticed they were frozen too.

Great, I'm gonna get pneumonia. I just hope they all get Ebola.

The bus arrived just as her teeth had begun to chatter, and she stood up, ready to board, her arms wrapped around her body for warmth, the make-up dripping off her face.

All of a sudden, someone put their hands on her. Penny yelped, trying to wriggle away in that vast sea of rain.

It was Marcus, looming out of the darkness behind her.

14

MARCUS

She's wrong if she thinks I'm gonna tell her she looks pretty, but then maybe she doesn't expect that. She acts like someone who doesn't know she's attractive, let alone expect other people to think she is. She's nervous and in a rush. All she wants is for me to put on a good act. She's not expecting bullshit, corsages or photos posed in front of a blinding flash. She just wants us to get on with the evening so she can forget about her school days forever.

We take a taxi. I pay for it, or she pays for it, since I get two hundred and fifty dollars for this whole charade. In the cab she's trembling like a leaf. I can't stand it when she's like this; I prefer it when she's tough. When she acts like she's made of glass, I instinctively want to grab her so she doesn't fall apart. Damn it, Penny, they're not seven-headed monsters – they're losers! They were then and they are now too, I guarantee it.

I get my confirmation of that as soon as we arrive. The boyfriend, the one with the asshole name, is a total jerk, and he's high on something. Not light stuff either – probably something more like coke. Penny's enemy, Rebecca, is a well-dressed slut, but a bitch all the same. She looks older than her years – I'd take her for at least thirty. She doesn't seem as high as her dwarf boyfriend, but she's taken something too. As soon as they see me, they react just like everyone else. He feels threatened, she's turned on. I'm used to it. Nothing new there.

Then I intertwine my fingers with Penny's and the show begins. I've never held hands with anyone for this long. Francisca doesn't give a damn about all that crap, and also we usually needed to keep our hands free, ready to kick someone's ass or hold a knife. For a moment, just one, not even so long as the blink of an eye, I have the strangest feeling, which makes me think of the first time I drank alcohol when I was ten. That first gulp of beer. The coolness of it, the thrill and the dizziness. But then it passes, and now it's gone.

One thing is certain: Rebecca hates Penny and that guy with the curly hair wants to do her. He doesn't stop staring for a moment, and gives me a nasty look when he thinks I'm not looking.

I notice Penny's seen him and is blushing and this pisses me off.

But why does it piss me off?

It makes no sense.

I'm only here to earn two hundred and fifty dollars, not to spin theories about who wants to be with who and who blushes when she sees who else, right?

Maybe she was the one he liked in high school, but he never went for it. Maybe, in addition to infuriating Rebecca, Penny hoped to get revenge on this idiot who snubbed her back then. Why he would have snubbed her at school, I don't know, but the fact is that now he wants her and he hates me.

Dancing with Penny is strange. I've never actually danced with anyone before, except once as a kid with my mother. I have a lightning-quick and totally unexpected flashback to me aged eight or nine, already taller than she was, offering her my hand and performing a ridiculous imitation of a bow. I'd forgotten that, but now the memory's returned, and I can even remember her words. She said to me, 'One day you'll invite your girlfriend to dance a waltz.'

It's crazy how romantic she was, in spite of everything. She thought my future was full of heart-pounding waltzes and red roses for some unique and perfect woman who would suddenly appear, like a barefoot Cinderella on the steps of a crystal palace. My mother believed that love existed somewhere in the world – beyond her room, her body and her life. She tried hard to convince me, but she never succeeded. I liked to listen to those stories of hers, like a hopeless patient wants to believe the pitiful lies of some quack, but even then I knew they were only fairy tales told by a wannabe princess disappointed by life. The love that I saw as a kid was always a stack of bills left behind on a bedside table, a slew of curses, the mingled odours of sweat and blood.

I'm dancing with Penny, and her hair smells of wild strawberries. I hold her close and her body is rigid and hesitant against me. I wonder if it's me or just the whole situation that's bothering her. Maybe she'd rather dance with that loser with the golden curls, and the sheer thought of it pisses me off all over again.

So we're playing spin the bottle like idiot kids when it lands on her, and that's the end of it. The moron approaches, and suddenly I'm drowning in rage. *Don't you dare touch her, you prick!* I kiss her and my mind goes blank. All I can think about is her mouth, her tongue, her breath and her strawberry-scented hair. If we were alone right now, I'd lift up her skirt and take her with all my might. But we're not alone here, and all too soon the background sounds rush back in, and I feel confused and terrible and really mad at her.

When I feel this way, I insult people; and I don't know why, but somehow I feel easier with myself when I treat Penny like shit. The truth is that I want to drag her behind a door, behind a curtain, behind a screen, and slip between her thighs without a single word of explanation. OK, it's a fact: I have a thing for her. It's nothing mysterious – I'm a young man and all my parts are in working order. I repeat it to myself ten times over while spewing a bunch of bullshit at her. *I'm just a man.*

Then, suddenly, Rebecca drags her away.

I follow them, hang around near the staircase they went up. After a while Rebecca comes down, and as soon as she notices me, she does the same as any other slut: mouth gaping, tongue hanging out, wide eyes, a smirk – the full shebang. She grabs me by the arm, tells me Penny's coming down in a minute, and in the meantime I can go to the basement with her to grab some wine.

Of course I'll go to the basement with you, my dearest little bitch.

Her boyfriend with his douchebag face doesn't even notice, or maybe he's just happy every time someone does him the favour of fucking his woman, since he's barely able to stand with all that coke up his nose.

We go downstairs to a temperature-controlled room, all wood and white plaster, packed with rows and rows of bottles. We reach the far wall, where the rarest, most expensive vintages are kept.

Rebecca begins to run her hands over the necks of the bottles as she watches me, then she takes one and caresses it in a suggestive way. There's a strange blue light in her eyes as she comes up to me, and now she's running her hands up and down her body, twisting and turning like a snake, only one thing on her little mind. She's stroking my arms, my stomach, the crotch of my pants. 'You're very sexy, you know, Marcus.'

'I am. And you?'

'I'm better than Penny.'

I give her an oblique smile. 'Are you sure about that?'

'Yup.'

'Let's see. Take your clothes off.'

Rebecca gives a low laugh and starts to undo the zipper at the side of her dress. She slides it down, all sensual and slow. The dress falls on to the dusty floor. Now she's standing there in a lace bodysuit, squeezed into it like a herring through the eye of a needle.

'Take it all off,' I command.

She's loving how firm I am with her – she's licking her lips and her face is flushed. She's fully naked now, with her small but perfect tits and her Brazilian wax.

I shake my head. 'No,' I say in my coldest voice. 'I can see now. You're not in any way better than my Penny.'

Her eyes widen and she looks like a rabbit caught in headlights. 'But . . .'

'I'm sorry, but my dick just won't cooperate,' I tell her. 'In fact, seeing you naked like that just makes me want to fuck Penny even harder.'

'That bitch! I'm sure she's paying you! But I'll give you more – I have my chequebook upstairs. How's two thousand dollars sound to you?'

'I'd need a whole lot more than a couple of grand, believe me. But it's not a question of money – I just find you repulsive. I have no intention of getting down in the filth and slime alongside you, you know.'

With that, I turn my back and leave her, naked and pissed off. I think I can hear her swearing at me, but I don't care enough to know exactly what she's saying.

I can't find Penny. For a minute, I'm afraid she's stuck somewhere with that creep – the one who looks at her like she's a lollipop he wants to suck. I can't stop myself from clenching my fists.

Then I see him.

'Where is she?' I ask, and he frowns.

'If you're referring to Penny, she left. If you're referring to Rebecca, you should know better than I do.'

'She left? When?'

'About ten minutes ago, after discovering you're a scumbag.'

Another time his comment would bother me, but right now I'm worrying about Penny, and he leaves me strangely indifferent.

'Where did she go?'

'What do I know? She didn't want me to go with her.'

'Did she take a taxi or what?'

'She didn't even take her coat – she practically ran out of here. You know, you're a piece of shit. If you have someone like Penny, what would you need with Rebecca? But maybe it's true what they say – the bigger the muscles, the smaller the brain.'

I grab the collar of his shirt. 'You'd better hope nothing happened to her.'

'You too.'

He's not wrong. It's not his fault. I came here with Penny tonight. I'm the one who should have protected her. I hold back my desire to crush his balls with my knee just for the sheer enjoyment of knocking that accusatory expression off his face, and I leave that evil house.

It's raining. I look around but there's no trace of her. My heart starts racing.

OK, take it easy. She's not a child. It's true you went to the party together, but you didn't exactly sign a deal in blood. So she left, did she? Well, that's her business.

But I can't convince myself not to worry. Part of me realises I'm a fucking liar. I think back to her frightened expression before we arrived – her moist, glistening eyes – and I get seriously pissed at myself.

I try to call her on her phone but it just rings. I fire off a few expletives.

She didn't have enough money with her, so she couldn't have taken a taxi. Maybe a bus?

I ask a couple where the closest bus stop is, then start running like crazy.

She's in a bus shelter that's actually not giving her any shelter at all. She's sitting on the bench staring out at the muddy street. The bus arrives, spraying water everywhere. Penny gets up to climb on board. I don't really get what I'm doing here, and most of all I don't really get what I'm feeling; I only know that as soon as I embrace her from behind, wrapping her tightly in my arms, I feel like I've conquered some essential part of myself.

15

Penny winced at the sight of him, and her tears soon turned into a strangled sob.

'Asshole!' she said, struggling to get away from him. She got on the bus and Marcus followed.

It was empty apart a few souls slumped in the front seats. Penny sat somewhere at random, her hair dripping like a leaky downpipe. She stared out the window in a grotesque display of indifference. A pool of rainwater had collected on the floor, and she stared out through the window as if Marcus were invisible.

In reality, it was the opposite. She was trembling all over, a little from the cold and a little from anger, clenching her fists as if to signal imminent and ceaseless conflict between them both.

'You should have waited for me,' Marcus told her.

She turned and gave him a fierce look, but it was a fragile ferocity that risked melting into a sea of tears. Then she imagined Marcus and Rebecca having sex in the basement and laughing at her, and once again was overwhelmed by rage.

'Get away from me!' she ordered him. 'You didn't keep your end of the deal. Go sit somewhere else – I don't want you here. You disgust me.'

'Stop talking bullshit,' he replied in an icy tone that irritated her even more.

She got up from her seat, scrambled past him with her nose in the air, and went to stand by one of the doors, clinging to the metal bar. Marcus quickly joined her. They stood there in silence – Penny soaked through and tottering on her high heels, losing her balance with each brake and turn, his arms always ready to catch her. Every time it happened Penny told him not to touch her, but every time he did, and her heart skipped a beat, making her feel miserable as well as helpless.

At one of the many stops, Marcus took her hand. 'Let's get off here,' he said, pulling her from the bus.

'No! I'm not home yet.'

He showed no sign of listening to her, but continued holding her hand, as if leading her off in a specific direction. The rain had let up but it was still mercilessly cold.

Marcus stopped in front of a diner that was like a portal back to the era of flared trousers and feathered hair. They passed through a glass door with a polished brass frame, stamped with the words 'The Gold Cat'. Marcus greeted an older lady behind the counter as if he knew her.

'Hi, Sherrie. Could you please bring us a towel?'

The woman nodded at his request. She was plump and petite, around sixty years old, with a bright, yellow-gold crest atop her white hair, which was styled like Farrah Fawcett's in *Charlie's Angels*. The room itself was decorated in different shades of yellow, from the floor up to the pendant lamps. Three or four customers sat in booths devouring mountains of mashed potato doused in gravy or slices of apple pie à la mode, and there was someone else seated at the bar, eyes glued to an old TV with the sound turned low.

Marcus dragged Penny towards the ladies' bathroom. It was small and unadorned – unlike the bathrooms at Tucker's house – but clean, and there were no snakes slithering around. He went in with her, ignoring the stylised symbol of a woman with a skirt on the door. He seemed to know exactly what he was doing and punched the button on the hand dryer. It fired a jet of hot air that would uproot an oak.

'Come here,' he ordered. 'Dry your hair. Sherrie's on her way.'

Penny looked at him in shock. 'Where are we, and who's Sherrie?'

The woman with the flossy white hair came in. 'Oh my goodness, you're all wet! You'd better dry off before you catch your death of cold! And you get out of here, you rascal!' she said, turning to Marcus. 'This is the ladies' bathroom.'

Marcus gave Sherrie an easy smile in return, and left with her. Penny stayed under the stream of hot air and soon felt like a new woman. After a while, she heard a knock at the door.

'Can I come in?' asked Marcus.

Penny was horrified by her reflection in the mirror – she looked like something the cat had dragged in. Her hair was sticking up all over the place, her make-up had trickled down her face and her nose was as red as a tomato. She tried combing her hair with her fingers, but the final result didn't look any better.

Oh, what the heck?

Marcus entered without waiting for Penny to respond.

'Feeling better?' he asked. 'Let's go eat.'

'I'll eat at home, thank you.'

'Eat something here – have some pie at least.'

'You're not normal.'

'I never pretended to be. Is your dress dry now?'

'Yes, but . . .'

He walked over to the dryer and punched it again, silencing it. 'It's the only way to turn it on and off.'

'And when you're not around to sneak into the women's bathroom, how do they do it then?' she asked sarcastically.

'They don't. Let's go.'

'Stop dragging me around like a schoolbag; it bothers me.'

'I don't want you to run off again.'

'I didn't run off.'

'You ran from that house full of assholes.'

'I didn't run off – I left of my own free will, and if I want to leave again, I will.'

'Don't even think about trying it.'

'You threatening me?'

'I just want you to have something to eat, rest for two seconds and hear me out. Come on. Sherrie put on some fresh coffee and she makes an excellent apple pie.'

Penny was hungry in spite of herself, and couldn't resist the offer. Within five minutes they were sitting at a booth by the window, which had a gold decal of a smiling cat with long whiskers and a definite purr. Penny gobbled down the pie and drank the coffee as if she didn't know where her next meal was coming from.

'Look how much you're eating! Are they starving you back home? You want more coffee?'

'No, I'm fine.'

'So, you gonna be less of an idiot now?'

'I was never an idiot!'

'You sure were when you ran off like that. Will you listen to me for once?'

'No.'

Unexpectedly, Marcus reached across the table and took her hand. Penny jerked it away like she'd had an electric shock or something. He frowned and then said, 'Look, nothing happened with Rebecca.'

'I don't give a crap what happened!' Penny exclaimed, but then she immediately blurted out, 'Actually, you know what? I do care – a lot! We had an arrangement! So I order you to report on everything that happened while you were working for me.'

'Don't, Penny. I'm not working for anyone. But I didn't fuck Rebecca, so are you happy now?'

'You don't actually need to fuck someone to have done something wrong,' Penny grunted, annoyed, as she stared out the window.

'Nothing happened.'

'Nothing? So why did you go down to the basement with her?'

'Because I knew what she wanted from me. I wanted to see how far she'd take it and then send her to hell.'

'And . . . ?'

'And I sent her to hell.'

'Are you serious?'

'Why does that surprise you? She's a dirty whore, and one of the bitchiest women I've ever met.'

'You think . . . she's ugly?'

'I think she's rotten, inside and out.'

'But how did you know that . . . that you wouldn't like her? And then if . . . while you were down there . . .'

'It didn't happen. While I was down there, I just thought about how damp it smelled in the basement.'

'You are so not normal, Marcus.'

'I have standards, that's all. I don't aim for just anything with a hole, you know.'

'Now she's going to hate me even more than before.'

'Do you care?'

'Not really. Can I have another piece of pie?'

'You're paying.'

'I get it. You're getting a separate cheque, aren't you?'

'Something like that.'

'You're an asshole. I've honestly never met anyone so obsessed with money.'

Marcus nodded to Sherrie, who had arrived with more pie. He smiled at her fondly. Once they were alone again, Penny asked him, 'So who is she? How do you know her?'

Marcus was silent for a few seconds, and Penny interpreted this to mean *Mind your own business*, but then he answered.

'When I was a child, I called her my aunt, even though she isn't really.'

'When you were a child?' Penny exclaimed in amazement. 'So you did already know someone in this city!'

'Yeah. That's really why I chose to come here, so I could check in on her – nothing strange about that.'

'It's wonderful you have someone around from when you were young. If it weren't for my grandma, I wouldn't have a home town either.'

'Actually, I prefer to forget about my childhood, but I love her anyway. None of it was her fault.'

'Her fault?'

'Have you finished stuffing yourself yet?'

'Yup.'

'The rain's stopped. Let's try to get home. It's not so far from here.'

Shortly before they left, Sherrie came up to Penny and gave her a hug.

'Thank you,' she said as Penny left, thinking that, for whatever reason of her own, Sherrie was pleased she'd come.

◆ ◆ ◆

Why do I feel so good when I'm around him?

She asked herself this over and over as they walked together in a darkness as thick as molasses.

They exchanged a few words, and suddenly Marcus asked her, 'Are you cold?'

'A little, but we're almost there now.'

Without another word, he took off his leather coat and handed it to her.

'I'm fine, thanks,' Penny replied, pushing it away.

'Put the fucking coat on.'

'You have good intentions but bad manners.'

'If you don't want it, I'll take it back.'

Penny bit her bottom lip. She really was cold. 'OK, thanks.' She put the coat on, and it was like donning a metal cape. It was huge, heavy and very long, but it kept her warm and smelled of Marcus.

They continued in silence for a stretch. The sky was clearing and the stars looked like shards of glass.

'I think I know why Rebecca hated you in high school,' Marcus said after a while.

'I know why too – because I wasn't rich and beautiful, and she felt contaminated by my simple existence.'

'Maybe that too, but more because that guy liked you . . . What the fuck's his name?'

'Who?'

'The boy with the curly hair.'

'Igor?'

'They all have such shit names!'

'Why does everyone keep saying Igor liked me?'

'Who else said it?'

'Um . . . he did.'

'He actually told you he liked you?'

'Yes, but he was only leading me on.'

'When did he tell you?'

'While you were in the basement with Rebecca.'

'And he told you he still likes you?'

'What is this? An interrogation?'

'I wanna know.'

'You want, you want . . . You're always ordering me around. Anyway, yes, he still likes me, but I didn't really believe him.'

'So what about you?'

'What about me?'

'Do you like him?'

'Stop it!' she grumbled, wondering what the point was to this whole conversation.

No, I don't like him. I like you, you asshole.

'In any case, Rebecca was jealous of you,' Marcus concluded. He took out a Chesterfield. It occurred to Penny that he hadn't lit one for hours, and it had been strange to see him without that pale appendage hanging from his lips. He smoked furiously for a few minutes.

'That's just nonsense. I don't want anything to do with any of them,' Penny said.

'Including Igor?'

'I'm not stupid. I'm not going to fall for him just because he looks at me twice.'

Marcus lit another cigarette, sucking down mouthfuls of poison as if they were fresh air. After a few minutes, he turned to her and said, 'Was he batting his eyelashes at you and everything?'

'Well, hell – I mean, yeah, I do have that effect on some guys. I'm no heartbreaker, but I have impressed the odd guy or two. Of course, so far they've mostly been psychos, but it's not my fault. Don't be so surprised that other people see something in me.'

'You sure have a short memory.'

'What?'

'I thought I'd made it clear that I also find you . . . um . . . fuckable.'

'Ah yes, and since you're not attracted to every single hole you see, I guess I should be flattered. Something tells me you fall into the psychopath category.'

Marcus laughed for the first time that strange evening. 'I take your point,' he admitted.

'Do you really like me . . . in that way?'

'In the fuckable way? Sure. But don't worry, I'm not gonna fuck you.'

'Why ever not?'

'Because it would be a trap.'

'A trap?'

'I can't just fuck you and be done with it, and I'm not looking for a relationship. I'm already in one.'

'But what if I swore to you that I'm not after any kind of relationship either? What if I just wanted to fuck you and be done with it?'

Marcus frowned. 'Don't make jokes like that, Penny.'

'Who said I'm joking? Look, I'm twenty-two years old, not eight, and I'm made of flesh and blood, same as you. I'm not gonna do it behind the club, of course, but I could also use a . . . temporary and uncomplicated arrangement. So what do you think? We know each other well enough – but not too intimately. You wouldn't be just anyone, but it wouldn't have to be a big thing either. Somewhere in the middle.'

'I said quit joking around, OK?'

'The truth is you don't like me. You're just making excuses now.'

They had arrived home. The building stood out in the dark like a crumbling monolith. The light was out again, and Penny pulled her phone from her bag.

There were several calls from Marcus, then three from unknown numbers and as many texts. She read them by the door while Marcus paced up and down, chain-smoking like a madman.

The texts were from Igor.

How had he got her number?

Are you OK, Penny? Did you get home safe? It's me, Igor.

Please, I'm worried about you. You were so upset.

If Marcus pisses you off one day, please reach out to me.

'Look, you see? If you're going to act like some precious virgin princess, I'll go console myself with Igor.'

She held up her phone to show Marcus the messages. He didn't look at them; he didn't look at anything but her eyes. He threw his cigarette in a dramatic arc and it plopped into a distant puddle with a faint hiss. Then he grabbed Penny by the wrist and, with his face menacingly close to hers, said to her, 'No one has ever called me a "virgin princess". You win. Come on, I'll show you what kind of princess I am.'

They'd been in the attic for ten minutes and Penny's heart was in danger of choking her. Marcus had taken off his sweater and shoes and was walking around the apartment half-naked. In the dim light, his tattoos looked like dark warning signs. He was no longer wearing his leather necklace, and when he turned his back to her, Penny noticed another Maori stingray, this one larger than the one on his chest, spreading its wings all the way down to the base of his spine. She watched him, hypnotised; his every movement seemed to bring life to the markings on his beautiful bronze skin.

'D'you want a coffee?' he asked as he fumbled with an old coffee maker. 'I do. I'm going to need a lot of energy tonight.'

Penny answered with a silent nod. She had followed suit and taken off his long coat and her shoes, but then had remained standing in the middle of the room like an empty hanger.

'Make yourself comfortable,' Marcus said. His tone was ironic and his eyes gleamed like a raptor's in the dark.

'I'll make myself comfortable as and when I feel like it,' Penny answered crossly.

I know what you're doing. You're trying to bait me. You think I won't have the guts to go through with this madness – you're trying to scare me out of it – but I'm not going to chicken out. And besides, the one thing you don't know is that I love you.

That private confession had somehow appeared in her general thoughts, swift as a pistol shot.

I love you.

When had it happened? How and why? Penny didn't know, but she knew it was real all right. It was the first time she had admitted it to herself. It was a whole new feeling, fizzily lightweight but terrifying, starting from that one little organ in her chest, pumping blood and love and longing to every goddamn part of her.

If I wait for you to love me back, I'll die a virgin, so my feelings will just have to be enough for the both of us.

Then, in one brazen step, she went over to the bed and sat down on it. Marcus was pouring coffee into the cups and didn't notice right away. When he saw her, he frowned and spilled some coffee on the table.

'What the hell . . . ?'

'Could you hurry up with that coffee? I'm also going to need a lot of energy tonight.'

Marcus walked towards her, both serious and furious. 'Tell me you're kidding and we can quit while we're ahead.'

'I'm not kidding at all. Don't get the wrong idea about me. I'm not some fairy with tinsel wings and I'm not looking for your

153

love – just pure sex. Fuck me like you fuck the others, and don't pretend you have any scruples.'

'Penny, you don't know what you're getting into.'

'I know perfectly well.'

Marcus pointed to his jeans and Penny saw exactly what she was getting into. A glaring erection strained against his pants.

That's for me?

Marcus sat on the bed. He gave her one last angry look and then, without any more hesitation, squeezed the back of her neck with one hand and kissed her. Penny ended up lying on her back, her tongue once again working its way over Marcus's lips, mouth and teeth. Marcus licked her in turn, panting like someone who knows what he wants. Maybe Penny should have told him she was a virgin, but if she had, he would have stopped, she was sure of it. And she didn't want him to stop.

Marcus fumbled under her dress, which rustled like a swarm of bees. He must have done the same to a million women. Or maybe just her, here, now, tonight? He moved as if he knew where everything was: zippers, hooks, things to raise and things to slide. He pulled the dress over her head and Penny shivered with total love and a fear she was doing her best to conceal. Her heart pounded like she was about to have a heart attack, with all the strength of one last goodbye bang. She found herself in her bra and panties under the heat of Marcus's gaze, and wondered if it was all a dream, one of the countless fantasies she'd been having over the last few weeks. But then his hands removed the last of her clothing and his tongue tasted her skin – slow but impetuous – telling her that this was all too real. He bit her nipples gently and stroked them with his fingertips, sending chills of pleasure throughout her body, in sync with the rhythm of her heart.

Then he moved down her belly, parted her legs and kissed her down there too. For a moment Penny lost all sense of place and time. With her eyes fixed on the skylight bathed in fallen rain – without actually seeing it, because her vision was filled with tiny sparks of pleasure and delight – she enjoyed his voracious touch at the centre of her body and stopped thinking about anything else; if she could have, she would have stayed that way for the rest of her life. But Marcus suddenly broke away from her. He stood up and stared down at her with the eyes of a hungry predator, remaining like that for a moment, beside the bed, in the shadows. Finally, he let out a sigh that was almost a rattle and took off his pants. Penny trembled for a moment like she had done back in the alley, but the fear of having him inside her was less strong than the need.

Marcus pulled a condom out from a drawer. He quickly opened the wrapper with his teeth and started to put it on, but Penny stopped him.

'Can I do it?' she asked.

Where has this shameless hussy been hiding? From which novel, film or soap did I learn to be so forward?

He nodded, and she saw his throat twitch as he swallowed, as if watching something new and mysterious, even though it must have been the millionth time for him. Penny tried to stop her clumsy hands from shaking. She tried not to look stupid or let on that she'd never done this before, but although she had indeed never done it, and she did feel a little stupid, she managed better than she expected.

She lay back down. Marcus kissed her again, a kiss so good Penny could have happily orgasmed simply from the way his tongue intertwined with her own. Then he took her hips in his hands, raising her up a little, and entered her body.

The pleasure disappeared, replaced by a sharp pain. It was as if her skin had been cut by a red-hot metal blade. She would have had every right to shout at him, 'Stop, wait, do it slowly – I'm fragile!'

But she didn't say anything at all. She only uttered one small cry, which could be mistaken for pleasure, and held back her tears.

Marcus moved with the impetus of a man making no concessions for someone who was doing it for the very first time. He thrust back and forth inside her like a battering ram, at the same time kissing her, licking her throat, squeezing her breasts, and gripping her thighs to make her body arch. Penny kept her eyes open so she could see him: his arms, his chest, his stomach glued tight to her own, the key to her lock that was opening for the first time in her life.

Suddenly he whispered to her, 'I'm coming,' and Penny said 'Yes', excited, almost as if she were about to give him a gift, and she felt him go deeper, so deep she was afraid he'd reach her ribs, and then the rhythm became even more frantic. He growled in her ear, his tongue becoming a spear, and finally he exploded inside her like a supernova.

Marcus collapsed on top of her, breathing like a sprinter crossing the finish line. Penny desperately held back her urgent need to tell him, *I love you, I love you, I love you!*

They stayed like that for a while, melted into each other's skin and sweat, until Marcus rolled onto his side and lay down on the bed, nestled into her body.

Penny wondered, *Should I leave now or can I wait? Can I say thank you or would that make me look stupid? How long will it take for him to forget about me?*

Then something happened that broke the fragile spell. Marcus sat up. He was about to take off the condom when his eyes, still clouded from his mighty orgasm, became masked with anxiety.

'Penny!'

She didn't immediately understand why Marcus's face wore a look of horror.

'What the . . . ?'

And then she understood.

The condom was stained with blood and a crimson patch had spread between her open legs. It flowed out of her skin, staining the duvet on the bed, enough to betray her secret.

'Penny!' Marcus exclaimed again. 'Tell me that's not what I think it is.'

She shrugged her small shoulders. 'I think it's what you think it is.'

Marcus placed his hands over his face and began to breathe hard and fast.

'Are you mad because I stained your duvet?' Penny asked, trying to smile. 'I'll pay to have it cleaned.'

'Why the fuck would I care about a duvet?' he snapped, springing to his feet.

'If it's not a problem for me, it shouldn't be one for you either. I'm not dead. It's a completely natural thing.'

Marcus started moving around the room like an angry lion on a chain. Penny got dressed in an instant, without bothering with her underwear. She covered her wound, hoping that once it was out of sight, out of mind, Marcus would stop hating her.

Suddenly he stopped, and Penny looked at him, enchanted by the thought of what had just happened, of his body on hers, of the two of them who had been so distant becoming one, and she was so lost in remembering that she didn't hear his question, not until he said it a second time.

'Did I hurt you?' His voice came out in a whisper and a gasp.

'Not that much. Not really.'

Marcus looked for a cigarette. He walked around the apartment, naked and beautiful, his hands shaking with rage. He managed to get a spark after three false starts with the lighter and took a long drag. 'You should have told me!'

'It's no tragedy. I'm still alive, aren't I?'

'Damn it, I hadn't even noticed. I mean, you were very tight, but I thought it was because you didn't do it often, not that you'd never done it in your life. And besides, I've had no way to compare. The women I'm with generally have their doors wide open.'

'Really?'

'Do I look like someone who fucks virgins?'

'So it was a first for both of us.'

'Why did you lie to me?'

'I have a wild imagination, but I know it's bullshit.'

'It really is.'

'I can distinguish a dream from reality, and I know it would never have happened that way in real life. The whole Prince Charming thing with the music, the flowers, the beating hearts. I know those things don't exist.'

'And what does exist? Someone who splits you in two without a word?'

'It was a beautiful experience for me, really.'

'You even enjoyed it when . . .'

Penny bit her lip. 'I . . . uh . . . I don't think so, not in the sense you mean.'

'There is only one sense, Penny. Did you feel pleasure?'

'I was happy . . .'

'I'm not talking about happiness. I'm talking about an orgasm.'

'No, I didn't have an orgasm, but . . .'

Marcus sat down on the bed and rubbed his forehead with one hand. Penny stood up, picked up her few belongings and smoothed her tousled hair.

'I'm leaving,' she said, smiling. 'Don't worry, I'm fine, and I'm happy anyway.'

'Happy about what, damn it?' Marcus exclaimed, annoyed.

To have done it with you. That you were my first. That I can still taste you in my mouth.

'To have it out of my mind. I'm nearly twenty-three. It was getting ridiculous. Now everything will be easier. I hope I didn't disappoint you.'

Marcus looked across at her as she got to the door. 'You were in no way disappointing. A man can't fake that, you know.'

She didn't tell him that she wasn't referring to his body. She knew his body had wanted it. She wanted to ask him how he was feeling; if it had felt right when he kissed her; if he felt that no taste could be sweeter than her tongue; if he had felt their souls merge when he entered her.

But she couldn't ask him any of those things and, above all, she didn't want to know the answers. She was sure they would kill her.

So instead she opened the door and said, a second before she left, 'Thank you, Marcus.'

16

MARCUS

She avoids me, she wriggles away, she tries to escape like a frightened gazelle. If I let her, she'd jump off the bus while it was still moving. I don't want her to get soaked, and if she doesn't dry off soon, she'll risk getting sick.

Why do I always have to take care of her? I get the distinct impression she ought to be paying me more for what I do. I have to protect her ass from Grant and pretend to be a good boyfriend, and now I have to look after her health.

Maybe I feel sorry for her. Yes, that's definitely it – I feel sorry for her. She really touches my heart at times, but never more so than tonight. She looks like a stray cat lost in a rainstorm. There's nothing more to it than that, of course: even assholes like me can still pity someone like her.

So I take her to the Gold Cat. While Penny's drying off, Sherrie comes up and winks at me. 'I like this one,' she says with a smile. She's always had a soft spot for me. If it weren't for her, what happened in my past would have destroyed me.

'What do you mean?'

'This girl is the one.'

'She's not my girlfriend.'

'I know, your girlfriend is Francisca and blah, blah, blah, but it's only because you're used to Francisca. She's the only stable thing you've had in years, you've gone through hard times together, and that can make you think you love someone, but love wouldn't destroy you the way she will.'

'Francisca doesn't destroy me.'

'No, but she lands you in prison.'

'Please, Sherrie, will you just drop it? Penny means nothing to me, OK?'

'You weren't looking at her like she meant nothing.'

'What, me?' I exclaim, genuinely puzzled. Sherrie used to be a prostitute, but that doesn't mean she spares me any of her lessons on romance. She and my mother were two whores with heads full of fairy tales. 'And just how exactly was I looking at her?'

'With tenderness.'

'"Tenderness" is not a word I know. "Compassion" might be nearer the mark. Did you see how wet through she was?'

'I've seen many things in my life and I'm sure of this: it's compassion, not a sense of revenge, that can turn into love.'

'Look, just go make her some hot coffee and something to eat, will you? Any more compassion from the two of us and she's gonna catch pneumonia.'

I can't stand it when she talks about Igor, but she insists on teasing me about him, and personally I don't find that funny at all.

If I were less stressed and tired after my particularly shitty evening spent chasing after some little fool in order to explain – as if I owed it to her – that I did not in fact fuck her former classmate, a small flicker of intelligence might lead me to wonder why on earth she gets to me quite this much, but I am tired and stressed and

I'm not asking any questions. I just think I'd better take care not to reveal anything about Rebecca's offer of two thousand dollars, which I refused without batting an eye, I might add. I didn't say no because I have feelings for Penny – no romance here, just a little common sense. I could have used that cash, but I've had my share of dirty money and maybe it's time I earn some without sacrificing my own conscience.

I'm not sure quite how it happens, but my conversation with Penny suddenly takes a strange turn. *Don't push me too far, baby, don't do it. I've been wanting you for weeks.*

And then, with those texts from that moron Igor just adding to my frustration, and Penny boasting about them and trying to read them to me, all I wanna do is lift her dress and shove it inside her right now.

Don't push me, Penny – I barely need an excuse. One more challenge from her, and then there's no holding back.

I'm so hot for her, but I try to give her the space to leave. Maybe she'll think about it and realise the mess she's about to get into, and that I'm not the right man for a girl who wants princes and violins. I don't know how to speak words of passion. If she wants sweet whispers and poems she should go.

I begin to undress in an attempt to scare her, but she's not scared. She watches me as if I were a puzzle without an answer, then sits on the bed and calls me over with her eyes.

And that's good enough for me. She's not a little girl anymore, is she? And if it's OK with her, then who am I to say no?

I put my tongue in her mouth, and she tastes good, sweet and juicy, so I devour her. I sink between her lips, and I'd like to stay like that for an hour, just kissing her, biting her nipples, licking her pussy, before spending the rest of the night fucking her in every corner of the bed.

But it's not possible. There's no time – it would be absurd and I can't be indulging in all this crap. I just need to fuck her. Guys like me don't bother with foreplay.

I'm undressing her and suddenly my lungs are expanding, like I've suddenly inhaled several tons of air all at once, and when she's finally naked in front of me, my erection becomes one of the most immense I've ever had in my life. The blood is literally singing in my ears, flowing from my brain all the way down to my legs. I just don't know what the hell is going on with me.

She's tight, so tight and sensual that I multiply inside her. I look at her, and I push in again and again and again, as hard as I can, until I come, I come and cry out, I come and I want to call her by her name, her full name, Penelope, and it's so strong, this wanting to do it, but I manage to stop myself.

I don't want her to leave yet. We have to do it again. Once is not enough for me – it's really not. I still have so many things I want—

And then I see the blood.

Blood on the condom, on the bed, on her skin.

I'm paralysed for a moment, looking at this sign that's unmistakable. She was a virgin.

My memory rewinds to the moment when I entered her, and I see my passion, my violence, my rhythm, and I feel like someone who's torn a lamb apart with his bare hands.

'You should have told me!'

The idea that she might hate me now, the suspicion that what I did was horrible for her – it pisses me off and makes me feel weak, all at the same time. I need a damn cigarette. I have to think.

Think about what?

I'm sinking into a swamp of paranoia here, and it's not my fault! She told me she'd already done it, and now she's not even trying to make me feel guilty.

So why on earth do I feel so guilty?

She's pulling her clothes on and I have to stop myself from going over to her. I'd like to take her gently in my arms and hold her close.

I've never wanted to hold a woman after sex before. Even with Francisca, we pull apart, we turn our backs, as if being that intimate makes us want our own space. But when I look at Penny, she seems so small to me, even more fragile than she did before, and I think back to her lily-white skin and her ruby-red blood, and I remember the exact moment when she cried out: she cried out because I was hurting her, because I stole her innocence without even knowing it.

I have to stop obsessing about this. It's done, it's over, it happened.

OK, so we fucked and she's no longer a virgin, but she wanted it, she made a choice. I had my pleasure, and that's enough. When do I ever worry about the feelings of the women I fuck?

But when she leaves, more or less dressed, shoes in hand, her hair mussed up and that smile all her own, she even thanks me, and all I wanna do is ask her to wait, stay longer, tell me how you really feel, let me touch you again, but slowly, gently, without any pain this time. Let me make you come.

Luckily, I don't. I watch her leave while I continue to sit there and smoke, and I close my eyes and tell myself to stop it, *Marcus, stop it. This has gone on long enough already.*

17

Penny couldn't sleep that night. When she arrived home, her legs were shaking, and it wasn't just from emotion. They hurt like she'd been doing ballet splits.

Well, hell, it sure felt like I was doing ballet splits.

She didn't shower before lying down on her bed in her party dress with no underwear: she wanted to keep some trace of Marcus on her. She thought back to all the moments that had just passed, and it seemed strange that the merging of their bodies was no longer merely in her imagination but something that had happened in reality.

She cried like a woman full of regrets for something precious that was lost, even though she had absolutely no regrets – and all the madness of the past night had resulted from her own conscious decisions.

So I'm not a virgin anymore. Am I any different? Am I better or worse?

She didn't know, she wasn't sure. Maybe she was only ever herself, with or without her ruptured hymen. So what had changed?

She thought also of Marcus's expression when he'd found out. Was it anger? Disgust? What was the message in his eyes exactly? She wanted to understand it better, to read it correctly, but she couldn't: he'd seemed sorry, yes, but why? Because he had hurt her, or because he hadn't given her an orgasm?

She didn't care that she hadn't come. She only cared how hard life would be for her from that moment on – not because of what had happened to her body, but to her heart. Marcus would be able to forget all about it: for him, apart from the blood, it had been a fuck like any other.

I'll never be Francisca, but then that's not exactly news. I knew that already and chose Marcus all the same.

And so Penny cried, but not from the pain of her particular wound. How would she behave when she saw Marcus tomorrow? What would they talk about when they walked home at night? Would he continue to have sex with other women?

Am I actually no better than that girl behind the club, in fact?
Does every woman seem the same to Marcus, except for Francisca?
And how will I get through the days once he goes away with her?

Following her sleepless night, Penny got up at dawn. She tidied the apartment and made breakfast for her grandma, then showered and changed – not to cleanse herself of Marcus, but to try to shift her melancholy.

She was brushing out Barbie's long hair when it suddenly came into her head to ask, 'Do you remember John, Grandma?'

Penny saw Barbie's smiling face reflected in the round mirror she held in her hand. 'Of course I remember. How could I ever forget? Great loves are never forgotten.'

'Was he in love with you?'

'Of course he was, my darling, otherwise I would never have done what I did.'

'What did you do?'

'Something you're not supposed to. I'm a little ashamed – I've never told anyone before.'

Penny stopped her brushing for a moment. 'What was it? You can tell me.'

Barbie sighed like a lovestruck teenager. 'He was my first in every sense.'

'You mean that you . . . ?'

'Yes, that's what I mean.'

'You never told me.'

'Because you've never been in love until now.'

'But I . . . don't know if . . . if I am in love.'

'Yes, you most certainly are, but remember: no kisses without a ring, or he'll leave and you'll have to marry someone else because you're pregnant.'

Penny dropped the brush and bent down to pick it up, her mind in shock, her movements slow, like those of someone underwater. 'You mean you fell pregnant?'

'Yes, but I never told anyone. I agreed to marry your grandfather right away, so no one ever knew a thing about it.'

'You mean my dad . . . wasn't the son of Grandpa Ernest, but . . . John?'

Barbie turned and looked at her with glistening eyes. 'Are you mad at me, sweetheart? Maybe I shouldn't have told you.'

Penny knelt in front of her and took her hands. 'Don't worry, Grandma, it's OK. If you were in love then you did the right thing, and it makes me happy when you confide in me.'

Barbie smiled again and Penny perfumed her hair with her favourite rose talc. Meanwhile, she wondered how much more there was to the story. Probably very little and maybe nothing at all; Barbie often reworked memories in her own way, twisting the past and the present, flavouring them with a good helping of imagination. Maybe this John never existed at all, or maybe he was John

167

Wayne himself, an actor she'd fallen in love with as a girl and had turned into a myth to brighten the story of her past. Barbie had not had an easy life. Penny had lost her parents when she was too small to remember, but her grandma had lost her son while her mind was still fresh and clear. Maybe her gradual mental decline had started right at that point, when she was battling with that unbearable pain, and then her stroke had delivered the final blow. Maybe that was why she now told stories, a thousand stories – always new, always enriched by some little nuance she'd never revealed before.

Anything was possible.

Anything except for this: to keep the promise Penny had just made to her. Because even in the absence of a ring and a pledge of lifelong commitment, she had already given Marcus everything she had to offer.

She saw the letter when she left the apartment to head to the library. It was lying there on the floor, slipped under the door by the mailman perhaps. It just had to be from Francisca.

She took it and stared at the stairs leading up to Marcus's attic. She could have gone up there and put it under his door, but instead she put the envelope in her bag and set off for work.

All afternoon she felt as if she were sitting on a time bomb that could blow up the library. She also felt guilty, because part of her wanted to burn it and pretend she had never got it in the first place.

She tucked herself away in a secluded corner, the one dedicated to Russian writers that almost nobody read, and pulled out the letter. She sniffed it but could detect no trace of perfume. Francisca's pen had scored deep grooves into the surface of the envelope. Who knew what she might have written, but above all, who knew what he would write back in reply? Would he tell her about Penny?

You know, I fucked that little girl who came to see you in prison. What do you want – she's doing us a ton of favours and I had to throw her a bone, but don't worry, it wasn't great. She was stiffer than a statue, and can you believe she was still a virgin! The bitch stained my bedding.

No, Marcus wouldn't say a word, nor did he think of Penny in that way. She was convinced he did love her in his own way. That strange night of hot, wild sex – though certainly not memorable to him, except for the small detail at the end – would remain their secret.

We have a secret.

Sliding the letter back into her bag, she heard a male voice say 'Hi!' behind her.

Her first thought was Grant. He'd been gone for weeks now, but that didn't mean he'd given up. She had only one weapon with which to defend herself: a book. She could hit him with a copy of *War and Peace* – that would hurt quite a bit. She reached out and grabbed the bulky tome, then spun around.

It was Igor.

She was so stunned that she stared at him for a good thirty seconds, as if he were some bizarre hallucination. It was Igor who snapped her out of it.

'Well, I can tell you're surprised to see me,' he said with a smile, 'but I'm not sure if you're pleased or not. Were you planning to clock me on the head with that?'

Penny, frozen like a shot-putter mid-throw, shook her head and then placed the book back on the shelf.

Igor was holding a bag emblazoned with the logo of a famous city bakery. He was wearing jeans and his usual tweed jacket over a T-shirt printed with the Mona Lisa sticking out her tongue.

'Er . . . yes,' Penny admitted. 'I never dreamed I'd be seeing you again.'

'And why would you think that? I thought I'd told you that . . . well . . .'

'I didn't give any weight to last night's bullshit.'

Igor didn't comment on the bullshit she was referring to, but instead asked her, 'So how did it end up with you and Marcus?'

Penny shrugged in a show of indifference. 'Oh, who cares?'

'Nothing happened with Rebecca.'

'How do you know?'

'Because after you left, she came back up from the basement in a total fit. I mean, she didn't look like she'd had fun, let's put it that way.'

'I see.'

'I'm sorry if I sent you those messages. I was a little worried.'

'How did you get my number?'

'Rebecca had it. I took it off her phone when she wasn't looking.'

'I'll have to block her. I don't want to get invited to any more of those parties.'

'Don't worry, if there's another party she'll invite you in person, to make it harder for you to say no and to see the ugly, horrified look on your face, when in actual fact she'll be the horrified one because you're so beautiful.'

'I'd rather avoid you commenting on my appearance. I think it's all bullshit – you know how it is.'

'Sooner or later you'll realise that I absolutely mean what I say. In any case, I didn't come just to tell you how beautiful you are. I came to bring you two things.'

'What two things?'

Igor went over to one of the long, empty reading tables. From his bag he pulled out a decorative round paper carton, along with Penny's favourite wool coat.

'Oh, thank you!' Penny exclaimed, happy to have her coat back. 'And what's in there?'

Igor winked and pushed the carton towards her. Penny raised the lid and couldn't help smiling. Inside sat nine beautiful cupcakes the size of tennis balls, each iced with a different miniature cover of a famous book, nestled on a bed of delicate tissue paper.

'Can you eat these?' Penny asked, astonished by their beauty. It seemed criminal even to want to touch them.

'Yes, and they're delicious. Which one do you want to start with? *Little Women* or *Harry Potter*?'

'I think I'll taste *The Hound of the Baskervilles*. I think that one's chocolate.'

They sat at the table, very close, and began talking and eating. They didn't discuss the party or the past. Penny discovered that Igor had majored in art history and now painted sets for a small theatre company.

'I never would've predicted that. I thought you'd become a lawyer.'

'Like my father? Never! What about you?'

'Nothing, really. I work here and there, and I try to save some money.'

'To do what?'

'Just to have a bit of a cushion.'

'That's not true. I can see a spark in your eyes. You have a secret dream you don't want to tell me about.'

'I don't reveal my secret dreams to the first person I meet, you know.'

'We've known each other since we were sixteen!'

'But we've never been friends.'

'Then let's become friends, and I'll ask you to tell me your secret.'

'Who knows what you're hiding, Igor.'

'Nothing, I swear to you. Rebecca didn't send me, if that's what you think. I don't really like her or her cokehead boyfriend, to tell you the truth.'

'He's a cokehead? I thought he was a total jerk, but I didn't see that coming.'

They laughed together, and then Igor pointed to a cupcake with *Anna Karenina* on it.

'This seems appropriate, don't you think?' he said, pointing to the 'Russian Literature' sign above the shelves.

'True, though it doesn't have a happy ending. Better in my belly than on the railroad tracks.'

With those words she took a bite of the cupcake, and the soft cream filling gushed out on to her chin. Igor stretched out an arm, pointing to a sticky patch near her mouth, looking amused.

'You have Anna Karenina on your conscience!'

'Not me, but that asshole Vronsky.'

Igor pulled a handkerchief from his pocket – an actual pocket handkerchief, made of fabric and not tissue paper.

'It's there, right below your mouth. Let me get it.' With extreme delicacy, he dabbed at the splash of cream.

'Thank you.'

'Now for *The Divine Comedy*.'

'And then *Hansel and Gretel*. Are you like the witch who wants to fatten me up?'

'I like a woman who doesn't live on air and amphetamines. Though you don't seem like you eat much either.'

'We're coming back to compliments, and I hate compliments.'

'I agree, and also because I'll admit I'm pretty scared of Marcus.'

'Why?'

'No offence, but he seems dangerous.'

Penny put down the cupcake with *Dante's Inferno* written on it and shook her head. 'No, you're wrong about him actually. He's not dangerous at all. He's the nicest person in the world.'

Igor smiled. 'When love is blind, everyone else stops hoping.'

'Who does? Hoping for what?'

'Nothing, it's just a quote from the play I'm doing the scenography for. It's called *Thistles Aren't Flowers*. And now let's share *The Wizard of Oz* – there's apricot jam inside.'

'All right, but let me make a wish first. The cowardly lion wanted courage, the tin man wanted a heart and the scarecrow wanted a brain. There's something I want too.'

'And what's that?'

'I can't tell you, otherwise it won't come true.'

She closed her eyes and made her wish before savouring the exquisite cake.

'Thanks for the cupcakes and the coat, but I need to go back to work now.'

Igor nodded. He held out his hand to give hers a squeeze. 'You have my number – call me if you want to. No pressure, but I really hope to hear from you.'

Penny offered the cakes that were left over to Miss Milligan, who accepted them with an innocent enthusiasm. While biting into the hippogriff on the cover of *The Prisoner of Azkaban*, her elderly boss asked her, 'What did that boy want with you?'

'He's an old classmate of mine who I just met again recently. We had a chat.'

'I didn't mean him, my dear – I meant the tall muscular young man in the blue jacket.'

Penny winced and gave her a questioning look. 'Who . . . who do you mean exactly?'

'The one who was here when you were chatting with your friend from school. He asked me where you were and I showed him.'

'I didn't . . . didn't see him . . . Did he leave?'

'I don't know. I think so.'

With her heart in her throat, Penny began to scour the library in search of Marcus. She couldn't find him anywhere. She wondered why he had come, and above all why he had left without speaking to her.

Did he want to tell me something important? Was he worried about me?

Her confident smile faded as she remembered the money she still owed him.

Maybe he'd just come to collect his two hundred and fifty dollars.

To imagine for one moment that he might have come simply because he was worried about her or wanted to seek out her company was the best way to set herself up for a major disappointment.

She was standing in front of the closed attic door, already in uniform for her job at the Well Purple. In one hand she held Francisca's letter, and in the other an envelope full of cash. She had already walked up and down these steps a few times without being able to decide on what was best to do.

To knock or not to knock?

Most of all, she felt embarrassed.

All of a sudden she made up her mind to slide both envelopes under the door, to postpone the awkward post-sex chat.

Just as she was bending down, the door suddenly opened.

Marcus stood there before her, looking more enormous than ever. He was shirtless and must have just finished a workout, because he was sweating and his hands were bandaged.

'Fuck it, Penny!' he exclaimed. 'Could you please avoid making suspicious noises outside my door? I was about to slam you in the face!'

'I wasn't making any suspicious noises . . .'

'Footsteps and breathing where there should be silence count as suspicious noises.'

'You must have exceptional hearing then. Can I come in?'

He frowned and went back inside, leaving the door open in a clear invitation for Penny to follow.

He ignored her for the first few minutes, instead beating the hell out of the red leather punch bag with his fists and feet, and Penny could hear him gasp in rhythm with his movements as the floor of the attic vibrated with the force of his blows. She couldn't take her eyes off his muscles as they stretched before unloading monstrous energy, or the sheen of sweat on his back, his contracted face, the tattoos that seemed to dance as he moved.

Eventually, she watched him go into the kitchen and gulp water from a bottle. He ran the back of his hand over his mouth and at last seemed to remember her presence.

He stared at her, and Penny felt a desperate need to lie naked on his bed once again. She swallowed, bit her lip and remembered why she had come.

'I brought you these,' she said, showing him the envelopes. 'Francisca wrote to you, and here's the two hundred and fifty dollars I owe you from yesterday.' She felt her cheeks flush, thinking of the double meaning of that statement, as if she were paying for his sexual performance. 'For taking me to the party, I mean,' she hastened to specify.

Marcus had a hard look on his face, cold as iron. 'Leave it on the table,' he ordered.

She nodded and went to put down the letter, but it seemed glued to her fingertips. 'OK, I'll go then.'

Penny was on her way to the door when Marcus caught up with her in three long strides. He was sweating, but didn't smell bad – if anything, he smelled dangerous, and Penny liked it. She liked it a little too much. She turned to find him towering over her, and had to tilt her head back like a flower in the wind just to see his face.

She'd been hoping for something to happen, but as usual Marcus took her by surprise. Somehow Penny needed to get it through her head that Marcus and romance were not brothers or even distant cousins – either that, or he and romance remained total strangers unless he was actually in love. And since he wasn't in love, he wasn't going to be wasting any time on words. He was very nearly trapping her against the wall, without even touching her, and then he said, 'I want to fuck. How about you?'

By rights, she should have said, *No. Yesterday was a mistake, so let's just leave it. Best not to mess with these things.* But instead she just breathed, 'Yeah, okay.'

Marcus's hand, still wrapped in its bandages, landed on her shoulder and pulled her to him. His tongue searched her mouth like it was a thief's fingers in a secret drawer. His other hand began to tinker with her underwear, and Penny soon found herself without stockings or panties and her skirt raised up to her navel, revealing her smooth naked belly.

She had no idea how she ended up on the couch, but there she was, perched on the sapphire blue blanket, her legs open wide like the petals of an iris and Marcus's lips kissing the moist folds between her thighs. Kneeling on the floor with his face buried in her, he seemed like some good and beautiful god, and Penny tenderly stroked his hair.

Her head dropped down to the back of the couch as she released a sigh of pure pleasure. She felt as moist as dewy grass, fluid as molten gold, and Marcus's mouth on her body took away all the cares of her world as her mind went blank – she could think of nothing except his tongue as it conquered her entirely.

At one point, he picked her up and carried her over to the bed. The bloodstained duvet was gone, leaving only a simple white sheet. He laid her carefully down with her head on the pillow and then lay down beside her, spread her legs and touched her with his fingers. Penny bit her lip and stifled a confused whisper as Marcus's index finger parted her tender flesh, but it didn't hurt. It was an indescribable sensation, a tingling, a tremor, a heartbeat, a panting desire. His finger moved slowly – so slowly and so delicately that it surely could not belong to the same hand that only just now had been unleashing those powerful blows on the punch bag.

Penny barely heard his voice in her ear asking, 'Does this hurt?'

She whispered back an absolutely sincere 'No'.

So he moved more decisively, touching her inside as if he had a hundred hands on one finger. Penny closed her eyes in the face of those sensations, the pleasure that opened her up like a rose – first a bud, then an open flower, alive and pulsating. It was as if she had another heart down there, a hidden heart. When at last she came, she cried out the sensual and ancient song of a woman in ecstasy. As she emptied her lungs, Marcus kissed her on the lips as if he wanted to swallow her voice, and it was so hard for Penny not to shout 'I love you' directly into his mouth.

She thought it though; oh goddammit yes, she thought it all right.

I love you love you love you love you . . .

With this humming in her head, she opened her eyes and looked at him and saw that he was watching her intently.

'I owed you an orgasm,' he told her, his eyes both lost and aroused.

He started to get up, but Penny shouted 'Wait!' which came from her soul to his.

'I want . . . I also want to . . .'

He frowned and shook his head. 'You owe me nothing.'

'Not because I owe you! I want to do it. I want to touch you . . . like you touched me.'

Giving him no time to say another word, she grabbed him by the arm and made him lie down, tugging at the thin cord of his sweatpants. She held her breath as she touched him and felt a sublime joy, like holding precious briarwood wrapped in velvet. She wanted to kiss him, taste him. She wanted to know every inch of his body, every hiding place and secret. She was unrecognisable to herself. She felt lost in the face of such obscene desire, but was determined to continue. Dropping her gaze briefly, she then looked up at Marcus, saying, 'I'm sorry if I'm no good. I've never done it before, but . . . I want to try.'

'Oh my God, Penny . . .' he whispered in despair and disbelief.

'Don't you want me to?' she asked, surprised and a little sad.

'You haven't done this either?'

'No, I haven't. I'm sorry.'

And so, with enormous courage, she did what she had never done before. She was embarrassed, insecure, and her desire far exceeded her ability. She liked everything about Marcus, every corner of his body, every innermost nook and cranny. She tried not to think if and how much she was messing up, or whether Marcus was bothered by her inexperience, but then she looked at him for a moment and realised that he wasn't bothered at all.

He was raised up on his elbows, his mighty legs parted, head bent back, with a hoarse low groan in his throat. He was enjoying her awkward kisses and the caress of her fingers as if she were helping him manage some brief respite from all the difficulties of his life.

Suddenly, Marcus put his hand around Penny's, moving it faster now to show her he was ready to come. She nodded and, complying with his silent request, observed him with dedication and enchantment, her lips slightly parted, breathing lightly, as if he were a living work of art, and these actions and their accompanying soundtrack were precious memories to gather to her heart, eternal moments never to be forgotten.

Eventually, after emitting a longer, harsher, hoarser moan, Marcus fell back on the bed. He ran a hand over her head, lightly touching her forehead, her eyelids, her cheeks. Penny thought he was maybe trying to shoo her out without being too direct.

Why do beautiful things last for so little time, and why does the darkness seem so much darker when they end?

Penny slipped off the bed and retrieved her clothes. She would have to go back downstairs to put herself together again. In her chest, her heart was like a nightingale that dies after singing its last note.

As she headed for the door, Marcus called out to her, 'Penny.'

She spun around, frightened almost at the tone of his voice. 'What is it?'

He sat up and stared at her. He was so provocative, so naked and strong, like some ancient statue decorated with ancestral signs, that she wanted to repeat every gesture, go back to that bed and relive all the kisses, the hands, the tongues, and his body everywhere, though she'd have been equally content simply to take a photo of him and keep it next to her heart forever.

Marcus opened his lips as if he wanted to say something important, but then he just said, 'Nothing,' and fell back heavily on to the bed.

◆ ◆ ◆

That night, they walked home from work under an unusually starry sky, with Marcus smoking and Penny lost in thought until she broke the silence by asking him why he'd come to the library earlier.

He inhaled a great lungful of smoke and said, 'I wanted to know why Francisca's answer hadn't come yet and to remind you to bring me that money, but I saw you were busy so I left.'

'I wasn't busy. I was only talking to Igor about . . .'

Marcus gave her a wry smile, expelling smoke through his nose, the corners of his mouth pulled up, his eyes dark except where they glinted with tiny reflections of the streetlamps.

'Why should I care what you and Igor were talking about?'

'You could have stayed.'

'Oh no. I saw your game and I wanted to let you play it.'

'What game?'

'You're clearly looking to be with some rich jerk like your slutty friend Rebecca, huh? You tried it with Grant but it went wrong, so now you're throwing yourself at Igor. I don't blame you, OK? You should try to get out of this shithole any way you can, if you can't use your own brains to do it.'

Penny stumbled so hard with shock that she had to spread her arms slightly to keep her balance. 'What on earth are you talking about?'

'No need to overact. I'm not buying it.'

'I'm not jumping on Igor, and I sure as hell didn't jump on Grant! How dare you? You really are an asshole, aren't you!'

'Is that news to you?'

'Sometimes you look almost human, Marcus, but other times you make me regret . . .'

'Sucking me off?'

'Stop that!'

'That's what you did, wasn't it? And I have to admit that it wasn't so bad in spite of your lack of experience. You have a natural talent for that kind of work.'

Penny whirled around, poised to hit him, but Marcus was faster and stronger and stopped her, slowly bringing her wrist behind her back.

'I know your game, Penny, and actually I like it,' he said. They stood in the middle of the sidewalk, in a pool of darkness that hollowed out their features.

'I'm really not engaged in any games! And let go of my arm, will you?'

'I said I like it. You show Igor your good-girl face and use me as a fast fuck – and that's what I'm made for. We're on the same page. Of course, you would have done better to lose your virginity to him, just to give him the satisfaction. I'm sure you would've gotten a nice ring and who knows how many other expensive gifts out of it.'

Penny pursed her lips and stared at him in horror. Her cheeks were on fire and her heart felt skewered, like he'd stabbed her with a sword, but she had no intention of letting Marcus win by crying or humiliating herself. She wanted to repay him with his own cynicism, so as not to seem weak and defeated. She would far rather he saw her as a whore than a victim.

'Let go of my arm,' she told him again. And then she added, trying her hardest to maintain a similar level of confidence, 'I'm glad we agree on at least one point, namely that the sex is good. You use me and I use you. Anything else is our own business.'

'I like it when you set clear boundaries. So shall we go do it?'
'Hell yeah!'

They started making out on the stairs. On each floor, in the usual darkness of that hour, Penny felt Marcus's hands under her skirt. For the first time in her life, she wasn't afraid of the dark. Suddenly, he leaned her against the wall and kissed her in a way that made her blood shoot hot and cold through her veins. Her arms pinned over her head, his leg between her legs, his tongue soft as melted chocolate, deep and very hot, his lips biting hers.

They finally made it up to the attic, and made a dash for the couch where he yanked down her stockings with a kind of disdain, ripping them into shreds. He pulled a condom from his pocket and discarded the wrapping with his usual fury. Penny felt a brief flash of anger at the thought that he had brought it with him, and wondered if he had more in the same pocket and had already had sex with other women tonight and she was merely the last in his string of conquests. She felt hurt and disgusted, but nevertheless let him slide into her, and this time it was easier. He slipped in without resistance or pain, and with each stroke it was as if the world had contracted, the universe had disappeared and nothing else existed beyond this one piece of him that filled her whole body with tremors of lust and pure sensation. Their ragged breaths blended into one single hoarse cry as they came together.

Soon after, Penny rose to gather her coat from the floor. Marcus remained on the couch, sitting with his pants down to his thighs, hunting for the lighter in his pocket. A cigarette dangled, ready, from his lips.

Penny tried to ignore him, leaving the attic in silence, with no kiss, no smile, without a word, closing the door with just enough force to communicate that she despised him, even though she had just given herself to him.

And yet she knew that she loved him.

How these two things went together – a piercing hatred alongside an equally piercing need for someone – she had yet to discover.

18

Marcus

As soon as I wake up I go for a run. I'm dead tired. I don't want to think about anything, and above all I don't want to think about Penny and what I stole from her. When I return, I stop for a moment outside her door.

What am I going to do?

Knock?

To tell her what?

Does it still hurt after I broke you? How are you? Are you disgusted by the very sight of me?

But even if I do disgust her, what do I care? It's not like I actually raped her. If she'd told me, I would have been less aggressive.

No, if she'd told me, I would have opened the door and seen her out. Guys like me aren't cut out for that kind of responsibility. I have no time to waste on petting and make-out sessions like I'm sixteen or something. What good is it if you can't fuck hard?

So I don't knock, but go up to the attic instead and try to forget all about it.

But then my eyes fall on the stained bedding, so I snatch it angrily off the bed, put it in the shower and give it a good scrub, then I wash myself too. I stand under the jet for at least half an hour, as still as I can, and even if I try and try, and I'm tired and my mind should be blank, I just can't get Penny out of my head.

What. Is. Happening. To. Me?

I go out again and see Sherrie for a bite to eat. The place is full of people. You can eat well for very little. I sit down at a free table and Sherrie approaches me with a wink.

'You alone today, baby?' she asks, handing me a plastic-covered menu that I know by heart.

'I'm always alone,' I reply. 'Bring me a medium-rare steak and a beer, will you, and then a slice of your amazing cheesecake.'

'All right, honey, but next time you bring Penny along.'

'I don't want to disappoint you, Aunt Sherilyn, but there's absolutely nothing between Penny and me. I'm not bringing her here, or anywhere else for that matter.'

'Bad call. That girl is like a breath of fresh air. She's clean like the March waters in Montana when I was a child. I used to get up early to help my parents in the barn, and for a good five minutes I'd stay out in the snow and breathe in fresh oxygen! Even now, when someone asks me what's the best thing I've ever eaten, I think of that air there, the pure air of my childhood, but anyways . . . I meant to ask you, does your parole officer know you hang around here?'

My lip curls at the thought of that snoop Malkovich. 'I doubt it. He's not exactly stalking me. He knows I wrote to Francisca because the prison administration told him, but it's not like he can constantly monitor everyone on parole.'

'If he knew, he wouldn't be very happy about it.'

'You're family, Sherrie, and if that asshole puts his nose where it doesn't belong, I swear I'll make him remember why they sent me to prison in the first place.'

'Don't talk like that. You have to behave yourself. You have your whole life ahead of you, and now there's Penny to think about. Don't ruin your future because of your past – not again.'

'You know I care about you, but quit all this crap about Penny. And bring me my food. I'm hungry!'

Sherrie smiles and walks away. I look at her: she's well over sixty but she doesn't look it. When she was young, she was beautiful – she's shown me some of the photos she keeps in a tin; she looked like one of those babes in the movies. She tried to be an actress, in fact. She left the mountains and all that fresh air she misses so much and moved to New York City, but instead of becoming a star on the big screen she became a prostitute. The line between a dream and a nightmare can be dangerously thin, and when you get hungry and nothing else comes your way, you learn to adapt. And that's when she crossed paths with my mother. Who knows just how long fate had been planning to turn them both into whores? And when I say whores, I mean it exactly the way it sounds.

◆ ◆ ◆

I devour the steak and all the fixings, and then Sherrie brings me a cup of coffee. She sits across from me and gives me a strange look.

'I've been watching you, my boy,' she tells me.

'What do you mean?'

'You've been here for an hour and I've been watching you.'

'Did I do something you didn't like?' I ask her, with a provocative smile.

'Well, first of all you look awful. Those dark circles under your eyes are scaring me.'

'Time doesn't do me any favours, I guess.'

'It's not that – I'm afraid it's your bad ideas that aren't doing you any favours. Don't get yourself into any trouble, promise? No fighting, no wrong crowd, no alcohol.'

'I don't go out and I'm honest as a choirboy, I swear.'

'Until she gets out of prison.'

'Would this be Francisca you're talking about?'

'Obviously, and as soon as she gets out, you're gonna be back in trouble, won't you? So you'll end up with more vacation time on the state's dime and ruin yourself forever.'

'You're just like Malkovich – you don't understand: I was ruined long before I met Francisca.'

'That's not true. You had issues, yes, and you were rebellious and desperate, but you'd never killed anyone.'

'By some miracle. I'd have killed that other shit if you hadn't stopped me.'

'That shit wanted to hurt your mother and you defended her.'

'The shit I did kill wanted to hurt Francisca. The only difference is you can't stand her.'

'It's not that I can't stand her, my boy, but try to understand me: I think we're put on this earth to find our missing half. D'you know that story? No? They say that in the beginning, every human being was a kind of monster. Two heads, four legs, four arms, but despite being hideous, we felt complete. We breathed even better than we do now, like how I breathed back in Montana – I know what I'm talking about. Then some jealous god, one of those who flies into a rage at the sight of a happy human, divided us in two. Each new person had two arms and two legs and one head, but above all each had a single heart, you follow? And when the same angry god split everyone in half, he sent their parts to opposite sides of the world like a magician shuffling the cards. So all of the people who used to be complete are now looking for their other half. I have nothing against Francisca, but I'm absolutely certain that she's not your other half. It's like when you go crazy trying to force the wrong pieces of the puzzle together, and you end up joining a strip of sky to the tip of a cat's tail, and it's quite obvious that what you just did is totally wrong. Know what I'm saying?'

'All I know is that you should open a matchmaking agency instead of a diner. Someone out there will buy these dumb stories.'

'They're not dumb. Listen to me.'

'So you're saying Penny's my other half?'

'Yes, I truly think she is. There was such great energy between the two of you.'

'It wasn't energy, it was the onset of pneumonia.'

'Then answer me this . . .'

I laugh again, uncertain of where Sherrie is heading with this. She looks at me with a half-smile and then asks a strange question. 'Don't turn around, just stay as you are and tell me this. There are two beautiful women at the next table. How are they dressed?'

I laugh again, not understanding what she's after. 'There are no beautiful women at the next table. What is this? A trick question?'

'My boy, since you walked in, those two have done nothing but try to get your attention. They were clearly hoping you'd invite them over to your table, and you didn't even notice. You've been here for an hour looking like a sorry combination of sad, tired and crazy. The fact you haven't noticed them means either you're going blind or you have something else on your mind, and I have a strong feeling that thing is Penny.'

I shake my head for the umpteenth time. Not that she's all wrong – I really have been thinking of Penny, just not in the sense that Sherrie means. And there are no beautiful women. I'd have noticed. I have a radar for pussy, wherever it is and whoever I'm with. Francisca and I had a game where she'd identify the most beautiful woman in the room and then ask me if she was more beautiful than she was. So far, I've never seen anyone more beautiful than Francisca.

Curious, I look over Sherrie's shoulder and almost choke on my last sip of coffee.

At the table on my right there really are two women. They're around twenty, scantily dressed. They've been there for a while, because their lunch is almost gone. They were probably sitting there when I walked in.

And I didn't even notice them.

Since I got here, I've done nothing but think of Penny and what happened with her last night.

I'm not one to repeat myself but . . .

What. The. Fuck. Is. Happening. To. Me?

I lose a little time but then decide. I have no idea what I'm going to tell her, but I can't just stand out here forever. The library is warm and welcoming and has a strange atmosphere, almost holy, like in a church. I look around but I can't see her anywhere. Everyone stares and follows me with their eyes like I'm some alien. It's my curse – I can't go anywhere without people noticing me. If I tried to pull off a robbery I'd get recognised in a line-up for sure.

I ask an old woman who seems to work there where Penny is, and she points me towards the Russian literature section. I feel like a perfect idiot. It's not like Penny and I have great things to say to each other.

I slip into the fantasy section. Two kids are sitting with their noses glued to the pages. They seem to love what they're reading. A blinding flashback transports me back into the past, to many years ago when I too would take refuge among books in search of a better place to live. I didn't go to school regularly and I couldn't consider myself any kind of genius, but I did like reading all right. Until I reached a certain age, that is, when I finally understood how foolish it was to try to sneak away from real life because real life will suck you right back in. Before that, reading took me beyond the walls of my filthy room, and it seemed like everything was more bearable when I was hypnotised by a book, less mired in bullshit and blood.

But the Marcus who dreamed of growing wings and flying away to discover some secret treasure or travelling down a river on a raft soon became the Marcus who dug a pair of scissors into the flabby back of a fucking piece of shit. I hope these thirteen-year-olds here never have to experience the same transformation.

Finding the right section, I peer into the empty space between two volumes and I can't help it but my stomach gets so knotted it might bring up the steak I just had for lunch.

Penny's with Igor – if that truly is his name. They're talking, laughing and eating I don't know what. He even reaches out suddenly and touches her lip. I pick up a slim book and grind it to a pulp.

Bitch!

I can't think of anything else.

Bitch.

I see her game now. She's not stupid. She's a bitch but she's not stupid. Look at how she's smiling at him. She wants a man with money.

It really is true then: all women are like that. Ultimately they're all whores, every one. And to think I was worried about her – but no, it really wasn't worth the effort of coming here.

Now I understand what she's really after, I'll give it to her all right. I'm gonna ruin her. I'm gonna eat her up, and in the end there'll be no way back to all the innocence she lost along the way.

◆　◆　◆

I go home seeing red. The punch bag becomes my mortal enemy. I beat it like I want to kill it. All my thoughts disappear into a void, black as tar.

Suddenly I hear noises outside the door and go to open it. Penny's shaking so much she looks like she's about to fall backwards down the stairs.

I let her in, but ignore her for a while and just keep punching the bag to soothe my overwhelming rage. In the end I'm exhausted, sweaty – but calm. Getting physical through sports has always stopped me from taking apart every single person I wanna kill. In this case, Igor. Him and his golden fucking curls.

I look at Penny as if to ask her what the hell she wants, and she shows me Francisca's letter and the money. Money? What money? Ah yes, the money for yesterday. Two hundred and fifty well-deserved dollars.

For an instant Penny's blood flashes through my mind, her grimace of pain, my unknowing brutality, and I make a rapid decision.

I owe her an orgasm. I owe her a little pleasure to make up for yesterday's pain.

And then I start to do it nicely with her, taking my time, just so she doesn't hurt too much.

I pretend like I'm sixteen again. I'm stopping at third base. I touch her with my tongue and my fingers. She has the taste and feel of an angel.

It's ridiculous but I like it. I like it! It excites me to think that I'm the only one who has ever touched her in this way; violated her. I think that every man, once in his lifetime, wants to be with a virgin, for the perverse flavour of having been the first and only one.

But the most shocking thing happens afterwards, after she comes with a whisper that seduces me more than a hundred grunts or yells. It happens when she asks if she can put me in her mouth. She's so uncertain, so hesitant, so blushing, bold and scared all at the same time, and this turns me on even more. Her combination of fragility and boldness makes me almost explode.

I don't recognise what I'm feeling.

I don't know what it is.

I don't know.

It's not the usual thing.

It goes beyond the relief of my penis in her hands and her mouth.

It's some feeling that's mysterious, nameless.

Half an hour ago I was furious, and now I look at her and I don't understand anything anymore. She's a bitch, she's certainly a bitch, but I like this bitch way more than I should like any woman who's not Francisca. As she's leaving, I have to bite down the temptation to ask her to stay, to tell me exactly what's going on between her and Igor, to order her never to speak to him again.

But I don't, damn it, I don't. I've never been jealous before – it would be crazy if I started now. People who get jealous are losers – weak, insecure people, the kind who need to feel safe so they don't get swallowed up in all the emptiness of this shitty life, but I'm not like that. I'm alone by choice. I don't have doubts, I don't get vertigo, I fill up the space and deny my fears, and I will beat back these unknown sensations that are trying to fuck with my head.

But I think about it all evening, even when I'm working at the club, and all the time I'm thinking about Penny like crazy. A beautiful and provocative woman shoves it in my face, and I say no.

Me, say no?

Yeah. I do it without thinking. *No thanks, go away, I have shit to do.* She goes away looking confused, but actually I'm even more confused than she is. She was a babe, like the women at the diner I didn't even notice.

This is starting to piss me off.

When I close my eyes all I can see are Penny's lips, her closed eyes; I can hear her breathing, smell her skin. I can't get her out of my head. Even in the midst of the deafening music, all these posers – this mess of a hard night – the whole film of her naked body, her shivers and quivers, her aching sighs, plays through my head on some crazy kind of loop. I'm going totally out of my mind here.

Maybe I need to toughen up.

No violence, no, but I need to put an end to this whole useless charade of confusion and upset.

From now on I'm gonna fuck anyone.

It doesn't matter where, how or who.

I can't only be with Penny, and I'm not gonna be gentle with her anymore either. I have to show her zero regard, zero pause, zero consideration. From now on we're only gonna fuck – no more of this making love.

In the midst of all this, the weirdest thing is that when Penny leaves at six o'clock in the morning, I still haven't read Francisca's letter.

19

Everywhere. They did it everywhere. In the afternoons, before going to the library, Penny would go up to the attic and there'd be no talking, they'd just fuck, straight and simple.

He'd wait for her and undress her and then take her and enjoy being inside her body.

She'd go upstairs and undress him and take him and enjoy him and his body equally.

At night it was the same. Sex, just pure sex – hungry, rude, panting – and nothing more.

Penny thought about it all the time, unaware that Marcus was thinking about it even more often than she was, because the more either of them thought about it, the more they wanted it for real.

By now Marcus's body held no more secrets for her. She had learned to decipher his tattoos and gone online to discover their meaning. Just as she had imagined, they were symbols of power and courage. She didn't yet know the significance of the pierced heart, but it didn't feel quite appropriate to ask him. After all, he was continuing to act as though he hated her, as though he was merely using her flesh and fucking whatever came his way. Sleeping with him gave her pleasure and that was enough for her.

He's leaving with Francisca in three weeks, in any case.

Who knows what Francisca said to him in her letter?

Why hasn't he responded yet?
In exactly three weeks' time, he'll be gone from here.
But I don't want to think about that just yet.
For now, I just want this.
In exactly three weeks he'll be gone.

◆ ◆ ◆

Barbie wanted to go to the hairdresser so Penny went with her. She'd been neglecting Barbie recently and wanted to devote an entire day to her. She gave her a wonderful morning of pampering, a fun manicure and helped her apply strawberry-coloured lipstick. Penny refreshed her own dyed lock of hair, and in place of the fading pink, there was now a vivid and hopeful emerald green.

On returning to the apartment, however, fate gave her something else to think about. Penny was just settling down to prepare lunch while her grandma was busy admiring her new manicure, when there was a knock at the door.

Penny started when she saw Marcus leaning against the doorjamb, looking not exactly joyful. He beckoned her on to the landing for a moment.

The novelty of this request wasn't a problem – at least they were talking now in addition to rolling around together on any surface capable of supporting them – but Marcus's face betrayed disquiet, and this concerned her.

'What's going on?' she asked, wiping her wet hands on the apron tied around her waist.

It was strange to welcome him like that, with the air of a virtuous housewife dedicated to simple and healthy things like making meals and feeding an elderly relative. It was especially strange after recent days which had overflowed with sweaty moans and deep kisses.

'Mr Malkovich would like to see you. He's back on my case. Can you come upstairs for a second?'

'That's fine, I'll come now. Did something happen?'

'What happened is that he's not happy unless he's busting my balls.'

Marcus's comment was soon explained. When he saw Penny, the parole officer expressed the reason for his visit.

'My wife and I would like to invite you to dinner over at ours.'

Penny stared at Marcus in amazement, while he, standing by the bathroom door, rolled his eyes sardonically without it being noticed by his unwelcome guest.

'At yours? And is . . . well, is this standard?'

With a big smile on his face, the man nodded. 'As a parole officer I like to take the occasional former convict under my wing – especially the ones I consider most deserving: the ones who are good at heart and just got mixed up with the wrong people. That way I can keep half an eye on them, but it also lets me extend a few perks. My wife helps and supports me, and given the affection she has for our boy here, it seems natural to extend the invitation to you too, Miss Miller.'

'Oh . . . er . . . of course. I think it's a great idea.'

Behind Malkovich's back, Marcus made a face and raised his middle finger.

'So if you're not busy tonight, would you like to come over? Would that be possible? I promise you won't be late for work. We'll have you out by ten.'

'That's fine with me. I . . . I go wherever Marcus goes. We're basically joined at the hip,' Penny commented, hoping that Malkovich wouldn't notice her blushes. He did, however, notice, and he interpreted it correctly: not as a clear indication of a lie, but as a timid expression of a very genuine emotion. Marcus, still standing behind Malkovich, mouthed a silent 'Lying bitch!' in Penny's direction. She held back the urge to return his look with one of her own, or at least something along similar lines, as she needed to maintain an air of detachment.

They finalised the arrangements for the evening and, when Malkovich had gone, Marcus lit a cigarette and said through the smoke, 'He's looking for the best way to send me back to prison but he can't find it.'

Penny shook her head. She didn't see it that way at all. She saw kindness in this gesture from the man who had just left.

'You tend to see evil everywhere, in others as well as yourself. You can't even imagine that someone could like you unless you happen to like them back, and yet you don't even really know how to like another person. I, on the other hand, think he wants to protect you and set you back on the right track. He seems like a conscientious man who's just doing his job, and a good person who's going above and beyond to help you.'

'You got all that from him during this one short visit?'

'Learn to trust people more and you'll be surprised.'

'I don't even think about it.'

'Yeah, it's all shit for you, isn't it? Only three things count for you: Francisca, fucking and money – and not necessarily in that order.'

'While *you* have these great ideals,' Marcus countered ironically. With his usual cigarette between his lips, his five o'clock shadow and the tough look on his face, he absolutely looked like the epitome of someone who could only ever feel hate for other people. Recently it had been even worse between them. All that sex had somehow turned him away from her, and despite taking and touching each other in every conceivable fashion, somehow they both sat on separate planets, light years apart in the giant cosmos.

Penny shook her head, sensing the usual pang that threatened to split her fragile heart in two every time she remembered that

Marcus could never truly be hers. 'I believe that good things happen. I want to love and be loved, to help other people and make my dreams come true.'

Marcus laughed mirthlessly. 'You don't say? Well, I think you'll need a whole ton of money for these beautiful dreams of yours.'

'What are you trying to say? If I had money of course it would be easier, but I'm going to manage it anyway, even if I have nothing.'

'Get together with Igor with the golden curls and the money should come flooding in.'

'It's not surprising you think I'm a whore, since I sure act like one when we're in your room, but let's leave it at that, OK? I don't want to hate you, because otherwise I might not be able to pretend that I'm crazy about you tonight when it counts.'

Marcus stubbed out his cigarette in a glass. 'That said, take your clothes off, please. I need to burn off some stress.'

Penny marched to the door, her face set. 'No,' she answered. 'If you need to burn off your stress, you can take care of yourself. I'm a woman, not some kind of sex doll, OK?'

◆ ◆ ◆

Penny dressed simply, to give the impression that she was a good girl, even though she knew she wasn't. She wore a pleated skirt with a blouse and flat shoes, her hair was combed straight around her face, and she'd applied almost no make-up. In her backpack she'd stuffed far-less-chaste clothes, which she'd change into later at work. She looked like one of those dangerous murderers who go to their sentencing dressed modestly to try to deceive the judge.

Marcus, on the other hand, didn't give a damn about his appearance. He wore black jeans, ripped at the knee, leather boots and a leather biker jacket. He still hadn't shaved, so he looked even more dangerous than normal.

The Malkovichs lived in a suburban neighbourhood that was in no way high-class but was surrounded by plenty of greenery, and this made them more sympathetic in Penny's eyes. Anyone who chose to live among trees could not be counted as a bad person.

Marcus went through the front door with a cigarette in his mouth, as if to spite his hosts. Penny handed the lady of the house a plate of cookies she'd baked for her, and her hostess's face lit up with joy. She was a small, plump woman with a heart-shaped mouth, honest eyes and a 1920s hairstyle, soft waves sculpted with the aid of who knows how much hairspray.

She showed Penny around, proudly pointing out all her little things: her collection of glass swans, the beautiful tapestries she'd embroidered in the bedroom, as well as photos of their son. Especially the photos of their son.

He was a sturdy boy with vivid dark eyes, and for a moment Penny felt as if she already knew him – then she understood. He kind of looked like Marcus. Pissed off with the world.

That's when the lady let her know, in a somewhat-sad voice, that Cameron (that was his name) was gone. Penny understood that he had not simply left but was dead. She was so sorry that she felt like bursting into tears. The lady saw her glistening eyes and was moved.

'You're so sweet, Penny. When Monty told me that our Marcus had finally found a good girl, I didn't believe it right away, but now that I've met you, I'm so happy. He needs it, you know – he's suffered so much.'

Penny felt a thrill. It probably wasn't right – in fact, it certainly wasn't right, because if Marcus had wanted to talk to her about his past, he would have done so already – but Penny was unable to quell her curiosity. She had no idea how else to learn more about him, and since they were alone and the lady seemed inclined to talk, she ventured, 'I know, he told me something about . . . his mother.'

Annie Malkovich nodded sadly. 'A woman can't do . . . well . . . that kind of work – if we want to call it work – at home, with a child in the next room. That poor fellow barely went to school. The house was always full of scum, often violent men, because whoever does that kind of thing certainly can't call himself a good person. And on top of all that, Mary was an alcoholic. Our poor Marcus had the most terrible time growing up.'

'It must have been awful . . .' Penny, for whom this account explained everything, whispered. She imagined Marcus as a little boy, locked in a room, plugging his ears while on the other side of the wall his drunken mother fell prey to violent men. Unlike Annie Malkovich, Penny didn't judge Marcus's mother for what had happened. She felt sorry for her. She too seemed a victim of unhappy circumstances. Just like little Marcus.

This time, she was unable to stop the tears from flooding her eyes.

'That's right, dear,' Annie went on, 'I can't think about it without crying either, especially given what happened later. It's no surprise if a child who was witness to all kinds of abuse against his mother grows up and tries to kill someone.'

Penny shivered, the tears still rolling down her cheeks.

'Fortunately he only wounded him, but that's when social services finally woke up to what was going on in that house, and took the boy away. It was the right thing to do, mind you – they couldn't have gone on like that any longer – but I'm not sure that the institution was the best solution, considering that's where Marcus met Francisca Lopez.'

'She was there too?' Penny blurted out.

'He didn't tell you? Well, I'm not surprised he didn't. Maybe he didn't want to make you jealous. Francisca Lopez didn't help him at all – she only dragged him down. She was a violent kid – so violent she burned down her stepfather's house right after her mother died. And she was a real thug, the kind who beats people up for fun. She and Marcus brought out the worst in each other. That's why Monty and I were so happy when you came into Marcus's life. You know how to give him the love he's never had. Francisca only gave him hate.'

Penny put her hand over her heart. She imagined the two of them, all alone like two flowers far apart in the desert, scarred by their violent childhoods, immersed in a perennial darkness, meeting and then finally blossoming. She thought back to the photo she'd seen of those weary young faces and the anger that seethed in their eyes. She understood once and for all, like a youngster being told Santa Claus isn't real, that nothing she could say or do would ever replace all that complicity between them. Marcus and Francisca kept one another afloat when the stormy sea threatened to pull them down, they fed and quenched each other's thirst, they had grown up together and were destined to remain united until the end of their days, however long that might mean.

But still Penny wanted to cry, because hers was an ordinary love, a selfish love. She simply wanted Marcus all for herself, but she could never have him.

Annie Malkovich put a hand on her arm, interrupting her train of sad thoughts.

'Life isn't easy for anyone. We all need people to help get us through. Thank goodness Marcus now has you in his life. Let's go downstairs now. Dinner is ready.'

◆ ◆ ◆

Penny felt too sad to eat, but tried to do justice to the dinner Mrs Malkovich had prepared. She had the distinct impression that

Marcus was throwing her questioning looks. She replied with enormous smiles for the benefit of their hosts, who interpreted these glances and expressions as exchanges of love and were more than satisfied with what they saw.

After dinner, they found themselves chatting in the living room.

'Please keep it up, Marcus,' Monty Malkovich said at one point. 'Work, home and Penny. I wrote a very satisfactory report to the judge about your progress and I have good news for you in return. I gave my personal guarantee that you won't be trying to leave the state, and they gave me this for you.'

From a drawer he drew out Marcus's driver's licence and handed it to him.

Marcus let out a grumble – maybe a thank you or maybe a nothing – and slid the licence into his pocket.

'Thank you so much,' Penny said on his behalf.

'I know, of course, that a licence without a means of transport is fairly lacking in value, so I reached out to a good used-car dealer – here's his address. He's trustworthy and honest, and he'll take good care of you.' He handed him a business card bearing the stylised logo of a car.

Marcus accepted it without saying a word.

Penny once more thanked Mr Malkovich, convinced now of one thing: he and his wife were certainly passionate about saving young men from the road to perdition in general, but they felt especially protective towards Marcus because he reminded them of their dead son.

Around ten, Marcus and Penny called a cab and Malkovich paid the fare back to their neighbourhood. Before setting off, Penny embraced Mr and Mrs Malkovich with sincere affection. Marcus limited himself to two silent handshakes.

As they were leaving, Penny turned to look back at them, and they looked old to her, like two abandoned parents trying to save other people's children because they hadn't been able to save their own.

◆ ◆ ◆

In the cab, Marcus looked at Penny with curiosity.

'Can I ask what the problem is? You're pale as a ghost. What were you doing with Mrs Malkovich upstairs for half an hour? When you were gone, I had to put up with a million bullshit questions from Malkovich.'

'They're good people. Don't speak ill of them.'

'Why were you crying when you came down?'

'I was moved by Annie's collection of glass swans.'

'Bullshit. What happened up there?'

'Nothing serious. Just . . . she told me about her dead son, and I couldn't hold back my tears.'

Marcus studied her, unconvinced. 'Are you sure she didn't tell you some tearjerker story about me?'

'Of course not.'

He was about to reply when Penny saw something out the window that caught her eye. She leaned over to Marcus's side, practically leaping over him.

'Stop!' she ordered the cab driver, who slammed on the brakes in reaction.

'What's going on?' the tired-looking guy asked.

'Keep the rest of the fare. We'll get off here.'

She dragged Marcus out to an enormous winter carnival that stretched, colourful and grandiose, for the length of two or three blocks. There was cheerful music in the air, and although it was only November, to Penny it seemed like Christmas.

'Can we go?' she asked, her eyes shining.

'No way. It'll all be kids and couples, and besides, I have to work.'

'OK, you go then, I'll stay,' Penny said, barely able to conceal her disappointment. She had no intention whatsoever of leaving. She desperately wanted to experience a winter festival like the ones in the movies. Doing it alone wouldn't be so fun, of course, but she'd make do.

Marcus stopped in front of the entrance, where a small crowd had lined up to go inside, one hand on his hip, the other holding a freshly lit cigarette.

'You're a fucking bitch,' he muttered.

'See you later!' she exclaimed, heading for the line.

He grabbed her by the wrist for a moment. 'We have to leave at eleven.'

'Does that mean you'll stay?'

He studied her silently. The burning tobacco at the tip of his cigarette glowed more brightly for a moment as he took a drag without taking his eyes off her. 'You're quite a mystery, in your own way,' he said finally.

'What do you mean?'

'I can never understand what's going on in that head of yours. Sometimes you're like an actual adult and other times, like right now, you pull all these faces and I get the terrible suspicion that I'm having sex with a little girl in disguise. You really twenty-two?'

'Don't worry. You're not going to prison for child corruption any time soon. I'm twenty-three years old on the 20th of December. In any case, we're never just the one thing, are we? You think you have one persona, but I'm pretty sure you also have a nice little tangle of different personalities going on. OK, let's go! I don't want to waste any more precious time just talking.'

She instinctively reached for his hand, with no thought for the significance of the gesture or his possible reaction, and only once they were inside did she realise he hadn't withdrawn it. She squeezed it harder and thought that happiness smelled of cotton candy on a cold night, with Marcus smoking and grumbling by her side.

Penny had a great time. There wasn't enough time or money to stop in front of all the attractions on offer and play every game, but even wandering around was fun. She was thrilled by the novelty of shooting at a stack of cans with a wooden gun and winning a stuffed toy with a battery, so that if you pressed its back it said, 'I'm the coolest!' She didn't keep it for herself though; she gave it to a little girl who was crying because her cotton candy had fallen on the ground.

Suddenly they found themselves facing an elaborate structure in the shape of a palace, with two beckoning entrances: one, painted in pink, had a shining sign saying 'Tunnel of Love'; the other, all black, was called 'Labyrinth of Horror'.

'Don't even think about it – I'm serious,' said Marcus, looking at the pink castle like it was a steaming heap of manure.

'You mean, don't think about entering the Tunnel of Love?' she said. 'So how about the Labyrinth of Horror then, big man? Let's see what you're really made of.'

'What is there to be afraid of? Plastic skeletons?'

She laughed. 'You never know, maybe you'll be more scared than you think. I promise we can go after this one last thing, OK?'

'All right then, but if it's just an excuse to touch me, know that you don't need one. Just tell me and take your panties off.'

'You're such a gentleman, Marcus, so discreet – but don't worry, I don't want to touch you. Right now I'm pretending to be ten years old, and I just want to have fun and eat cotton candy. So can we go inside?'

◆ ◆ ◆

The carnival's other clientele must have been very romantically minded, as the Labyrinth of Horror was deserted, except for a few blindfolded mummies and a couple of fake zombies that suddenly leapt out of the darkness. Penny and Marcus followed a long path that occasionally branched off and made them run into various types of monsters, who popped out with pre-recorded diabolical laughter and spooky music.

Suddenly, however, in a spot barely illuminated by a flashing neon light, Penny let out a scream. When she realised what had scared her, she burst out into nervous laughter. It was only herself, reflected in a funhouse mirror. She looked three times taller and fatter.

Reflected in the same mirror, Marcus, already tall and huge to begin with, looked positively gigantic.

'I told you it was an excuse,' he said.

Penny pulled back, realising only now that she had been clinging to his chest.

'Sorry,' she muttered, moving away.

'You don't have to apologise,' he replied mockingly. 'What are you sorry about? Did I give you the impression I didn't want to be touched?'

She didn't answer him, just bit her lip and walked on. Escorted by the music that repeated itself obsessively, they walked in silence through the rest of the labyrinth. A few new monsters popped out, but by no stretch of the imagination could they be regarded as terrifying. Penny was much more afraid of what she was about to say.

'I lied to you,' she whispered, as if she didn't really want to be heard.

'When?' Marcus asked, sounding slightly alarmed.

'Mrs Malkovich told me about you, and I encouraged her. Forgive me. It was intrusive. If you want to kill me and bury me right here and now, go ahead.'

Marcus said nothing. He looked for a cigarette but couldn't find one.

'So, what did she tell you?' he asked.

Penny gave him a quick summary of the revelations, without including the negative comments about his mother and Francisca.

'I'm sorry,' she said when she was done.

She saw him shrug his shoulders in the shadows. 'So you were crying for me.'

'Yeah, that too.'

'There's really nothing to cry about. You can spare me your compassion.'

'It's not compassion.'

'Oh no? So what is it then?'

It's love, you asshole.

'I'm sorry because you . . .'

'. . . stabbed that son of a bitch in the back? I'm only sorry I didn't kill him, but it wasn't up to me. If they'd have let me, I'd have slashed his jugular. Unfortunately, Sherrie got in the way.'

'Did she live with you?'

'Close to us. She'd just finished up with some guy, heard the screams and came and took the scissors from me. I'd sharpened them on purpose. It was premeditated, you know. That guy had already tried to hurt my mom the one time, so I was prepared when he came back. I loved seeing his blood splatter. He was a useless piece of shit. The kind of guy who beats his hookers.'

'You're right.'

'What?'

'You're right that he was a piece of shit. It would have been no great loss to the world if he'd died, but I'm glad Sherrie stopped you.'

'That's when social services put me in an institution. It was a horrible place, but after a couple of years I met Francisca. They didn't want us to be together, but at night we'd jump the gates that separated the boys from the girls and do whatever we wanted. It was hardly a maximum-security prison. That part was fun.'

'Was she your first?'

Marcus laughed. 'Nope. My first time was back when I was fourteen. She was a twenty-year-old hooker, a real bitch – I mean, one of the many girls my mom used to hang out with, though don't imagine she forced me or whatever. They were decent whores. They didn't even touch me by accident. I had to ask for it. I insisted and she finally gave in. Francisca and I got together a whole lot later. We had a great time, she and I, we became one, and when we fucked, we forgot about everything around us. So we fucked a lot, because we both had a lot to forget.'

'Have you ever had sex just for love? Just for the pleasure of being with someone, and not to forget or to take your mind off something else?'

Marcus laughed again, so loudly this time that his voice, mingling with the disturbing music, seemed almost gruesome.

'That's what sex is for, Penny. In all the pleasure you forget all the disgust you're carrying around. There is no other kind of sex.'

Penny looked down at the bumpy path, covered with a long black carpet. Her heart shrank so small that it disappeared somewhere, lost in the vast cavern of her ribcage.

'So did you see your mom again?' she asked, to change the subject.

'Yeah, after I left juvenile detention, though by then she was dying.'

'Dying?'

'She got cancer – uterine, like some demon wanted to punish her.'

'And your father?'

'Can a whore's son ever know who his father is? Even she had no idea. Not that I ever gave a shit.'

'And you and Francisca . . .'

'We've stayed together. I've had a crazy life with her. We've done the most stupid and dangerous things, but then that mess happened and we ended up in prison.'

'And now you're here.'

'Now I'm here. We don't have long now.'

'Just until Francisca gets out?' Penny asked, shaking her head in defeat at the thought of this special bond between Marcus and Francisca. It was too much for her to take in. There was no possibility that the present she and Marcus were sharing could ever measure up to his extraordinary, crazy, violent past with Francisca, full of sex and violence.

'No, I mean we're at the end of the maze. There's a light and the music's stopped. Hurry up now or they'll fire me, and I don't know about you but I can't afford for that to happen.'

◆ ◆ ◆

'OK, I'll get out here. See you later,' Penny said, jumping out of the cab they'd been forced to take so they wouldn't be late. She was still dressed up like a schoolgirl and needed to change.

But as soon as she got out of the car, she felt like she'd been catapulted into a burning well. Grant was standing in front of the Well Purple entrance, and she was sure he was waiting for her. He was prowling nervously, checking his wristwatch and maybe wondering why she hadn't shown up yet.

Penny stood, paralysed.

'You OK?' asked Marcus.

'Yes,' she lied, staring at Grant, who still hadn't noticed her.

But Marcus must have picked up on something in her voice, the uncertainty of her lie, some forced vibration, because he followed her out of the cab and looked over in Grant's direction.

'What's going on?' he asked again. 'And don't bullshit me.'

Penny forced herself to smile. 'Nothing, really, it's just that it's late. I should go or I'll get in trouble.'

She walked faster, wriggling out of Marcus's grip on her shoulder, and rushed past Grant in the hope that he wouldn't notice her and would leave, thinking she wasn't there. But he turned around and caught her just as she stepped over the threshold, and a snake-like smile spread across his face.

Penny crossed the human tide that was already beginning to fill the room and entered the tiny staff area to change. She kept her eyes glued the whole time to the folding door, which had no key, fearing that Grant would come bearing some evil surprise. She was just putting on her shoes with some relief when suddenly there he was, right in front of her. The music and the voices outside had drowned out the hiss produced by the door as it opened. Now he was standing there, staring at her with his usual menacing leer.

'I've been so worried about you, my love,' he said. He came slowly towards her with a delighted expression on his face, as if he were about to offer her a bouquet of flowers, but his eyes betrayed all the ferocity of a demon wearing a halo of fire.

She rose to her feet and tried not to show that she was terrified. 'Get out of here. I need to get on with my work.'

But Grant didn't leave. He moved closer, forcing Penny to step backwards, even though she hated acting like the victim, or prey.

'You're more beautiful every time I see you. Did you do something new to your hair? You reek of sex. You're absolutely to die for.'

'If you don't move . . .'

'I'll move, I'll move, but I hardly want to have you for the first time in here. I just wanted you to know that I didn't disappear on you. I really do care about you, and sooner or later I'll put that in blood.'

Penny turned her head away; she couldn't stand his breath on her face. He had doused himself in some expensive cologne that made her feel nauseous. He was too clever to attack her in here, where someone might catch him, but his very nearness to her was aggressive and turned her stomach. So when Grant reached out to grab her shoulders, even if that gesture didn't necessarily signal a full attack, Penny remembered what Marcus had taught her and moved swiftly to thrust his arms away, then raised a knee and kicked him where she knew it would hurt the most. Grant wailed and folded over on himself, groaning insults at her.

Penny had expected him to plummet to the ground, gasping like some poisonous insect, but Grant didn't fall – on the contrary, he remained on his feet and shuffled awkwardly backwards. That's when Penny saw Marcus appear behind Grant; he was too tall and imposing not to notice. He grabbed Grant by the shoulder, bent his arm behind his back and slammed him against the wall with such violence that she thought he would break something.

'What the . . . ?' muttered Grant, nose and mouth squashed against the wall as if he were about to kiss it. Blood dripped from his nose as tears of pain streamed down his cheeks.

Marcus held him firmly in that position. 'You total piece of shit,' Marcus said in his ear. Even without his monstrous hold on the other man, his tone alone would have been frightening. 'First I'm gonna cut your throat, then I'm gonna tear you limb from limb and burn your body. They won't even find your teeth when I'm done with you.'

Grant continued to whimper like the coward that he was, with his broken nose and bruised balls. Penny grabbed Marcus's arm and gave it a squeeze.

In his eyes, she saw an armed murderer, the same boy who had wanted to kill the man attacking his mom, only bigger – so much bigger – and way more lethal.

Penny couldn't allow him to kill again. She would do what Sherrie had done long ago. She would take the scissors away. 'Please, let him go,' she said.

Marcus loosened his grip on Grant's arm. He stared at Penny, who stared back in a silent plea for him not to go any further, not to destroy himself in the process of destroying Grant. Penny's eyes were bright, clear and tender. Grant, meanwhile, took advantage of the moment to wriggle free and make a run for it. He escaped without even looking back at his aggressor, holding one hand over his nose and limping conspicuously.

Marcus lunged in Grant's direction, as if he wanted to catch him, and Penny had to use both hands to hold him back.

'If you hurt him, it'll hurt you more. He's a piece of shit but he didn't hurt me.'

'Not yet! Fuck, Penny, with some people there's only one solution. They have to die. If he doesn't die, then sooner or later he will hurt you – you or someone else.'

'Then let's hope he does die, but not by your hand. Please go to work now. Something tells me he won't be back in a hurry.'

Marcus shook his head.

'I've already called the Maraja to tell them I'm not going in tonight. I'm gonna stay here, and if he does come back I'll take him to the alley and smash his head against the wall. I'm not kidding, Penny.'

'I know you're not kidding but . . . I'm not going to let you ruin your life. In three weeks Francisca will be out and you can leave all this behind. I'll manage like I've always done. Now let me get to work, or Debbie is going to start making my life even harder.'

Penny moved towards the bar. She realised she was shaking and only had one shoe on. She found the other one and felt tired – so tired that she seemed to be carrying the weight of the whole building, including all the people and their hearts, their thoughts, and the vast amounts of alcohol they were busy drinking. Including Marcus, who was staring at her and not looking away; Marcus, with his murderous eyes, who whispered to her a moment before leaving the room, 'If he touches you, he dies – and that's a promise.'

Just like he said, Marcus did not go to work that night. He stayed at the bar – ever present, watchful and seething – until the end of Penny's shift. Penny, who was already upset for rather more serious reasons, had to stand by and watch a million women hit on Marcus, although all of them eventually gave up, resigned.

Suddenly, two of the women approached the bar to order a drink.

'So how did you do it?' one of them asked, after requesting a gin and tonic.

'Excuse me?' Penny asked right back.

'Get with that stud,' she said, nodding towards Marcus. 'And he must love you right back. He didn't even want to give me his phone number. He said he's with you. How did you do it?'

Penny buzzed with a ridiculous thrill at the fantasy of being Marcus's real girlfriend instead of what she was – an excuse to hold women off because he wasn't in the mood.

'I have a few hidden skills,' she replied coolly, resisting the temptation to spit in the woman's drink.

Grant didn't come back, and they were quiet on the walk home. Marcus had calmed down, but he was still mad, like the glow of heat beneath cold embers.

'I'm going to walk you to work and then I'll come get you. Anything happens, you call me,' he said in a resolute tone.

'Marcus . . .'

'No, really. That's the way it's going to be.'

'Our contract is about to expire. This is no longer your problem.'

'You're not taking this seriously enough.'

'I am taking it seriously – I am. I'm the one he's after,' she protested. 'But it's my problem, not yours.'

'It's my problem too!' Marcus barked, suddenly stopping in his tracks. He pulled her towards him, and without any warning Penny found herself in his arms, without any kind of preparation for her poor little heart to feel so full and so empty all at once.

'Why?' she whispered.

'I don't know why,' he answered, 'but that's just how it is.'

'Thank you for looking out for me, but . . . try to stop it, OK? And now let's go home. I'm freezing and exhausted.'

Marcus nodded, his face dark. He stalked along with his hands in his pockets and didn't even smoke. He seemed immersed in a billion thoughts of his own – and these remained private.

On arriving back at their building, he took out his flashlight and shone it on the front door, waited for her to enter and then left, without a word or a nod.

Penny changed and went to bed in record time. She felt utterly destroyed. So many emotions had been concentrated into one short day. She thought back to what she'd learned about Marcus, and cried into her pillow.

After a while a noise made her jump. She sat up and saw him on the fire escape. Afraid that something serious had happened, that he had gone in search of Grant and finally killed him, she opened the window full of dread. He stood there, smelling of soap and cold.

'Come in, you're going to freeze to death out there,' she told him, noting that he was only wearing a T-shirt and jeans, no socks, and that his shoelaces were still untied. 'What happened?'

He ran his hand over his forehead as if wanting to bring order to a whole jumble of thoughts, then faced her and said softly, 'Promise me that even after I leave you'll look out for yourself.'

Penny nodded, trying not to think of that no-so-distant moment. 'I promise.'

'Did he touch you before I arrived? Did he do anything to you?'

'He tried, but I stopped him. What happened, Marcus?'

'Nothing. I mean . . . I don't know.' He fell silent for a few minutes, his gaze lost, three horizontal lines marking his forehead. After a while he stared at her and asked in one breath, 'Am I like him?'

Penny couldn't prevent the shudder that ran down her body. 'Like Grant? What do you mean exactly?'

'I was thinking about it, and I don't think I'm any better than he is. Maybe I'm even worse. I've gotten into so much trouble, Penny. I'm so full of the wrong stuff.'

'We all have, trust me, and please don't compare yourself to Grant. He's a maniac.'

'And I'm not? I'm a beast, Penny, and you know it.'

'I mean, you're not exactly a prince. You're a bully, you're foul-mouthed and you're basically a shit, and in bed you're a . . . a total delinquent. But you're yourself – don't go acting like you do and

215

then force me to tell you otherwise. I'm sure if I told you no, you'd stop. And you're kind in your own way. You always ask me first before you do something – not in words, but with your eyes. And you want . . . you want me to feel good when . . . when we do it. You're not selfish in bed, and even if you are a beast, that kind of makes me one too, since I like what you do to me and how you do it. And I can be frank too, remember? So don't compare yourself to that asshole, OK?'

Marcus smiled down at her, and suddenly it was as if a light had illuminated part of the darkness inside of him. 'So if I tell you I wanna do it right now, you won't judge me?'

Penny stifled a laugh. She locked the door and pulled the curtains shut, then walked back to where Marcus stood watching her and went up on tiptoes to give him a kiss on the lips that was as light and innocent as freshly fallen snow.

He in response took her in his arms, sat down on the bed and lowered her into his lap. Holding her gently, he unbuttoned her pyjama shirt and began to caress her breasts. He stared at her as he did it, gazing at her skin in the quiet half-light of the room, her small round nipples, her exposed neck. Then he went down further, brushing against her abdomen, her hips, her silken belly. He pulled down her pants and continued to caress her legs with his fingertips. He went on like this for a long, long time, without penetrating her in any way, except with his piercing eyes.

Then he undressed her completely and stepped out of his own clothes. They were now naked on Penny's bed – which wasn't used to such encounters – under the covers, touching each other as if they had never met and needed to learn a map to save their lives.

'I didn't bring a condom,' he whispered in her ear. 'I can't be inside of you.'

She nodded, but for a moment – just one – she thought about how she wanted him there anyway, how she wanted his flesh and his seed and his child.

Immediately afterwards she brushed off the thought as sheer craziness and contented herself with his fingers. When she came, Marcus closed her lips with his thumb, smiling at her mischievously as he moved his own hips along with her exquisite spasms. When he came into her hands, Penny silenced him with a kiss.

She was sure she would never get more; that night, in that slow and silent exchange, those kisses, those caresses, were the closest thing to love that Marcus could ever give.

20

MARCUS

We fuck non-stop, Penny and me. I lose my mind whenever I see her. I can't think of anything else. When I'm at work, I want to go home to be with her. I wake up in the morning, waiting for her to arrive, and when she does I drag her inside and undress her and take her like I haven't done it in a thousand years.

I go through two boxes of condoms in a week: it's a record even for me. Sometimes I stop to think about it: it's crazy that I'm fucking someone who was a virgin weeks ago. I can't think straight, I seriously can't. I can't think about anything else besides her and what I'd like to do to her, and when I do it, I start thinking about what I'll do to her next time.

I like it, I like it too much. It's just sex, obviously, but it surprises me because I've never fucked so long with the same girl. Except with Francisca, of course, but Francisca is Francisca: she's beautiful, she's my woman and we share a long history.

Penny, on the other hand: who is she? What does she want? Some hot, wet sex, a few orgasms so she can forget the fucking world? Or maybe she's trying to pass the time before she finds her Prince Charming.

Just the thought of it sends me into a rage that I take out on the bag instead of Igor. I still don't get why he makes me so mad. There's no reason why I should lose my mind by imagining Penny with someone else.

And yet . . . she's fucking mine.

I'm going crazy, I'm definitely going crazy, there's no other explanation. And the more I think nonsense like *she's mine*, the more it torments me, and the more I fuck her without a word or a kiss like she's some whore, hoping it might lead me to despise her, hoping it keeps me from whispering in her ear when I come inside of her: 'Please tell me you only want me.'

There's a knock at the door but it's not Penny. It's that asshole Malkovich. He wants to invite us to dinner at his house, and Penny accepts like it's no big deal, like she actually thinks it's a great idea. She's talking to him and I hate her with my whole being. Bitch! She pretends to be in love with me, and in the meantime she's flirting with that rich kid. But I'll take it as a lesson on how to live, trust, love and all the rest of it. When Malkovich leaves, she refuses to give it up to me. What an absolute asshole.

Malkovich gives me a sermon on how to behave and what kind of friends I should have. Suddenly Penny disappears off with his wife, and Monty takes me aside to sing the praises of this extraordinary girl I've chosen, how sweet and good and right she is for me. What does it even mean that she's 'right' for me? What should I do according to his God? Marry her, go live with her grandmother, have half a dozen kids and get a fucking office job?

Would that be the right life for me? To stay in this shit city? That would be death, not life. Me, I've always been on the run. I try to move on from a place as soon as possible, even more so now that I was locked up for four years, and stale air makes me feel like I've been buried alive.

If Monty Malkovich has that kind of future in mind for me, I guess he's gonna be disappointed, because as soon as Francisca gets out, I'll be out of here too.

Penny will forget me soon enough, I'm sure of it. As soon as I see Francisca and hold her in my arms, everything will reset. I'll stop feeling like this and go back to how I was before and what I truly am – the same old Marcus Drake who fucks life before life fucks him.

◆ ◆ ◆

Penny returns with Mrs Malkovich and I can see straight away she's been crying. What happened? I'm dying to know all the way through dinner, but there's no way to get her alone. These two are so fucking annoying.

I finally ask her when we leave, and she tells me that Mrs Malkovich told her about her dead son. I know that story. She told me too. His name was Cam, I think. He was a good boy initially, according to his mother's words, but then, after a really bad heart-break, he got depressed and fell in with the wrong crowd. Drugs, alcohol, gambling, stuff like that. Then he tried to rob a store and was killed by the guy who was cleaning up – he was armed and he defended himself. Not the first time I've heard a story like that. It's tragic, but I don't understand why Penny would be crying for someone she never even met.

Once we're in the cab, she changes the subject and almost dives out the window. I don't know what she's seen, but the fact is that she orders the driver to stop: she's crazy.

Carnival lights reflect off her face and she's smiling like a child.

If she thinks I'm going with her, she's wrong. I've never been to a carnival, not even as a kid, and I don't plan to go to one now.

I tell her, and read the disappointment in her eyes. It looks like she's about burst into tears, but she doesn't, just tells me to leave. Still, I can tell she's upset. I shouldn't give a damn. I have work to do, and she can go alone, but dammit, I can't leave her. I hope I can stop being manipulated by tears – and especially ones I've only even imagined. I'm turning into a jerk, the kind who can't say no to a little girl who takes him by the hand and drags him into a carnival, laughing like it's Christmas.

In the end, the funfair is actually kind of fun. It's a mess but it's full of happy people. Kids, parents, lovers eating cotton candy. They may be pathetic, but at least they're not hooligans. I look at Penny, glowing in all this light, and hold her by the hand because I'm afraid of losing her. She plays games at the different stalls, shows me this and that, has this dangerous air of complete innocence, and she confuses me, scrambles me, like I'm on the brink of something big, something that could destroy me. I need to be careful, keep my head together – I can't fall into her trap.

I don't even know what kind of trap it is, to be honest, but I look down at her as she leads me into the Labyrinth of Horror and I'm afraid. I'm not afraid of all the puppets emerging from the darkness with their hysterical laughter; I'm afraid of her. I'm afraid of her shining eyes, of the way she holds my hand, of her lips that have kissed me and only me. I'm afraid of how much I want her all the time, and how even now that she's probably found out everything about my past from Mrs Malkovich, she's cool with it. I should disgust her, but somehow I don't. She cried for me. No one has ever cried for me – not even Francisca, and I certainly never cried for her. That's how life is for the two of us: we keep on going, we laugh behind the backs of the dead – we, who are alive – because we don't know how much longer we have ourselves.

But Penny cries for me, and she listens to me, and she holds me by the hand, and she squeezes harder when the story gets worse.

So what does she want from me?

What the fuck does she want from me?

As soon as we arrive at Well Purple I immediately notice that there's something wrong. One second she's happy, the next she's upset. She's lying when she says there's nothing wrong – I know she's lying. So I think back to her description of Grant. Some dude who's half crazy. I'm sure that's the guy who's waiting for her by the entrance. She looks at him like she's staring into the fiery abyss. Plus he looks familiar to me, and finally I realise: that same asshole was at the Maraja a few weeks ago, pestering Grace, one of our waitresses. Jason threw him out and told him not to come back. This scumbag has a thing for bothering women.

I call in to say that I'm not going to work tonight. If it's not OK, they can go hang themselves. Meanwhile I follow the asshole inside. I lose sight of him for a moment in the crowd and then see him slipping into the staff area. My blood shoots up to my brain.

I find him nearly on top of her, muttering something into her ear. I slam him against the wall and feel his bones crunch like bar snacks, and now I'm about to take him outside and kill him and burn his body and free the world of another piece of shit.

But then Penny begs me not to with her eyes.

When I first put my hands on the asshole who wanted to hurt Francisca, she egged me on, urged me, 'Finish him, finish him off, finish him off!' while giving him a good kicking herself. Penny, on the other hand, is begging me to let him go, and while the asshole's struggling and then running off, she's holding me back.

She doesn't realise that he'll try again. Guys like that are always out to hurt someone. Guys like that don't deserve to live.

◆　◆　◆

I stay at the bar, but no one leaves me in peace. It's just one after the other in a sea of pussy. If it were another night I might be game, but not now I have to keep an eye on Penny. I also have to be careful that asshole doesn't come back. If something happened to Penny while I was off messing around, I couldn't forgive myself.

And, to be honest, I don't want any of them in any case.

Suddenly I even find myself saying, 'Listen, I'm here with my girlfriend. I'm really not interested.'

'I don't believe it,' this chick says. 'You trying to play hard to get or something? So who's the lucky girl?'

I point to Penny, who's currently serving a cocktail to some jerk who's staring down her cleavage. My God. I have to force myself to stay where I am. How many cleavages have I stared at in my time? Looking is hardly a crime.

The woman looks over at Penny. 'What, you mean that one there?' she asks, stunned.

'That one right there. You got a problem with that?'

'No, it's . . . She just doesn't look your type.'

'I know what my type is.'

'Maybe you can give me your number just in case?'

'Look, doll, I don't want you, now or ever, so get out of here.'

The woman goes away, flushed and perplexed, and I'm sure she hates me, but I don't care. I can finally go back to monitoring the situation. If Grant comes back, he's a dead man. But he doesn't come back. Not that this makes me feel any better. I'm afraid he'll get his way when I'm not here to do anything about it.

I'm distracted on the way home. I'm thinking about what happened when something starts bugging me.

Yes, I'd like to kill Grant, but am I really, truly, any better than he is?

When I'm alone, I try to remember how I behave when Penny and I are together.

Do I force her? Have I ever done anything against her will? I can't remember, dammit, I can't remember. The suspicion of having been – if not violent – too persuasive, of having ignored any refusal on her part, like I ignored her pain that very first time, makes me feel so bad that I get out of the shower, dripping, and go down to see her.

I can't knock on her door because her grandmother would hear, so I head out the window and climb down the fire escape to her room. When she lets me in, surprised and frightened, I can see immediately that she's been crying again.

For a man, admitting that he's more of a bastard than his enemy is not easy, but I admit it: I suck more than Grant does. I pretend to deliver justice by wanting to get rid of him, but I'm worse than he is. You don't have to be arrogant or outright violent to hurt a woman. I have violated Penny in a thousand other ways and I feel like shit.

But she denies it and keeps on defending me. My pride hopes it's true, but inside I know I've done wrong.

Penny . . . I've been such a mess since you came into my life. Everything I thought was logical is turned on its head, and I'm left with some impossible puzzle. I feel like I'm walking on a wire suspended over an endless void. I don't recognise myself and I'm scared to know what's going on inside my own head. This is why I try not to think about it, just bury my head in the sand and ignore the words screaming in my mind. I don't want to understand what's happening. I want everything to go back to the way it was before.

In the meantime I look at her, want to touch her. She's all mine, for now at least. We don't need to rush tonight. Let's take this slow.

We touch each other in silence so her grandmother can't hear us. We do it in a different way, we're less hungry about it, even though I'm as horny for her as ever, but the orgasm is the same, the orgasm shakes me from head to toe. When she touches me and looks at me with her sweet smile of near astonishment, my pleasure is amplified in a way I can't explain, and I come in her white hand, on her virgin bed.

When we're done, I put my arms around her. I want us to spend the whole night together, and this confuses me. I want to pull the covers up and sleep alongside her, and do it with her all over again as soon as I wake up.

But that would be going too far. OK, I admit that I like her way more than I expected, but I can't just turn my whole life upside down. I can't die and be reborn in a day. I can't bury who or what I am quite so radically. I can't do that for anyone or for any reason.

So, even if my need to stay is fighting like a storm in my chest, I put on my clothes and go back to where I came from.

21

Penny woke up to the deafening racket of hail on the windows, as if God were pelting sugared almonds on to the earth. Penny shivered, opening her eyes, and thought of Marcus, and how cosy it would be to watch the storm with him.

But it would also be foolish for her to hope that he might. Last night he'd given her something close to love, but Penny knew it was an imitation and not the real thing. She needed to keep her feet on the ground or she'd end up with a broken heart.

You already have a broken heart, baby.

So she sat alone and watched the hail come down.

Suddenly her grandma was at her door, trying to come in and finding it locked. 'Penny? Are you OK?'

Penny opened the door and gave her a reassuring smile. 'I'm fine. I was so tired last night I accidentally locked the door.'

Barbie smiled at her, tilting her head to one side like a sparrow. 'You're so very much in love with that boy, aren't you?'

Penny turned red as fast as a cotton swab dipped in cochineal and wondered if her grandma had understood the significance of the locked door – or if she'd even heard them.

She looked at her and replied with a simple, 'Yes'.

Barbie sucked air in through her lips then changed the subject, as she always did when she was on to a thought, but it then slipped her mind. 'Come on, I made pancakes for breakfast.'

Penny got ready to pretend to enjoy pancakes with ketchup or – worse – with toothpaste, but instead she found the table carefully set and a stack of delicious-looking pancakes. Even the aromas in the kitchen seemed how they should be.

Reassured, she tentatively took a mouthful and it was good. It was a real pancake with no surprise ingredients.

'Wow, these are delicious. Thank you!' she said to her grandma, embracing her.

'But we're out of maple syrup,' Barbie muttered, a little disappointed.

'Don't worry. I'll go ask Mrs Tavella if we can borrow some.'

Penny put her coat on over her pyjamas and left the apartment. She was happy with recent events, which had been a pleasant surprise: Marcus had shown her a fleeting glimpse of love, and her grandma had finally made something she could actually eat. These things were definitely cause for celebration.

Out on the landing, she gave way to temptation and headed up to the attic. Not to ask Marcus for maple syrup, but to invite him down to have breakfast with them. He'd no doubt be regretting his kindness towards her the previous night and turn down her invitation. There had been that one time he'd invited himself to lunch, but breakfast was different. Breakfast was not a meal to be shared with just anyone.

She smoothed her hair down with her hands and wrapped her coat more tightly around her body.

Like he hasn't already seen you in your pyjamas, and out of your pyjamas, and all upside down and in every position. Sometimes literally upside down.

She knocked on his door, blushing at the thought of how close they had been only hours before, full of kisses, caresses and stifled moans. Her heart was thumping so hard and threatening to leap from her chest that she was afraid of losing it on the stairs, like ripe fruit that had fallen from the tree.

But no one answered. She knew he couldn't be sleeping. Could he possibly have gone for a run in the middle of the hailstorm?

Somewhat disappointed, Penny went back down to see Mrs Tavella. Her neighbour, in a patched purple robe, was pleased to see her and willingly lent her a bottle of syrup.

'So how are you and Marcus?' she asked, winking at her.

Penny wondered if the strange brood of old women in the building, many of whom seemed almost blind and deaf, were all in fact a little sharper than she realised. Or whether the love oozing from her every pore was so obvious – a kind of marker; some eternal thunderous pulse – that everyone could see and hear and understand. She didn't answer, but thanked Mrs Tavella for the syrup and dashed home.

In one split second, and just a step away from the door, the whole joy of that morning evaporated as Penny heard a deafening crash from within the apartment, like the sound of a pile of dishes breaking.

She flung open the door to a chilling scene.

Barbie lay on the ground, unconscious or dead. Somehow she'd dragged the tablecloth and everything on it down to the floor as she fell – pancakes, plates, cutlery, even the vase of artificial flowers. Penny screamed and dropped the bottle in her hand, which fell and bounced, syrup splashing everywhere, dripping like golden blood.

◆ ◆ ◆

The hospital was grey and distressing. Penny, still in her coat and pyjamas, stood pale and very scared, waiting for someone to tell her how her grandma was doing.

She could still hear her own voice screaming, quickly joined by a chorus of neighbours who rushed out of their apartments en masse to see what was going on. She could hear the siren of the ambulance and see Barbie's cold hand under her own, her colourless cheeks, her closed eyelids.

She didn't die, she just fainted, but she seemed dead.

At the hospital they took Barbie away somewhere, leaving Penny alone in a corridor with walls as white as ice and a few plastic chairs. She sat and waited. Occasionally a paramedic would pass her by, or confused voices would rise up in the background, all of which Penny ignored. She just sat there, replaying the same tragic scene over and over in her head.

After a while, a doctor appeared – literally materialized – right in front of Penny, who had isolated her mind and ears in a kind of state of hibernation.

'We've established that your grandmother has had a stroke.'

'Can I see her?'

'Yes, but she's still unconscious.'

'Will she recover?'

'It wasn't a very strong one, but considering that she's experienced this kind of event in the past, we still need to evaluate the precise extent of the damage this time around. She may have a hard time with speech and movement. We'll need to determine a treatment plan for her. Follow me.'

The doctor led Penny into a dim room, silent except for the sound of machines. Barbie was lying on a bed with her eyes closed. She looked so pale that she appeared dead, though her heart monitor said otherwise.

Penny stayed at the hospital for hours, sitting in an uncomfortable chair, holding the hand of the only person she had left on earth. She was practically frozen in place with the fear of losing her, as if moving even a single millimetre might invite death into the room. Then, little by little, the beeping of the monitor calmed her. Barbie's heart never once stopped beating. Her grandma was still alive.

After a few hours Penny began to feel cold, and she suddenly remembered she was still in her pyjamas, a light coat and no socks. She looked at the clock on the wall and realised to her surprise that it was already late afternoon. There were no windows in the room, but she was sure that the sun was about to set.

The doctor told her to go home and Penny agreed, but only because she was afraid of getting sick herself. Who would look after her grandma if something happened to her?

Outside, it was hailing again. The falling ice was no longer hypnotic and graceful, as it had seemed in the morning, but intimidating. Worst of all, because of her rush to get to the ambulance in the morning, Penny now didn't have a single dime on her.

How do I get home? Will I have to ask the doctor for a loan?

Her feet were frozen and she started to cry. At least the tears were hot enough to warm her cheeks.

In the midst of all this ice and desperation, she suddenly felt as if she were losing her balance. For a moment she thought she'd slipped on the wet road and waited to feel the thud of her bones on the sidewalk, but then she realised it was something completely different.

Marcus, as if by magic, was taking her in his arms. It almost gave Penny vertigo. She wasn't used to flying so high. She wasn't used to flying at all.

'Let's go,' he said firmly.

'But you . . . how . . . ?'

He didn't reply, just continued to carry her through the incessant hail. Finally he approached an old red Chevy Camaro parked next to the sidewalk. He placed Penny carefully back on her feet and opened the door for her. She looked at him strangely.

'It's not stolen, if that's what you think.'

Penny, a bit confused, didn't have to be told twice. She got into the car, vaguely wondering whose it was, while Marcus got into the driver's seat and started the engine.

He asked her how her grandmother was.

Then he asked her how *she* was.

Then, as he drove, he took her hand. 'Wow, you're freezing.'

And he didn't let go of her hand until they were home – not even when he changed gears.

Everyone back at their building wanted to know how Barbie was. Penny passed on the news and got many words of encouragement in return, but as soon as she crossed the threshold of her apartment and saw the mountain of pancakes and crockery and the maple syrup all over the floor, it was like reliving the same trauma and the same pain all over again, and she had to stifle a cry with her hand.

Marcus had come in with her, and he closed the apartment door. Penny felt his looming bulk behind her, then heard his voice.

'Go get yourself a hot shower,' he said – or rather, ordered.

She nodded limply and shut herself in the bathroom. She stayed under the jet until the hot water ran out, her muscles finally loosening so she could at last bend her fingers and toes. Then she dried her hair with a towel and pulled on a pair of heavy socks, old sweatpants and a yellow sweatshirt with a crocodile on it.

Back in the kitchen, she gasped in surprise. Marcus had scooped everything off the floor, thrown away all the broken bits and cleaned up the rest. Now he was standing in front of the stove, cooking something.

She looked at him as if there must have been some mistake. 'What . . . ?'

He sensed her presence and turned around. 'Sit down. I'm no great shakes as a chef, just so you know. I hope you like your omelette with everything in it.'

Penny plonked herself down on a chair, still unable to process what was happening, and Marcus served her a large portion of omelette.

Penny realised that, despite what had happened, she was famished, and she ate greedily. Marcus poured her a glass of chocolate milk, and she drank it down to the last drop. All the while he stood watching her, his back against the stove and his arms crossed over his chest.

After she had eaten every morsel, she asked him, 'Did you get the car today?'

'Yeah, I went to that dealer Malkovich suggested.'

'It's cute.'

'More than anything else, it's useful.'

'Thanks for all this.'

'Quit that. I can't stand it when you thank me.'

'OK, so how about this? You asshole, you didn't have to come and get me at the hospital, clean up and cook for me.'

Marcus smiled. 'That's better.'

'How did you know where I was?'

'I came back and the whole building let me know.'

'They're dear and lovely people.'

'And how are you feeling now?'

'Better. I'm really worried about my grandma, but I am feeling better.'

'She'll recover.'

'I hope so.'

'Meanwhile, if you don't want to get sicker than she is, curl up on the couch under a blanket.'

'Yeah, I need to rest. Especially since I have to work in a few hours.'

Marcus followed her to the couch, sitting next to her. He occupied the space almost entirely and one of his knees was pressed firmly against hers, as if in recognition of the indisputable trust that now existed between them and he no longer feared contact. 'You're not going back to work in that shitty place.'

Penny frowned. 'Of course I'm going back.'

'No, you need to find another job – not a night job.'

'But listen, that's my job and I'm going back there.'

'Do you like it?'

'What do you mean?'

'Is it your passion? Your secret dream?'

'No, of course not, but you can't always satisfy your dreams! Is it your secret dream to be a bouncer?'

'No, and I don't plan to do it much longer.'

'I didn't think you believed in dreams.'

'Let's just say I've had it up to here with all kinds of prisons, including low-paid, shit jobs.'

'OK, but your case is different. You're leaving soon. You can live under the stars, in a barn, wherever you want. I have to stay here and I have to work, whether I like it or not.'

'You can find another job.'

'Marcus, if I could have found another job I wouldn't have ended up at Well Purple. I don't have any qualifications, I didn't go to college, and it's not like there are these great jobs out there just waiting for me to show up.'

'What would you like to do?'

'The thing I want to do I can't do here.'

'What is it?'

Penny curled up on the couch with her legs tucked beneath her. She bit her lip for a moment and then shrugged. 'I'd like to live in the country and take care of animals, cut wood and sell whatever I produce on the farm for a living.'

For an instant Marcus stared at her quietly, as if absorbing some new revelation, until finally he said, 'That seems like a great dream to have.'

'Yes, so how do I make it come true? Start growing basil on the fire escape?'

'No, by finding another job that's somewhere between shit and your dream.'

'There's nothing in this neighbourhood, Marcus. I've already looked.'

'Maybe you'll have to change neighbourhoods then.'

'That's crazy. First of all, I'd spend everything I make on my commute, and second, I need to stay as close as possible to my grandma, even more so now.'

'I'll drive you.'

'Of course! You'll drive me! So how long will that last? For a week or two? And what happens then? Let's just drop it – I have a headache.'

She switched on the TV to some random channel. She wanted to hit him. It was all so easy for him to say – easy for someone who would be off with his magnificent Francisca so soon.

For a few minutes, the TV croaked on in the silence that lay between them. Penny was sitting with her knees pulled up to one side and her arms folded defensively across her chest. Suddenly she heard a rustling beside her, and Marcus moved closer, resting an arm around her shoulders.

'I don't want you to go to Well Purple anymore, Penny,' he said stubbornly.

'You have no right to ask me not to.'

'Yes, I do.'

She glared at him. 'And why would that be?'

Marcus scrutinised her rather than offering any kind of explanation – the silence full of things that screamed out to be spoken – then finally reached out his other arm towards her. He placed his hand on her cheek, brushing her lips with his thumb. He did nothing else – only that slight movement, only that finger, which for one enchanted moment parted her sulky lips.

Penny didn't yield to his gesture and again went on the attack. 'You have a terrible face that looks like a butt. Did they ever tell you?'

'"Buttface" is practically my middle name.'

She let out a snort of exasperation. 'I'll remind you that I also still happen to owe you money. You think it grows on trees?'

Marcus said nothing. He remained still, his arm around her shoulders and the hand that had just caressed her clenched in a rough fist in front of him, his eyes fixed on the TV, which was playing some old movie in black and white. Penny felt a pang in her heart when she realised it was a western with John Wayne. She thought of her grandma and her mysterious John and had the urge to call out to her, 'Barbie, come – look who's on TV!'

Suddenly Penny understood what it would be like to live without her. Loneliness and silence. No one to love and be loved by. She had no brothers, sisters, aunts or uncles – she had no one but Barbie. With no warning at all, she suddenly burst into floods of tears, her head now between her knees.

She was in so much pain at the thought of it that she didn't notice until after her sobs had eased: Marcus's arms were wrapped tightly around her. She leaned into his chest, sniffling, looking at John Wayne pointing a gun, his hat cocked to the side with that crooked, ironic smile on his face.

'Let's do this . . .' Marcus suggested. 'Tonight you rest, and tomorrow we'll talk about it.'

'The two of us have nothing to talk about,' Penny muttered, her sentence punctuated with great, shuddering sobs. 'I don't understand. You don't even care about me.'

'I care a lot about you.'

'I know you want to console me after what happened today, but don't lie to me now, even if it is for my sake.'

'It's no lie. I care a lot about you.'

Penny leaned away for a moment to look at him. 'You're being too kind to me tonight. I'm going to have to make you pay for it,' she murmured sadly.

'Make the most of it, because it's not going to last forever.'

'I never expect things to last, Marcus. I don't need warnings. Forever doesn't exist. Santa Claus is more likely to exist than forever.'

'Stop thinking and talking. Close your eyes and get some sleep.'

'I can't. I have to stay up in case they call from the hospital.'

'I'll stay up.'

She looked at him in wonder. 'You're staying here?'

'Don't you want me to?'

'What about work?'

'You said it yourself, it's not exactly my dream to be a bouncer. If they fire me, who cares.'

'So what is your dream?'

She felt Marcus's hand caressing her hair.

'I wanna be free,' he replied. 'But really free. To go places, do things, have things but also to have nothing. I'm tired of chains. I lived for fifteen years in a brothel and – I say this in a literal sense – without a moment of peace. I was in juvenile detention for three years, even if I wasn't a delinquent, just because my mother was a whore. Later I was in prison for four years, just thinking about getting out as soon as possible. It's a pattern. A life sentence. I may look free at the moment but I'm not free. I will never be forgiven. I will forever be the boy who stabbed a man and the man who killed a boy. Which is true – that's who I am. Blood doesn't lie.'

'Freedom starts from within, Marcus, and forgiveness comes from your own conscience. Give yourself time, stop seeing yourself as the son of a prostitute condemned to be a scoundrel because it's written in your DNA. You talk about your mother like that, but who was she really?'

Penny didn't think he'd answer. The question was a gamble. In the background, in the silence that followed, John Wayne grabbed his rifle and fired it, at the same time mounting a stallion.

But Marcus surprised her again. 'She was a simple woman. She had a dream of her own: to be an actress. It failed.'

'Did she love you?'

'I think so.'

'She definitely loved you. Don't think of her with a grudge. Think of something beautiful you did together and try to remember that and forget all the bad stuff.'

Unexpectedly, Marcus slipped two fingers into the neckline of his sweater and pulled out the ring he always wore on the leather cord around his neck.

'This was from her,' he explained, and Penny's heart throbbed. 'When she died, she only left behind a few things. I didn't take anything except this. She wore it when she was eighteen, when she left her small town for the big city in search of fame and fortune. It's worth nothing, but it meant something to her. When I was about ten, she told me I should give it to my bride. She actually put it that way, "Give it to your bride." She was so naive in her ideas.'

Penny tried to imagine Francisca with this trinket, seemingly made for a little girl. It was a delicate silver thing, a crocodile wound round in a loop, with a small residue of green enamel around its snout and two splinters of red stone for its eyes. She couldn't imagine the beautiful brunette she'd met in the prison wearing that little thing on her finger. The woman she'd met in prison was more like a giant crocodile herself, waiting to gobble it up.

I'm jealous, thought Penny. *It's jealousy, along with a million other awful feelings.*

'Thank you for telling me,' she said. 'You got so upset the first time.'

Just when you were about to kiss me.
And you were beautiful, and arrogant, and fragile, all at once.
And I wasn't afraid.
And I've wanted to make love to you ever since.

'I didn't get it . . .'

'Get what?'

'That you really wanted to know.'

'I really care about you too, Marcus.'

Silence, and John Wayne saving the good guys. Penny watched the movie for a minute. The volume was on low, the sounds muffled. Marcus's hand was in her hair, while his other arm held her tight. His large body, like that of a stone angel, sat close by her side. He certainly didn't have the look of an angel, but he felt like one with his presence. All at once Penny was flooded with the notion that Barbie would make it, that Marcus would stay here with her, that she would find a fantastic new job and that life would be beautiful and full of forevers.

She fell asleep with that dream in her head, as childlike as the ring around Marcus's neck.

22

MARCUS

I can't sleep. I think of Penny and I can't sleep. She trusts me, *she* trusts *me*. Usually women offer me what little I ask of them and leave taking what little I give. Francisca has never given me all of herself, she always holds back – there's always a secret, a hostility in the way she lets herself be penetrated. It's normal after what happened, and I never ask anything more of her.

With Penny something so extraordinary is happening that it scares me. She gives me her soul. When I touch her, it feels as if her heart is beating under every inch of her skin. Her eyes speak to me even when she's silent. Her smile is like a punch in the gut. I enter her and it's an unknown world. I'm not talking about what she has between her legs, but what I feel when I'm there. My own needs are amplified, and suddenly what I have is not enough, what I am is not enough. I want more, but I don't know what this 'more' is. Or maybe I do know and I'm denying it because admitting it would be too much for my pride.

One thing is certain: I'm not gonna let that asshole hurt her. Even to imagine that he's thinking of her in his vulgar way arouses something primitive in me. I feel like I could kill someone again, but not in the heat of the moment; I could plan to kill him, like

I did with the man who wanted to hurt my mother. Sharpen a weapon, prepare myself, position myself and strike. There is no other way. I have to leave soon, and I can't leave Penny alone with this danger lurking.

I have to leave soon.

I can't leave her alone.

Why do I have to leave?

I want to leave.

And in terms of her being alone . . . why does my leaving mean she has to be alone?

I'm too full of myself here. She's not gonna be alone – I'm nobody to her.

But if I'm nobody, why does she offer herself to me in that way, why does she open her eyes and let me into her emotions? Why is it that when she does it she seems to be doing it for me, and not just for herself?

Damn it, maybe I have a brain tumour or something. There's no other way to explain this insanity.

And it doesn't explain why, whenever I think of Francisca, I can only think, *I need to tell her; I have to talk to her.*

What do I have to talk to her about?

We talk about us or we don't talk at all. We're about to find out how much we miss each other after four years of no sex. We'll leave this shithole, and fuck Malkovich if he says otherwise.

Yeah, maybe Francisca is the cure for this unknown sickness . . .

I leave home early for that used car dealer. I buy an old Camaro on instalments. The guy trusts me because Malkovich vouched for me. If he knew I was leaving so soon, he'd sure be pissed.

Then I go to the Maraja. During the day the club is closed to the public, but not to the staff. I'm looking for Jason and I find him. It helps my case that he has a thing with Grace and made quick work of that asshole Grant when he bothered her. I ask if he remembers him and he immediately nods and swears. He knows him all right – Grant's a shit who likes to hang around and insult the help. He lives in some snooty neighbourhood and is always bragging about it when he wants people to know he's rich.

We talk about something else and I tell him that I won't be able to work for a few nights, that I'm busy, and he doesn't ask any questions.

I have shit to do, yes. If I wanna smash that piece of shit, I need to understand how he moves, where he goes and when would be the best time to smash his face in.

First, I'm going to find out where he lives. It's even easier under the cover of the hailstorm. All this icy water hides stuff, and since I'm not the type that goes unnoticed, it helps me not to stand out like a bright splotch on the landscape.

Turns out, Grant lives in a snooty neighbourhood about a mile away. I pace the streets a few times over the course of an hour, trying to do long laps so no one notices. Suddenly I'm convinced that whatever god is up there – assuming there is someone – wants to see this asshole in pieces, because he passes right under my nose in a Mercedes SL, driving out of a gate that looks like it belongs to some mega-mansion. His nose is still swollen, and who knows how he explained that one. I'm sure he didn't tell the whole truth or even part of it, considering that no one has come around yet to accuse me of anything. Maybe he knows that if he lets on where he lives, he'll end up under the ground. Who knows how many other girls would come forward to accuse him of things if they weren't so afraid to do it. He's no fool, this guy – he's a calculating monster.

I throw away my cigarette and follow him in my new wheels. He leaves his neighbourhood for another that I'm sure he thinks of as a slum. It's similar to where Penny and I live, in fact. He's going hunting again. He looks for his prey among women he considers inferior, women like Penny or Grace, or this one right here . . .

An assistant in a kind of trinket shop. Nothing precious, all 'Made in China', though I'm no connoisseur.

I can't go into the shop because I don't want him to notice me, but through a window I get the gist. The woman is flattered by his attention. It doesn't seem possible to her that someone like him should have noticed her. I think of Penny and imagine how she felt. I imagine the night he brought her who knows where and tried to put his hands on her. I imagine her fear and grip the steering wheel until my knuckles go white. *When the time comes, you'll pay for it all, you piece of shit. You'll pay for the fact that you forced yourself on her. I will reduce your face to a mask of blood.*

But I have to do it properly. No one can suspect me and no one can guess it has anything to do with Penny. I'll never tell her. This will be my parting gift.

I'll kill this reject so she no longer has to be afraid.

If I looked like your average guy I'd follow him all morning, but in reality I'd risk tipping him off. So after a while I leave. I'll be back very soon, and before he dies I'll find the right moment to make him understand exactly how other people should be treated.

As soon as I get home though, I walk into a mess. The whole building is in turmoil; the old people are rushing around and remind me of ants. Finally they tell me what happened, and straight away I find out which hospital Penny and her grandma have gone to.

'Straight away' is all relative, of course; you always get endless explanations where the elderly are concerned. In the end, I find that it's not too far so I go there.

Penny. All I do these days is think of her, for one reason or another. I think of her while we're making love, when I'm on my own, when I'm planning to kill someone who's hurt her, and actually right this minute. I've done nothing but think of her since the second I woke up. Or since I tried to fall asleep that is, since I didn't sleep a wink. I'm fairly sure all I've done is think of her for nearly two months now. That's an infinite amount of time for someone who usually thinks very little.

And just when I'm thinking about her, I see her right there. All alone on the wet sidewalk, and she's still wearing her pyjamas from last night, the ones I took off her with my own hands. She's wearing a pair of soggy sneakers and is hugging herself in a thin red coat. She stands out like a bloodstain against the cloudy backdrop of the hail. Even from here, I can see her teeth are chattering. She looks cold and lost.

I can't stand it any longer. I get out of the car, run to her and take her in my arms.

Penny, you have to stop forcing me to think about you all the time. You have to stop it. I can't go on like this, I can't; whatever you're doing to my life, stop doing it or I'll be screwed.

She's been crying, she's in shock and very frightened. While she's in the shower I try to clean up what looks like a bar fight. I rummage around in the fridge and find some eggs. I'm not much of a cook, but I can rustle up an omelette. When she appears in the kitchen, I realise I must be in a bad way if a woman dressed like she is – in a hideous old sweatshirt with some faded design on the front, thick socks and ancient sweatpants – still excites me to the point that I'm ready to go, but that's just how it is. Even when she's dazed and tired and is having to force a smile, and her hair is damp and she's not wearing a trace of make-up, I can't stop wanting her. She sits and eats and thanks me, and I think about how I'm sorry to see her like this, and how I'm sorry for her grandmother, I'm sorry for everything in the goddamn world but . . . if only she gave me the nod, I'd do it with her right here on the table, in the midst of all the dishes. I'm sick, yes – I'm definitely a sick man.

Anyway, I don't push the sex thing – that wouldn't be right – but there's one thing I can't keep to myself. I don't want her to work in that lousy place anymore. I don't know how it's my place to tell her because I have no right to ask, I just know that if she goes back there, I'll be pissed. I like how she challenges me; I've always liked that side of her. Her traces of fragility, her pride, the way she tells me to fuck off just like that, the combative look on her face, the force with which she clenches her fists and prepares to go up against the world. I like it, it attracts me, it makes me feel even more like fighting back. But the fact remains that she can't go back there. I can't bear the thought of Grant bothering her again. I can't stand that anyone would look at her and imagine a thousand and one ways to slip into her underwear. I can't let her do it, though it's still not clear to me why I have all these thoughts that turn my mind into a house ripped apart by a tornado, why I have this insatiable hunger for her, this need to protect her.

And I especially don't know why I have this urge to tell her everything about myself. Penny asks and I answer. I can't hold my tongue with her, not in any sense at all. I tell her about the ring, this silver nothing that I wear around my neck in memory of the only innocent thing my mother left me, the only thing that wasn't bought with the cash from some passing john, and that included my father. But Penny listens to me, and she always listens with an attention that seems one hundred per cent sincere. She speaks to me that way too, and her words remind me of things, of moments set aside at the bottom of a drawer.

She listens to me, and speaks to me, and then falls asleep, and I pick her up in my arms and carry her through to bed, leaving the TV on, buzzing in the background. I should leave now, I should walk straight out that door, or climb over the windowsill.

Damn it, Marcus, get out of here. You've done everything you can do. You'd be crazy to do anymore. A real loser.

It's all true, but when, in spite of myself, I decide to stay and lie on the bed next to her and watch her breathe, I don't feel like I'm losing something. I feel like I'm on the edge of that great abyss, perched on the very last sliver of it, but I remain suspended there and I don't back away, I don't go back to safety, because I have the impression that if I did then I really would be a loser.

So I stay awake like I promised, just in case the hospital calls, and wonder what will happen tomorrow, and the day after that, and what turn my life will take, what sense it will gain, what choices I'll have to make – and if I'm up to making them, or if I'll be too afraid. I don't sleep – I sleep very little these days, just pick up a few hours here and there and not even every night. I'm up until dawn. No one calls. I leave before she wakes up, with a powerful feeling that the abyss will be the beginning of something – and the end of me and who I was.

23

Early the next morning she took the bus to the hospital. Marcus had left at some point after she'd fallen asleep, and Penny decided not to call or involve him. She didn't want to get used to needing him for small things, like getting a ride somewhere that she could easily reach by public transport. She needed to get organised with work, outings, caring for her grandma. He had nothing to do with her life; he was a passing gift, a dazzling sun that wouldn't shine forever. Soon he'd go away, taking with him everything she had been in those two months. Penny in love for the first time. Penny becoming a woman. Penny suddenly full of hopes and wishes she'd never had before. Penny with a body that could feel pleasure instead of always feeling like the ugly duckling. Penny with a boundless tenderness for the very last person she would ever have dreamed would arouse her heart and all her senses – someone who looked like some barbaric warrior or dragon-tamer. Penny the little princess, desired, caressed, touched, seen at last as a grown woman. The same Penny who would soon need to open up a heavy trunk, plunge into it, and let herself be forgotten like an old wedding dress stored in mothballs.

She had to get used to it, and so she went out under a relentless rain.

Her grandma was awake. The news from the doctor was heartening. No fatal consequences, fortunately – perhaps even by some miracle. She'd still need to stay in the hospital for a few days, and once she was home she'd have to take a mountain of drugs.

Penny wept at the sight of the extremely pale Barbie, so close to her in looks except for her long, now slightly dishevelled hair. 'Thank you for staying here with me,' she whispered, though Barbie couldn't make it out through her sobs.

'I think I was a little sick,' her grandma said with a jaunty smile. 'Maybe I ate too much birthday cake, but you only turn eighteen once.'

'Well, eat a little less next time, all right?' Penny whispered. 'You have to stay here for a few days so you can rest and get back on your feet, and then we'll go home.'

'All right, but you make sure to lock the door at night and have Marcus keep you company.'

'Do you remember Marcus?' asked Penny, a little disturbed at her grandma's selective memory. She had just said she was an eighteen-year-old girl who had had too much cake, just back from the revelry of her own birthday party, but Marcus was still there in her thoughts.

'Of course, darling, he's that handsome boy who lives upstairs. The one who's so in love with you.'

'Er . . . yes . . .' Penny mumbled. It would have been better if she had forgotten him so Penny wouldn't have to explain why he was gone in a few days' time.

She left the hospital a couple of hours later, quieter and more hopeful. The rain fell and stopped and then fell again. Bundled up in her red duffel coat with the hood up and her bright green lock of hair peeking out, she thought of the doctor's last words. Barbie could not be left alone; she now needed supervision 24/7. A return to Well Purple was therefore out of the question, and she would need to find another job. A neighbour could keep Barbie company during the day, and she was sure that the ladies in the building would willingly lend her a hand, but there was no one who could help her at night without pay. In the end, Marcus had won.

◆　◆　◆

She did not immediately realise where she was going until she found herself in front of the window with the smiling golden cat. The Gold Cat was packed at that hour. Its retro air, with its mustard-yellow wallpaper decorated with psychedelic flowers, and the large pendant lights, Formica shelves and, along the walls, numerous movie posters from the Seventies, attracted a young and lively clientele. Sherrie waited on tables, assisted by a lady in her forties dressed in a similar yellow dress and with an identical cotton-candy hairdo. Many of the clients were women, and Penny thought they must feel comfortable in an environment run by other women who were neither young nor beautiful, which didn't foster a competitive environment.

Sherrie recognised her immediately and went to greet her with a smile.

'Come on in, honey, there's a free table for you. I'll be right over.'

Penny sat between the counter and a golden jukebox that may or may not have just been for show. She scanned the menu, but she wasn't there to eat. After a while Sherrie approached her table, as bouncy as any twenty-year-old, and the first thing she said to her was, 'Isn't Marcus with you?'

Penny blushed like a girl caught red-handed just as she's about to kiss a photo of her favourite star. 'Er . . . no.'

'That's a pity. I wanted to ask him a favour. I got a delivery this morning and wanted to ask him to bring it home for me. It's a little heavy and I know he has a car now. So how are you?'

Penny shrugged; she was so tired that this one ridiculous little movement felt like an earthquake in her body. In a few words she told Sherrie about her grandma, and the kind-hearted waitress, who for some mysterious reason seemed to have a soft spot for her, sat down beside her and squeezed her arm with her small, bony hand.

'Oh, my darling, she'll get better soon, you'll see. The worst is definitely over.'

'I hope you're right, but she's the only person I have in the world and I have this crazy fear of losing her.'

'You have Marcus. He'll help you. He has broad shoulders and a huge heart. You have your grandma, but you have him too now. And me, if you'd like.'

Penny looked at her like a frightened child might stare at a picture of her absent mother, and then suddenly and without warning, her cheeks felt hot and her eyes filled with tears. Because this woman, a former prostitute who should have had a million and one reasons to be cynical, was instead one of the sweetest people she had ever met. Affection from her was a most generous and wonderful gift, but even more wonderful was her taking for granted that Marcus wanted to give Penny his affection too. Neither Sherrie nor Mr Malkovich seemed to have the least idea what Marcus actually planned to do with his future. Did they really think he would stay in this city and become a prisoner of the rat race just to be with her? She was almost tempted to tell Sherrie, to explain to her using the same tone as an adult would in telling a child the truth about the tooth fairy, that magic mirrors, princesses with the glass slippers, and beanstalks reaching for the sky all cease to exist when people grow up. But Sherrie was so convinced and so romantic in her outlook that it seemed cruel to disappoint her, so Penny kept her mouth shut and ordered the cheesecake.

When Sherrie returned with the most enormous slice smothered in blueberries, Penny mustered up her courage and asked, 'Do you need another waitress here?'

Sherrie immediately grasped the meaning of her question and smiled at her kindly. 'You need a job?'

'Yes, but I can't start for a few days. I'm available once my grandma settles down a little. D'you think you could find something for me?'

'I'll talk to Lorna about it and let you know, but I think so. Where there's room for two, there's room for three. And if you're special to Marcus, you're special to me too.'

Penny thanked her, her eyes wide and limpid and so full of gratitude that Sherrie gave her a gentle pat on the head before going to wait on a table that had been calling her over.

As Penny ate the cheesecake more eagerly now, reassured by the hope of finding a job, she heard her phone ring. She rummaged among the usual millions of things that filled her bag, and somehow wasn't the slightest bit surprised to see Igor's name on the display. She answered after a moment's hesitation, and for a while they chatted about this and that. Suddenly Igor said, all in one breath, 'So are you coming with me to the theatre or what?'

'What?'

'Tomorrow night is the premiere of the show I did the scenography for. Will you be my date?'

'Er . . . I . . . can't. My grandma's in hospital and . . .'

Igor asked a few sensible questions about what had happened, then finally said, 'Maybe a distraction would be good for you. You can't be at the hospital after visiting hours anyway, can you? We'll have a good time together, and that way you won't be home alone. What do you think?'

'Actually, I . . .'

'I get it. The problem is not so much your grandma as Marcus. He's keeping you company, I guess. I'll confess, I had hoped you'd finished with him, but clearly you're still together.'

'No, he has nothing to do with it, but . . .' She stopped. As if the mere utterance of his name had conjured up his presence, Marcus, wet with rain, now plopped down opposite her at the same table. A sulky expression on his face, he was staring openly at her. He was wearing a dark blue waterproof jacket with a flame-red zipper. He was holding his customary pack of Chesterfields and flipped it to extract a cigarette, which he put to his lips, although he didn't light it. Penny remained silent for a moment.

'Are you still there?' Igor asked.

'Yes, I'm here, just . . .'

She heard a sigh from the other end of the phone. 'All right, I understand, but if you change your mind, you know where to find me.'

'You should invite another girl.'

'I don't want to invite another girl, I want to invite you.'

'But it doesn't make sense to wait for—'

As always, his reply was cheerful but firm. 'Penny, I've been waiting for you for over six years now. I can wait another day. You never know – miracles do happen. I'm not giving up that easily.'

She hung up, embarrassed by what Igor had said, which had made her blush a little, and noticed that Marcus was still watching her. He leaned on the table with one elbow, chin on hand, and fiddled with his cigarette, nervously flicking it against the Formica.

'Hi,' she said simply. She was sitting with her back against the wall, facing into the room, and couldn't help but notice that the looks of all the other customers, without exception, were aimed at him. Smiles, elbow nudges, murmurs, salacious comments for sure. One chick was licking her yoghurt spoon slowly and suggestively.

Penny wondered if Marcus had noticed, and what Francisca usually made of it: could she bear this weight of desire that exuded from all the strangers who looked at him, as if they wanted to strip him naked with their thoughts – and then with their teeth? But then she realised that Francisca no doubt attracted similar looks wherever she went, from any red-blooded male under the age of ninety. They were alike in that way – such a stunning couple.

'You been to the hospital?' Marcus asked, breaking the silence in a strange voice, as if the growl of a wolf lay barely concealed behind his attempt at kindness. 'Is everything all right?'

'Yeah, more or less.'

'I could have driven you. Just ask me next time.'

'I wish I could say how kind you are, but the tone of your voice is scaring me.'

Marcus lit his cigarette, paying scant attention to the 'No Smoking' sign that shone in red letters like a traffic light on the wall right over his head.

'Were you talking to Igor?' he asked her between two inhalations of smoke, while Penny picked at the remains of her cheesecake.

'Yeah, I was.'

'I tried calling you all morning, but you never answered.'

'Oh, I'm sorry. My phone was on silent in the hospital and I didn't hear you.'

'But you heard Igor calling.'

Marcus leaned across the table. He was about to say something to her, and from the look on his face she knew it wouldn't be nice, but Sherrie arrived at just the right moment and interrupted him.

'My boy!' she exclaimed. 'I'm so happy when I see the pair of you together! But you need to put out that cigarette – you can't smoke in here. Tell him, Penny. Smoking is bad for your health.'

'I'm afraid if I told him that he'd smoke twice as much just to spite me,' Penny said. 'Listen, how much do I owe you for the cake?'

'Nothing, baby girl, but can you guys do me a big favour? I got a little delivery from eBay. Could you drive it over to my place if I give you the keys? But be careful – it's fragile and made of mirrored glass, and if you break it you'll have seven years of bad luck!'

Marcus, the cigarette still lit between his lips, nodded slowly. While he was busy talking to Sherrie, he reached across the table to squeeze Penny by the arm to stop her from leaving, and his touch seemed to bring out the sun to warm Penny's blood in spite of the rain.

◆ ◆ ◆

Sherrie lived right by the sea. She'd ordered one of those huge disco balls, straight out of the Seventies, with glittering sequins and mirrors. Having warned them again not to break it, Sherrie looked apprehensive, like a mother who doesn't know if her child will be safe.

During the car journey, the rain continued to fall in sheets. After a few moments, as if he had been holding in a question for far too long, Marcus asked, 'So what did he want?'

'Who?'

'You know who. Igor.'

Penny shook her head imperceptibly and stared out the window. 'Why are you so obsessed with him?'

He ignored her question, and his sharp look gleamed with anger. 'Did he ask you out?' he insisted.

'Yup.'

'When? Where?'

'I don't ask for reports on your every movement.'

'Well, I'm asking for yours. What are you going to do?'

'Nothing. He wanted to meet tomorrow night. I told him no.'

Marcus gripped the steering wheel more tightly. Penny sneaked a look at him. He looked tired, with dark circles she'd never noticed, as if he'd slept little and badly – and not just for one night. She held back her impulse to touch his hand as it gripped the gearshift.

'Before you leave, can I take a photo of you?' she asked.

He turned with a startled jerk, as if he didn't understand what she meant, but his eyes grew even darker as he went back to looking at the road.

'I need it,' Penny explained. 'I won't show anyone and I promise not to steal your soul.'

Without even looking at her, Marcus murmured sharply, 'Maybe you already stole it.'

'I'm not a witch. I just want to remember you . . .'

Although she was sure she would never forget him, she didn't want to run the risk of ending up like her grandma, who only had her errant memory to rely on. She needed proof, something that could show her fifty years from now that Marcus had existed and not only been some romantic fantasy.

Just then, they arrived at the beach. Sherrie's house was a kind of wooden shack built directly on the sand, almost lapped at by the tongue of the sea. There was respite from the rain as a broken ray of sunshine pierced the clouds. Penny wondered how Sherrie felt about waking up every day with all this beauty before her eyes. Maybe, after so many years of compromising between necessity and horror, she had simply craved the innocent perfection of nature.

Marcus carried the huge box into the house. Sherrie's home was small and pleasant, painted in bright tones of orange, red and Persian blue, with decor and furnishings inspired by the Seventies, just like in the diner. On a multicoloured striped sofa sat a golden cat, the spitting image of the one on the windows of the Gold Cat, which looked at them absentmindedly and then began to languidly lick its paws.

When they left the house and before they reached the car, Penny took Marcus by the wrist and asked in a pleading tone, 'Can we please take a walk?'

He watched her as he had done since his arrival at the diner, with an intense and brooding look. 'OK,' he said. In natural light, his face looked even more tired.

They walked in silence along the wet sand by the furious ocean, which bellowed against the rocks on the shore. Penny pulled her hood up as her hair snaked around her face, and her emerald lock ended up in her mouth. She clung to Marcus's arm as they walked, his hands tucked into his pockets, his eyes downcast, staring at his shoes which sank into the sand with every step.

Without realising it, she began to talk to him. If she had dwelled on her own life, on her sick grandma, on Marcus's imminent departure, on what might remain for her after two amazing months in each other's company, she would have started crying, really crying, and not just tears and sobs but something more – something far, far worse. Maybe she would indeed have collapsed on to that fine sand and begged him to stay, saying, 'I love you! Don't leave me! How will I live without the man I love?'

So to avoid precisely this scenario, she rambled on about other things, commenting on the beauty of the ocean, the sky, the little harbour just visible in the distance, the fishing boats, the seagulls, and the shells which she imagined had been abandoned on the shore by mermaids.

Suddenly, in the midst of her idle chatter, just as it was starting to rain again, Marcus halted abruptly. Penny winced, fearing that she'd said something to upset him, even though she had spoken only nonsense. She found herself standing in front of him, and he was so tall and massive that he shielded her from the force of the wind. With his hands still in his pockets, he stared at her as if he wanted and had to tell her something important.

'Are you all right?' she asked, more and more worried by those dark circles, by that beard now long enough to be not the product of calculation but of neglect, by those tight lips.

For a while he said nothing and didn't move a muscle, just continued to gaze at her, and Penny saw the stormy ocean reflected in his silver eyes. Suddenly Marcus drew his hands out of his pockets and hugged her so tightly that she seemed almost a part of himself, then kissed her on the mouth.

Penny abandoned herself, bound to his tongue and his soul, as close to him now as if he were inside of her, as if they were naked and one.

Then he held her tightly against his chest, one hand on the back of her neck, and Penny could no longer stifle her concern.

'What is it?'

'I don't know,' was the only answer she got.

'You seem strange to me today. Did something happen?'

'My mind is on fire, Penny.'

'Do you want to tell me about it?'

'No. I have to try and get rid of it or I'll suffocate.'

'Did I do something wrong?'

'I'm the one who was wrong.'

'What do you mean?'

'To ever come to this city in the first place. To that damn building. To let you fuck with my mind.'

Penny stared at him as if he'd just slapped her. 'What are you saying?'

Marcus interrupted her, placing a finger on her mouth. His expression was far from romantic, despite the kiss he'd just given her. He looked furious and unhappy. Without allowing her to speak, he said, 'Let's just go, before the devil makes me say things I'll regret for the rest of my life.'

He refused to talk in the car, and as soon as they got home Marcus took refuge in his attic as if he were running away from her. Penny couldn't stop thinking about it, not even when she was at work in the library. What had he meant by all that?

She was just placing a copy of *Jane Eyre* back on the shelf when Edward Rochester came into her mind and stirred up a crazy idea. She thought back to the character's brusque ways with Jane and his faked interest in the beautiful Blanche. She thought of his torment and his secret pain, his jealousy over St. John.

A warm and dangerous emotion began to swell in her heart.

Could he be in love with me?

Maybe Marcus is in love with me!

She worked the rest of that afternoon with her head in the clouds, excited, agitated, hopeful. Her heart was pounding like a jackhammer. She had a ton of work to get through, but was so happy that it didn't weigh her down. Her grandma was getting better and would be home soon. And maybe Marcus actually loved her.

Marcus, Marcus, Marcus.

She arrived back home around dinnertime with a smile on her face, a smile so huge and unchanging that it could have been tattooed into place. On her return, she went straight to the attic, bounding up the steps of the spiral staircase with all the excitement of a teenager.

She knocked on the door, full of energy.

As soon as he opens it, I'm going to kiss him and tell him I love him!

And there on that landing, in front of that door, her happiness unravelled like a braid in the wind. Because it wasn't Marcus who opened the door.

It was Francisca.

She was back. Beautiful, dark, and pissed as hell.

She was wearing Marcus's T-shirt, the same one he'd worn under his shirt that morning on the beach, and nothing else. She had a lit cigarette between her fingers, and the smoke filtered slowly through her naturally scarlet lips.

On the floor behind her lay a long trail of clothes. Jeans, sweaters, socks, shoes. Underwear was strewn everywhere, scattered randomly on every surface.

Beyond her in the room, sitting on the edge of the bed, totally undone like someone who has just made love for the first time in almost four years, was Marcus. Naked, apart from his tattoos and the long bandages wrapped around the knuckles he used to punch the bag.

Francisca shot her a look that did not even try to hide her silent triumph. Weak and embarrassed now, Penny stumbled on words to explain her sudden arrival.

'I . . . uh . . . Sorry . . . I didn't . . . want . . . to . . . disturb . . . Wel— er . . . welcome back,' she stammered.

For a moment, it seemed as if Marcus was peering straight into her soul. It was as if he had slipped his hand between her ribs and pulled out her beating heart. She imagined him crushing it in his bandaged hands and then hurling it down the stairs.

Mute and defeated, she turned and trudged down the steps, her mind a painting where all the colours had turned to black. All she could do was repeat to herself, 'Be careful not to fall, be careful not to fall,' but as soon as she made it inside her apartment she collapsed to the floor like a loose-stringed marionette.

24

MARCUS

I can't sleep. I'm tired and stressed. I'm feeling things I've never felt before and I don't want to, damn it, I don't want to. I can't stand being dominated by an emotion I can't control. Love for Francisca never turned me into prey like this, never made me feel like I was about to break or choke. We were stronger together. With the pasts we have, we saw ourselves in each other.

But I don't need Penny to survive. I don't need her, and she doesn't give me anything I can't find anywhere else. She's not like me, we don't share a past, nothing unites us. We speak different languages and we're different in every way. We've known each other for two months – not even – which is nothing.

Yet I miss her. I have to see her again, I have to touch her, I have to hear her voice, I have to take her.

It's not good, not like this. I want to be free to eat, drink, smoke, sleep, get laid. Leave for any corner of the world whenever I want. Stop thinking about things that will destroy me. Things like, *What if I stayed?*

Stay where? Here? No way, José!

No way. Not even. If. They. Hang. Me.

Even if I were dead, I'd still want to get away from this place and never come back. Soon I'll be out of here, come hell or high water.

Meanwhile, I look for her everywhere. At home, the hospital, the library. I call her on the phone, but she doesn't answer me. Eventually I go to Sherrie's diner, by chance, and I see her there.

She's sitting at a table talking on the phone. I just know she's talking to that asshole Igor. So she ignores my calls and answers his, huh? A monstrous rage mounts inside of me, and this is another of those inexplicable emotions that floor me. Could I be jealous? It doesn't make sense. I have never once been jealous of Francisca, and yet just looking at her takes people's breath away and the way she walks turns all the men into loaded guns. But I'm jealous over Penny? She's just your average girl: short, slender as a nail, with ridiculous hair and big orphan eyes.

This is definitely not good. I want to kill Igor with my bare hands.

I agree to walk on the beach. I listen to her as she speaks and smiles and points to the water and the shells. A furious urge to kiss her comes over me. I'd like to throw her down on the wet sand, rip off her pants and be inside of her body. But I have to stop. I can't go on like this. Things have already gone way too far. I have to find a way – any way – to get her out of my system and return to myself, because otherwise I'll risk losing my mind.

The punch bag never fails me. Exercise calms me a little, distracts me, shifts the course of my thoughts. Suddenly there's a knock at the door. It can only be Penny. I'll tell her not to come up anymore, I'll tell her I'm leaving tomorrow, and as I think this, I realise I just want to get to the door, let her in, push her in the corner and kiss her to kingdom come.

I open the door.

But it's not Penny.

It's Francisca.

I look at her for a few seconds as if she were an apparition. She looks at me and smiles, tilts her head to one side and then throws her canvas bag to the ground. She's devastatingly beautiful. Those black, tyrannical eyes, the quivering nostrils, the fire-red lips, a body like a wild mare's. She leaps on to me, wrapping her thighs around my hips. She says nothing, asks for nothing, just kisses me like she's been thirsty for a century. I'd forgotten the taste of her tongue, the frenzy of her mouth, how her nails scratch my back.

We end up on the floor, and take off our shirts, jeans, shoes, and then she's naked above me, and she licks me and swallows me. Then she takes me and moves like only she can, in her same bold dance.

In the end she stares at me, sweating and wild, more beautiful than I even remembered.

'Did you miss me?' she asks.

'Did they let you out early?' I ask her in turn.

She frowns and assumes that pugnacious expression that I know all too well, that frown like she's about to shoot someone.

'I asked you a question first, *mi amor*,' she says, with those splendid killer eyes on my face. 'Did you miss me?'

'I did miss you,' I reply, but as soon I do so, I realise this is the first time I've ever lied to her. To tell the truth, in the last few weeks I have done nothing but think of someone else, but seeing her now and suddenly remembering everything that unites us, I realise that this is my woman, and her alone. We have a hundred universes in common. She's my salvation, the cure for the evil that devastated me. The cure for Penny. 'I am you and you are me,' I add, stroking her side. We used to say it all the time – it was our special way of saying 'I love you'. I say it and I think I'm free, that for me there is only Francisca, here and now, and that at last I am sure.

Francisca smiles and gets to her feet. She moves around the room naked – supple, muscular, solid, exciting. She takes one of my cigarettes from the pack on the table, brings it to her lips, lights it and takes a puff.

'You're a sight, *mi amor*,' she says finally, looking at me. 'Yes, they let me out early, so I decided to surprise you, and luckily you didn't surprise me back. I thought I'd find that little *chica* here in your underwear.'

I laugh, and as I laugh, I seem to be struggling, as if my cheek muscles aren't cooperating.

'Did you fuck her?' she asks, watching me carefully, her cigarette between two fingers, blowing smoke from the corner of her mouth.

Then I take a cigarette from the same pack and light it by touching the tip to hers. I sit on the edge of the bed and hear myself say, 'I just kept my cock warm for you, but why don't you stop the interrogation now? I feel like I'm back in prison.'

Francisca's tickled and just starting to laugh when there's a knock at the door.

I don't have time to think as she throws on my T-shirt and opens the door with almost-violent urgency.

Behind the door is Penny with a radiant smile on her lips, a smile that immediately dies. She looks at Francisca, looks at me, then at Francisca again. She understands in three seconds that everything is finished. Assuming there was anything to finish, of course. She stutters then leaves, apologising.

And as she goes, I hear my mind scream, *Penny!* I clench my fist, fight the instinctive urge to chase after her, to stop her on the stairs. It wouldn't make sense. I don't owe her any explanation. My woman is Francisca, this long-legged warrior, not the small fragile thing that just left. We were just having fun – it was quite clear from the beginning. I owe her nothing, let alone explanations. I will never see her again. That game is over forever.

25

She stayed where she was, leaning against the front door, curled into herself, for what seemed like forever. It seemed to her that for this whole time she had been unable to think of anything – and maybe she hadn't even breathed. Her mind was obscured by pain and panic. It was over, all over. She would never see him again, never kiss him again, never touch him again. Marcus and Francisca would be leaving very soon. They were a perfect couple. A damn perfect couple.

And Penny was a real idiot. Only an idiot could have believed – albeit for a handful of dazzling hours – that a man like Marcus could be something more to her than a fling. What had fooled her? The secret torments of Edward Rochester? What a complete idiot she was.

After that infinite time, during which every little creak made her jump because she secretly harboured the hope that Marcus would come downstairs and tell her he loved her, loved her, loved her, in spite of Francisca, against Francisca, against the entire fucking world – she got up and shut herself in the bathroom.

She stayed in the shower until the water ran cold, then dried herself with slow, mechanical movements, and finally slipped into her grandma's bed. She didn't want to stay in her own room – there were too many memories imprisoned between those walls and the fire escape.

Holed up under the covers in Barbie's bed, Penny cried all the tears ever created by God. She thought about all the time they'd spent together: the way they had first met, their first standoffs, their first kiss, their first time.

Though it hurt her, she wondered what Marcus and Francisca were doing. Were they making love again? Were they sleeping in each other's arms? Were they eating dinner together and laughing and catching up on their four years apart? When would they be leaving?

Will Marcus ever think of me?

Will I ever stop crying?

◆ ◆ ◆

In the morning, she left home early to go to the hospital. She had barely slept an hour, made up of minutes-long stretches when she'd managed to drift off, only to start awake again.

She spent the morning with Barbie, ate nothing and drank a disproportionate amount of coffee from the hospital vending machine. Her grandma alternated stretches of sleep with moments of confused chatter, and when she was awake, she began to cry desperately, wailing that her son was dead, as if it had happened only an instant before and not almost twenty years ago. Penny hugged her and cried with her.

Upon returning home, she felt as weak as a child with a high fever who'd been up all night vomiting. She walked slowly up the stairs, fearing she'd run into Marcus, hoping she'd run into Marcus. When she reached her own landing, however, instead of entering the apartment and closing herself in and shutting out the world, she let herself be led away by a delirious temptation.

She climbed the spiral staircase in silence, and put an ear to the attic door. What she heard was the absolute end of even her faintest

265

hopes. Marcus and Francisca were having sex – those sounds were unmistakable. She didn't doubt that they'd been doing it for hours, doing their best to make up for so many years of forced separation.

She put a hand over her mouth to keep from screaming. She wanted to shout his name, even if she didn't know why – maybe because saying it would mean he still existed for her and wasn't part of a past she had to bury.

But she remained silent. She went back downstairs, trembling, and vomited her coffee along with a sea of acid. Then she looked at herself in the mirror: her eyes were red, swollen and devastated with sadness. Her lips too were swollen, and bleeding. Her nose looked like a purple plum. Her emerald-green lock of hair was beginning to fade, turning now to a blue-grey – more grey than blue. And she realised she didn't deserve this much pain all at the same time.

So she did something she wouldn't normally do.

She called Igor. They agreed to meet each other that evening. He seemed really happy with the call, recognising it as the miracle it was.

In the hours beforehand, Penny got ready carefully – she even put on make-up – and put on the only provocative dress she owned. The one Marcus had criticised, the green velvet sheath she'd worn to visit Francisca in prison. She liked it. It was snug and short enough to suggest her precise intention: she would sleep with Igor – out of desperation and vengeance, and for her own oblivion – and she wouldn't look back.

◆　◆　◆

Igor arrived on time with an exultant smile on his lips. He got out of the car and held out his arm for her, opening the passenger door like a true gentleman. He wore a trench coat over his jeans, and a trilby.

Penny was about to climb in when she felt her heart jump into her throat. Without understanding why she was suddenly falling, Igor's hand shot out and held her steady, thinking perhaps she had tripped because of her high-heeled boots. In actual fact, she had spotted Marcus and Francisca walking together just a few feet away. They were pressed against each other and holding bags as if they had been out shopping. That familiarity, which screamed, *We don't just have sex, we eat together, breathe together – we are as one*, hurt Penny more than their stolen moans through the door.

But Penny pretended not to see them. She pretended to be a happy girl who was going out for a real first date with her high school crush and saw nothing but him. She pretended to be a relaxed twenty-two-year-old in a green dress with a faded green lock of hair and a pink coat matching her pink hat, expressing her supreme happiness through all these colours. She even leaned over and kissed Igor on the cheek, dangerously close to his lips. The car moved off quickly, and she resisted the temptation to check the rear-view mirror.

Who knows when they'll be leaving? she wondered in a fit of melancholy.

But then she told herself she didn't want to know, didn't have to know. She just had to live. Have fun with Igor that night, really have fun, and start all over again.

26

MARCUS

Francisca's sleeping but I can't. It's almost dawn and I've been pacing around the apartment like a beast in a very small cage. I smoke and smoke and smoke some more, and a couple of times I stop at the door and think about going downstairs, but I don't. I don't have to do this. My woman is here, not somewhere else. I've been waiting for four years, and I'm not going to screw everything up for some random bitch. Sometimes I'd like to punch myself in the head to get Penny out of my thoughts. None of this makes sense; it's total madness, it's a disease. I'm here with the sexiest woman alive, and all I can think about is Penny. Can a man lose his mind in a few weeks? No. A man cannot lose himself in such a short time. And if that's true, then this can't be what I think it is, and it can't last. It's momentary madness, and if I refuse to give into it, it will pass.

I have beer in the fridge. I open one and drink it. Francisca gets out of bed and joins me. We smoke and drink and laugh and screw. This is the life I want. Tomorrow we're leaving without telling anyone. We'll be gone. Technically we're not allowed – I'm on parole – but fuck the rules. OK, I've had four beers and some Johnnie Walker and I'm drunk, but if something is true when you're sober, it's also true when you're drunk: it's better to die on the run than live in a prison.

◆ ◆ ◆

I finally fall asleep in a stupor of sex and alcohol. When I wake up it's dark. Either it's still night or it's night again. I think we must have slept for hours. I get up and my head spins; I used to be able to hold my whiskey but now, after four years of sobriety, I admit I feel like shit. A cold shower is the best thing to clear my head. I need to go out and buy something to eat.

While I'm dressing, Francisca wakes up.

'Wait for me, I'll shower and go with you.'

We go downstairs and deliberately ignore Penny's front door. I hold a cigarette between my fingers and take a deep drag and think *Fuck you* to whatever is behind that door. Luckily, we don't see anyone; I don't want to run into some decrepit old lady trying to make trouble.

It's no longer raining outside but the air is freezing. The store is nearby and we walk. It's strange to walk down this street with Francisca, strange to feel her next to me again. I thank Johnnie for the favour he has given me: I'm still too hungover to dwell on superfluous things, things that also include Penny.

But on our way back, each of us holding a paper bag full of gargantuan burgers and fries, my mission to stop thinking about Penny becomes impossible.

Because I see her in front of me, by the building, and she's not alone. She's getting into a car, and Igor is opening the door for her. She smiles, he smiles, and I stop smiling. The bitch is dressed like that day we went to the prison, and she's wearing make-up, and she kisses him on the cheek and gets into his car, and he looks like some athlete who just won a race. Then they leave and I immediately want to know where they're going and what they're going to do – if he touches her, I think, I'll tear off his arms. As this onslaught of thoughts hits me, I stop on the sidewalk and observe the car as it moves away. The whiskey is no longer enough, and I suddenly feel high, as if I've been drinking gallons of coffee, and yet suddenly foggy, all in the same infernal moment, but this is a different kind of fog, which has nothing to do with alcohol. It has to do with a murderous jealousy that's invading me and threatening to set off World War Three.

I set off towards the house, go up the stairs, and don't notice Francisca until I'm inside my apartment again and drop the bag on the table like I'm weak from some kind of fever. Then I see her standing next to me, staring into my face.

'Are you in love with that girl?' she asks directly.

I start laughing, hard and bitter. 'What the fuck are you saying?' I exclaim, looking for a cigarette.

Where did I put the cigarettes? Where did I put those fucking cigarettes?

I find them and take one and light it and take a drag and laugh again, but Francisca doesn't laugh at all.

'Me, in love with her? Did you see her?'

'I did, but I also saw how you looked at her.'

'And how exactly did I look at her?' I ask, in a teasing tone. Francisca and Sherrie are in competition with each other for who is more full of crap.

'How you should have looked at me when I came back.'

'Don't talk bullshit, Fran.'

'Then can I ask what's up with you?'

'Nothing. It's nothing, OK?'

'Did you fuck anyone else besides her?'

The question makes me jump. 'What?'

'It's a simple question. Since you've been with her, have you fucked anyone else?'

'No,' I admit, 'but that means nothing.'

'Did you kiss her during sex?'

'Fran, that's enough. Don't break my balls over this.'

'You're the one breaking my balls. I just want to understand what's happening to you. I've never seen you like this.'

'Like what?'

'All out of sorts. Your hands are shaking. You have a look in your eyes that I didn't even see when we killed that guy. Did you kiss her while you fucked her?'

'Yes, but what does that even mean?'

'I don't know, but I want to know if I still have a place in your life.'

'Of course you do! I only screwed Penny and, yes, I kissed her, but to go from that to asking me if . . .'

'So if, for example, I said to you, let's start now, immediately, delete her, and you'll never know where she went tonight or what she did with that guy and you won't see her ever again, what would you say?'

I laugh, nervously stubbing out the cigarette in an empty beer can. 'I'd say fine, let's leave now! I'll pack my bag and we'll beat it! But do you really think that I . . . care about . . . about that one? You're out of your mind, Fran, you're out of your mind. We only dated because she paid me! And I fucked her here and there. What's the big problem? I didn't think you cared where I park my horny cock when you're not around.'

'I don't care about that, but I do care where you park your heart.'

I laugh even louder now, and I fear myself, because my voice with its strident edge, which seems capable of cutting diamonds, sounds like the shrill laugh of a devil with no hope.

271

'I'll get my things ready and leave, OK? So you can stop talking bullshit,' I say firmly.

I take the bag and begin to fill it furiously, just to show her, and while I'm doing it, I turn my back on a silent Francisca and can't get the image of Penny and Igor out of my head. She was smiling – smiling! She was happy, and kissed him next to his lips, and I swear to God that tonight he'll try to screw her, and since he's no idiot he won't be violent like Grant, and she will say yes, she will say yes, she will open for him like she opened for me.

I stop and I hurl the bag against the wall with brute force. A diabolical blasphemy comes out of my mouth as I hit the punch bag with such force that it falls to the floor, which vibrates and creaks like a tree.

Francisca is still motionless in the middle of the room – tall, proud, shiny as a scalpel. Merciless, as she always has been, she goes back on the attack. 'Are you in love with her, Marcus?'

And then it's useless, it's useless to try to get around it, like it's useless to sweep away dust, fog, defences, or give a different meaning to something that only has one. I've never lied to Francisca, and I didn't plan on starting today. I just didn't understand. Damn it, I didn't understand.

At this point, I hear my breathless, desperate voice saying only 'Yes'. And then it says, 'Forgive me.' So without even turning around to face Francisca, I grab a jacket and my car keys and race out of the apartment like a man who's running for his life.

27

The play did Penny more harm than good. It was the story of a woman who goes in search of true love, and before she finds it she experiences a long list of tragicomic false starts. All heightened with music played by a live orchestra and hand-painted scenography in a style that imitated the rich and vivid brushstrokes of Van Gogh.

Sitting in the second row next to Igor in a small cosy theatre all trimmed in blue, Penny tried to smile. She had turned off the sound on her phone to be polite. Every now and then she checked it for fear of missing a call from the hospital, and was astonished to find that Marcus had phoned. The temptation to call him back was enormous, but she didn't give in. Maybe he just wanted to know how she was, maybe he wanted to apologise, maybe he wanted to say goodbye because he was leaving.

He loved me in his own way. It's not his fault I'm not Francisca. But I don't want to talk to him again.

Whatever the reason for those calls, she didn't care. They had nothing more to say to each other.

At the end of the show, Igor introduced her to the people in the theatre company and Penny shook hands and smiled until her cheeks hurt, realising with sadness that the play was continuing to the bitter end and she was now the lead. She was pretending to be cheerful and nice, in that same damn dress that was far too short, with her face made up and her heart in black and white. Fortunately, Igor didn't seem to notice. It was to Penny's advantage that she had never been a particularly outgoing girl, the kind who commands the room, the kind people notice when they fall silent. After all the pleasantries and pats on the back and mutual compliments and fake smiles, she and Igor left at last.

'Would you like to come and have dinner at my house?' Igor asked her. 'I'm a very good cook.'

Penny accepted at once, thinking that fate was a pimp. Fate wanted her to sleep with Igor, or just maybe, given that her clothing that evening was channelling a girl who barely bothered with wearing her underwear, she had sent him a message loud and clear all by herself, which he had gratefully received.

On reaching his apartment, Penny saw that it was small but colourful and whimsical. It featured abstract paintings, certainly by his own hand, with the same dense brushstrokes as the scenography, as well as a low table made from an old barn door, and quotes – phrases taken from famous poems – drawn by hand on to a wall that was a mosaic of bricks in relief. Even the glasses were extravagant: some shaped like stills in a distillery, others with huge hollow cubes inside, others shaped like the headless, sinuous bodies of women.

Penny sat down on a couch and Igor handed her a bottle of beer, then he sat down beside her and asked frankly, 'So, do you want to tell me what happened?'

'What do you mean?'

'Why are you here with me instead of with Marcus? You seemed so decided yesterday, and I was confused when you called today.'

'In a good way, I hope.'

'In a great way, but . . . why this sudden change?'

'We . . . er . . . we broke up.'

'Can I ask you what happened, or is that too much?'

Penny took a sip of beer and tried a casual smile. 'Nothing special. It just didn't work out.'

'So suddenly? It seemed like it was very much working out.'

'I was . . . I'd been thinking about it for a while, actually. It was just a physical thing, nothing more, and I want more.'

Unexpectedly, Igor reached out and took her hand. 'Miracles do happen then. I want more too. I know it's early, but . . .'

'It's never too early,' she said, a little agitated, wondering what the hell she meant by that remark, tossed out to fill a void and hide a heartbeat.

'So if, for example, I kissed you, you wouldn't think I was an asshole taking advantage of your vulnerability?'

'I'm not vulnerable at all,' she said firmly, feeling as fragile as a house built on sand.

Igor smiled, continuing to hold her hand. 'I am really trying, of course, but I don't just want that. I do really like you. I've always liked you, ever since I first saw you. You were sixteen and you wore a braid over one shoulder and a sky-blue coat with big buttons.'

'You still remember that? Grandma sewed it for me, but I stopped wearing it after Rebecca made fun of it. It made me feel like some poor kid.'

'But you were delicious, and so original, so different from the others. So different that I believed Rebecca's lie. I was a boy. I was stupid – I should have asked you out anyway.'

Penny gave him the best smile she could muster just at that moment.

'Come here,' he urged. Igor had no intention of saying it twice. He leaned in and kissed her on the lips.

Penny waited for the world to turn upside down, for her heart to leap into her throat and hands and legs, yet nothing happened. But she didn't try to wriggle away. She was determined to stay and make it to the end. So she placed the beer bottle on the floor and moved even closer to this angel with the blond curls and the cornflower-blue eyes. She looked at him as if she were begging him to throw her a rope while she was falling over the edge and into the abyss. Igor, despite his fairy-tale appearance, was still a man – a man who moreover had always had a thing for her, and he didn't stop to think about just why she'd so impulsively rushed into his arms. He simply welcomed her.

They found themselves one on top of the other on the couch, which was very different from the one in Marcus's apartment, in that it was not a worn-out, patched-up old thing but a comfortable chaise longue in bold stripes of indigo and yellow. Igor was holding her tightly, with Penny intent on wiping the slate clean to forget her painful memories. Their long kiss wasn't in any way bad, but it was only a kiss. Fully aware of the difference, of her utter failure to put her memories behind her, unable to think about anything else but Marcus, wondering why the hell she had loved him so much and how it was possible to love him so much and if six weeks were long enough for her to love anyone so much, Penny began to cry like a hopeless fool.

Igor couldn't help but notice; he pulled back, concerned. 'What's going on?' he asked.

Lying beneath him, Penny squirmed until Igor moved aside and she got up, her eyes flooded with tears. All she could repeat was, 'Please excuse me – I'm sorry, I'm so sorry.' She kept repeating it as she put on her coat and made for the door and left the house and walked out of Igor's life forever.

Running down the stairs, she repeated the same words over and over in her mind. It was nothing to do with Igor, it was all her fault and because of her stifling way of loving, her exclusive need for Marcus, even though he didn't deserve her, even though he was the last man on earth who could offer her the hope of a nest and safety and a future.

◆ ◆ ◆

She arrived home distraught and took off her boots, hurling them into the corner as if they were on fire. Suddenly there came a loud knock at the door, and she rushed to open it in a burst of childish desire, hoping against all hope that it would be Marcus.

But it wasn't him.

There on the threshold stood Francisca. Seeing her, Penny couldn't hold back a sudden intake of breath. Francisca parted her lips and squinted, staring at Penny with a somewhat-bemused look on her face.

'Can I come in?' she asked, entering without waiting for permission.

Penny went on the defensive. 'What do you want?'

'I should be asking you the same thing, *chica*. What do you want from Marcus?'

'Nothing.'

It wasn't true – she wanted everything, but for someone who wants to imprison a rainbow in a box, everything is like nothing.

Francisca sat on the couch, pulling up her supple legs, which were wrapped in a pair of tight jeans that highlighted her perfect body. Penny felt a sense of annoyance at the confidence expressed in this gesture, and at the same time some relief. Francisca had a naturally threatening air – she was so strong and solid, with her powerful jaw and eyes blacker than ebony, and for a moment Penny had feared that she wanted to attack her. Instead, it seemed that her strange guest was there to talk.

'Marcus and I share a special bond,' Francisca continued. She seemed as comfortable on the couch as if she were the host, while Penny, barefoot, remained standing. Despite her apparent position of supremacy, she felt low and defenceless.

'I know. Why do you feel the need to remind me?'

Francisca didn't answer her question and went on cryptically, 'He needs to feel free, not oppressed by anything or anyone. He's lived in a cage since he was born. There are so many different types of cage, you know?'

'Really, I don't understand what—'

Francisca cut her off. 'We love each other in our own way. We don't suffocate each other, we don't fear each other, we don't force ourselves to be together.'

'I still don't—'

' . . . understand – I know. And now I'll explain.'

Francisca pulled up a sleeve of her sweater and showed her the scar Penny had noticed in prison. 'I did this trying to kill myself when I was twelve. My stepfather abused me in ways I don't want to remember. He was a horrible man, but after my mother's death he got custody of me. Unfortunately I survived, but I made him pay. I set the house on fire with him inside. He didn't die, but at least they sent me away from there. The juvenile detention centre was my salvation. Marcus was the only one I ever really talked to about my past. Everyone else thought I was just an ungrateful, rebellious teenager. I thought I'd never be able to have sex with a man, but he . . . You see, he looks like a murderer, he looks like a bull on the mountainside, but he treated my wounds with patience. In exchange for his special love I gave him my special love: a very strong but secret love, never jealous, never declared. Because I knew that if I shouted it at him, if I tried to hold him back, to tell him "I want you just for me", he would have left. He has this weakness: he remains at your side with all his soul as long as he sees an open door, an escape, the air, the wind, the road. He had other women, I never demanded exclusivity. If I had, maybe he would have listened to me for a while, but then he would have made a run for it. I had to let him be free.'

Though she didn't understand the full meaning of this long story, Penny couldn't help but be struck by it in the deepest part of her heart. She saw Francisca was holding back tears. For a second she didn't see a woman who was exceptional for her appearance as well as her way of being, but a young child at the mercy of a cruel man. A little girl who had tried to kill herself so she would be saved. She imagined Marcus taking care of her. The thought of how much he loved her made Penny feel as insignificant as dirty water from the mop on a cheap tile floor. Mere dirt and water. Francisca and Marcus had loved each other and still loved each other – in their own way, to be sure, but it was a special way and different from a million others. But Penny was still confused as to why Francisca had opened herself up to her like that.

'I'm sorry for you,' Penny said in a whisper. 'I truly am sorry for you. And maybe I should feel sorry for myself too, because I don't understand what you want, and I'm certainly not very perceptive.'

Francisca, rising to her feet and becoming the tall, triumphant warrior again, said to her, 'I want you to let him go when he tells you he wants to stay here with you.'

Penny wobbled and had to hold on to a chair to keep from falling. Her cheeks were on fire and her heart was cramping. She looked at Francisca as if she were crazy or drunk, wondering if she was saying this to get revenge on Penny for wanting her man. 'What is this? Some kind of joke?'

Francisca shook her head; her face darkened, and her black eyes told Penny it was anything but amusing. 'Not at all. Marcus believes he's in love with you. Maybe he is and maybe he's not, I don't know, but the thing I want to know most is this: Are you in love with him?'

Penny didn't answer right away. She was too focused on what Francisca had just told her.

Marcus is in love with me?

Maybe she's drunk?

What is she talking about?

Is Marcus in love with me?

Penny's hopes started to enter her thoughts before she could stop them. Her heart began to beat at breakneck speed, making her ears ring.

'Do you love him?' Francisca asked her again.

'Yes,' Penny replied firmly.

Francisca, paradoxically, smiled. 'Good – so turn him down. If you truly love him, you won't let him stay in this shithole with a shitty job and a shitty life. If you truly love him, you won't turn him into a prisoner. His dream is to be free. You want to be the one to kill his dream? He's burning to get out of here. After four years in prison do you want to land him in one that's even worse? What would he become here? The good man who listens to his supervisor at some crap job, comes home early in the evening and watches some stupid old man on TV? But even if you were that selfish, you do realise you'd soon be paying for it with interest? Because I know Marcus – sooner or later he'd tear off the shackles and leave you anyway. Marcus needs an open window, an escape route, and what escape would he have in this life? He'd die inside, he'd be like a chained wolf, a tiger in a hamster cage. It's up to you. You decide to keep him and you risk killing him as well as yourself when he leaves you anyway – or you can decide to let him go now and show him that you really care. And that you're less stupid than you look.'

With that parting shot, Francisca got up to leave.

Penny called after her in a choked whisper. 'You're such a liar,' she said.

Francisca shook her head. 'I didn't lie to you about anything.'

'Yes, you did. You said you never forced him to stay with you, but isn't that what you're doing now? You just don't want to get your hands dirty.'

Francisca's eyes filled with rage. For a moment Penny thought she was about to set aside her subtle violence and attack her outright. Instead, Francisca continued to emotionally blackmail her.

'If you love him like you say you do, you know what to do. I'll leave it up to you.' And with that, Francisca walked out of Penny's home – and her life – forever.

28

MARCUS

I don't know what my intentions are, I just know I want Penny. I need to find her, I need to talk to her. I try to call but she doesn't answer. Does she not hear it or is she ignoring me?

I drive in the car to nowhere in particular, like a madman who knows he's crazy and doesn't even bother to hide it. I stop for a while at Well Purple and the Maraja, but to no avail.

Penny's not here and I have no idea where she is. She could be anywhere, along with that asshole who's wanted her for six years and hopes to have her tonight. If I find him, I'll rearrange his priorities all right.

And since I'm pissed off and don't know where to go and don't want to go home to Francisca, who stared at me like I'm some stranger, and I have to unload all this painful anger that's making me feel drunker than when I had all those beers and the whiskey, I decide to pass by that woman's shop, the one who sells trinkets.

I'm lucky – or unlucky, depending on your point of view – but the shop is just closing, and Grant is there, waiting for the woman and pretending to be a gentleman while thinking about how to force himself on her. I see them walk away together towards his car, and I am so furious with those preppy types who show off their wealth to compensate for their small dicks that I follow them.

Grant's car slows at a hilly area on the outskirts of the city. A kind of park, where couples come to fuck if they can't do it anywhere else. I immediately remember Penny's story: I realise it's the same place he brought her, and my anger becomes a raging fire.

I lose sight of them for a moment. It's all dark, he's turned off his headlights and he's holed up who knows where, and it's ten minutes before I find them, but then suddenly there they are – didn't Grant get the memo that he needs a less conspicuous car if he wants to hurt people in it?

I park and get out. I notice some movement inside the car and hear voices. At first it just seems like they're getting busy, but I know that's not the whole story. And then I hear the girl scream, and not out of pleasure. I think of Penny, who may have screamed in the same way, and I open the door. The asshole didn't even lock the door on his side. I am certain, however, that there will be no escape from her side.

I open the door to a predictable scene. The woman is terrified, dishevelled, sweaty: her eyes are huge, and she's looking confused. The asshole has his cock out, limp as a worm, and the expression of a pervert. OK, now I'm really gonna take care of him.

I grab him by the collar and pull him out of the car with one hand. I don't think, I don't reason, don't calculate the possible consequences: if I kill him, I end up back in prison, and if I beat him to within an inch of his life, I'll do time for that too, but I don't give a fuck right now, I just want to make him pay. For Penny. For this woman I don't even know. For my mother. For all the women forced to accept advances they don't want.

I slam him against the car and start laying into him. He doesn't even try to defend himself, at most just kicks a little, terrified, bewildered, and he may even be pissing his pants. The woman gets out of the car, her make-up all smudged by her tears, panic in her eyes. She stares at me in silence, and for a moment I think I see Penny: Penny begging me to stop, like she did at the bar; Penny taking my arm and restraining it.

Then unexpectedly I stop. Anger evaporates from my body like a gas. As soon as I release my grip, Grant falls to the ground like a deflated balloon, reeking of piss and sweat. He no longer looks like some fake prince. He looks like a beat-up piece of shit. I leave him there, like the heap of trash he is, and turn to the woman. 'D'you want me to take you to the hospital?'

She whispers a weak 'no', and then adds, 'Home, I want to go home.'

She gets into my car voluntarily and without suspicion, and I stifle the urge to lecture her about trusting the wrong people – even one who may have saved her skin. But I don't say a word because I'd scare her and she'd think I want to hurt her too. I look more the type than Grant. She's silent the whole way home, pulling at her cheap skirt, her hands on her knees, staring straight ahead at the road. She shows me where to stop, and when she gets out of the car she staggers, like a doll with a broken leg.

'Are you sure you're OK?' I ask her again.

'Yeah, I'm fine.'

'Do you have anyone at home to be with you?'

'My mom.'

'Go on then. I'll wait until you get in.'

She nods and starts to walk towards the door. After two steps she stops, returns, and bends to speak to me through the open window. 'Are you an angel?' she asks me.

Penny asked me the same question the first time we met, in the darkness of the staircase. No, I'm not an angel. Never have been. There's nothing angelic about my life – I'm more of a fucking devil. But I don't say anything, just shoot her a vague smile as she walks off. I leave her with the illusion that I'm some kind of protective spirit, a good one, even if I'm only made of hatred and revenge.

But maybe that's not all I'm made of. There's also love – an unexpected, violent love that I hadn't expected to find. Totally different from what I feel for Francisca. New and dangerous, because it makes me feel vulnerable, like a soldier without weapons or a shield. I finally let the feeling inside of me and into my messy life; I welcome it in and now it's here to stay.

◆ ◆ ◆

I sprint up the stairs in our building. I knock on Penny's door like someone who's been buried alive and is trying to break through the walls of their coffin. I'm agitated, nervous, pissed off. Then she opens and I see her again and it's like I haven't seen her in centuries. She's still wearing her short dress, she's barefoot and she's been weeping – I can see that immediately. And not just a little: her mascara is running, there are trails of salt on her skin and her lips are swollen. I go in and close the door and ask her, 'What happened?'

She shakes her head and looks at me anxiously. 'What did you do to your hands?' she exclaims.

My hands? I look at myself and only now do I realise they're stained with blood – Grant's blood, the filthy blood that spattered from his face.

'It's nothing serious,' I whisper, wiping them. I want to understand why she's been crying, or it's gonna drive me crazy.

'It looks serious. You have blood on your jacket too. Can you please tell me what happened?'

'Grant and I had an exchange of opinions.'

'What?'

'I don't think he'll ever be quite so beautiful again.'

'Did you . . . ?'

'I didn't kill him. Unfortunately he's still alive, but it'll take all of his daddy's money to fix his face. Now, tell me what happened to you. Did Igor bother you? I'm already covered in blood, so one more . . .'

She shakes her head again, more decisively than before. I approach her and want to touch her, hold her. I want her to tell me that nothing happened with Igor, nothing at all, but the more I move towards her, the more she shrinks back.

What did you do to me? What do you want from me? Why do you hold me in suspense with your weeping eyes? Why do you move away from me like a butterfly escaping a hawk? Fuck it, Penny, I'd never hurt you.

And yet she shrinks back, and suddenly she's against the wall and can go no further.

'You have to go now,' she tells me, standing there like she's my prisoner. Yet I don't touch her; she's afraid of me, even if I don't know why she's afraid of me, and I don't touch her. I only look at her, look and realise that I'm scared too. Damn it, she's tiny and made of tears, and yet I'm afraid of her. Then, dropping my voice, I say to her, 'What if I told you . . . if I told you I want to stay here?'

I see her throat move as if she were swallowing a big mouthful of something. Her lips tighten and for a moment I sense that all the pain in the world is passing through her small body. Finally, she whispers, 'What a load of bullshit,' and my heart stops. 'What a load of bullshit,' she goes on. 'Why on earth would you stay here?'

I realise I'm clenching my fists as I say, 'To be with you.'

She opens her eyes, holds her breath, looks down and avoids my gaze. 'Bullshit, Marcus,' she repeats.

There's something like a storm roaring in my chest, fury swirling into desperation. I reach out and almost put my fist in the wall behind her. With one hand I lift her chin. My touch makes her quiver. She scrutinises me with apparent contempt.

'So when exactly did you decide you wanted to stay? Before or after you fucked Francisca?'

I keep her face up even though she's trying to look away. My darling, beautiful little Penny. Could six short weeks, a mere blip in time, a snap of the fingers, really change the world I've lived in for twenty-five years, so utterly and absolutely?

'After,' I reply, and realise how stupid that sounds. But it's true. I wasn't sure until after. Before, it was a worm of an idea, a shadow, a paper cut. After, it became a full-blooded truth. 'But then I realised that it's you I want – you and only you.'

She's trembling and I try to hug her, but she walks away from me, struggling out of my arms. Am I hurting her? Bothering her? What, damn it – what's wrong?

'Well, I realised the opposite after fucking Igor,' she says.

My reaction is immediate and instinctive. My knuckles hit the wall, straight as a ram. Straight away, I move away from her, walk away because there's an earthquake happening inside of me; I walk away because I am the earthquake. I hit a chair and it jumps violently into the air. My arms are burning. The thought of the two of them together is unbearable. For a few minutes I lose all sense of reason, just walk around her apartment like a bear with an arrow in my heart. She says something to me but I don't hear her. The sounds of my body are deafening: the blood in my veins, the beat of my heart, even the gnashing of my teeth, the flexing of my muscles and the creaking of my bones.

After a while, however, I force myself to think again. It makes no sense to get mad like that. Who am I to preach celibacy? I did it with Francisca only a few hours before, and not just the once. But how can I explain to Penny that I only did it because I'm a man and she jumped on me and I used to love her and had to work things out? Yes, I loved Francisca, but not the way I love Penny. I will love Francisca forever, but not like this, not like this.

Suddenly I realise that the worst thing that just happened is not that Penny slept with Igor. The worst is the other thing she said. That she realised the opposite. The opposite of what?

'What do you mean, "the opposite"?' I say.

Penny makes a face I can't interpret – and don't intend to – and states firmly and clearly, but with an undertone wobbling on the edge of hysteria, 'I don't want you.'

I stop in the middle of the room, squinting as if I want the scene to come into focus. I look at her and she looks at me and then she nods and adds, 'OK, so we fucked, Marcus, and it was nice, but I need someone like Igor. He makes me feel safe. You're great in bed and you're undeniably hot, but let's face it, you've been in prison, you have a shit job, you fight with everyone and we have absolutely nothing in common. I've known Igor a long time and I've known you for all of six weeks – enough time for an exciting adventure, but not for a great love.'

She hasn't even finished talking and I'm standing over her. I pin her back into the corner. A single word flashes in my head. *Bitch. Bitch. Bitch.* And then . . . *God, I love you, bitch. I hate you and I love you.* I squeeze her neck with the fingers of one hand. I feel her throat moving. We're so close that our breaths mingle.

I'd like to do something, anything – kiss her, fuck her, insult her – but instead I do nothing. I feel like a tree that's been struck by lightning. I have a fire in my chest and my thoughts are colliding with each other and I can't understand a thing.

All I know is she doesn't want me.

Then I explode with laughter – even though I have no desire at all to laugh – I step back, let go of her slender throat and stare at her for an instant that will kill me for the next hundred years. I stare at her and think this is the last time I will ever see her with her fiery hair, peachy lips, eyes full of tenderness and trouble – especially now – and her body which is no longer mine and mine alone. This is the last time I will ever see her and I feel like the world is a deep abyss that I'm gonna fall into in exactly one minute's time, as soon as I walk out that door. I leave the apartment and slam the door behind me. I will never see her again.

I run up to the attic, holding my breath. Francisca is there, waiting. I look at her and say, 'Let's go, right now, this minute.' Tomorrow, I think, I'll have time to die.

29

FRANCISCA

I hated her as soon as I saw her. Without knowing why, or maybe somehow I did know. It bothered me that Marcus had talked to her about himself, about us, but I couldn't show I was jealous; I never have. Even when I wrote to him, I held back, smothered the fire. Instead, I wrote to him about us, told him what life was like behind bars, told him what I'd do to him as soon as I got out. I wanted to eat him up.

When I got his reply, I wanted to break through the bars and get to him as soon as I could, because his letter was concentrated bullshit. Bullshit about his life, his apartment, how he was waiting for me. Not even a nod to that fucking angel face. A page of bullshit, as if he were afraid that if he let himself think, he might let on too much. And what was there to let on? That he was falling in love with Penny.

I don't think he did it on purpose, I really don't, but you don't live for twenty-four years in this shitty world without learning to pay attention, because if you're not careful, you'll leave it without understanding what you need to understand. You get smart, and when you love someone a lot, you get doubly smart.

I haven't laughed since I was twelve.

Marcus is the only man who has ever touched my body without it feeling dirty.

I can't stand being touched by anyone else, not even by mistake. Imagine how I react to the ones who do it on purpose. If Marcus hadn't killed that bastard at the club, I'd have done it myself.

I even hate it when people stare at me in the street.

I hate being photographed.

I hate any person who wants to capture me, steal from me, stop me, get something from me.

Marcus is all I have.

But I'm no longer all he has.

I get out earlier than expected and go to his place, hoping to surprise him, but he surprises me instead. He's surprised, yes, but not in the way I'd hoped. His eyes hide a million questions. He makes love as if it were his duty.

At night I watch him as I pretend to sleep. He smokes as if he's immersed in the fires of hell. Then he takes a cold beer from the fridge. We drink like in the old days, and finally he's free, but I don't feel any better about the fact that he can only screw me properly when he's drunk.

We go buy something to eat, and there, on the sidewalk, everything becomes so clear that I almost vomit. Just a few feet away I see the face of that fucking angel. She's with a boy. They get in a car and drive off.

Marcus looks like a murderer who wants to shed blood like a farmer sows his seed. I see how he looks at them, I see how he looks at her. My legs are shaking, and I suddenly feel empty, empty, empty, and pissed off, and lonelier than a child who's been raped and who's cutting her veins with a razor blade. We go upstairs and I ask him. It's useless to pretend that years haven't passed – and especially these last weeks. At first he keeps moving down the same old hall of mirrors, but then he slips. When he finally admits he loves her, I feel like there's no tomorrow. I'm still in prison. No – worse. I'm still back in my old bedroom with my stepfather on top of me.

◆　◆　◆

She loves him. Fucking angel face loves him. I look at her and there's nothing left for me to do but use their love against them. I don't lie to her but I exaggerate, and I don't reveal the most painful secret to her. I don't reveal what I've read in his eyes: hunger, love, jealousy, and an unexpected and terrifying vulnerability. She listens to me, believes me, and I have proof of it later.

A few hours later, in fact, when Marcus finally returns home. His eyes are all steel and ice again. He packs his things in the same bag he first threw against the wall. I get ready and we leave.

30

Penny turned towards the window to watch the deluge outside. She wondered where the sun had gone these days. She'd almost forgotten the warmth of its rays on her face and the beauty of a world not plunged into darkness. She'd seen nothing but rain for days, and without the sun, the city became one big grey maze of alleyways.

'Miss, I'm waiting for my fried chicken,' a skinny woman called over to her. Penny apologised and placed her meal in front of her.

That's when she saw him, standing by the entrance, awkwardly fighting against the whims of an umbrella caught in the wind. He was soaked through, and his long khaki raincoat simply wasn't up to the job of protecting him from the inclement weather. He managed to close the umbrella only by dint of a few acrobatics, and then he finally came into the restaurant, depositing the dripping umbrella in a corner.

He recognised her immediately as she stood there in the middle of the room, dressed in yellow, with her little waitress's cap on her head and her green lock of hair, which by now had faded to a dusty grey. He gave her a soggy, weary smile. Penny welcomed him as if she were the evening's hostess, even though this was not her home and Mr Malkovich was not her guest. Though he was definitely there for work. She had been expecting him to come; in fact, she was surprised it had taken him this long. She sat him near the jukebox and asked if she could bring him a coffee.

'Yes, please – hot, if that's OK? I'm worried I'm catching a cold. But . . . I'm here for another reason.'

'I know,' Penny answered.

'I'd also like to see Mrs Grey. Up until now I've only been monitoring her, since I've always known Marcus pays her visits, but now I really need to speak with her.'

'I know. I'll get her.'

'Wait, I'd rather talk to you first. Can you sit for a second? Why are you working here?'

'I left my night job to take care of my grandma after she had a stroke. Sherrie almost saved my life by hiring me. She's a wonderful person.'

'I know. I don't judge people by their past, only by their present.'

'Maybe it would be better if you didn't judge them at all.'

Behind the counter, Penny picked up the pot and poured coffee into a cup, then sat down across from him, aware of what was about to happen. Marcus had left over a week ago. He had fled in the night, silent as a cat, though even if he'd crashed his way down the stairs, Penny wouldn't have been able to hear him over her sobs. That evening, as soon as he'd shown up at her place, Penny had understood that Francisca was right. Imprisoning him would have been like killing him, a slow death, a trickle of compromises, a slow progression of identical days, which would soon have led him to hate her. Lions must be free, even to live in a violent savannah, even to be killed – to die a savage death, a death in their prime. Seeing him wounded after assaulting Grant had been the tipping point. What if Grant reported him? Would he end up in prison again? So she had let him run off to chase after the wind. It wasn't easy and she had cried for days. She still cried every time she came home and saw the spiral staircase that led up to the attic. She cried for all the cruel lies she'd had to spit out at him, and she cried for his sad eyes, because behind his shield of anger, the look in his eyes had been truly tragic.

'So, where is Marcus?' asked Mr Malkovich after a few restorative sips of hot coffee.

Penny answered him sincerely. 'I honestly don't know.'

He shook his head, displeased. 'I was so hoping he wouldn't do anything this foolish, and I was afraid Francisca might come back. She's always made him do the dumbest things.'

'She . . . she loves him.'

'If she really loved him, she wouldn't have let him violate his parole like this. If they catch him, they'll send him back to jail.'

'Maybe they won't bother going after them? Marcus and Francisca are hardly terrorists or serial killers. They're not exactly going to have the FBI breathing down their necks, are they? They're small fry, and if they're careful, they may just get away with it.'

'But what kind of life can you live if you're always on the run?'

'An exciting one.'

Mr Malkovich looked astonished at this statement of hers, and a bit melancholy. 'I really thought you two were close. I was hoping that you . . .'

'I think we were close,' Penny corrected him. 'But no one can force someone to live a life they don't want.'

At that moment, a voice interrupted them.

'Table five are asking for their French onion soup, my dear,' Sherrie said. 'Can you take it over to them, please? Hello, Mr Malkovich. Have you finally come to question me? We don't know where Marcus is, and even if we did, we wouldn't tell you. And please don't bother this poor girl any more, OK? She's upset enough already. She's hardly eating – can't you see how thin she is?'

Monty Malkovich nodded, as if only now did he notice Penny's dreadful state. She'd lost weight, which she could barely afford to lose in any case, and she was pale and could barely drag herself around.

Penny shook her head as Malkovich took it all in. 'I'm fine, honestly. I'll go get that soup now.'

Before he left, Malkovich stopped her. 'Please, Penny, if he shows up, tell him to contact me. I haven't reported him yet. I love that boy, but if he doesn't help me, I can't help him for much longer.'

Penny nodded with a slight sigh.

'If he shows up, I'll tell him, but it's not going to happen. Listen to me – Marcus has gone from our lives forever.'

Barbie's hair was silken and once more smelled of roses. Penny brushed it for a long time every day. It was almost evening and darkness had settled on the streets outside. They were sitting together on the couch on her return from the library.

Penny's grandma needed constant assistance and her mental gaps were now chasms. One particularly bad morning, she had woken up, seen Penny and asked, 'Who are you?' Penny's heart had fallen to the floor and smashed in two on hearing this. Fortunately, Barbie had recognised her again a few hours later, but from that day on Penny lived with the constant fear of losing her. Not physically – the doctor had assured her that with treatment she could still live a long time – but mentally. Her memories were part of her, they were her family and the certainty of having had a past, they were even the certainty of existing now, of being someone who counted for someone else, but if Barbie's mind went, what would Penny have left? Only a giant and destructive black hole at the centre of her universe.

So she stayed with her grandmother whenever she could, even slept with her, and by day she worked and then ran home with all the urgency of a mother returning to her small child. She was thin and tired, but she wasn't giving up.

Two months had passed since Marcus had left. In those two months she had turned twenty-three, Christmas had come and gone, a new year had arrived, and so had the snow. Grant hadn't shown up again, and neither had Igor. And nor had Marcus. Monty Malkovich had given Penny his number, and every now and then Penny called him and sighed with relief when he told her that Marcus was still free, that he hadn't yet been captured and carted off back to prison. She hoped he'd be free forever. Alive and free.

But oh, how she missed him. She missed him like people in the Arctic Circle yearn for the sun during their six months of darkness.

One day, when she was brushing out Barbie's long hair, her grandma said, 'A letter arrived for me today. Is it a love letter from John, do you think?'

'For you? Show me!' Penny exclaimed.

Barbie drew an envelope from her cleavage in a gesture harking back to long-lost times, when a woman would tuck money away there as a safe place that no decent man would ever dare to violate. Well, it sure didn't look like a love letter; it was indeed addressed to her, Barbara Rogers, but it looked more businesslike. Maybe it was a bill, but for what? Penny opened it, worried. It was from a lawyer requesting a meeting on a certain day and time for an important notification concerning Barbie. Penny didn't recognise the name. She asked her grandma if she did, knowing her memory tended to preserve the strangest details, but Barbie shook her head, genuinely unaware.

'Too bad it wasn't from John,' she added with regret.

Penny picked up her phone to call the number on the letter. The call was answered by a dignified-sounding secretary.

When Penny found out what it concerned, she watched her grandma dab perfumed powder on her cheeks, smiling at her own reflection. She mused on love's many colours – far too many to count. A wound that never stops bleeding. A teeming throng of memories. Remorse for what you did and regret for what you wanted to do, but also, above all, a perfumed handkerchief that dries your tears when memory fades and life draws closer to its end. Love is that golden four-leaf clover, that warm blanket, that distant music, that miracle which comes back one evening at sunset, when everything seems lost forever, and makes you feel eternal because someone out there has never forgotten you.

31

FRANCISCA

February is a real shit month. Except I don't think it's the fault of February exactly. It's not the cold or the rain, it's Marcus. We're still together but we're not together. We've crossed seven states. We've done a ton of odd jobs. We've travelled miles on foot and by bus – it's easier for them to find us if we drive. We've fucked in dozens of motels. No one has come to look for us. But he's no longer mine.

And yet, I make do. I don't want to lose him. I'm satisfied with the scraps he allows me, with his mere shadow, his dazed looks, the snarling and distant sex, after which he immediately gets up and goes for a cigarette as far away from me as he can, before coming back to bed without a word. One night I can't resist going up to him. Marcus is standing in front of the window with the blinds half-drawn, glaring out at the grim panorama of the parking lot beyond. I take a couple of drags from his cigarette, then ask him, 'Are you still thinking of Penny?'

Call it impulsive curiosity. Suicidal curiosity. It's not like Francisca Lopez to be this stupid, to humiliate herself and remind him of his heartfelt admission of love two months ago. But I'm so different now. We're both so different.

He stares at me, his eyes narrowed to slits. 'What the fuck are you talking about?' he spits, and he looks so mad it scares even me.

I should back off, but I don't. 'You said that you—'

He laughs bitterly, and takes a few drags of the cigarette in turn. The blue smoke surrounds him and then escapes from an invisible crack in the window.

'I said shit I didn't mean. It happens, doesn't it?' he goes on. 'I don't even remember what she looks like anyway. Fucking is just fucking. I was using her for a few weeks, that's all.' He stares at me, smiles at me with malice, grabs my wrist with his hand.

He crushes the cigarette on the windowsill, leaving the butt there, crumpled, then pulls the blinds down to shut out the light. We land back in bed. Having sex with Marcus is like being in a hurricane.

He means everything to me. This panting, sweaty sex is everything. He is my angel and my demon.

But when he's inside of me, I'm afraid. I'd like to cry and to punch him with my fists. Not because of what he's doing, but because of his eyes, which look at me without seeing me. Because of his glittering metallic eyes that don't know what they're giving away. When he fucks me, he's fucking with Penny – or fucking against her, for revenge – and he doesn't even know it.

Another time it's raining when we walk along the main street of a town whose name I can't even remember. We have a few beers at a bar, then walk around town, try to stay out of trouble. Marcus paces ahead of me with his long loping stride, not so far as to forget all about me but enough to be able to ignore me. He keeps trying to light his cigarette in spite of the downpour.

'Hey,' I call out to him, 'good luck with that.'

He looks up at the sky as if he's only just realised that God is chucking it down. He squints, and the water is running down his eyelashes, his nose, the beard I'm still getting used to, his leather jacket. 'Yeah, it's too wet,' he replies, and he throws the cigarette into the river that's suddenly coursing down the middle of the road.

Then he glances down and his whole expression changes. He looks like someone who's seen a ghost. I follow his gaze and stop in my tracks.

On the road, in the middle of all that water, there's a woman. Is it her? No, it's not her, but they're very similar. She's small, thin, clumsy, with absurd brown hair dyed red and purple and who knows what else. She's dropped something and she's struggling like an ugly swan, groping around in a puddle. Books? Can they be books? What is that idiot doing with books in the rain? But it doesn't matter who she is or what she's doing, it only matters that Marcus – proving that he remembers Penny very well indeed, given that he only needs to mistake someone for her to go crazy – rushes across the street through the puddles and lets himself be battered by the rain like he's a horse galloping through the waves and the spray along a shoreline.

He stoops to help her, the storm beating down on his back like it's a drum, and just as I'm standing there thinking, *There's nothing I can do, there's nothing I can do, his heart is with her, his body is with her, and what the hell did she do to him, what on earth did that inno-cent bitch do*, a car comes speeding around the corner. The driver must be drunk, high or crazy. He veers off to one side, skids, loses control, then heads straight for Marcus and the girl.

It all happens in a second.

I scream.

The woman screams.

Marcus doesn't scream, and shoves her hard towards the sidewalk.

He takes the full blow.

The books fall to the ground. Marcus falls along with the books, among the books, in a puddle already red with his blood, while the car crashes into a wall on the other side of the street with a long, hysterical honk, and I scream out loud now all my hope is gone.

32

Spring in Vermont was suspended between the snow and the flowers. Nature was trying her hardest to overcome the cold. Walking out of the store with a bagful of groceries in her arms, Penny was doing her best not to slip on the frozen ground.

She was about to open the car door when Jacob called her back, poking his head out of the shop, 'Penny, you forgot the chocolate!'

She smiled at him gratefully. Jacob was a tall boy with white-blond hair, green eyes and strong, lumberjack arms. He had a slight crush on her and sometimes they went out together, but their friendship had never managed to transform into anything more.

Which was fine with Penny.

For two years and three months now, her heart had remained as cold and solid as an icicle. A sinister winter had settled in her chest, and she was no longer able to experience anything that even came close to a feeling of love. The only love remaining in her life had been reserved for Barbie.

But now Barbie was gone and Penny had been alone for six months, with no ties to anyone beyond what lay in her memories.

She climbed into her pickup with her weekly food shop, settled herself on the seat and adjusted the long braid that snaked out of her pink wool beanie.

She'd been living in Vermont for over two years now. After accompanying her grandma to visit the lawyer, Penny had been left speechless on discovering the full extent of what the woman had hinted at on the phone; Barbie, on the other hand, had had a lot to say. She was full of gratitude, but not as surprised as someone else in her position might have been. Maybe because she had always known that John – or Thomas, in reality – had truly existed, or maybe because her mind was still living back in those romantic years of her youth. So she hadn't been as shocked as Penny to learn that Mr Thomas Macruder, recently deceased, never married and with no children, had left her – his beloved and never-forgotten Barbie – everything, every dream he'd cultivated in his solitary life. A farm in Vermont with a white wooden house, a red barn, maple and apple trees, green and golden lawns, endless space and air, mountains with forested slopes and a vast immensity that soothed the soul.

So they'd quickly moved into their new home, and Penny finally broke free of the chains that bound her and began to move with the fleetness and agility of some creature of the wild. There they lived in total isolation, with just the wildwoods for company, without even a computer – only a phone for emergencies.

Until her dying day, Barbie continued to believe that she was sixteen years old.

Penny never found out whether her grandma's stories about her past were true, and about Thomas, who was perhaps her real grandfather, but he did have thick, burnt-copper hair like her own – not blonde like Barbie's, or brown like Penny's parents. Not scientific proof exactly, but enough to get her thinking.

All she knew was that, thanks to this man, her secret dream had become a reality. Maybe there really was a God somewhere between those mountains and that snow, a God who listened to mortal prayers and tied a knot in his handkerchief so he'd remember to make them come true, sooner or later. Maybe it was magic, destiny, the plan of the angels. Maybe. In any case, it was always better to hope than to die of pure melancholy.

And so Penny continued to hope for two years and three months, without interruption.

◆ ◆ ◆

Penny drove under the wooden arch with the sign she'd painted in red letters. Under the outline of what looked like a happy mermaid, the inscription stood out: 'The Home of Barbie and Thomas'.

She drove up the driveway lined with apple trees and parked near the house, in a space that she had shovelled that morning, piling all the snow to one side and in a fit of playfulness patting it into the shape of a fat little snowman, like the ones she used to make with her grandma. She got out of the car with her shopping bags. For miles around, patches of snow alternated with sprouts of green. There was still a lot of work to do. She wanted a few horses, but in the meantime, she was happy with her orange cat. She had sown oats, corn, potatoes, barley and wheat, and she picked the apples. Whatever she couldn't eat herself, she sold. A couple of people would come up from the village at harvest time to help her and she paid them back in grain. She was planning to turn an unused stable into a small apartment to rent out to tourists – other lovers of nature and quiet, just like herself.

She walked inside, and her cat Tiger came to rub against her legs in his usual sinuous dance. Penny caressed his soft fur lovingly, then dumped her bags on the massive farmhouse table. While organising her groceries, her eyes fell on her reflection in the door of the old steel refrigerator.

None of her neighbours in Connecticut would recognise her now. Physical work had built her up and made her stronger, and her cheeks were crimson from the cold. She'd stopped cutting her hair, and it reached down to her waist – smooth, with brown and auburn highlights, and no weird colours anywhere in its length. She often tied it back, like now, in a messy braid that hung over her shoulder and on to her breast. Her current wardrobe featured only jeans, flannel shirts, fleece gloves, chequered jackets and rubber boots. Not that she'd considered herself elegant exactly in the old days, but now she was quite the peasant girl, without a scrap of make-up or even the odd manicure. These days she kept her nails short and clean, and that was all.

She noticed suddenly that the basket of wood for the fire was getting low, so she went out and round to the back of the house. Tiger followed as he always did when the weather was mild enough. He dodged the clumps of snow, jumping from one patch of grass to the next in a network of green that was slowly expanding with the imminent arrival of spring, on the lookout for a warm spot in the sun where he could stretch out like a lazy little dog, licking his parts and purring graciously at the world. With her newfound boundless energy, Penny split a few logs with an axe. The sound of wood on wood relaxed her as it always did.

Suddenly her cat-dog jumped to his feet in the midst of a loud yawn and arched his back. He always did that when a fox or squirrel was passing by, even at some distance. Penny didn't give it too much thought. She gathered up as much wood as she could manage, smiled at the cat, who sat poised like a lion in the savannah, and turned to go back in the house.

Glancing up, her mouth fell open and her eyes widened in surprise. She lost all strength in her arms, and the wood fell around her like an avalanche of rocks on the mountainside. She didn't know whether to laugh, faint or cry.

33

SHERRIE

It was good to live by the sea. After the mountains of her childhood and the hellish city of her youth, the beach house was a whole new chapter. She would never go back to Montana. She couldn't risk sullying the precious purity of those memories from her early years.

It was Sunday, and Sherrie was sitting on the front steps of her house, enjoying the sun in spite of the lingering bite to the air. On the beach, a few daredevils were running around in the cold. The waves were long and high, curling like the talons of a hawk. The wind caressed her face and made her flossy hair dance.

She heard someone approach, the sand crunching with each step, and turned absently, imagining it would be the person who used her yard as a short-cut to the beach every day, but it was not. Her smile turned into joyous laughter.

'My darling boy!' she said, leaping to her feet. She embraced him, so moved that the tears began to flow down her cheeks. Marcus smiled at her, touching her soft white hair.

'When did you get out?'

'A few days ago.'

'Let me see you! How are you? You look fit – physically, at least.'

'I'm well, thank you.'

'Come, sit down. I was going to make some coffee. Would you like some?'

Soon afterwards, they found themselves sitting on the steps, warming their hands around big mugs of strong, hot coffee. The air was full of salt spray and fine sand. Every now and then, as the clouds shifted, the sky darkened and everything turned silver, only to brighten again when the sun returned.

Sherrie, leaning to one side, watched him carefully. Her baby was beautiful as ever, even though he was no longer a child but a twenty-seven-year-old man. Yet he looked tired, with deep circles around his eyes that dulled their special spark. When they had drained the last dregs of their coffees, he took a cigarette from his pocket, lit it and smoked it slowly. A drag and a thought. A drag and a look at the sea.

'So, tell me something,' she urged.

Marcus shrugged. 'I don't have much to say. I've been inside. It's not like I've seen much.'

'I was so scared when that guy called me . . .'

'You mean Malkovich? What did he say?'

'That you'd had a fatal accident. I almost had a heart attack!'

'It wasn't that serious. I had a head injury and a sprained wrist and I got all scratched up, but when I got to the emergency room, they ID'd me and sent me back to prison. But you know . . . it was better that way.'

'Better?'

'Yeah. I was sick of wandering around like some tramp.'

'I thought you liked it.'

Marcus took a long drag from his cigarette. 'I used to, but then . . . I don't know . . . it lost its meaning. It got boring. At least when you're in prison you're looking forward to something. When I was on the run I didn't look forward to anything. I felt like an empty beer can being kicked around. Without the accident, it would have been left to me instead of destiny. I would have made it all up somehow.'

'There's nothing better than freedom, my love.'

'I used to think so too, but freedom is overrated if you have no place to go and no one to go with.'

Sherrie smiled to herself, but Marcus didn't notice. He kept staring out at the ocean.

'How is she now?' Sherrie asked on impulse.

Marcus spun around and looked at her, frowning. 'I don't know. I was gonna ask you.'

'Why would I know how Francisca is?'

Marcus pursed his lips, the cigarette between his fingers, smoke coiling from his nose like from a dragon's nostrils. 'I thought you were talking about . . .'

'Penny? What makes you think that, my boy? I was referring to Francisca. I know she lived with the Malkovichs for a while.'

Marcus shielded his eyes for a moment, as if the sun were too bright. Finally he murmured, 'She's still with them. When he came to the hospital expecting to find me half-dead, Francisca was there, all alone and desperate and deader than I was, so they invited her to stay with them. It's kind of a miracle. They talked all kinds of shit about her and now they love her. I went to see her. She's working and studying and looks like anybody else. I don't know if she's happy exactly, but she's keeping herself out of trouble.'

'That's good. I knew Malkovich had come to see you. He told me how you were and that you were back in prison. I wanted to visit you or write to you, but he told me it was better if we all left you in peace for a while. He said that's what you wanted.'

'It's true. There were too many people around, too much pressure – Francisca, the police breathing down my neck like I was some serial killer or something, Malkovich and his wife. I was in agony, totally broken.'

'Broken because of all the people around you or the one who wasn't there?'

Marcus stared unflinchingly into her eyes. 'The one who wasn't there,' he admitted. 'Where is she? I went to her apartment but another family was living there.'

Sherrie shook her head disconsolately.

'I wish I could help you, but I don't know. She worked for me for a few weeks. One day, suddenly, she comes to tell me that she and her grandma are moving, kisses me on the cheek and leaves me an envelope with some money for you.'

'What?'

'She said it was a hundred dollars she owed you for some work. She told me that if you came back, I should give it to you, and if not, I should give it to charity.'

Marcus jumped to his feet and flicked his cigarette into the sand. His face, which until then had seemed carved from the finest pale marble, now twisted in fury.

'What am I supposed to do with her fucking money?' he exclaimed. 'I was hoping, dammit, I was hoping you at least knew where she was! How am I gonna find her?'

Sherrie watched him with tenderness. Her baby. Her broken-hearted baby. Her baby in love. She thought back to the day Penny left. How she'd cried in Sherrie's motherly embrace. Who knew where she was now; who knew how she was?

'I'll go get you that money. Throw it away if you want, but I have to give it to you. I promised her I would.'

When Sherrie returned with the small envelope Penny had left her, still sealed after all these years and tucked inside a copy of her favourite fairy tale from when she was a child, *Sleeping Beauty*,

Marcus was already on his feet. He grabbed the envelope and walked briskly towards the shoreline.

Sherrie didn't tell him that she'd held it up to the light, trying to discern if the envelope contained something like a letter instead of cash. She didn't tell him that she'd been very upset when, without a shadow of a doubt, she'd spotted no more and no less than the face of Benjamin Franklin.

Sherrie watched Marcus go, and prayed he would find his way. Even Francisca was making progress. But there was no more strenuous a road than a stretch of sand leading to an angry sea. Her baby had already suffered enough, and he deserved all the best life had to offer.

34

MARCUS

I can't say I didn't try, but I definitely didn't succeed. I'd thought of Penny non-stop after leaving that night. The accident was a good thing.

So I went back to prison. It's the best place for someone who hates his life on the outside. If you want something you can't have, if you want it with all your being, if the world suddenly feels too small because it's suffocating you and too big because you can't run far away enough to forget, a spell in jail is a good compromise.

Francisca wrote to me for a while, and this time Malkovich didn't stop her. I answered her once or twice and that's it. Penny never wrote to me. I imagined her with Igor, happy and satisfied, and I was thankful to be where I was so I couldn't fuck him up like I did Grant. Not for fear of being sent to prison again, but for fear that Penny would hate me.

I kept wondering what this thing was that I felt. I'd like to be smarter, so I could find an explanation in the books, but I'm just not intelligent like that. I'm just a poor sad bastard who thought he was made only of muscle and temptation and found himself dying of love – for someone who didn't even want him. It would be kinda funny if it wasn't so damn tragic.

The first thing I do when I'm out is to go back to that building, to that apartment. I know, it's bullshit. She made it very clear over two years ago that we're on different planets and that she prefers Igor, but I can't resist. Penny doesn't live there anymore, and her grandmother's gone too; the neighbours tell me they moved out a few months after I left, but no one knows exactly where.

Then I go see Malkovich. He's not home, but his wife drags me in and showers me with praise about Francisca. First she was the devil incarnate, now she's an angel. She tells me that she's taking classes, that she studies a lot, that she's working a decent job in a very chic café (her own words) and that she and her husband absolutely love her. She even sleeps in Cameron's room.

As Mrs Malkovich is talking, Francisca comes downstairs. My Fran – beautiful as a precious stone. Diamond and lava, both together. She smiles, and this makes me feel good. The last time I saw her she was crying because she thought I was going to die.

We hug. My heart doesn't break. Desire doesn't overwhelm me. I feel only a deep affection.

'Hey, kid,' I say to her, even though she's no kid now, 'you're looking great.'

'You too. How are you?'

'I'm fine.'

'Me too, you know? It's strange, and even a little scary sometimes, but . . . it's like I'm a kid again. They treat me like a twelve-year-old with the flu. I don't know how long it'll last. Maybe I'll sneak out one night and take all the silver with me, but for now . . . I kind of want to be twelve. I never got to have that.'

Then, without further comment, I shoot her the question I've been dying to ask. 'Did Penny come by here before she left? Do you have any idea where she is?'

Francisca cocks her head to one side and looks at me. 'You're still in love with her,' she says. It's not a question, it's a statement.

In an instant, the spark in her eyes disappears and her gaze clouds over. I don't know what she feels for me after two years and everything that's happened. I stopped her from writing to me; I rejected her without words. I abandoned her, but she never stopped being special to me; she is me, she's my sister, she's my mother. She was my pillar during those broken days of my youth. My blanket on cold nights. Without her I'd have died at sixteen. She saved my life when I was hungry and when my heart was more fragile than an eggshell. She offered me her wounded body. And now she's looking at me with these sad eyes like two inkblots, and it almost seems like she's about to cry black tears. And yet I cannot and will not lie to her. No more bullshit, no more words that say no when my thoughts and my blood are screaming the opposite. So, quite simply, I nod and stare back into her eyes. It's the truth – a truth that has kept me in hell for two years and three months.

Francisca slowly looks down, bites her lip and seems to be struggling with some thought of her own. For a moment the warrior girl of the past returns, the one we both want to pack away into legend now. Finally, her new self admits in a melancholy little voice, 'Please believe me, but I don't know. All I heard was that she went away just before you went back to prison. But . . .'

'But?'

'But I do know she loved you.'

She leads me to the couch, sits me down and tells me a story. I listen to it, giving no indication of how I'm feeling inside, which is to say I look exactly the same as ever, but feel like I've just swallowed a ball of flame. I think back to that night, to her words, to her face and her trembling body. My need to get her back is so strong and painful. For a moment I close my eyes, my fists clench, hard as iron, and I feel more alone than any castaway. Francisca, meanwhile, is watching me uncertainly; I guess she's expecting me to explode any minute, but instead I stroke her cheek. I can't be mad at her, even if what she did probably wrecked my whole life and any chance of happiness. I can't bring myself to be mad at her, with those beautiful sad eyes – the eyes of a goddess.

As I leave I think, *I love you, my little Fran, the light of my youth. You helped keep me alive when I was a boy. And yet, I don't know how it happened, I don't know why . . . but as a man, it's Penny I can't live without.*

◆ ◆ ◆

She's just gone. Vanished. Not even Sherrie knows where she is. I've tried calling her number, but it's no longer active. All I have left of her is a banknote in a crumpled envelope. I wish I could set the sea on fire. I wish I could shatter the sky.

I take out the hundred-dollar bill and hold it up by the corner in the wind. It flaps and quivers like a wounded bird. I'm about to let go when I notice there's writing on the back. I frown and turn the note over; it's still lurching and squirming like a bird that's wanting to fly. My gaze is fixed on a few small letters, written in pink: 'I love you. If you still want me, you can find me here. P.'

Next to it is the name of some town in Vermont. I crumple the bill in my hand, slap my forehead and swallow hard. I was about to throw it away. I was about to give it up. The very thought is enough to floor me, and I sink into the sand with all the weight of my body. Right now, the sun is scattering the clouds and I laugh like an idiot in front of the churning sea. I laugh and laugh, and as I do, hope begins to rise within me once again.

She's not hard to find. The village is small. After all the many mistakes I've made in my life, fate is finally on my side. At this precise moment, Penny's just coming out of a store – not a moment before, nor a moment later. I recognise her immediately, walking towards an old apple-green pickup. I look at her and can't breathe. Yes, she's changed, but it's still her all right. I want to undo that braid with my fingers, knead her hair in my fist, kiss it and touch it for hours. I want to hug her, sleep with her, wake up with her, for all of this life and all of the next. I want her with every drop of my blood.

Then the man at the store calls her back and I see how he looks at her, and I'm afraid. Has she forgotten me? Does she have someone else now? She doesn't even notice me, because she's lost in who-knows-what thoughts, and I hang back behind the parked bus at the terminus.

It's been more than two years now. Does she still mean what she wrote on that bill?

35

Could it really be him? Marcus?

She stared at him in disbelief, captivated at the sight of him. When she left, she had wanted to challenge fate. She'd reckoned that Marcus would most likely never come back, or if he did – who knows when and who knows how or why – he'd most likely have spent that cash on drink, or else he'd have come looking for her sooner.

He'd finally come looking for her.

Standing there in his black leather jacket, a green army backpack over his shoulder, he stared back at her, as if he couldn't make his mind up whether Penny was real or imagined. Penny knew all right – it was really, truly him. His eyes, his lips, his throat with the top edges of his chest tattoos peeking out from his shirt, those same imposing shoulders and the strong legs in his usual jeans. So tall he made her feel like a sparrow in comparison.

◆ ◆ ◆

Penny's heart felt like all the hearts in the world, all joined together and thumping so loudly they could probably hear it over the border in Canada. Instinctively, she tucked a lock of hair behind her ears, as if she wanted to make herself look presentable, and it occurred to her that she must look hideous – with her hair all mussed up, any old clothes on and sweaty from splitting the wood, plus she was wearing no make-up – on the precise and glorious day that Marcus finally decided to show up. A long time had passed and she was now a woman of twenty-five who had been through hell and high water, but she suddenly felt as weak and insecure and tearful as a little kid caught in a gust of wind.

It was like her tongue had a knot in it. She couldn't think of a single sensible thing to say. After a silence that seemed to stretch on forever, she heard her own voice pipe up, as though it had a will of its own. It said, 'Will you help me carry the wood in?'

Will you help me carry the wood in?

Marcus looked confused for a second, but then nodded.

They walked around the outside of the house, her in front with a few logs in her arms and him behind her, carrying the rest of the load, the cat following in their wake and treading carefully to avoid the patches of snow. Penny cursed herself a million times for the first words she'd said to him. She should have jumped on him, clasped him in her arms, kissed him from here to kingdom come.

They entered the house, and Tiger curled up on the couch in a beam of sunshine. Marcus and Penny put the logs in the basket, and then Penny stood with her back to him, struggling with her emotions, while he fumbled with matches and kindling, lighting the fire. And then she said another idiotic thing: 'Are you visiting the area?'

What had happened to her brain? Was she in some kind of trance? Her mind was almost blank, filled only with tumbleweeds and a vague sense of panic. Her grandma and Thomas smiled down at her in encouragement from their photos on the shelf, two pieces of the puzzle that was Penny's life. Penny couldn't move, couldn't breathe, except to utter that one ridiculous question.

'No,' Marcus replied firmly. 'I finally found your message and I came. Are you glad to see me? I want you to tell me: should I stay or should I go?'

His body was talking to her too, and as he spoke, he took a few steps closer to where she was standing, still and full of pent-up tears, with that one long braid on her breast, her cheeks flaming like the sun, and a tumult of love pounding in her chest. The fire was blazing now as he rose to stand behind her, his arms drawing her into his embrace.

'I love you, body and soul,' he whispered, and Penny's legs went weak. Her grandma, from the photo, told her not to be afraid, reminding her once again that love is a miracle.

So she turned to look Marcus in the eye and said, 'Not as much as I love you.'

He stared solemnly at her for a moment, running his eyes over every millimetre of her face, one hand on the nape of her neck, his other thumb running slowly along the line of her mouth, as if painting it with his fingertips. And then he pulled off the band fastening her braid so that it spilled out into a cascade of liquid copper, and finally he kissed her. Penny's heart flew past the tops of the maple trees outside, thirsty for the spring. Marcus's kisses were deep and sensual, sending shivers of longing throughout her body. Gentle, but with a bold promise of mischief to come, his hands began to wander and she grew desperate to feel his weight upon her.

They slipped down on to the patchwork rug, under Tiger's lazy gaze. Marcus removed his jacket and sweater, the broadness of his chest thrilling Penny as much now as it had in the old days. She remembered his silken skin, his firm muscles, his bold tattoos, the leather cord around his neck with the silver crocodile, and was as enchanted by it all as she had been their very first time together. She touched him delicately, like he was a painting, feeling the soft roughness of the canvas beneath her fingers. The tribal tattoos, the stingray, that heart pierced by thorns . . .

'What does that one symbolise?' she asked.

'That's how I used to be,' he replied, 'once upon a time – back when I knew nothing, back when I didn't know you. Enough talking now.'

He ripped off her chequered jacket, only to find her button-down shirt underneath. Hoarsely, he whispered, 'Any more layers – maybe you got a wetsuit on under there? Shit, Penny, I'm gonna die if I don't get to fuck you soon.'

'Refined as ever, I see,' she quipped.

Stripping off in front of him made her feel small and exposed, but only for an instant. Seeing his naked body in front of her lit a burning desire, pure and brutal, deep within her. An intense answering hunger gleamed in Marcus's eyes, and yet she saw him stop and make a face, as if he'd suddenly remembered something essential, and he murmured in pain and frustration, 'If I can't be inside you I'm gonna have a heart attack, I swear, but I don't have a condom on me.'

She pulled him to her, their bellies rubbing together. 'Be inside me anyway.'

Grabbing her hair in his fist, Marcus shoved his tongue in her mouth, before saying, 'You really mean it?'

'Yeah, it's OK. I just finished my period and . . . I haven't done it with anyone else but you.'

Marcus continued to hold her hair in his hand like a bunch of severed stems, his breath uneven. 'You really mean that?' he repeated. 'You're still all mine and mine alone? Fuck, Penny, you're making me even harder.'

'I've been waiting and waiting for you, my darling poet.'

'You know I'm no poet, but I am so goddamn crazy about you. For two years and three months now I've done nothing but think of your eyes, your lips, your beautiful thighs, every single fucking day.'

'Then come to me, my love – come.'

He stared at her in silence. Penny misunderstood his hesitation and was disappointed. Marcus was right to be cautious, but she felt like she'd been robbed of a promise.

'OK . . . so let's not then . . .' she whispered.

Even while she was talking, Marcus suddenly took possession of her, moving his body in a delirium of thrusts and moans and kisses. There, on the rainbow carpet, prey to a pleasure that transcended her flesh and clung to her soul and ravaged her mind, Penny cried tears of pure joy, while Marcus came inside her, naked within her nakedness, giving her that part of himself as a pledge of an infinite future together. Her whole body thrummed as she came, almost lifting her from the ground, like a spirit rising to the heavens before landing safely back in his arms.

They remained locked in an embrace in front of the blazing fire, which was beginning to make the room feel toasty – her leaning against his chest while he kissed her brow and her hair, caressing her all over.

'Am I wrong, or did your boobs grow?' he asked suddenly.

'Please, Marcus, you're far too polite. Could you be a little more direct possibly?' she protested, laughing. 'And no, they didn't grow, I just put on some muscle.'

'You smashed those logs like a real lumberjack. I'll do it next time. I need to find work if I'm gonna stay. Are you looking for someone to help you here? I can get up at dawn and break logs, draw water from the well, groom the horses, clean the stables and drag the plough. And I promise you that no matter how tired I am, I will fuck you to tears every night.'

Penny pressed herself into his body. 'You really want to stay?'

'You really doubt it? Penny, I want to stay here and help you realise your dream and make love to you until the end of my days. And in the meantime . . .'

'In the meantime?'

'In the meantime, I want to give you two things.'

Without giving her time to ask what, Marcus reached for his backpack and pulled out an envelope. He handed it to her and Penny threw him a questioning look. She opened it and all of a sudden was sitting dumbfounded in front of a stack of banknotes. It looked like more than five hundred dollars. She stared at him, perplexed.

'What the . . . ?'

'It's the money you paid me over two years ago for walking you home,' Marcus explained. 'The exact same bills, including the last hundred dollars you gave Sherrie.'

'You never spent it?'

'Not a single dime. I felt like shit accepting it, but I didn't want you to know that I'd have done the same job for free. I didn't want you to know that you were fucking with my head just by breathing. I was messed up, Penny. I was going through hell. I couldn't understand why you made me feel the way you did. I ended up in prison again and they confiscated my things, but when I got out they gave it all back. It's yours now and that's it. You never paid me, baby, never. I did everything I did for you because I wanted to.'

Penny smiled at him and thought back to that time of fear, and lies told out of fear. She whispered a feeble 'Thank you', followed by, 'And there's something else?'

In silence, Marcus pulled the leather cord with the crocodile ring on it from around his neck. He took it off and held it between his fingers for a moment, then slipped the ring on to Penny's left ring finger. It fitted perfectly, like it was made for her.

Penny kissed that worthless ring as if it were the most precious jewel in the world.

'Thank you,' she said again, stroking his chest.

'And now we have all the formalities out the way, let's get back down to us. I have two years and three months to make up for, and I'm a hungry bastard.'

Penny thought about how she also wanted to make up for lost time. And then she thought about how there is no lost time when you learn to know yourself and prepare your heart, body and soul for that one person who will one day come to complete you in every possible way.

She still had so much to ask him, but that could all wait for now.

Then Marcus kissed her again, a kiss as deep as the sky at the bottom of a well, and Penny thought that, yes, her questions could absolutely wait.

ACKNOWLEDGMENTS

Acknowledgments are always the hardest part of any story, because there are so many people whose contribution, however minor, helped that I always worry I'll forget someone. But they're also the best part, because I realise how many friends I have around me, how much loving support I've received along the way. Writing is a solitary activity, but it's like a seed: to make it blossom and flourish takes teamwork.

Thanks to Laura Ceccacci, my agent who is always full of ideas and diligence; to Alessandra Tavella of Amazon Publishing, whose kindness is something magical. Doubly magical is the fact that, before I met her, I had already included a character with her less-than-common surname in the plot – Mrs Tavella, in Penny's apartment block. Clearly it was destiny that brought us together. Further thanks to my editors at Thèsis, whose advice has been invaluable. Thank you also to Patty and Rosy, the first ones to read a story I didn't think was working, but who encouraged me not to press Delete.

Finally, last but not least, thanks to Penny and Marcus, who appeared in my mind one day, asking me to tell their story.

ABOUT THE AUTHOR

Amabile Giusti lives in Calabria, Italy. She's a lawyer but doesn't feel like one. She has been writing novels since 2009 and is always working out how best to start or finish a story, even when she's at work. She loves reading Jane Austen novels as well as Japanese mangas, collecting blue china and tending to her collection of cacti – the thornier the better. She hopes to age as slowly as possible, because she wants to live to one hundred but always stay young inside. She's a great listener but not very chatty, although when she starts writing she just can't stop.

This is her ninth novel, and the second to be translated into English. She has ideas for many, many more.